Rolling ☆ Thunder

ROLLING THUNDER

☆ ☆ ☆

Mark Berent

G. P. PUTNAM'S SONS NEW YORK

G. P. Putnam's Sons
Publishers Since 1838
200 Madison Avenue
New York, NY 10016

This is a work of fiction. All of the characters in this book are fictional and bear no resemblance to real life personages either living or dead. (Sometimes I think the Vietnam war bore no resemblance to real life.) However, in striving for authenticity, some of the organizations and public figures exist or existed at the time. Note that not all actual events occurred in the exact chronology presented.

Map illustration copyright © 1989 by Lisa Amoroso

Library of Congress Cataloging-in-Publication Data

Berent, Mark.
Rolling thunder / by Mark Berent.
p. cm.
ISBN 0-399-13439-5
1. Vietnamese Conflict, 1961–1975—Fiction. I. Title.
PS3552.E697R65   1989   88-31615 CIP
813′.54—dc19

Printed in the United States of America
1 2 3 4 5 6 7 8 9 10

*This book is dedicated to the KIA, MIA, and POW
aircrew from Air America, the U.S. Air Force, the U.S. Army,
the U.S. Coast Guard, Continental Air Service, the U.S.
Marine Corps, the U.S. Navy, the Royal Australian Air Force, and the
men of the U.S. Special Forces.
"We stand to our glasses ready."*

ACKNOWLEDGMENTS

The list is long. It starts with John Williams, a USAF public affairs officer in Los Angeles in the sixties and runs up through Special Forces Captain (Retired) Jim Morris and Ethan Ellenberg in New York in the eighties. In between are writers and editors such as Stefan Geisenheyner, Peter Lars Sandberg, and USAF Colonel John Frisbee, former editor of *Air Force Magazine,* all of whom played a vital role in convincing me to write. Then there are editors like Ed Breslin and Neil Nyren who knew when and where to shape the manuscript. I am indebted to these people.

Yet nothing would have happened had it not been for my wife, Mary Bess, who found me in Paris in the seventies reliving the war instead of writing about it. She brought me back.

Rolling ☆ Thunder

Part ☆ One

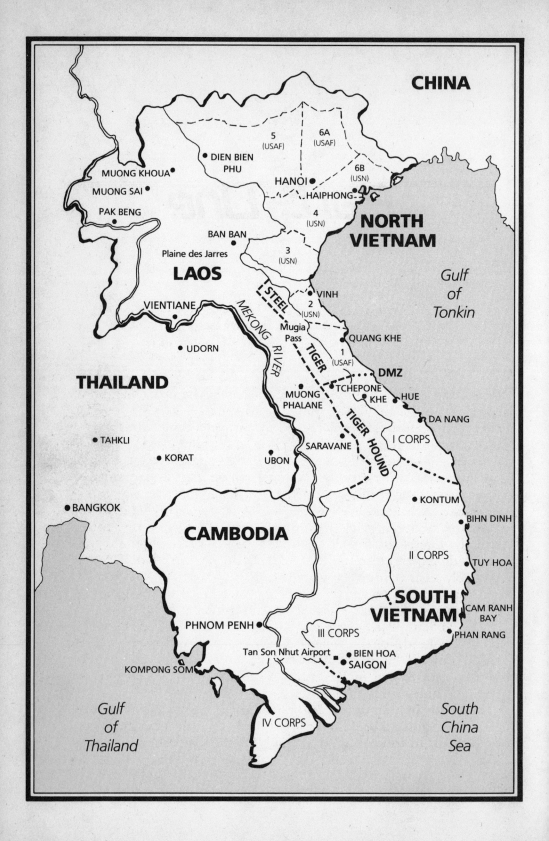

1

☆

A crashing jet fighter breaks up in different ways, depending on its speed, its angle of impact, and the topography of the ground it strikes. A high-speed impact at a ninety-degree angle ensures small pieces mashed into a near circular hole, with narrow wing trenches extending from each side. Depending on soil consistency, the engine can burrow down thirty feet, its twelve-foot length compressed to three. Lesser angles of impact splash the wreckage in the direction of flight and up balloon billowing clouds of greasy black smoke and red flames. A near-zero glide angle on smooth terrain is another matter entirely. Unless the aircraft cartwheels, which it often does if one of the landing gears collapses, the wings usually remain intact, although probably separate from the aircraft. Large sections of the tail assembly and fuselage also remain. If the pilot is not killed upon impact, he may survive. If the wreck doesn't burn. Usually they burn.

United States Air Force Captain Courtland EdM. Bannister knew all this as he delicately babied his shot-up F-100D Super Sabre jet fighter toward his home base of Bien Hoa, located fifteen miles northeast of Saigon in III Corps, South Vietnam. There were six half-inch holes in his airplane, two nearly lethal.

Less than an hour earlier, Bannister and his flight leader, Paul Austin, had been scrambled from runway alert to aid an American Special Forces unit in trouble up near Loc Ninh in War Zone C. In pairs,

Bien Hoa F-100D pilots pulled three types of alert: runway, cockpit, and standby. Each flight of two could be airborne and streaking toward a target in one minute, five minutes, or twenty minutes, respectively.

Almost all Bien Hoa missions, whether scrambled from Alert or scheduled the night before on the portion of the operations order called the frag order, were air-to-ground, doing what the USAF had been sent to Vietnam to do: support U.S. or Vietnamese troops in battle. The weapons hung under their wings were a mixture of bombs, rockets, napalm, and cluster bomb units known as CBU's. Each carried 800 rounds of ammo for the four 20mm cannons mounted internally under the scoop nose of the fighter.

A radar controller in a small dark room had Bannister on his scope.

"Ramrod Four One, I have you twelve miles out on the two-seven-five radial of Tacan Channel Seven-three. Squawk Three Four, acknowledge, Bien Hoa."

"Bien Hoa, Four One, squawking Three Four. I have a situation here. I need a straight-in. I'm leaking bad; gas and, ah, hydraulic fluid. Get me down quick, you copy Four One?"

"Roger, Four One, GCA copies."

The Ground Control Approach controller had picked up Ramrod 41 from Bien Hoa Approach Control, who advised him the pilot had declared an emergency owing to battle damage and low fuel. Bannister had not mentioned he was bleeding. Approach Control also said they had no contact with Ramrod 40, Bannister's flight leader.

As the controller prepared to transmit, another voice broke in. It was neither as low pitched as that of the GCA controller nor as calm.

"Four One, this is Ramrod Two speaking, Ramrod Two. You got gear? You got three good ones down? How about flaps? You got flaps? Where's your flight leader?" Ramrod Two, Bannister's operations officer and immediate commander, had channeled into the conversation using the squadron radio.

Bannister didn't have time to answer his nearly hysterical operations officer. He was busy keeping his crippled airplane aloft. Suddenly a red warning signal lit up, drawing his attention to a small hydraulic gauge on a lower panel in his cockpit. The needle of the gauge bobbled twice before yielding up the few remaining pounds of utility hydraulic pressure as the main pump ground to a halt, then violently broke up deep inside the big fighter. Bannister thought he could feel the grinding. He quickly raised his eyes out of the cockpit to see if he could spot the runway. He had to squint and to blink away blood. All he could see was the jungle canopy a thousand feet below stretching out for miles into a reddish haze.

Several slugs from the big quad-barrel Russian ZSU-4 12.7mm antiaircraft gun had stitched his Super Sabre from its scoop-shovel nose to just short of the tail section. They had punctured and ripped tubing and control lines, causing a loss of hydraulic fluid, which required Bannister to engage his emergency flight control system. That system was powered by a ram air turbine, called RAT. The engine itself was untouched. One slug, however, had ripped a small hole in the belly fuel cell, allowing fuel to stream out behind the F-100 like a smoke trail.

Another slug had crashed through the starboard-quarter panel glass of the windscreen, smashing the gunsight and zinging fragments of metal and glass into Bannister's face. His helmet and oxygen mask protected all but the area around his eyes and forehead. He wore no sunglasses and had not lowered either the sun visor or the clear plastic visor mounted on his helmet. The fragments had etched a few minor lacerations above Bannister's right eye. While neither particularly painful nor disabling, the wounds produced prodigious capillary bleeding, effectively causing Bannister to lose the sight of his right eye. Wiping with his gloved hand smeared it worse. Bannister unhooked his blood-filled oxygen mask and let it dangle. Pooled blood splashed down the front of his parachute harness and survival vest and mingled with his sweat. He heard the measured cadence of the controller through the headset in his helmet.

"Ramrod Four One, check gear down. Prepare for descent in one mile."

Bannister cupped the mask to his face with his right hand, bracketed the control stick with his knees, and pushed the transmit button on the throttle with his left hand. He countered a right wing drop with a leftward motion of his knees pressing on the stick.

"Bien Hoa, my situation is a bit worse. No utility, flight one is out, flight two is going, and I'm not getting much RAT pressure. Yeah, and I only got about a hundred pounds of fuel." Bannister still didn't mention the blood. He did not consider himself wounded, merely inconvenienced at a rather harrowing time.

"Where's your leader, where's Four Zero? Ramrod Four One, answer me."

"Get off the air, Ramrod Two," the GCA controller broke in. "There's an emergency in progress and I've got it." His voice was brittle, not the calming one he used with Ramrod 41.

Bannister shoved down a lever with a replica of a wheel on it. The lever released the lock pins, allowing the gear doors to open and the heavy wheels and struts to fall free. Then he pulled the lanyard that shunted emergency hydraulic fluid into the last two feet of hydraulic lines locking the nose and left main gear into place. The right main didn't lock, causing its cockpit indicator light to remain red. Bannister pushed to test the green indicator bulb. It worked. He already knew his flaps wouldn't go down; he had tried them at a higher altitude while doing a damage check. His flight leader was not there to assist him and report whatever damage Bannister could not see.

"Ah, Bien Hoa, the right main is still red. I don't think it's locked in place. And this will be a no-flap landing. Put the barrier up, I've got to make an approach-end engagement." Without flaps he had to bring his plane in fifteen knots faster. Bannister didn't intend to eject unless the engine quit.

He punched a button activating a solenoid that released a heavy steel bar extending under the aft section of his plane. The bar had a hook on the end. If he touched down in the right place, the hook would snatch the cable stretched across the approach end of the runway and yank him to a stop in a few hundred feet, exactly the way Navy fighters engaged a cable during an aircraft carrier landing.

"Roger, Ramrod Four One, Bien Hoa copies. Barrier crew notified. This is your final controller, how do you read?"

"Loud and clear," Bannister yelled into his dangling mask. From here on he needed his right hand on the control stick, his left on the throttle.

"Ramrod Four One, you need not acknowledge further transmissions. Steer right two-six-five degrees and start your descent . . . now."

As he talked, the controller kept releasing his mike button for an instant, in case Ramrod 41 had to make a transmission that his emergency was worsening.

Bannister concentrated on his heading, but did not start the standard 600-feet-per-minute rate of descent that would give him a smooth three-degree descent angle to the runway. He needed to hold his altitude until the last minute in case his engine quit from fuel starvation. Then he would decide if he was close enough to glide in or if he would be forced to eject. He blinked his eyes rapidly as he scanned his instruments every few seconds while simultaneously searching for the runway. His right eye cleared. When he finally spotted the white concrete landing strip he started to breathe more rapidly as he estimated altitude and distance to the point of touchdown. His airspeed gauge indicated 200 knots. He was flying into a five-knot headwind, giving him a speed over the ground of 225 miles per hour or 338 feet per second. In twenty-three seconds he would be on the ground, one way or another.

The controller's voice faded as Bannister concentrated on aligning his craft and deciding when to start his last-minute descent. If he was too late, his steep descent angle would cause him to overshoot the runway, which would force him to bail out or crash, since he did not have enough fuel to go around and try again. If he started too soon and the engine quit, he would also have to bail out or crash short of the runway.

One mile from the runway, Bannister decided it looked right and started an abnormally steep descent. He could see the crash crew lined up along the side of the runway: red foam trucks, a yellow wrecker, and a blue ambulance. At 800 feet above the ground and 4,000 feet from the end of the runway, his engine sucked up the last drops of JP-4 jet fuel and quickly unwound.

"Flameout," Bannister yelled into his mask.

The big plane wanted to quit flying, but Bannister held his speed by shoving the control stick forward, which forced the nose down more. His rate of descent increased to 1,000 feet per minute. Airspeed had to be high to spin the ram air turbine and give him hydraulic pressure to work the flight controls. He would need a lot of control response to break the glide and flare for touchdown. Though Bannister's heart rate went up another notch, he felt confident he could make it. All the numbers were right. He calculated he had enough altitude to trade for airspeed to make the touchdown point where his hook would grab the cable. The camouflaged airplane plunged closer to the jungle, barely cleared the palm trees, streaked across the half-mile clearing before the concrete, then flared smoothly as Bannister applied enough back pressure on the control stick to break the rapid descent but still make a firm touchdown so the hook wouldn't bounce over the barrier.

It all worked. The hook snatched the cable with the immense force generated by seventeen tons of mass in motion at 300 feet per second. The four-foot brake drums on each side of the runway feeding out cable screamed and smoked, absorbing kinetic energy as they decelerated the big fighter. The jet slewed sharply left; then, at 100 knots, the right main gear collapsed, slamming the right wing to the ground and starting a cartwheel.

Bannister's head banged against the canopy as the wing hit the ground. He grunted as he pushed without result on the now frozen control stick and rudder pedal, trying to counter the violent movement that could end in a fireball. Of the three remaining forces acting on the plane—forward momentum, right roll, and hook deceleration—the hold-back by the hook was the most powerful and won out. The left wing rose ten feet off the ground, the plane pivoted thirty degrees on the crushed right wing tip, the hook held and slammed the flat-bottomed airplane back onto the concrete runway. Bannister's seat survival pack absorbed most of the impact for him, but his head, weighted by the three-pound helmet, thudded down on his chest harness so hard the metal snap gashed his chin. The violent impact left him dazed, and for an instant he was on the edge of unconsciousness.

The fire trucks and crash crew surrounded the wreck almost before it settled. They shot great streams of sticky white foam over and under the plane, around the hot engine and aft section. Without fuel there was little chance of a fire. Four firemen in aluminum suits, looking like bulky astronauts, ran to the airplane, two to each side. One jerked the external lanyard blowing the canopy off while the others positioned a ladder and ran up to get Bannister, who was rapidly coming around and was able to undo his own helmet, harness, G-suit, and oxygen connections. The years of programming himself to perform all the ground emergency egress actions instinctively were paying off.

The fireman at the top of the ladder on the right side thought so much blood in the cockpit was unusual. Usually a guy hit this bad wouldn't make it back. He passed Bannister's helmet to another fireman, who, facing aft toward the open cockpit, was straddling the nose of the aircraft like a horseback rider. "Are you okay, sir?" the closest fireman asked through his helmet faceplate.

"Yeah, chief, fine, thanks. How about fire? We got any fire?" Bannister, thinking the plane would blow up, was struggling to get out.

"No, no fire. No sweat, sir, just hang on a minute." The fireman gently placed his gloved hand on Bannister's shoulder. He held the groggy pilot down until the flight surgeon from the ambulance could climb up the ladder and check his condition.

"Hey Court, how ya doing? Where ya hit?" Major Conrad Russell, M.D., asked as he leaned over Bannister to wipe away blood and assess damage. He saw the facial rips and tears where the blood had already clotted. He thumbed up Bannister's right eyelid and noted that the eyeball looked intact and functional. The nick in the chin was barely oozing.

"No place. I'm not hit. Just some junk in my face. Is my right eye okay?" Bannister asked. He looked up at Russell, squinting his gray-blue eyes as much from the residual blood as from the sun behind Russell's back. Bannister's brown hair, released from the confines of his helmet, soaked with sweat and plastered against his head, was trimmed almost to crew-cut length. His close-shaven sideburns ended at midear. His face was square, his jawline strong. Bannister was six-foot-one and normally trimmed out at 185. Vietnam heat and O-Club food had dropped him to a dehydrated 170. He was thirty and had been a USAF fighter pilot for ten years. This was his first crash.

Major Russell, his preliminary check complete, said, "Come on, let's get out of here. We gotta clear the runway. Other guys want to land too, you know. Your eye will be fine." He tugged at Bannister to get up and climb down the ladder.

The flight surgeon started to smile and hum as he moved his bulky figure down the ladder, accepting the helping hand of a nearby fireman. Doc Russell was doing what he loved best. He wore standard Shade 45 USAF blue two-piece fatigues that were now smelly and stained badly by the foam. His name, rank, and flight surgeon wings were embossed on a piece of leather stitched to his left breast pocket. Russell was overweight—rotund, in fact. His round, young-looking face vaguely resembled that of Baby Huey, the cartoon character, and so of course that was the nickname that had been given to him by the fighter pilots at Bien Hoa, particularly those of the 531st Tactical Fighter Squadron, the squadron for which he was responsible. Russell, a thirty-four-year-old major, would have been a pilot were it not for vision problems so bad that his eyes tended to cross whenever he was tired.

He walked Bannister to the ambulance. The letters and devices on the leather nametag on the pilot's left breast stated he was "Courtland EdM. Bannister, Capt., USAF." A star above his pilot's wings indicated he had flown at least seven years, had amassed 2,000 flying hours, and was rated a senior pilot. Below his pilot's wings were the parachutist's wings he had been awarded after training with the Special Forces in Germany. Bannister still wore his G-suit and survival vest, and carried an olive-green bag stuffed with his helmet, kneeboard, and maps. On his feet were Army-issue jungle boots, which were perfectly suited for tropical wear but would provide no ankle support in a parachute landing.

Standing next to the squadron jeep by the blue USAF ambulance, watching them approach, was Ramrod Two, Major Harold Rawson: five-ten, black hair combed straight back, a pencil-thin moustache over his thin upper lip. He looked the type who missed the days of puttees and riding britches. He wore, instead, the standard K-2B cotton one-piece green flight suit with the standard thirteen zippers. On his head was a regulation USAF blue flight cap with silver officer piping on the rim and the gold oak leaf of a major pinned front left. Rawson was the operations officer of the 531st Tactical Fighter Squadron, second in command to the squadron commander and responsible for day-to-day fighter operation. The commander, Lieutenant Colonel Peter Warton, was back in the States on emergency leave, which left Rawson in charge. He felt burdened with the unexpected responsibility.

Rawson watched Bannister and Russell approach, barely resisting the temptation to run up to Bannister crying, "What in hell did you do?" Instead he waited until the two men drew closer.

"Where's Four Zero?" he asked. Then, unable to contain himself, "How could you lose your leader?"

Before Bannister could answer, Russell shoved him toward the ambulance and said to Rawson, "Look, Harry, I've got to check this guy out before you or anybody from Intel gets to talk to him. Now back off."

Bannister's face had colored. He seriously considered slamming his fist into Rawson's small, turned-down mouth, which seemed perpetually to sneer whenever its owner spoke.

"I didn't *lose* anybody, goddammit. Austin got hit and went straight in," Bannister said in a tight voice over his shoulder as he climbed into the back of the ambulance. As the double doors swung shut, he turned to see Rawson struggling to control himself, with only limited success.

In the coolness of one of the nested trailers that served as a hospital on the Bien Hoa Air Base, Russell remained silent until he had finished swabbing the cuts on Bannister's face. They would not require stitching and would heal quickly if kept clean.

"Well," he said straightening up, "all that blood and these cuts are worth a Purple Heart."

Bannister stood up and walked to one of the small sliding windows that looked out. He had taken off his G-suit and dark-green net survival vest. The sweat beneath was crusted white with salt and starting to dry on his flight suit. He dug a crushed pack of Luckies from his zippered left sleeve pocket and lit one before he answered. The Zippo he used had a thick rubber band around it.

"Forget it." He inhaled deeply, held it, and blew the smoke out in a long sigh. He could still see the fireball that Major Paul Austin's plane had made after it hit the ground.

"Why?" Russell asked after a minute.

"Too piddly."

"Well," Doc Russell said, "I guess I understand that." He stood up. "At any rate, Paul Austin will get one." He was silent for a moment. "Hell of a way to earn it, though." After another pause he added, "Isn't his dad a general in the Pentagon?" He nodded to himself. "Sure he is, a three-star. So that's why Harry Rawson is so distraught." He looked at Bannister for corroboration.

"That's the one," Bannister said. He picked up his gear and started for the door. "I've got to go debrief. There's big stuff going on up there near Loc Ninh. We stumbled into something hot and I don't mean just gun barrels."

"Okay," Russell said, nodding. "Keep your dirty mitts off those cuts. Maybe I'll see you tonight at the club."

Bannister walked out the door thinking about the intelligence debriefing session he was about to face in the wing headquarters building. He knew he could convince the lower-ranking Intel people that something was up at Loc Ninh, but he wasn't at all sure whether the high-level ones at Saigon would agree. They had their own concepts and didn't like input that upset them. That was one problem he could probably deal with. He wasn't so sure about the other.

What weighed on Bannister's mind far more than the Loc Ninh buildup was the lie he planned to tell the flying safety officer about why Paul Austin had crashed.

2

☆

As Bannister walked out of Russell's dispensary at Bien Hoa Air Base, Braniff International Flight B1T4, a four-engine Boeing 707, began descending from cruise altitude twenty minutes out of Tan Son Nhut Air Base, the sprawling airfield and U.S. command complex on the northwest side of Saigon.

Braniff International, out of Los Angeles by way of Norton Air Force Base, California, was one of the half dozen U.S. airlines flying Military Airlift Command (MAC) contract flights to and from Vietnam. American, World, Continental, and the others carried G.I.'s under a government contract to augment the USAF's MAC, which didn't have enough transport airplanes and crews to ferry troops to and from Vietnam. MAC hadn't been set up to perform that task.

At first and subsequent glance the Braniff airplane was astonishing. What the eye didn't want to believe or adjust to was the color. From tip to tail, the 150-foot airliner was painted chartreuse. The irreverent called it the chartreuse goose. Inside, also under Braniff's new-look plan, the women wore Pucci ensembles of sleeveless blouses and culottes in bright pink and yellow, and flat-heeled multi-colored shoes that replaced the calf-high boots they wore off the plane. After hearing throaty rumbles, Emilio Pucci had decided not to change the traditional uniforms of the cockpit crew.

The plane banked left over the azure water of the South China

Sea, preparing for its run up to the base. To avoid ground fire, it would not descend below 4,500 feet until the last minute before landing approach, and then it would descend very quickly, more quickly than any civilian passenger would have understood, or put up with. It crossed high over the beach at Vung Tau where the sand was so white it looked like a band of purest flour.

On board the Boeing 707 were three cockpit crew members, five cabin attendants, and 165 military passengers crammed into seats better suited for small tourists on short flights. The G.I.'s, all in uniform, previously talkative and alert, became silent and glum as they stared out the window ports watching verdant jungle, peaceful-looking as Hawaii, slide beneath the wings.

Oblivious to the first view of a nation where his fellow countrymen were dying, First Lieutenant Toby G. Parker, United States Air Force—blond hair, oval-shaped blue eyes, good features, good teeth, the quintessential college frat man, more eager to party than to participate in anything that might require mental or moral effort—sat in aisle seat 1C directly facing the forward bulkhead, where three stewardesses were strapped into jumpseats facing aft. The configuration was peculiar in that the three girls sat knee-to-knee with the men in the front row, the row in which Parker had maneuvered to be seated.

Figuring he would see enough of Vietnam during his upcoming year-long tour, he concentrated on the stewardess he had been bird-dogging during the entire flight from Clark Air Base in the Philippines. As regulations required when their aircraft was landing, she was now buckled into the crew seat facing Parker. He had been trying for her attention since takeoff, hours earlier. She was finally settled in one place.

"Hey, really," he said, leaning toward her, "what's your name? Can I write you? Do you have a layover here or are you on a turn-around?"

Parker was proud of the lingo he had learned from dating so many stews in L.A., where he had been posted to the big USAF unit, SAMSO, in El Segundo. What he should have known was that even the newest MAC contract girl could spot a stew bum from forty seats away.

The girl, short cropped brown hair slightly awry, looked over. She read his name from the blue plastic tag over the right pocket of his tailored 1505 khaki shirt.

" 'Hey, really' yourself, Parker. Behave." Her amber eyes looked tired but faintly amused at this guy trying so hard to get her attention. Cute but boyish, she thought, as she smiled at him.

Encouraged, Toby made what he considered the best move he could under the circumstances. He reached over to take her hand and by his warmth impress her with tones of sincerity. Might even turn her on, he thought, though not too likely under these conditions. She made a movement he barely saw and suddenly his right hand felt numb from the wrist.

"Ouch. Damn. What did you do?"

"Karate." She smiled sweetly. "Just a mild chop on a nerve. I have a brown belt. I told you to behave." She adjusted her skirt and sat primly as the pilot dove the huge airliner toward touchdown at Tan Son Nhut Air Base, Republic of Vietnam.

The plane vibrated and shook as the slipstream tore at the gear and flaps the pilot lowered in the later part of the descent. This wasn't how it was done in the States, where no one fired at you from the ground, and some G.I.'s rolled their eyes at the humming and rocking movements. One, to his great disgust, threw up quietly into his hat.

The pilot expertly flared the big craft, and the main gear greased onto the runway with contented squeaks, then rumbled as the struts absorbed the unevenness of the concrete surface.

The Transient Alert crew of the 8th Aerial Port drove the service truck with the white steps to the front left of the liner. When the amber-eyed girl and one other unlocked and pushed open the big door, the warm, humid smell of Vietnam rolled through the cabin like swamp gas. The cabin filled with the steamy air that smelled of fresh palms and fetid jungle underbrush, and rotting garbage, perfume and formaldehyde. Over it all hung the odor of burnt jet fuel smelling like stale bus fumes. At first sniff it was sickening. It became worse with each inhale. It was an odor one wasn't likely to forget. Each G.I., as he breathed in, instinctively knew that this was a one-time moment in his life. Some, the more sensitive, shivered.

Parker was oblivious to all of this. For him Vietnam was just another adventure before he quit the Air Force. He intended to make the most of the year tour for which he had volunteered, starting right now.

He hung back to be the last out, so he could have more time to hustle the amber-eyed girl. She was busy with the others: stacking trays, opening galley hatches, letting the Vietnamese cleaning crews in by the galley doors so they could watch them to be sure they cleaned and did not plant bombs in out-of-the-way places. Parker was finally urged off the plane by a G.I. greeting official, a harassed army captain who said to get his ass down the stairs and into the terminal or he'd kick it there. Military officers didn't talk that way in the States, Parker thought, as he grabbed his blue AWOL bag and deplaned. At the foot of the steps, Parker dug out his folded flight cap and crammed it on his head at just the right angle. The airliner's captain and navigator had already left the ship to file a flight plan for the return leg, which would carry G.I.'s who had finished their tour of duty in Vietnam back to the States. The copilot remained behind to supervise refueling.

The 707 was parked on the civilian ramp in line with Air France and Air Cambodge Caravels, a Pan American 707, and an Air Vietnam DC-4. Parker could see military aircraft on a far ramp in several new parking revetments of corrugated steel and sandbags. Other revetments were under construction from one end of the two-mile flight line to the other. There was an aura of bustle and sweat about the field. Nothing moved slowly. Blue USAF maintenance vans and dirty white French-built civilian trucks bearing airline logos raced up and down the ramp, meeting airplanes, carrying parts, or transporting harassed contractors and workers.

Civilian airliners vied with camouflaged fighters as they lined up along the taxiway waiting to be cleared onto the runway for takeoff. Civilian passengers could look down on helmeted pilots sitting in the cockpits of their bomb-laden fighters waiting for takeoff to fly a combat mission. Military control tower operators of Tan Son Nhut's dual runways were experiencing well over 800 landings and takeoffs a day and were expecting double that in the coming year. At a distance Parker could see two-story wooden watchtowers on stilts alternating with brown sandbagged bunkers forming part of the perimeter defense.

Though December was one of the cooler months in the Asian monsoon season, the heat and humidity hit Parker like a fist as his lungs absorbed the steamy air. In minutes, as he walked to the terminal, he felt water starting to roll down his sides as if his body had turned on a small garden soaker. Before he reached the door, his shirt had a wide sweat-soaked V down the front and the back, with circular dark patches under each arm.

He shoved open the swinging glass door lettered FOR MILITARY PERSONNEL ONLY, and lugged his AWOL bag into the MAC side of the terminal. In less than an hour he was processed, his shot record was checked, and he had picked up his one duffel bag and slung it over his shoulder. Lieutenant Parker was on his own now and didn't have to report in until 0800 the following morning at the 6250th Combat Support Group administrative office, where he would take over as assistant to the assistant administrative officer or some such inconsequential job. Although he had to volunteer in his primary duty specialty as a code 7024 administrative officer, he had planned all along to seek a more exciting job once in Vietnam. He had heard such things were easy to do.

He pushed through the milling crowd of khaki-clad G.I.'s and went out the door to the front side of the deteriorating French-built terminal. Headed toward the base bus stop, he glanced through the tall windows and saw the stewardesses from his airliner near the small civilian bar at one end of the long, dirty, crowded area that passed for a passenger lounge. The girls were waiting for their airplane to be released by maintenance. They looked tired and wrinkled after their long trip.

Parker entered and elbowed his way up to the end of the bar, where the girls stood sipping warm Cokes through straws, talking about the new crew lounge that would be ready by their next trip. They had put on Portland Red wraparound skirts over their culottes and carried identical beige purses slung over their shoulders. But no one wore the pillbox hat that Pucci had worked such long hours to design. Parker dropped his bags at the end of the bar.

"Hi," he said to the amber-eyed girl. She turned to stare at him. She showed no surprise at his being there.

"You are persistent," she said, finally. "Aren't you due some place? Like a war, maybe?"

"I don't report to the war until eight o'clock tomorrow morning. Have dinner with me tonight. There must be an Officer's Club here someplace."

"There is and I can't," she said.

"Do you fly back today?" he asked.

"Right now," she said.

Toby had never seen such eyes, the amber and the flecks of gold were deep and hypnotic. He was about to tell her exactly that, when a dark-haired, medium-sized civilian stepped abruptly between them, grabbed the girl by the arm, and tried to pull her off to one side. He wore dark pants and a short-sleeved white shirt. Clipped to his shirt pocket was a red laminated photo ID card.

"Goddammit, Nancy, this time you got to talk to me," he said. His face was pursed in agitation. He exuded a faint odor of whisky. He released her arm and stood very close, looking down at her from a two-inch height advantage.

Not the least intimidated, she set her jaw as she put her hands on his chest and pushed him back.

"Bubba, go away. There isn't anything to talk about. There never was. Go away."

The place was crowded, hot, and smoky. The other girls didn't quite catch what was going on, because Parker was between them and the pair. He did hear one of the stews answer another's question by saying Bubba was Curtis Bates, the assistant station manager for Alpha Airlines.

Parker, edging closer to Bubba and Nancy, saw him grab her arm, twist and jerk it, while saying something using a lot of swear words. Never one to get involved, Parker surprised himself. Maybe it was the environment. He felt a surge of adrenaline and, without making a conscious decision to do so, reached out, grabbed Bubba's arm and swung him around. Instantly Parker found himself stomach-down on the dirty cement floor looking at ankles and mashed cigarette butts. He rolled over, jumped to his feet, swung at Bubba, missed, and was flattened again.

He got up in time to see Nancy do something with her hands and arms that doubled Bubba up and caused instant sweat to pop out on his forehead.

"Do you understand now, Bubba? Do you?" she asked, jerking his arm higher behind his back. Parker noted she had somewhat thick ankles and rounded, muscular calves. Bent over, Curtis "Bubba" Bates nodded his head and mumbled what could be taken for a yes. She released him as two Caucasian civilians pushed through the parting crowd and led Bubba away. They wore identical black trousers and white shirts and red ID cards. A dozen feet away, Bubba Bates, face so flushed he appeared near a heat stroke, looked back at Parker, nodded to himself, then turned and walked on, slamming his fist into his palm several times.

Nancy, seeing the look, took Parker's arm, "Oh look, I'm really sorry. But you shouldn't have interfered, you know. Everything was under control, really it was." She reached up, surprisingly tender, to touch Parker's face, then fingered the gathering bruise under his eye. "Damn. You're going to have quite a mouse."

Not at all in control of the situation, Parker stared at her for a second. He thought he could feel his face begin to swell.

"Brown belt, huh," he said.

She nodded. The other girls had gathered around. They pointed in the direction of the airplane and said it was time to board.

Parker could only stare into her eyes. He was totally out of ideas, beginning to suspect he was outclassed. Nancy looked at him for a moment.

"Okay," she said, "write me. Here, take my card."

She dug into her purse, handed him a finely embossed card, shook her head once as if amazed at what she had done, then ran after the other girls.

Parker stood still, watching the girls move off. Nancy didn't look back to wave or to say goodbye. With a sigh he glanced down at the card he held in his hand. "Hey," he half shouted, running after her, "there's no address."

He caught up with them as they went through the CREW ONLY door to the flight line.

"There's no address," he yelled, waving the white card.

"Write me at the airline office in Oakland," she shouted back as the door swung shut.

Parker stopped and looked again at the expensive card in his hand. The Gothic script identified the owner as Mrs. Bradley L. Lewis.

By 2100 hours that night Parker was ready for the bar at the Tan Son Nhut Officer's Club. Earlier he had checked into the Bachelor Officers Quarters and found his tiny room on the second floor. He had showered in the communal ten-head shower that had slimy slippery wooden grates over an even more slippery cement floor. The building was one of six in a row of identical pale-green, two-story wooden structures hastily erected to house the lieutenant and captain company-grade officers. He felt stiff, abused, tired from two days of travel, and humiliated. His eye, though puffy, was not showing the purple bruise of a mouse.

He had found the clothes-washing facilities in a service area down the hall. The white washers and dryers didn't require coins and were battered and stained from much use. Padding around in thongs and leopard-skin briefs, he had sprinkled and ironed a flight suit scrounged from a supply officer friend back in the States. He had never worn a flight suit and wasn't authorized even to own one, but felt things were much different here in Vietnam than at SAMSO, the Space and Missile Systems Office in L.A. He carefully smoothed a printed leather tag attached to the left breast that spelled out his name and rank. Nonrated people did not wear flight suits during their off-duty time, much less on duty. Being rated meant having earned a set of wings by completing the appropriate technical school. The graduate was rated as a pilot, navigator, gunner, crew chief, or other aircrew position. At a stateside air base such an act would be considered pretentious, and Parker knew the nonrated wearer would be in for heavy verbal abuse. In a combat zone, he figured most personnel flew on all sorts of different missions and his flight suit would merely be one of many. He climbed into the dark-green cotton flight suit and zipped it up.

2200 HOURS LOCAL, 17 DECEMBER 1965
OFFICER'S CLUB,
TAN SON NHUT AIR BASE, REPUBLIC OF VIETNAM
☆

Parker found the Officer's Club, walked in, hesitated, then walked to the crowd at the bar, four-deep and well on its way to becoming raucous. He elbowed his way to the long wooden bar. A ten-foot, Air Force–issue, spangled MERRY CHRISTMAS banner hung slightly askew on the wall above the bottle racks behind the bar. He had to wait several minutes to order a double scotch and water from one of the three off-duty G.I. bartenders. They were rushing and sweating to keep up with the demands of the fast, hard-drinking officer and civilian crowd. Parker sipped his scotch and decided he should have ordered beer. The place was not like any Officer's Club he had ever seen in the States. It was more like a saloon in the Klondike boom-town days. The humid atmosphere was thick with smoke and loud talk, pushed and mixed by three ceiling fans into a stupefying melange of sound and smell. Parker looked around.

The crowd wasn't only USAF or Army transients. Tan Son Nhut was where MACV, the command organization trying to prosecute the war in Southeast Asia, was located. MACV was an acronym for Military Assistance Command, Vietnam, the 3,200-man unified command under the Commander in Chief of the Pacific Command (CINCPAC), based in Hawaii. Air operations were controlled by the 7th Air Force under MACV. Commander U.S. MACV (COMUSMACV) answered directly to CINCPAC, who had to answer directly to the Secretary of Defense, a black-haired civilian who had had only two years of World War II supply service before going to Ford Motor Company and thence to the Pentagon. COMUSMACV had thirty-one years of active duty, of which six had been spent in combat leading troops in three wars.

Parker was surprised to see that most of what he took to be MACV people wore hideous Bermuda shorts, raunchy Hawaiian shirts, and tennis shoes without socks. Less than half wore fatigues or flight suits. Only a handful wore the class B khaki uniform. It was much too hot for blues.

He stood outside the crowd at the south end of the bar, starting to relax with his drink. Glancing around, he noticed three Army men—officers he guessed—in jungle fatigues huddled around a small black Formica table with wobbly legs. Standing on the table was a forest of beer bottles of a greenish hue with the numbers "33" in big numerals on the logo. It was a French beer made in Vietnam, called Bamuiba, Vietnamese for "33." The G.I.'s called it "Bomb-me-bad" and swore it contained a large percentage of formaldehyde. It certainly smelled as though it did. Bamuiba produced monumental hangovers that drilled and pounded an area of the brain no American beer ever penetrated.

One of the men was eminently noticeable: sparse black hair shaved close to a squarish skull, bulky bone covered with bushy black eyebrows overhanging dark-brown eyes, burly arms covered with a pelt of curly black hair. He could have posed in an ad for a jail-and-bail movie. His scowl was deep and fierce. With a start, Parker realized the scowl was aimed at him.

Cripes almighty, what now? Parker thought as he looked away. He decided to try conversation with the man standing next to him.

"How late does the bar stay open?" he pleasantly asked a thin first lieutenant in Army fatigues.

The lieutenant turned and studied Parker's wingless nametag a long moment before replying. "Beats me, I'm usually drunk by ten." The first john turned back to his companions, pointedly ignoring Parker, who was beginning to get the idea something was wrong but couldn't quite put his finger on what it was. He thought maybe his face was swollen. He reached up and touched the skin around his eye. The area throbbed but didn't feel swollen.

He swiveled his head around and, uncontrollably drawn, glanced back at the three men at the table and wound up staring at the brown pieces of cloth stitched where their rank should be. Still scowling, the burly man caught his eye and motioned him over. Parker turned away to order a beer.

He gave a slight jump when a raspy voice too close to his ear said, "What in hell you doon, flyboy?"

Parker tried to ignore him, but was trapped by the crowd from moving more than a foot or two. From the corner of his eye he could see the man stood at least three inches shorter but wider, much wider, than himself. He smelled like an old tennis shoe left too long in the bottom of a locker.

The stocky man grabbed Parker's arm and spun him around, "What you *doon*, flyboy?"

Parker saw the name Lochert stitched in black letters parallel to the man's slanted right pocket flap. On each shoulder he saw brown bits of cloth in the shape of an oak leaf. He decided he was confronted by a Lieutenant Colonel Lochert who, for some reason, wanted to know what he was "doon."

"Nothing, sir, just drinking," he said, considerably more cheerful than he felt.

"I can see that, shithead. I wanna know what in hell you're doing." He dragged the word out to two syllables. Parker could see he was drunk and fairly belligerent. Why, he had no idea. He decided to play it safe. All in all, it had been a hell of a day.

"Nothing, Colonel Lochert, nothing at all. As a matter of fact, I probably don't even belong here. I'm not even a—"

"I'll say you don't belong here," the man interrupted, "and I ain't no colonel."

Thoroughly confused, Parker tried to ease away. Lochert, christened Wolfgang Xavier, grabbed him again. Breathing the staggering smell of used Bamuiba into Parker's face, he boomed out in a voice more suited to drill fields or heavy combat, the perfectly articulated words. "My rank is major. I'm a grunt, a snuffy, and you, you straight-backed, perfect-toothed, blue-eyed shithead have eye-runned your frapping flyboy suit. You ain't no fighter pilot. Fighter pilots don't eye-run their flight suits. They like their green bags DIRTY."

He held Parker by the biceps in a grip that nearly paralyzed his arm. It was getting to be a bit much, especially considering what Mrs. Bradley L. Lewis and Mr. Curtis "Bubba" Bates had already done to him that day.

"Were you out dropping bombs today? Are you the shithead who short-rounded two of my slopes today? Are you the Air Force puke that killed my men?" The surrounding crowd took notice now and moved to form a circle around the two officers. Parker's face was absolutely white as he stared at the Army major who mistook him for a pilot. He had no idea on earth what to do. He could feel his heart thumping in his chest. He reflected briefly that he had never been in a fight in his life before being flattened twice earlier this very day.

The major looked even meaner, glared more fiercely at Parker as his voice boomed, "I said what the fuck—"

"WHAT THE FUCK WHAT?" Parker suddenly screamed back, out of control now, acted on by the heat, the flight, the girl; flattened twice already, he just wasn't going to take any more of this. He grabbed the lapels of Major Wolfgang X. Lochert's jungle fatigues and tried to shake the man. He expected death at any minute, but was too far gone to care. It was like trying to shake a hundred-year-old oak tree. The major gave a mock look of surprise and started to say something, when a tall slender man in shorts, tennies, and an abominable sport shirt with the word JAMMER sewn across the back wedged himself between the two. He pressed on Lochert's forearm with his thumb in such a way that Lochert released his viselike grip on Parker's arm. Parker, resisting the urge to rub his left biceps, his temper cooling rapidly, stepped back as the slender man in civvies whispered something into the Army man's ear. Lochert's eyes squinted in concentration as he listened, thought for a second, then nodded his head. He looked at the guy in civvies, said something so low even those close by couldn't hear, glanced once at Parker, pulled his lips back from his teeth in what could have been either a grimace or a grin, boomed a loud cackle that might be construed as a laugh, and strode back to his table.

The bar noise resumed as the crowd nearby realized the entertainment was over. Parker figured he had better make the acquaintance of someone who could tame a wild man so quickly.

"Buy you a drink, sir?" he asked as the man started back to the group he had been standing with.

"I have one, thanks anyway. But you come join us."

Flattered, Parker followed the man back to the group, whose members ranged in age from mid-twenties to late forties. They all wore Bermudas or cutoffs and had a variety of shirts with nicknames stenciled or sewn on the back. Tweaks was talking and laughing with Buzzer, as they and Flash Cart greeted Jammer. An older man with a cartoon blackbird holding binoculars and the words OLD CROW embroidered on his shirt handed Jammer his drink.

"Nicely done, boss," he said to Jammer. He knew better than to ask what Jammer had said to the major. Not so Parker, who, as he entered the group, blithely asked Jammer that very thing.

Jammer only laughed and introduced Parker all around. No names or rank were given, just the nicknames. This flustered Parker, whose name and rank were obvious from his own nametag. He didn't know whether to say "sir" or not to the others. He decided to do so on the basis of age. They all greeted him in a friendly enough fashion, then turned to their own conversations, all but the Old Crow. Parker thought it strange that no one asked him where he was stationed or why he was at Tan Son Nhut. He listened to them chatter among themselves and answered a few questions put to him about when he had arrived and where he was last stationed. After a half hour of this he'd had about enough drink to be, as he thought to himself, boldly inquisitive.

"What do you guys do, anyhow? Are you Air Force, at MACV, Seventh, or what?" Parker asked.

"A variety of things," the Old Crow said. "Some of us are Thirteenth Recce Tech, others TAC Recon, PI, stuff like that."

Parker caught on. It confirmed what he had begun to suspect. These people were in the reconnaissance business; Tactical Air Command, Photo Interpreter, electronic, and maybe other kinds. Whatever it was, he figured it might be exciting.

"Look," Parker said, "I'm looking for a job here at Seventh. You guys got any use for an admin type?"

"Can't say at the moment," Old Crow replied. "Come see me tomorrow if you can. Bring a copy of your orders. Here, take this." Old Crow scribbled in a pocket notebook and tore it off. Parker looked at it and read *"Col. Leonard Norman, Tiger Switch ext 5777."*

"Thank you, sir, thanks a lot. By the way, what do you think Jammer told that Army major?"

"I think Jammer told the major he was being addressed by Major General Stack and that he, the major, had best be nice. And," he said, eyeing Parker's wingless nametag, "he probably told him you are nonrated and couldn't possibly have short-rounded his troops. He's known the Wolf for a long time."

"The Wolf?"

"Wolf Lochert. He's an adviser to the ARVN in Three Corps. Yesterday an F-100 from Bien Hoa dropped a short round that killed some of his people. But understand, the Wolf was in deep trouble and had called the air strikes in close. When he debriefed us he said he figured they'd all be dead anyway, so the short round was a cheap price to pay for survival. He didn't even officially report it. Maybe he knew you were nonrated and was only testing you. He's a good guy. Tomorrow he'll probably be in church."

"Short round?" Parker asked.

"A short round is what we call any ordnance that hits or falls on friendly forces. When the artillery guys do it, it's called friendly fire."

My God, Parker thought, there's a whole new language and way of life out here. How can being shelled by your own side be called friendly? And some idiot Army guy testing me. Is bashing my brains out, for who knows what reason, a test?

"Thanks, Colonel Norman. I'll call you tomorrow about the job." Parker pocketed the colonel's card, had two more drinks, and left the club. Several men in flight suits and shorts had gathered around an old upright piano in a corner and were starting to warm up with some dirty fighter pilot songs. Nuts, Parker thought, walking out, the sound of a song about a girl named Mary Ann Barnes fading, I'll never belong here.

As First Lieutenant Toby G. Parker, USAF, stumbled through the dark to his BOQ, he realized he never should have worn a flight suit without wings. He made two vows. He would never wear the flight suit again unless he flew, and he would somehow learn how to fight.

Far to the east, lightning rumbled and flashed. Artillery did the same to the west.

3

☆

Power in the Pentagon is situated on the Third floor, E Ring, between Corridors 8 and 9. From here, the Secretary of Defense (SecDef) exercises direction, authority, and control over the Department of Defense (DoD), which encompasses the departments of the Army, the Navy (including the Marines and the Naval Aviation Corps), and the Air Force in addition to the Joint Chiefs of Staff (JCS), the unified and specified commands, and various other defense agencies. What this means is that the SecDef has 3,374,808 men and women to assist him in his duty to support and defend the United States Constitution and to ensure the security of the United States, its possessions, and other areas vital to its security. At that moment, like it or not, an area called South Vietnam, which was 12,500 miles from the SecDef's office, had been declared vital to the security of the United States. This Asian country halfway around the world currently had 460,202 of the SecDef's military people stationed there. An additional 40,000 were cruising around offshore in the South China Sea, while 35,000 more were at a half dozen air bases in Thailand.

The SecDef's main office is located in Room 880. His Deputy SecDef is on the same floor, in Room 944. The Chairman of the Joint Chiefs of Staff, whose job is to administer to the JCS while advising the President through the SecDef, is located almost directly beneath in 2E872. Scattered about are the offices of the Chiefs of

Staff of the Army (3E666) and the Air Force (4E924), and the Chief of Naval Operations (4E660). The Commandant of the Marine Corps is a half mile away in the Navy Annex on Columbia Pike.

Down the corridor 200 feet to the right from the SecDef was the office of USAF Major General Albert G. "Whitey" Whisenand, who held the position of Director of Operations and Planning, Special (Detached). Whitey Whisenand's job was unique in that he worked directly for the SecDef, not for his service chief or any other military boss.

As a two-star, Whitey was old in grade at age fifty-five. He had flown his first airplane, a 3,000-pound P-26, for the Army Air Force in 1933. In World War II he flew Mustangs. He flew his last fighter for the USAF, a 12,000-pound Lockheed F-80 Shooting Star, in Korea. On his eighty-third mission he crashed and burned on takeoff when his water injection failed. He had been medically grounded since. At fifty-five, he looked a senatorial sixty, owing to his expanding girth and white hair. He was not tall. Because of his burn scars he had a slightly rosy and grainy-textured matte around his upper cheeks and eyes, which made him forever appear as if he had just removed his oxygen mask after a long flight. The rest of his face was smooth and pink. His eyes were pale-blue and generally compassionate. Behind his normal expression of benign curiosity, he hid a high IQ and an enormous interest in what made people tick. And now, as he sat at his large oak desk sipping steamy Brenny's coffee from a chipped Ansley bone-china mug, he thought of the odd position he was in.

His job for the SecDef was threefold:

- to evaluate target requests sent from MACV via CINCPAC to the President for approval;
- to generate other targets to fulfill the President's requirements;
- to rank-order the results and weigh them against public opinion, then throw out or refile those targets that might cause public unease.

He spent long hours with an Air Force colonel and a Navy captain determining which among the targets were best suited for an air attack that would hurt the enemy, but not damage the U.S. image. SEA, meaning Southeast Asia, was the term used to encompass all areas where the war was being fought, Laos and Cambodia as well as Vietnam. The enemy was considered to be all Communist forces in

SEA, whether NVA (North Vietnamese Army), VC (the Viet Cong in South Vietnam supported from the North), or the PL (Pathet Lao Communists) in Laos.

Once they arrived at the final list, Whisenand then had to present the results and his recommendations to the SecDef, who would add his own ideas before carrying the whole package forward to the President, who had *his* own ideas.

The President would then confer, almost always at a Tuesday luncheon, with the SecDef and other civilian cabinet members and advisers, who had *their* own ideas. The results were sent back with the SecDef to be implemented. Whisenand was in the return chain for information purposes only. He could not protest any decision he felt to be faulty or out of line with sound military precepts.

It all went back to early 1965, when the war in South Vietnam had reached crisis proportions and airpower was selected as an interim answer. The previous CINCPLAN 37-64, a three-phase, twenty-eight-day attack against ninety-four targets in North Vietnam, which the JCS had been sure would effectively stop the flow of Communist supplies to the South, had been rejected.

Instead, the SecDef and the President had decided to gradually bomb northward from the 17th parallel of the DMZ, the demilitarized zone, toward Hanoi, in hopes that at some point the Communists would realize the pain wasn't worth the gain of trying to take over South Vietnam.

The program, code-named Rolling Thunder, set in motion highly limited air strikes. The policy, as stated by the President and as written by his Secretary of Defense, was that the Rolling Thunder air strikes had three combined and mutually supportive aims:

- to penalize Ho Chi Minh for supporting aggression in South Vietnam;
- to cut the infiltration of men and materiel into South Vietnam;
- to raise the morale of the South Vietnamese.

The strikes were supposed to roll thunder farther north each time the Communists did something the White House didn't like. The attacks' size, weapons, and time on target were dictated by the White House, a methodology that, Whitey was finding out, was killing fighter pilots.

Whitey suspected no war had been run quite like this—by committee, civilian at that—since the time of George Washington. And considering Valley Forge, not then either.

In addition to advising the SecDef, Whitey Whisenand was on the National Reconnaissance Organization board, a highly classified agency trying to set up clandestine reconnaissance in North Vietnam and Laos. The NRO used teams on the ground, Compass Cope drones at low altitudes in the air, U-2's at high altitude, and satellites in space. They were having a hard time getting support for all but the satellites. The SecDef loved satellites. His idea was to build an electronic fence between North and South Vietnam that ran east and west along the 17th parallel at the DMZ. Satellite coverage would relay information instantly to Washington, where he could absorb it, and relay back to the field commanders orders on exactly how to react to enemy actions. Whitey despised this arrangement of excessive civilian control, and the SecDef knew it.

Whisenand knew he would never get his third star because he was too old. In truth, there was no job for him. He was only on active duty at the sufferance of some highly placed admirers in the Congress who felt his contribution to the intelligence community belonged in the military. Whitey was independently wealthy, and he liked the United States Air Force. He was good at what he did, and saw no reason to retire merely to seek employment elsewhere.

He was the top intel specialist in the USAF; it was said he could spot a camouflaged gun emplacement at ten feet from a three-inch negative. He could identify all the Spoon Rest and Fan Song series Russian radar by their transmission sounds, and had a feel for enemy intentions that made some think he personally paid agents inside their cabinets to provide information.

Whisenand knew his time with the SecDef was limited. Whitey was sure that sooner or later his intellectual temperament and dislike of autocratic persons would prevail, and he would inform the ex-Detroit whiz kid exactly where his and the President's air war plan should be stuffed.

He sighed, put his coffee cup down, and picked up his latest target request list. He stared at it for a moment and threw it down as he looked at the chart board his Air Force and Navy assistants, fighter pilots themselves champing at the bit to get to Vietnam, had shown him. Draped with black crepe paper, it listed shootdowns. They had been told they would be in deep kimchi for negative thinking if the SecDef ever saw it. They felt it was the only way they could call some attention to and show some tribute, albeit minor, to the air crewmen who had paid such a high price to obtain a goal that didn't seem to be understood by their Commander in Chief. Whitey had them leave the board in his office. He looked at it and his face tightened.

AIRCRAFT SHOT DOWN OVER NORTH VIETNAM 148
PILOT/NAV MIA, KIA, POW 102
SUCCESSFUL RESCUES 46

"Those POW's are rotting in cells in the Hoa Lo prison in Hanoi," Air Force Colonel Ralph Morgan had said.

"Boss," Navy Captain Jim Tunner had said to Whitey, "we've got so many guys in there now, the troops over at Casualty Recovery have got a new name for the place."

"Oh? What's it called?" Whitey had asked.

"The Hanoi Hilton."

4

171430Z DEC 65
FM 3RD TACFTRWG BIEN HOA AB RVN
TO RUEDHQA/CSAF//RUWHNF/DEP TIG USAF NORTON AFB CALIF
RUHLKM/CINCPACAF\RUMSAL/7TH AF TAN SON NHUT AB RVN
C O N F I D E N T I A L 3SA 04281 DEC
SUBJECT: COMBAT LOSS: REF APEX BEELINE SENT 161630H
DEC: PRELIMINARY REPORT OF AIRCRAFT COMBAT LOSSES.
FOUO SPECIAL HANDLING REQUIRED.

A. 17 DEC, 1330H, PACAF, 7AF, 3TFW, BIEN HOA AB, 531TFS
B. TWO (2) F-100D'S, SN 56-3437, 56-3405
C. 1.) AUSTIN, PAUL W., MAJOR, FR46L57, FLIGHT LEAD,
      CALL SIGN RAMROD FOUR ZERO (40), ACFT 437; 2) BAN-
      NISTER, COURTLAND EdM., CAPT. A03021953, NR 2,
      CALL SIGN RAMROD FOUR ONE (41), ACFT 405.
D. 1.) LOCATION LOC NINH XT 486687, WAR ZONE D, RVN,
      PILOT AUSTIN MIA/PRESUMED DEAD/BODY NOT
      RECOVERED, ACFT 437 DESTROYED DIRECT RESULT
      GRND FIRE.
   2.) LOCATION BIEN HOA AB RVN, APPROACH END TO RUN-
      WAY 27, PILOT BANNISTER (WIA), ACFT 405 CLASS 26
      INDIRECT RESULT GRND FIRE.
E. 1.) FAC COPPERHEAD 03 (01-E) AND RAMROD FOUR ONE
      REPORT UNUSUALLY HEAVY GROUND FIRE FROM
      MULTIPLE QUAD 12.7MM ZSU-4 SITES. LEAD SITE XT
      458587 USED TRACERS TO DIRECT OTHER NONTRACER
      SITES.
   2.) RAMROD 40 NOT OBSERVED BY CO3 AND RR41 TAKING

HITS. NO RADIO TRANSMISSIONS HEARD FROM RR40
AFTER RR40 CALLED ROLLING IN ON TARGET.
3.) WEATHER NO FACTOR (BRKN OVERCST 18M, CLEAR, 10
PLUS VIZ).
F. SURVIVING PILOT (BANNISTER) STATEMENT TO FOLLOW
IAW AFM 127-1. FLYING EVALUATION BOARD NOT
APPLICABLE.
G. ITEMS G THROUGH X FOLLOWING IN ROUTINE CLASS TWX.
Y. JONES, K.L., MAJ., WG FLYING SAFETY OFF REPORTING.

0730 HOURS LOCAL, 18 DECEMBER 1965
HEADQUARTERS, 3RD TACTICAL FIGHTER WING,
BIEN HOA AIR BASE, REPUBLIC OF VIETNAM

☆

Captain Courtland Esclaremonde de Montségur Bannister, face a bit battered, cuts shielded by two flesh-colored Band-Aids, sat on a steel-gray metal chair facing the standard-issue USAF gray steel desk of Major K. L. Jones, 3rd Tactical Fighter Wing Flying Safety Officer. Jones was considered a "good guy." He had gone through the accident investigation school at USC, he took his job seriously, and he didn't automatically look for pilot error in his investigations. Jones was a Reservist with nineteen years' active duty and had been passed over for lieutenant colonel twice. He was forty-five, had no big screw-ups on his record, but it was simply that the USAF didn't promote many reserve majors to LC. The promotion boards had to save the few slots available for officers of the Regular Air Force, at least that was the rumored excuse. Jones knew he'd be flushed at twenty years of total service, but he still did his job. He flew the F-100 in an admin slot assigned to the 90th Squadron on combat sorties about once a week.

It was 0730 hours on a Saturday looming hot and humid. Both Jones's and Bannister's flight suits were already darkening with sweat. A tech sergeant prepared to record the conversation and statements on a Sony 3RT reel-to-reel tape recorder set on the edge of Jones's desk. The microphone was pointed between the two officers. The sergeant monitored the volume control, trying not to look interested in what was to follow. Jones looked up at Bannister and began to quote the flying safety manual from memory.

"Captain Bannister," he said in a formal tone for the machine that was belied by the pleasant look on his face, "be advised the purpose of this investigation into the crash and subsequent death of Major Paul W. Austin is not to obtain evidence for use in disciplinary action, or for determining liability or line-of-duty status, or for use before a flying evaluation board. Do you understand that?'' After Bannister said he did, Jones asked him if he would be so kind as to answer the questions about his name, rank, and experience level from the card he handed him. ''Be further advised that your statements are considered to be voluntary. Do you understand?''

''Yes, sir.''

''Do you have any questions?''

''No, sir.'' Bannister had been sitting with his hands on his knees. When Jones started talking he sat back in his chair and crossed his arms over his chest, then leaned forward to take the three-by-five card handed to him. The tech sergeant pointed the mike toward Bannister.

''I am Courtland Bannister,'' he began in a low but firm voice, ''Captain, AO3021953, 531st Tac Fighter Squadron, Third Tactical Fighter Wing, thirty years old, a senior pilot with about 2,300 total flying hours, 2,100 jet, over 600 in the F-100, sixty or so hours combat. I have flown thirty-eight combat missions in SEA in the F-100 and am qualified as a flight leader. I do hereby make the following voluntary statement.''

Having answered the questions for Jones, Bannister handed the card back to him, then pulled a folded piece of notepaper from his left breast pocket and began to read what he had penciled down earlier that morning.

''At approximately 1245 local time on 17 December I was cleared in on my third ordnance pass, a Mark-82 500-pound bomb, when I heard the forward air control, Copperhead Zero Three, call my leader, Ramrod Four Zero, several times. When he received no reply he told me to finish my pass wet and drop my bomb, then orbit high and dry while he recce'd the target area. As I pulled off I observed a column of greasy black smoke and red flames of the size usually associated with a jet fighter crash. The smoke was to the south of the target area and north of the Michelin rubber plantation. I told Copperhead Zero Three what I was going to do and flew over to take a look. He cleared me to orbit the crash site but to stay above small-arms fire. I orbited the site and confirmed it was the remains of an F-100. Neither Copperhead Three nor I saw a parachute. We didn't hear any beeper or survival radio.''

Bannister stopped his recital, folded the paper, and looked up at Jones. ''I know Austin is . . . ah, has bought it.''

"Why do you say that? He could have ejected at low altitude and you or the FAC didn't see the 'chute."

"I went down and looked. The ejection seat fired on airplane impact. Austin was still in it. I saw him, it, lying just outside the fireball."

"How could you see that well from forty-five hundred feet?"

"I went down on the deck. Later, when a helicopter went to get the body, it was gone. So was the ejection seat."

Jones looked at Bannister for a moment, then turned the mike toward himself and signed off with the time and date. He motioned the tech sergeant to shut off the machine, then told him to go get a cup of coffee. The tech left the room as quietly as he could.

"Court, the FAC told you to stay clear of small arms. Is that when you got hit?"

Court sat straight up. "Yeah. You want to investigate that, too? I busted the bird up bringing it in." Bannister was trying to keep the defensive tone out of his voice, though there was no reason to be defensive about his crash landing. He could as easily have bailed out of his damaged F-100, in fact that would probably have been the smarter thing to do, and no one would have said a word. Instead, he tried to save it and wound up laying a pile of smoking junk on the Bien Hoa runway.

Major Jones stood up and walked to the window in his room in Wing Headquarters overlooking the flight line and, in the distance, Runway 27. "No," he said, "the report on your airplane has gone out as a Class 26 due to ground fire. Your ops officer might press it, but I'm not. I hear he's pretty upset losing Austin, especially since he's the son of a three-star general."

Bannister checked the impulse to tell Jones that Major Harold L. Rawson was already pressing it. But he had no difficulty not telling Jones that Austin really augered in because he rolled in low and slow on his second pass, and hit the ground because he couldn't pull out in time. Austin busted his ass due to pure pilot error and Bannister didn't want to pass that information around. What the hell, Bannister had about decided while flying his shot-up airplane back from the mission, why let Austin's wife and the kids know their old man had splattered himself all over the field of glory because he screwed up? At the time, Bannister had become so preoccupied with getting his own bird back home that he didn't really come to the decision to cover Austin's error until Rawson started acting like such a horse's ass about *losing* Austin. So he had decided to report the crash as a combat loss, not a pilot-induced accident.

"Anything else you want to tell me?" Jones said as he rewound the Sony.

Bannister had a feeling Jones didn't want to go any deeper, if in fact he suspected anything. Paul Austin hadn't been known as the world's greatest fighter pilot by any means. But it's better to buy the farm defending your country against the godless Communist hordes than simply bust your ass like a second lieutenant the first time on the gunnery range at Nellis, because you stupidly asked your airplane for more, aerodynamically, than it could deliver. In terms of airplanes and pilots, the first was a heroic combat loss, the second a flying-safety violation reflecting great discredit on the USAF in general and the deceased's immediate chain of command in particular.

As a pilot on flight-leader status flying the wing of a known weak pilot (Austin had gained his time in MAC flying cargo planes, he hadn't been upside down since pilot training), Bannister had paid close attention to Austin's attack pattern; but he hadn't caught him in time on that last pass to say, "Roll out, level off, abort the pass." Instead, Austin had rolled in so close behind Bannister that by the time Bannister had pulled off target and jinked away from the ground fire up to the downwind, he had had only time enough to see Austin's F-100 slam into the ground in an extraordinary nose-high attitude. As an officer true to his oath, Bannister was torn between strict compliance with telling the truth and the desire to save Austin's family a lot of anguish.

Bannister had decided to forgo ruining Austin's official reputation as a combat pilot in the United States Air Force and maybe shaming his kids for life. Equally important, Court knew that no pilot's wife wants to live with the knowledge her husband is dead because of his own inept handling of an airplane she probably hated in the first place. Better to let her direct her grief-spun anger at the faceless enemy.

Bannister stood up. "No, sir," he said, bending over to fish his blue flight cap from his bottom right leg pocket, "I have nothing more."

"I'll have this transcribed," Jones said, indicating the tapes. "Stop around tomorrow and sign it."

"Do I meet a flying evaluation board?" Bannister asked.

"No FEB," said Jones. "Your airplane is a combat loss, not an accident. By the way, I read the Intel wrap-up last night. I saw what you said about the Loc Ninh buildup. How heavy is it really, and what do you think it's all about?"

"I'm not sure what it's all about," Bannister said, "maybe an attack on the Loc Ninh Special Forces camp, maybe a new permanent VC base camp, maybe an attempt to cut off Route Thirteen. But it was the first time that 12.7's have come up in this area so it must mean something."

"Very interesting," Jones said, standing up. "Well, Court, good luck and take care. Don't be a magnet ass," he added, waving Bannister out. "See you around. Oh yeah, almost forgot, Merry Christmas."

Bannister nodded, thanked him, said yessir, and left for his squadron area at the flight line. He had been told by Major Bob Derham, the assistant ops officer of the 531st Squadron, to report to Rawson immediately after his appointment with Jones.

The 1964–65 almost panic-driven escalation of USAF air operations in Vietnam required the immediate construction of eleven new air bases and the expansion of eight existing air bases to support combat operations. Quarters and mess halls had to be built to house and feed the troops. Runways had to be lengthened or constructed to launch airplanes sometimes loaded so heavily they rolled along nearly two miles of concrete before gaining enough speed to get airborne. An interim logistical effort, given the code name Project Bitterwine, shipped 82 million dollars' worth of packages providing instant air base—a food-service package, for example, contained all the equipment needed to outfit and operate a base mess hall.

The Bitterwine concept had the air-base buildup proceed in three steps. First, Gray Eagle kits containing housekeeping equipment to support 4,400 people in tent facilities were delivered to a new base. The next phase called for temporary structures such as inflatable shelters and prefab buildings to replace the Gray Eagle installation. In the third and final phase, civilian contractors completed runway construction and built permanent operational and support facilities.

There were special military organizations to undertake construction and repair of air-base facilities during the first two phases of Bitterwine. One such was the Base Engineering Emergency Force, or Prime Beef, as the acronym-loving USAF named it. Prime Beef was in the middle of Bitterwine Phase Two, the transition from tents to wooden huts for the USAF personnel at Bien Hoa.

Bien Hoa Air Base, named after the medium-sized village next to it, had been a small, sleepy Vietnamese Air Force (VNAF) base, built, French-style, of tin-roofed, thick-walled barracks for the enlisted troops and villalike houses with wrought-iron grillwork and red-tiled roofs for the officers. The VNAF used these facilities, which were run-down and tenement-crowded, while the USAF Prime Beef teams built what became known as Bien Hoa huts for the USAF people. The Bien Hoa huts were one-story frame buildings with corrugated tin roofs, wood floors, and wooden side louvers, like oversized venetian blinds, outside the screened sides. Both officer and airman used these huts, though not under the same tin roof, sleeping on G.I. cots covered with muslin mosquito netting. Though considered rough accommodations by new guys, the old heads knew they were far better than the Gray Eagle dirt-floor tent kits used by the teams of American advisers to the VNAF a few years earlier. Farm Gate, Jungle Jim, and Dirty Thirty were code names for these early USAF troops in Vietnam who came to advise the VNAF, then wound up flying many, almost too many, combat missions as U.S. participation escalated.

The building housing the operations, administration, and personal equipment of the 531st Tactical Fighter Squadron was an old French-built concrete warehouse hastily refurbished. Pacific Architects and Engineers (PA&E) would soon build new ops buildings, quarters for the pilots and airmen, and a second parallel runway 10,000 feet long, but it would be months before footings were poured. Meanwhile, white and brown dust stirred up by the giant yellow earth movers drifted and settled over the base like dried smog. Inside the 531st squadron ops building, wooden plywood partitions mounted on frames of two-by-four's had been set in place, light bulbs hung suspended from the rafters; and large floor fans standing six feet tall were stationed in each "room" to move the humid air. The floor was concrete, old and chipped. Crates and battered olive-drab filing cabinets lined the bare plywood walls. There was no lounge where the pilots could relax with a cold soda.

In the Personal Equipment (PE) room, the pilots' flight gear hung from big smooth hooks welded to two-inch metal pipe racks that supported their parachutes, helmets, and flight bags holding knee boards, maps, and other paraphernalia. Suspended next to the parachutes were green mesh survival vests the pilots wore to carry emergency rations (split C rats), survival equipment (hook, four each; signal mirror, one each; day-night flares, two each; and sixteen more items), and the most important piece of survival equipment a pilot could tote: his Urk-Ten (AN/URC-10) survival radio. About the size of a paperback book, the battery-powered radio gave a downed pilot the means to talk to his orbiting flight members and, hopefully, to a rescue helicopter. The Urk-Ten transmitted and received on 243.0 megacycles, known as Guard channel, which all airplanes with UHF kept tuned in for emergency use. The USAF called that frequency Navy Common. The Navy jocks said it was Air Force Common. The Marines could not have cared less.

Bannister passed by the PE room and went to the counter in front of the flying-schedule board. He looked up. Coiled around the rafters was six feet of green rock python snake. Looped twice around a two-by-four cross piece for stability, it had lowered its head down to a position where it could watch the traffic coming and going in the squadron. The rectangular head and jaws were roughly the size of a cigarette carton. Its rubbery tongue was constantly flicking in and out. The snake had been a gift from a FAC.

"Hey guys," Beaver 72 from the Mekong Delta to the south said one day as he walked in and placed a large cardboard box on the ops counter, "I brought you a present." Beaver 72 had brought presents before. He would fly his 0-1E up from the South to Bien Hoa, where his parent organization, the 504th Tactical Air Support Group, would work over his plane. Earlier presents included VC flags (sometimes real), or captured AK-47 assault rifles, and other battle memorabilia from grateful Vietnamese commanders. The 531st had been proud to display these trophies on their walls.

Beaver 72 had assumed an expression of benign altruism as the pilots gathered around, wondering what was in the box. "My God," one had whispered to another, "you don't think he has brought in some heads, do you?" One of the pilots opened the box and peered in. He didn't peer long.

"*Good God Almighty!*" he bellowed as he went straight up and back about four feet.

Stunned, the rest of the pilots froze in place as a very large snake head rose majestically from the box and calmly surveyed the stupefied onlookers.

As any fighter jock knew, snakes were slimy creatures that could poison you, eat you, twist your bones, crush you at their leisure, or plain give you the willies for days. That's what Lieutenant Dan Freeman said. Lieutenant Fairchild, a farm lad, knew better. But of course he had never seen anything larger than a bull snake. That was enough. Fairchild, Douglas T., was promptly appointed Snake Control Officer by the Squadron Commander, Peter Warton. By unanimous opinion, the squadron named the snake Ramrod. More precisely, Ramrod S. (for Strange) McNamara.

To be on the safe side, the Snake Control Officer and his cronies built Ramrod a cage that would probably have held King Kong in his wildest frenzy. After eating all the rats and mice provided him and graduating to larger food, Ramrod outgrew his cage and was allowed to roam the squadron. He had the whole area to glide around in; under counters, along the molding high up, in the rafters. It was his place. It was a bit disconcerting, however, for a visitor fresh to the squadron to have three or four feet of inquisitive snake, tongue darting, suddenly hang from the rafters to check him out. Rawson hated this and always entered the squadron in a sideways skedaddle to dodge Ramrod's attention.

Ramrod could unhinge his jaws to swallow an object the size of a chicken or a duck, which he did every two weeks as the pilots fed him. He would then sleep for several days (usually under the ops counter), awaken, deposit a large, white, odorless plaster-of-Paris-like lump, and shed his skin. The pilots would carry Ramrod by slinging him around their necks like an old flapper-style fur boa. Ramrod would wrap his tail around their chest for stability then position his head up and out facing forward from over the pilot's right shoulder. He would track and flick his forked tongue at whatever they passed.

Rawson's fear and hatred of the snake was becoming more evident every day, but as yet he hadn't done anything about it.

As Bannister walked past Ramrod, he saw Rawson behind the counter checking a staff sergeant who with a black grease pencil was printing up some sortie info on the clear-plastic-covered scheduling board. MERRY CHRISTMAS was blocked across the top of the board in red grease pencil. The staff wore fatigues, while Rawson wore an obviously tailored flight suit. Tailoring was cheap and easy to come by in Vietnam, and a few pilots had their uniforms and flight suits tailored to get rid of the baggy look. Officially categorized "Coverall, Flying, Man's, K-2B," the flight suits were made of cotton and had thirteen zippers, all guaranteed to rust shut while the green bag rotted off the hapless wearer's torso in a jungle survival situation. The K-2B's were not flame-proof. The Navy was starting to get flame-proof Nomex flight suits, and so were Army helicopter pilots. For obscure bureaucratic reasons, the USAF didn't have a contract yet. The wreath around the star over Rawson's pilot wings showed he had been flying at least fifteen years and was a command pilot.

Rawson motioned Bannister into the small room next to the ops counter and took a seat behind his gray steel desk, twin of all USAF desks in the world. Bannister stood in front. Rawson's pale blue eyes meandered over his desk top before looking up at Bannister. When they did, it was only for a second before his eyes began wandering around the tiny room as if searching for an elusive shadow, or a being that was not quite visible. Rawson plucked an expandable pointer-pen from his left sleeve pocket and began tapping it on some papers neatly stacked in front of him. Finally he spoke.

"I want to know, how did it happen?" he asked in a tight voice. "General Austin will be calling me and I've got to have an answer." Rawson's eyes never made contact with those of Bannister, which were supposed to be fixed at a spot about six inches over his superior officer's head, but instead were following Rawson's roving eyes. He hesitated, then answered.

"As I said in my official report to Major Jones at Wing, Austin was hit and went in. I saw him on the ground, outside the fireball."

Rawson stood up. "You mean he was still alive?" His eyes alighted for an instant on Bannister.

"No, sir, dead. In his seat. It must have fired on impact. An SF team on an Army helicopter tried to recover the body later, but it and the seat were gone."

"Why didn't you call out the ground fire? Why didn't you warn him? Didn't the FAC tell you there was heavy ground fire? Is there any chance he was still alive in the seat?" Rawson asked, eyes chasing shadows with renewed vigor.

Bannister had abandoned his position of quasi-attention and had put his hands on his hips when the questions started. When they finished he answered only the last one. "No chance, major. He and the seat were all crumbled and rolled up."

"Wait a minute," Rawson said, eyes widened and fixed for an instant, "how did you see all this detail? How low did you go?"

"Not very, enough to see what I could." Hell, Bannister thought to himself, I suppose I should have said I had field glasses, but I didn't. He knew what was coming. Several F-100's had been lost recently by pilots flying too low and slamming into the ground or mushing through trees as well as picking up lots of holes from ground fire. The word was out from 7th: Stay above 1,500 feet out of small-arms range. Or, if the VC don't get you, I will, implied the directive from the commander, 7th Air Force, Tan Son Nhut Air Base, Republic of Vietnam.

As the operations officer of the 531st, Rawson had his neck on the line to ensure that the squadron pilots carried out orders from above. If too many squadron jocks violated the regs and picked up too many holes, the ops officer would get tagged with supervisory error and never gain command of a squadron. Between that reality of USAF life and the fact that Austin's father, Lieutenant General Robert L. "Tex" Austin, Deputy Chief of Staff, Plans and Operations, in the Pentagon, would be ringing up via the hotline in Wing Headquarters, Rawson was, Bannister knew, on the verge of panic. "Did you go under fifteen hundred feet?" Rawson asked.

"Can't say, didn't look at my altimeter," Bannister said. Of course he hadn't looked at his altimeter, he had buzzed and orbited the crash site so low and slow he didn't dare put his head in the cockpit.

"Bannister, that's crap, and you know it," Rawson all but shouted, pointer-pen tapping frantically. "You know, you're a little too independent. You think you're something special." The pencil tapped faster. "Well, I'll tell you you're not. You're just a Hollywood showboat and those useless army parachute wings prove it. There's no reason for an Air Force pilot to have Army jump wings. You go off base running around with those Army thugs, maybe you impress them, but not me. So I know you went under fifteen hundred feet." Rawson paused for breath. "I'll tell you something: Effective immediately your flight lead orders are rescinded. You will fly nothing but wing from now on."

Eyes steady on Bannister for an instant, Rawson acted as if he expected a retort or an outburst. Instead, Bannister came to attention, yessired, saluted, and, without waiting for it to be returned, did an about-face and headed for the door.

"Bannister," Rawson yelled after him, mustache twitching. Bannister stopped, executed a precise about-face, and waited expectantly.

"You didn't wait for my salute." He stood up. "You're looking for trouble, Bannister, and I'm going to give it to you. I'm going to put you on every nasty detail and extra duty that comes up."

Court Bannister said, "Yes, sir" again, held a salute until Rawson, surprised, returned it, then went out the door.

5

☆

That night, in the squadron hootch, Bannister sat on one of the four rickety wooden stools in front of the bar the squadron pilots had built from scrounged sheets of plywood. They had built it at one end of their open-bay, wood-and-screen Bien Hoa hut barracks to have a private drink without going to the O-Club. They called it the Hawk Inn.

First Lieutenants Fairchild and Freeman, green-bag zippers down to their navels (the temperature was 92, the humidity at 86 percent), sat next to Bannister. Behind them, in the dark, was an aisle between the rows of a dozen or so mosquito-net–covered steel G.I. cots. Fairchild had turned Ramrod loose to investigate the hootch's rat population. Major Conrad Russell, M.D., USAF, was acting bartender. The small refrigerator behind the bar had cost ten K-Bar survival knives traded to an Army warrant officer over at the United States Army of the Republic of Vietnam (USARV) supply depot in Long Binh. A broken foot-high green plastic Christmas tree was propped on top of the refrigerator. The pilot's wife who'd mailed it to her husband had had unwarranted faith in the Army Post Office system.

The three pilots were drinking Budweiser beer. Doctor Major Russell had a scotch and soda. The squadron's Akai tape recorder, bought with money kicked in by the twelve hootch mates, was reeling off at 3¾ inches per second a tape of what the *Reader's Digest* said were the best songs of Christmas. Bing Crosby had just finished crooning his dreams of a white Christmas. Perry Como was now relating the tale of chestnuts roasting by an open fire. The pilots hadn't spoken much. Just some banal talk about how the day had gone—no hot missions; how the weather was—lousy; how the Bud tasted—cool, like in a real bar back in the world. The 3rd Tac Fighter Wing, they knew with relief, wasn't losing many pilots, maybe two or three a month. Nothing like the Thud and Phantom drivers that had to go North from Da Nang and bases in Thailand. Their losses over Hanoi, code-named Route Pack 6, were becoming staggeringly high, about five a week. The Hun drivers from Bien Hoa had a reasonably safe way of life going for themselves and they knew it.

"Whooee, that's good beer," said First Lieutenant Doug Fairchild, holding up his beer can so all could see this marvel of American know-how.

"But is it Christmas?" asked First Lieutenant Dan Freeman, not quite in the bag but getting weepy. He missed his wife and three-year-old daughter something fierce. This was their first Christmas apart.

"What the hell do you care whether it's Christmas or not, you're Jewish," Fairchild demanded, lowering the can.

"It's the season, you goy fink, to be jolly and I'm not jolly. I want to be home."

Freeman sighed and took another pull at his beer. "So what's a nice Jewish boy like me doing here anyhow, killing Buddhists to make the world safe for Christianity?"

"Now that's profound, Freeman, really profound. The only problem is, it's what you always say after you've had two beers," Lieutenant Fairchild said, trying not to laugh.

Though they'd heard it before, both Bannister and Doc Russell chuckled.

Fairchild and Freeman looked at each other, then at Bannister. "Too bad about Major Austin," Freeman said. "Yeah," Fairchild chimed in. "Was he really stitched or did he auger in on his own?"

Bannister took a long swallow of his beer, then fixed Fairchild with a sharp look, the humorous atmosphere rapidly dissipating. "Why do you ask that?"

"Oh, I dunno. Some of the guys might have heard something," Fairchild replied uneasily.

Bannister kept staring at the lieutenant.

"Unh, nothing big, Court. It's just that my crew chief said some tech from Wing might have heard something. You know how those wing wienies gossip, huh?'' Fairchild began nervously scratching his left forearm with his right hand. Bannister kept staring at him.

"Come on, Crapola,'' Freeman said, suddenly grabbing Fairchild's arm, "let's hie off to yon officer's mess and quaff a few for the jolly old king. What say, eh?''

"Yeah,'' Lieutenant Crapola said, climbing down from his stool and following Freeman's lead to the door of the hootch. "Unh, see you later, Court, Doc.''

The two lieutenants' boots clumped as they crossed the plank floor to the wooden screen door. Fairchild scooped up Ramrod and expertly fitted him to his torso. As Freeman opened the door for his friends, he hollered back up the dark path between the bunks to Bannister and Doc Russell, whose outlines wavered under the swinging overhead lamp, "God rest ye merry, gentlemen, Merry Christmas, and to all a cheery, beery good night.'' The squeaking screen door swung shut and they were gone, leaving the faint tune of Lieutenant Crapola humming "God Rest Ye Merry, Gentlemen.''

Doc Russell took a sip of his scotch. "Court, I paged through your medical records. You've got a hell of a middle name. I read Courtland Esclaremonde de Montségur Bannister. Do you mind my asking how you got that middle name? Is it a person, place, or thing?''

Courtland Esclaremonde de Montségur Bannister, grinning, nodded. "I wondered when you would ask.'' It was a long story that he told few people, but he figured maybe the Doc would appreciate it. He took a pull at his beer. "My Dad's first wife, my mother, was from Toulouse—southern France, right? About seven hundred years ago, part of her family, along with some two hundred others, were burned at the stake for heresy. They had held out at Montségur Castle for about a year. The ruins still exist. I've been there—about four thousand feet up on a plateau south of Toulouse and slightly north of the Pyrenees. Mother was proud of the stubbornness of her family in the Montségur Castle, I was her first child, so—she named me after the castle. Also an ancestor, a woman who was killed there named Esclaremonde de Perella.'' He waited for Doc Russell to make some comment. The expression on Doc's face was merely that of absorbed interest, with not even a grin about the female portion of Bannister's middle name.

Both men took a swallow of their drinks. Russell remembered old Hollywood screen magazine stories about Court's mother, the beautiful Monique d'Avignon of France's beau monde, who, as a teenager before World War II, had fallen in love with Sam Bannister, at twenty-three, already a movie idol. Bannister's face became more thoughtful as he continued. "She died when I was two. I never knew her. She and Dad had been married only a couple of years. Dad was running around a lot, so the de Montségurs helped raise me."

He looked at Baby Huey, this time a wry expression on his face. "I guess you know my dad remarried. Several times."

Silk Screen Sam Bannister had indeed married several times, as every Hollywood gossip columnist had screamed. Not since Errol Flynn had they had such a field day. Doc Russell remembered the rhyme all the young American men and half the population of Europe repeated.

> *Silk Screen Sam, the ladies' man.*
> *If he can't get in, no one can.*

"Yeah, I remember," Russell said, reluctant to ask further questions for fear Bannister would think he was probing. He'd always liked what he had heard about Sam Bannister, though. During World War II he had been a gunner on B-17's with the Eighth Air Force. He and Jimmy Stewart, Glenn Ford and Clark Gable had been some of the best-known Hollywood actors to volunteer for combat duty right after the Japanese attacked Pearl Harbor on December 7, 1941. Afterward he had picked up his acting career, made several highly successful adventure movies, and, with an old high school chum, invested the money in TV movies and Nevada desert real estate. Together they eventually bought up most of North Las Vegas. Playing only cameo roles now in selected films, Silk Screen Sam Bannister lived in the penthouse of his Las Vegas hotel, the Silver Screen, freshly divorced from his fourth wife. Sam was an accomplished world traveler who avoided the jet set.

"I have a half brother," Court went on. "His mother was Mary McDougal, Dad's second wife. His name is Shawn. Shawn Bannister. He's here in Vietnam someplace."

Doc Russell's eyebrows shot up. "As a G.I.?"

"Hell, no. He's a reporter for *California Sun;* it's a magazine published near Berkeley."

"I've heard of it," Russell said. "Sort of a left-wing scandal sheet, isn't it?"

"I guess so. Shawn claims it's a 'coupling of realism and existentialism.' He's hooked on Sartre and de Beauvoir."

"Sounds like a crock to me," Doc Russell said.

"Yeah, it's a crock." Bannister folded his beer can and tossed it into the trash. He stood up and stretched.

"Doc, I just don't feel like it's Christmas," Courtland said. "How about you?"

"Well, I'll tell you," Baby Huey began, shifting his bulk to pour another three fingers of Vat 69, "I don't feel so bad, but then I didn't ding on the runway either. All things considered, Court, you should feel pretty good about merely being alive."

"Alive? What do you mean, alive? Sure, I'm alive. I'm well and happy. Believe me, I'm well and happy," Bannister said, swinging his head from side to side to emphasize his words. He was starting to feel the beer. Only with conscious effort was he able to suppress a replay of the dead Austin in his seat and the sight and sounds of his own crash on the runway.

Russell looked at Bannister. "Why are you really here in combat, Court? I saw on your records yesterday that you volunteered for SEA. In fact, you broke an assignment to the Test Pilot School at Edwards to get recurrent in Huns and come to Vietnam. Why did you do a dumb thing like that? You had it wired. You probably could have gone on to the astronaut corps or something. Anything instead of this God-awful place," Russell said, somewhat belligerently.

"Doc, I plan on doing just that. Going to astronauts, I mean. I only put off going to Edwards for a year. I'll go there to the school after this tour and then, sure, on to astronaut training," Bannister said.

"You still haven't answered my question," Russell pressed. "Not *how* did you do it, but *why* did you do it? Wife troubles, finances, glory, country at war, boredom, all of the above?"

"What is this, Doc, the friendly flight surgeon's psychiatric evaluation?"

"Hell, no, Court, just a friend inquiring. Take me, for example. I'm here because I love flying, and fighters, and, yes, you guys who fly them. I want to see how you all fit together in a war." Doc Russell paused. "You don't have to answer if you don't want to."

Bannister liked Russell. He knew he was competent, hardworking, and, unlike many military doctors, not in the service merely to get his medical school tab picked up by the USAF, or simply to get the varied experience that would take a civilian ten years of general practice to acquire. That kind of M.D. usually snickered at the servicemen they treated and could hardly wait until they could get out and earn eighty grand a year and tell funny stories about the nincompoops in uniform.

With three dependents, Doc Russell was content with his $19,565 per annum and M.D. bonus pay as a major on flying status (he was required to log four hours a month). Court, a captain on flying status drawing combat pay, grossed $10,236 per year. Doc Russell might not be a warrior in appearance, Bannister thought to himself, but he sure was one inside. He was known to do anything, to buck any rank or regulation that prevented him from taking care of his boys. It was common knowledge that Baby Huey had earnestly requested an officious hospital commander more concerned with advancement than Aesculapius to go stuff his stethoscope where the sun don't shine, while he, Doctor Conrad D. Russell, went outside channels to fulfill an immediate need to replace a broken autoclave.

Bannister decided to tell Russell a bit of his story. Just enough to satisfy his curiosity. What the hell, he thought, I haven't really gotten to know anybody here. A few months in the squadron that's been together for years and I'm still the FNG, the frigging new guy. And, he admitted to himself, I have been off running around with the Army Special Forces guys quite a bit. And there was the aura of his father, because of whom most guys were afraid to appear sycophantic. Bannister was used to this understandable quirk in squadron life. It hadn't been like that at grade school in Hollywood and at the lycée in Paris, where everybody's father or mother, sometimes both, was a known personage. But in the Air Force, until his squadron mates accepted him as a good pilot who was serious about his profession and fought their self-induced intimidation, they usually remained aloof. Yesterday's events after Loc Ninh might open the door for him. Bannister also admitted to himself that he felt a bit tipsy and that a minor case of the lonesome Christmas blues was starting to set in. This conversation might be the needed catharsis. He took another pull at his beer.

"My wife and I were divorced about two years ago, when I was in the Air Force Institute of Technology program at Arizona State. I was carrying up to twenty-one hours of engineering each semester and flying ADC T-Birds out of Luke on the weekends. So I, ah, was gone a lot. My wife became more and more unhappy and finally said her mother didn't raise her to participate in a one-person marriage."

"No kids?" Doc Russell inquired.

"No. We had only been married one year. We had agreed, no kids until we were ready, but we were growing apart. We never became ready. She wanted to go back to her career."

"Which was?"

"Acting, dancing, singing . . ."

"Oh, my God," Russell said. "I just remembered. You were married to Charmaine, weren't you?"

Bannister nodded.

"Hey, she's here in Vietnam with the Bob Hope Show. I heard about it on AFVN."

"Yup."

"Are you going to see her?"

"Nope," Bannister said, crushing another beer can. "Not planning on it."

"Does she know you're here?"

"Can't say," Bannister said. "We don't write each other. I guess she knows I'm in 'Nam. Dad threw a bit of a wingding for me at the Screen in Vegas before I left." Bannister smiled. "Do you know what one of the movie fan magazines titled their coverage? *Combat for Cowboy Court.*"

"Cowboy Court?"

"Yup," Bannister said. "When I was nineteen, right before I became an aviation cadet, I was in a few cheap Westerns. Did a lot of riding but no acting. It was a lot of fun."

"What a life," Doc Russell said, shaking his head, "what a life. Why bust your buns so hard for the engineering degree?" he asked, resisting saying, "You certainly don't need the money." This courtesy did not go unnoticed by Bannister, who then really decided to open up.

"The moon, Doc. Because of the moon," Bannister said more intently than Doc Russell thought called for. "After the lycée, I had barely two years of college, general 'beer and broads' college at that. You need an engineering degree to get into Edwards. It used to be two years of math or engineering got you in, but the new Air Force Requisition 53-12 Regulation changed all that. I had to go complete my ME degree, in a bloody short time I might add, gutting my way through George Beakley's College of Engineering at ASU to be eligible for Edwards. Then, after I graduated from Edwards, I planned on going to Houston, to be selected for Houston, that is, for astronaut training. Then off to the moon. I planned on being the first man to walk on the moon."

"You're a tad late now, aren't you," Russell said. "Aren't all the moon guys chosen?"

"Yes, they are," Bannister answered. "I'll try the next round. I'm going to Edwards when this tour is over. By late '69 I'll be in astronaut training for a shot in the early '70's. That's how it will be."

The Doc placed his now empty scotch glass down on the stained plywood bar. "Court," he said, "you still haven't told me *why* you chucked a sure slot at Edwards to come to Vietnam."

"I'm getting to it. I called my old Squadron Officer School boss, General Herb Bench. He was Director, Personnel, at TAC HQ. He agreed that experienced fighter jocks were needed here and suggested I could give up my Edwards assignment, then reapply for the next class and hope I could pass the board again. He said he heard the board would look favorably on my reapplication." Bannister shrugged his broad shoulders. "That's about it."

Doc Russell, an intent look on his Baby Huey face, said "No, Courtland Esclaremonde de Montségur Bannister, that's not 'about it.' You keep giving me the 'how.' I want the 'why.' "

"Why should I give you the why? What the hell do you care?"

"Why shouldn't you? Besides," Russell said, "I do care."

Bannister stared at Russell for a long moment, took a deep breath, and started to talk in a voice so low Doc Russell had to lean forward.

"My country is at war—" The Doc started to say something, but Bannister held up his hand to stop him. "I have a lot of reasons, but that's the main one. It all started for me when the first two Thuds were shot down by MiGs. I didn't know the pilots personally but that didn't make any difference. They were our guys. They were at war and I was about to fat-cat it on the beach, while they were getting their butts shot off. What I'm trying to say without getting all tangled up, it's my duty to be here. This is exactly where I want to be." Bannister's voice had become louder as he spoke.

"There's more," said Russell, "isn't there?"

Bannister glanced at the Doc, then fixed his eyes on the beer can in his hands.

"Yes, there's more. Isn't there always?" Bannister tossed his empty beer can into a trash barrel in back of the bar, reached across the narrow plywood strip, and dug another from the reefer. He punched it open, took a long pull, put both hands flat on the bar and looked Russell in the eye.

"Doc, I'm a fighter pilot. I'm a single-seat, single-engine jock, up from F-86's, who has been training for this for nearly ten years. I'm telling you, it's my duty to be here. I'm a soldier, a warrior, an airman, a fighter pilot. Call it what you will, they all mean the same. It's what I get paid to do. It's why I've been drawing flight pay all these years. Maybe I'm like a boxer who trains and trains for the big fight that never seems to come off. He can get stale or he can quit. Up to now, for me, just the thrill of flying fighters and knowing I'm good keeps me from going airlines or, God forbid, back to Hollywood. You understand what I'm trying to say, Doc?"

"Yeah, I understand. Is that all?" The Doc knew full well there was one last bit. He was checking to see how honest with himself Bannister really was.

Bannister slapped his hand on the bar. "No, dammit, that's not all." He hesitated, then began again, his mouth twisting into a wry grin as he spoke. "Down deep I wanted to see if I could hack it when someone started shooting at me."

"Well, can you?"

"Damn, Doc, you don't give up, do you?"

"Well?"

"The guns are small around here, and I've only got thirty-eight missions so far. But yeah, I suppose I can hack it. Sure. The guys going North out of Da Nang and Yankee Station and Thailand, they've got it rough. Not us. Overall, though, at least we're winning the war. The guys are doing some real good stuff."

"What do you mean, 'not having it rough'? You just had an air-plane shot from under you and your flight lead shot down and killed, and you say we're winning the war. What makes you so sure?"

"I just am, that's all. I'm sure, Doc. Those shootdowns were a one-time thing. Let me tell you, here in Three Corps or south in Four Corps, if a squad-sized unit draws one, merely one, round of sniper fire—they've got three Huns overhead in twenty minutes with a full load of twenty mike-mike, nape, and CBU. Same thing in Eye Corps and Two Corps. We've got the VC on the run."

"That's in the air. How about on the ground?"

"Remember the headlines in the *Stars and Stripes* a few months back?" Bannister asked. "The SecDef said there was no reason we couldn't win if such was our will. The Commander of the U.S. Mil-itary Assistance Command Vietnam, General Westmoreland, said his search-and-destroy strategy would clean out the Cong one year from now, by the end of '66. McNamara says he sees the light at the end of the tunnel. And it's our will to win, so we'll win."

"How about up north then," Russell said. "You said yourself the losses over Hanoi are rough."

"Yeah, they are that," Bannister responded. "The guys are badly cramped by the Rules of Engagement. But if the whole Communist drive falls apart down here, then we won't have to go North any more. God, Doc, we got nearly a quarter million G.I.'s in-country now. And the USAF is building up to twenty wings and fifty-some squadrons of fighters and recce and transports here. Not to mention the Marines and the Navy. We're creaming the bad guys. You watch. They'll come around. Maybe even during this bombing halt President Johnson is starting."

"Court, look," Doc Russell said as he set his nearly empty glass down, "do you really mean all that? That we are winning?"

"Of course I do."

"What about the Loc Ninh buildup?"

"I said we're winning, not that the war is over. Yeah, the bad guys are up to something around Loc Ninh, and Intel doesn't believe it. They say the area shows no past or ongoing activity of any kind. I told them there was enough activity to shoot me down with guns of a caliber not normally seen this far south."

"Shoot *you* down? Why the singular? Didn't they shoot Paul Austin down too?"

Bannister looked straight at Doctor Conrad Russell for a minute. "No, Doc, they didn't," he said in a low voice. "He rolled in low and slow. Paul didn't leave himself enough room to pull out. I saw him, an instant before impact. He must of had the nose of that bird up thirty degrees, burner blowing and throwing dirt up like a rooster tail. In fact, he might have made it if he hadn't lit off his afterburner."

Doc Russell looked up, "What do you mean?"

"You know, you've been in the backseat of our F-model. When you bang the throttle outboard to engage the burner, eyelids on the aft section of the tailpipe open up about two or three seconds before the burner ignites and kicks you in the butt with the extra thrust. That extra open space in the tailpipe costs you about two thousand pounds of thrust when you need it most. But, the main reason I know he wasn't hit was what he said just before impact."

"I didn't know he transmitted. I signed off as Wing Flight Surgeon on the report you made to Keith Jones and I didn't read where Paul transmitted anything. What did he say that makes you so sure he wasn't hit?"

"When a pilot is hit, the first thing he does, if the plane hasn't exploded under him, is say, 'Lead's hit,' or 'Two's hit.' You let somebody know who you are and what happened. But when a jock screws up like Paul did and knows he can't pull out enough to avoid hitting the ground, he almost always says, 'Ah, shit,' in a long, drawn-out, low-key way. It's never a scream. Listen to some of the tapes the various air forces have of crashes from aerobatics or on the gunnery range when a guy screws up. You hear the same phrase in Japanese or German or French. *'Baka,' 'Scheisse,' 'Eh merde.'* It's a hell of a thing to hear. There's everything you've ever wanted and lost in life packed into that one phrase."

"And that's how you know," Russell said. "Paul said, 'Shit.' "

"That's how I know. Paul said, 'Ah, shit.' "

6

☆

"Have you signed in yet?" Colonel Leonard Norman, the Old Crow, asked Lieutenant Parker. Colonel Norman's office was a closed-in cubicle with piped-in cold air and a desk fan to trundle the coolness around the little room. There were one red and three black dial phones on Norman's desk, and a field phone was hanging in a canvas bag on the wall next to the desk. The room was designed to be secure: no noise, electronic emanations, or signals of any kind could penetrate or depart the office. The floor was linoleum, as was the hallway and, in fact, the whole temporary wood-frame structure that housed the newly formed 7th Air Force, Tan Son Nhut Air Base, Republic of Vietnam. Both officers were dressed in the 1505 summer-weight khaki uniforms, the kind with the wide, fruity round-tipped collars despised by officer and airman alike.

"Yessir, I signed in yesterday during in-processing," Parker answered.

"That's for Seventh," the colonel said. "Have you signed into your unit?"

"No, sir, not yet. I figured I'd better call you first to see if you really could find me a job."

Parker gave Colonel Norman his DD 201 record packet and a copy of his orders. The colonel flipped through the folder, stopping to study Parker's past assignments and length of service.

"So, you were the administrative officer for Colonel Werbeck's executive office at SAMSO in L.A. Says here you finished up your three-year active duty officers' candidate school commitment last month. You could have gotten out. Instead, you voluntarily extended for one year, provided you could spend that year in Vietnam. What's this all about? Have you decided to make a career of the Air Force?"

Parker looked uncomfortable. Nuts, he thought, how the hell do I answer that one? With most of the truth, he decided.

"No, sir, I'm not career. I thought I should spend a year in Vietnam, that's all."

Parker couldn't begin to tell the colonel he was only curious as to what it was like in a war zone. Besides that, he wanted to have something to say when his kids-to-be asked, "What did you do in the war, Daddy?" And, down deep, he vaguely remembered bragging to a girl that he was going to war. That was before he started his volunteer paper work, or even thought about doing such a foolish thing as volunteering for 'Nam. As it turned out, that statement was the final clincher to what became an interesting evening after a beer-drinking session at the Oar House in Santa Monica. Afterward, an obscure inside voice prodded him to follow up on his brag about volunteering for Vietnam.

Colonel Norman studied Parker's face. He rather regretted speaking rashly at the O-Club the night before, but he had been impressed with Parker's standing up to the great Wolf Lochert. Few people did. He knew Parker wasn't giving him the whole story, but he was also impressed that the boy was an authentic volunteer. Most youngsters his age were letting their hair grow while investigating the wonderful mind-expanding properties of cannabis. Exactly as his own son was doing, Norman reflected sadly. He made a decision.

"Sit tight for a minute, Parker."

Parker sat tight as Norman picked up one of the three black dial phones on his desk and spun out four digits. He got through to some other colonel named DeLong.

"Pete, Norm here. Yeah. Do me a favor. I'm sending over a first louie named Parker. SMOP his orders detaching him from the 6250th Combat Support Group and assigning him to me here at the Seventh Intel as special courier. And crank up the paperwork to have Detachment 5 OSI do a Top Secret Plus background on him."

Norman knew the exec officer could accomplish the required changes without the slightest difficulty, even though it wasn't even close to being his job. DeLong knew whom to call, and that's what counted.

Norman and DeLong were part of a small coterie of officers who knew that in time of war you didn't dick around, you went and got the job done the best way you knew how. They complemented one another in positions of strength: Norman was the chief of Intel, DeLong the executive officer to the commander, 7th Air Force; others held such positions as fighter wing commander, logistics chief, and personnel director. Each in turn had his own lines to buddies in the Pentagon and elsewhere. Hooked in with these officers was a network of senior NCO's who also knew how to get things done behind the scenes, without fuss, fanfare, or red tape. There was a war to be fought. Paperwork was lax here, which meant field-grade officers—majors and colonels and above—or senior NCO's could screw off and not get caught, or, conversely, they could get their job done far better than in the paper-and-inspection-soaked peacetime Air Force. More visible low-ranking airmen and company-grade officers— lieutenants and captains—could never screw off, only work hard. And, though they didn't really think so, many, the more promising ones, were being watched. The truly motivated got picked up by some master sergeant or colonel or brigadier and moved along toward the day they could really help their sponsor accomplish, in the best manner possible, whatever mission the sponsor was assigned.

Norman pressed a button on his desk. Staff Sergeant Dan Miloyka responded from his office next to the colonel. Both offices opened on the long hallway, as did all the others on the first floor of the building. Security air policemen, fatigue pants bloused into black jump boots, stood guard at each end of the hall. The upper-level floors had several two-room office suites for the more senior commanders.

"Dan, take my jeep and hustle Lieutenant Parker here up to Colonel DeLong's office, then over to Supply. Sign him out for fatigues, jungle boots, survival vest, weapon, and a Urk-Ten survival radio." Turning to Parker he asked, "What kind of a weapon you like, son?"

Lieutenant Parker cleared his throat. "Weapon?"

To Parker, who had studied ancient history a bit, weapons were clubs or bows and arrows or arquebuses or something like that. And why all the paraphernalia merely for working here at Tan Son Nhut? They weren't *that* close to the action.

Seeing the blank look on Parker's face, Norman told the staff to get him a .45 with holster, a web belt, and 100 rounds of ball ammo.

"Oh yeah," Colonel Norman added, "get the lieutenant one of our steel-mesh fifty-pound courier bags with cable and wrist cuff."

Wrist cuffs? A .45? "Unh, colonel," Parker began, "unh, could you tell me what it is exactly you do here and, unh," he cleared his throat, "what exactly *I* will be doing?"

"Sure, son. We process all sorts of agent reports, target requests, recce photos, and intelligence material, gathered from a hundred places. We correlate, collate, analyze, then disseminate the hard stuff to certain users. We utilize T-39's to get the stuff up-country and out of country, and 0-1E aircraft for delivery here in Three and Four Corps. You're going to be a courier. After you draw your gear, Dan here will teach you the finer points of courier duty, chain codes and the like. Your first run will be tomorrow morning."

"In the T-39?" Even though it meant working on Sunday, Parker had delightful visions of the T-39, a USAF executive jet with airliner seats, whisking him to Hong Kong or, at the very least, Bangkok. The 0-1E pilot, he figured, probably carried his own stuff—it was, after all, just a little prop-driven two-seat puddle jumper.

"The 0-1."

"0-1," Parker repeated. "Where?"

"Ultimately, to a small reporting station we have a bit north of here. Barely an hour's flight in the 0-1. You have to pick up some hard stuff there. But first you'll drop off some material at Bien Hoa," Norman said.

"Sir, what's the name of that small reporting station?"

"Loc Ninh."

1100 HOURS LOCAL, 19 DECEMBER 1965
THE CATHOLIC BASILICA,
SAIGON, REPUBLIC OF VIETNAM
☆

On Sunday, Major Wolfgang Xavier "the Wolf" Lochert attended Catholic Mass at the Basilica in John F. Kennedy Square in downtown Saigon. The church was crowded for the eleven o'clock High Mass. Christmas was barely a week away, causing increased attendance. Tilting rows of candles gave off a comforting glow. Incense smoke, shaken out of the golden thurible by the bearer as the procession slowly walked down the aisle to the altar, permeated every corner of the church. The organist played the Introit Hymn in muted tones as the Mass began. The familiarity of the beginning ritual encased Wolf in a sensation of comfort.

"Introibo ad altare Dei ad Deum qui laetificat juventutem meam." I will go unto the altar of God, to God, who giveth joy to my youth, the Wolf automatically translated, memories of his years as an altar boy

in Minneapolis and of his two years at the Maryknoll Seminary in New York flooding his mind. The Wolf followed the Latin from memory. He could recite either the priest's or the altar boy's part. For the next thirty-five minutes the Wolf followed the Mass until Communion, when he began the words he had prayed tens of thousands of times through the years.

"O Holy Spirit," he intoned to himself, "soul of my soul, I adore thee. Enlighten me, guide me, strengthen me, console me. Tell me what I ought to do and command me to do it. I promise to be submissive to everything Thou permittest to happen to me, only show me what is Thy will."

The Wolf almost wept at the penance he knew he was doomed to serve in his soul. He believed—ah God, how he believed—and wanted to serve Our Lord, but regardless of how hard he tried, he could not overcome his great weakness, the weakness that prevented him from becoming a servant of God wearing the cloth of the Maryknolls. For the shameful truth was that the Wolf, Wolfgang Xavier Lochert, since he had been old enough to comprehend the world around him, could not be submissive to anything that happened to him or around him. He questioned, argued, and ultimately resisted anything that he didn't agree with or approve of, be it a physical matter or a moral one. At each Mass and in his evening prayers, he sought and prayed fervently for humble submissiveness. He truly believed it was the secret of sanctity, and until he could obtain that state of grace, he was doomed to be His unworthy servant as a layman.

The big man knelt, forehead bowed over his knuckly hands folded in prayer, his giant body in gentle repose among the smaller Vietnamese.

Scattered throughout the church in clusters among the Vietnamese and a few East Indians were scores of Americans and Europeans attending Catholic Mass in a combat zone. Built to retain cool early-morning temperatures, the tall, vaulted cathedral with twin spires thrusting identical crosses 200 feet into the air imparted cool solemnity to those celebrating the mass. Outside, a company of white-uniformed Saigon police, the Quan Canh, called QC or, derisively, white mice, by the American military, stood and lounged indolently around Kennedy Square, guarding the huge red-bricked cathedral against a VC terrorist act. Their white uniforms were immaculate and tailored. Each wore the type of aviator's sunglasses that are issued only to aircrew. Directly in front of the center double doors, four of the policemen stood facing outward from the white Madonna statue that rose twenty feet in the air from its round pedestal.

Only two weeks had gone by since the terrorist bombing of an

American soldiers' hotel in Saigon. The previous week, two hand grenades had been randomly tossed into the throngs of civilians at the Central Market, killing six and injuring twelve.

As the Mass progressed past the canon and into the Communion several people left the cathedral early to return to work or to prepare a big dinner or, in the case of several demurely clad young cos (unmarried women), to return to the Tu Do street bars where they hustled Saigon tea from G.I.'s at an exorbitant price. Fully 10 percent of the crowd of 375 exited the church.

No one took any notice of the thin, mild-looking young Vietnamese man, dressed in a white suit with black tie, who slowly walked out with the others. Inside, no one had called his attention to the fact that he had left his pew without picking up his large Catholic missal. A few seconds behind the young man, his backup, an athletically trim, older Vietnamese called Buey Dan who was the assistant tennis pro at the Cercle Sportif, strolled into the bright Saigon noon sun. The young man, who had deliberately left the missal, was unable to resist circling JFK Square to observe the mayhem about to happen. He knew that by doing so he was violating all he had been taught. Buey Dan, seeing this as he walked in the opposite direction, shook his head imperceptibly, thinking with a measure of intrusive sorrow, that this was not consistent with party lines, that he would have to send this young man to a VC line unit: He was too impetuous to work undercover in Saigon. Buey Dan knew he would make the transfer, but he did not want to.

The blast and concussion of the bomb, though fabricated with only a quarter pound of plastique, was echoed and amplified and reechoed and reamplified vertically up amidst the pillars and vaulted ceilings and statues and stained-glass windows, to such an extent that it sounded as if multiple bombs of diminishing power had gone off in a ripple. Horizontally, the blast and the three hundred or so roofing nails wrapped around the plastique were absorbed by the backs and sides of people in the pew and by the wooden bench back itself, but the velocity was still strong enough to drive splinters and nail fragments into the bodies and chests of those behind the pew. Two Vietnamese tots in flowered white dresses who had been giggling at each other had stood almost directly behind the horrendous blast and were decapitated. Three adults were killed outright in that row, seven injured. In the row forward from where the young man had left the missal, the four closest to the blast were killed as nails laced their kidneys and spleens. Eight people next to and forward of those killed were injured. Two were American G.I.'s.

Major Wolfgang Xavier "the Wolf" Lochert dropped straight down as if poleaxed. He did not throw himself to either side. He lay in a crumpled mound as the stunned silence was shattered by screams and wails, and the people on either side of his body scrambled over each other to get out of the now smoke- and dust-filled church. Only after his pew was empty did the Wolf cautiously raise his head to look around. Clasped in his right hand was a Mauser 7.63mm automatic, the personal (he referred to it as the social) weapon he always carried strapped to his outside right ankle. He surveyed the scene in a circle about him and spent long moments studying the overhead structure. Still crouched, he returned his automatic to its holster, knowing there would be no one now to shoot at, and rose to his feet. Many VC terrorist bombers set a secondary charge to go off within a minute or so of the first blast, to catch the unwary who were still standing around. The Wolf had determined that such was not the case at this pre-Christmas Catholic Mass.

He moved to help the wounded, reflecting that though he did not like crowded places of any sort, he had put that reservation aside to go to Mass this day. His facial expression was one of total compassion for the wounded, as he knelt next to the closest torn body. At the proper time, the rage which was suppressed in the back of his mind would surface. Two of the Vietnamese priests knelt next to him as he tore strips of clothing from the crying and moaning wounded to start to tie off bleeders expertly and dispassionately. As the three men performed their tasks, the blood on the white marble floor stained the priests' robes as well as the knees and cuffs of the big man's pants. A squad of white mice, pistols drawn, entered the church shouting and waving their weapons about.

One French and two Vietnamese physicians pushed their way through the stunned crowd creeping back into the church to search for friends and family members. As the three doctors went to work, the Wolf stood up and walked toward the center of the three double front doors, eyes swiftly searching each face he passed. He paid no attention to the stares directed at his trousers, which looked as if they had ragged red patches sewn on them. Nor did he seem to notice the awed and frightened looks of those who saw his face fast becoming contorted and darkened with rage.

The white mice and ARVN troops, supplemented by roving American MP patrols, had begun cordoning off the area at the front of the church. The first ambulances, French bi-tone horns raucously making *pam-paw, pam-paw* sounds, threaded through the traffic of bicycles, pedicabs, and blue-and-yellow taxis to the carnage. A U.S.

MP, seeing Wolf's bloody pants, rushed up, saluted, and asked if he was hurt. The Wolf, wiping his hands on his olive drab handkerchief, barely took notice as his eyes busily searched the surroundings and the gathering crowd, trying to read the expressions on Oriental and Caucasian faces. As he stood there, his back to the Madonna statue, a furtive movement, one he had been looking for, caught his eye. In a series of motions considered impossible for such a big and bulky man, the Wolf drew his social weapon and sprinted to one of the tamarind trees lining the square. Darting behind the smooth-barked tree, he caught the thin young Vietnamese man in the white suit by the throat with his left hand and jammed the barrel of his Mauser into his right eye.

"Chinh may lam chuyen do, phai khong? You did it, didn't you?" the Wolf spat in the struggling man's face. The Wolf knew his VC. He knew how they looked and smelled after a successful strike. The Wolf might not be properly submissive in the eyes of the Holy Roman Catholic Church, but he was damn near a mind reader when it came to enemy thoughts and intentions. A natural-born psychiatrist, he instinctively read body language and movements as if they were seventy-two-point headlines. The Wolf nodded, *"Tao biet may lam chuyen do, quan cong san.* I know you did, Communist pig."

The Wolf hustled the thin man against the tree, where he pinned him with his throat hold, slipped the Mauser into its holster, pulled a stiletto from his left sock, and eased it into the young man's heart through his stomach. There was no blood, the Wolf knew how to avoid arteries. The heart's aorta blood pumped furiously inside the chest cavity but could not squeeze out of the small stiletto-made hole as the thin blade was withdrawn. The Wolf helped the dead man slowly fold into a sitting position at the base of the tree. The position hid the stain from the voided bowels, but not that of the bladder, so the Wolf carefully folded the man's hands in his lap, partially covering that stain. Returning the stiletto to its hiding place, he stared at the slack face for a second, remembering what he had seen in the church. He grunted and placed his right hand flat on the dead man's head and with what remained of the church victims' blood on his thumb, he traced the sign of the cross on the man's forehead.

Straightening up, he felt he was being watched, even though all the drama and activity was taking place over at the church. He wasn't worried, because he knew his actions, mostly hidden by his bulky body and the tree, had been fast, fluid, and not ostentatious. The Wolf knew he could melt away in the few seconds it would take any viewer to comprehend exactly what had happened under the tree.

Yet one man, standing in the doorway of an apartment building nearly two hundred feet away, knew exactly what had happened. Wolf didn't see the man, but Buey Dan saw him and memorized the Wolf's face, body size, and motions. Buey Dan knew someday he had to kill the man who had just slain his son.

The MP who had enquired of Wolf's health swung around the tree, eyes widening at what he saw. He looked at the Wolf, nodded in comprehension, and returned to his post, telling himself he hadn't seen anything that belonged in an official report.

Pulse and breath quickly returning to normal, his face smoothed somewhat, the Wolf started casually to drift down the tree-covered street away from the cathedral and toward the jeep he had parked on rue Tan Thuyen. Two Caucasians, a man in his midtwenties and an attractive, lithe girl, slightly younger, angled quickly across the street in front of Wolf, obviously intent on intercepting him. The man wore an expensive khaki safari suit with many bulky pockets. Slung around his neck were a Nikon 350 with telephoto lens and a Hasselblad 500EL. He was heavily tanned, with brown hair that curled below his ears, a square jaw, and a flashy smile that would melt the heart of the coldest spinster. The young girl wore light cream-colored slacks, low heels, and a high-necked, full-sleeved green blouse that accentuated her green eyes but deemphasized her ample bosom. Her shoulder-length deep mahogany hair was lush and thick. Wolf had briefly noted the handsome couple in church. Close up he recognized her as a girl he had seen in many movies. She was Charmaine, the dancer performing in Vietnam with the Bob Hope Show.

The smiling man walked up to Wolf, right hand outstretched for a shake, "Hi, I saw you back at the church. You really helped the wounded. I took pictures. I'd like to talk to you about it." The man insistently kept his hand outthrust. "You must be military and you must be known. Even if you are in civilian clothes, that MP saluted you. I saw how well you reacted back there. That's what I'd like to talk about. I'm from the *California Sun* magazine. My name's Shawn Bannister." His smile became strained as he kept his hand extended.

The girl with him, Charmaine, stood back a few feet watching the Wolf's face. Damn, the Wolf thought, flustered by her steady green eyes while simultaneously aware of the man's cameras. Did he snap a shot of me behind the tree, Wolf wondered. At first he was simply going to grab each camera and expose the film then take off, but the girl's eyes held him. He also knew he had to keep moving before the dead man was discovered and linked to him.

"Talk? Yeah, come on," the Wolf rasped, ignoring the outstretched hand. He strode by so quickly that Charmaine and the man had to trot to catch up. Wolf turned right on rue Pasteur and walked the few meters to where he had parked the motor pool jeep. He told the two to jump in as he put the rotor in the distributor, unchained the steering wheel, started the engine, and drove off. The girl sat in back.

Speeding around and through the Honda scooter and pedicab and Renault taxicab and bicycle traffic, the Wolf thought again of the film in the cameras and what might be on it. He decided to act. He jammed the jeep into a sidewalk parking slot. Without shutting off the engine, he grabbed the two cameras and twisted their carrying straps just enough to put firm but not fatal pressure on the man's throat. "Don't do that," the girl in the back seat half screamed. The Wolf ignored her as he quickly stripped the film from each camera and threw the glossy strips into the gutter. Still holding the camera straps, he twisted them sufficiently to make the man's eyes bulge. The Wolf stuck his face an inch from Shawn Bannister's nose. "Whaddaya wanna talk about, shithead?"

7

☆

Phil Travers, Captain, USAF, a.k.a. "Phil the FAC," call sign Copperhead 03, was flying a small gray Cessna Forward Air Control observation airplane, an 01-E in USAF nomenclature, at an altitude of 300 feet on a heading of 354 degrees. He was halfway between Tan Son Nhut and Bien Hoa with a passenger in the backseat. On the 01-E's engine cowling a big white-fanged red mouth had been painted by Captain Travers and his crew chief, Sergeant Mike Germaine. The red tongue extending from the mouth resembled that of an Irish Setter whose head was protruding from the window of a fast-moving station wagon.

Travers had stayed low, to avoid not only all the jet traffic and Army helicopters but also the cloud layer at 1,000 feet that had gone from scattered to broken since their takeoff from Tan Son Nhut. Once in the clear, he decided it was time for some fun. Humming to himself, he pushed the stick forward, rapidly obtaining the aircraft's maximum speed of 115 miles per hour, then added five more miles per hour for luck. He proceeded to perform smoothly two perfectly coordinated barrel rolls, one left and one right. At the finish of the second, he pulled sharply back on the stick and brought the little airplane through a loop so perfect he flew through his starting-position prop wash. He hummed along to some snappy music piped into his headset from his Automatic Direction Finder navigational radio tuned to the American Forces Vietnam Network station in Saigon. At any time Phil "the FAC" Travers expected his backseat passenger, a nonrated first john courier FNG he had never seen before, to complain bitterly about the rolling and turning airsick-inducing maneuvers. Travers was quite positive in his belief that all Air Force personnel, even those nonrated types, should know and experience the joys of flight. The idea that perhaps rapid rolling maneuvers, sudden g-forces, and complete inversion did not appeal to all such personnel never entered his mind. This is flying and flying is *fun*.

It was known that Travers flew his Cessna observation plane as if it were an F-100 jet fighter with hydraulic controls and 40,000 pounds of engine thrust instead of the one-ton (fully loaded with gas and two people plus parachutes), 213-horsepower propeller-driven aircraft with fixed landing gear it really was. The only hydraulics in the tiny aircraft ran from the rudder pedals to the six-inch wheel brakes, as in an automobile braking system. Patterned after the Army L-5 of World War II and Korean War fame, but with a much bigger engine, the high-winged 01-E had a tail wheel instead of a nose wheel like the later-model Cessnas. It also had a control stick instead of a control wheel.

"How ya doing back there, ah, what did you say your name was again?" Travers asked into the intercom via the boom mike attached to his headset.

"Hey, great. This is terrific," the passenger replied over the intercom in a happy voice. "I've never been in a plane this small. Let's do some more. Yeah, and my name's Parker."

Geez, I really love this, First Lieutenant Toby G. Parker thought to himself. I never thought flying would be so much fun. He felt absolutely exhilarated as Travers brought the 0-1E around in another loop. He even noted the airspeed, 40 mph, and altitude, 780 feet, at the top of the loop.

As they came down the backside of the loop, Parker swung his head to look out each of his side windows. Just outboard of the struts that extended from the fuselage to the wings were 2.75-inch rocket racks, each holding two Willy Pete—white phosphorus—rockets the FAC could fire into the ground to make big white-smoke aiming points for the strike pilots he was controlling talking over his UHF radio.

Travers had told him, in answer to his questions, that the big strike fighters flew too high and too fast to find the usually obscure ground reference points in the jungle needed to locate a target. The little FAC 0-1E's, flying low and slow, could see practically everything. They also carried the right kind of radio, an FM set, to talk to soldiers fighting on the ground who needed the firepower that air support could provide. Most FAC's lived in and flew out of tiny jungle airstrips, where they maintained close contact with their Corps Army DASC, the Direct Air Support Center, and the local Vietnamese province chief, Travers had explained.

Under the call sign Beaver, Travers had flown seven months in the Delta, reporting to Horn DASC. Now he was the FAC for Bien Hoa province, on call twenty-four hours per day, seven days per week. He knew his area like the back of his hand and could pick out a new VC supply point or trail within hours of its construction. Besides the .45 strapped to his hip, the only other armament in the airplane was the short-stock M-16 (CAR-15) Travers had wedged to the left of his seat. Even though they had first met at dawn, Parker could tell Travers thrived on this kind of life.

As Travers—Copperhead 03—was leveling his 0-1E, he was pleased that his passenger, even though an FNG, seemed to be appreciating the flight with obvious enjoyment. Glancing toward Bien Hoa he noticed some cloud buildups farther north that might affect his plans to fly the courier run up there after the Bien Hoa stop.

"Here, Parker, you fly it for a while. I got to make a few phone calls." Travers released the controls, checked that Parker indeed had the airplane control stick in his hand, and punched in Bien Hoa Tower on his UHF radio to ask for landing instructions. He fully expected Parker to refuse or at least ask questions about how to fly the little airplane. He was impressed when he did not and wondered if Parker had ever flown before.

Parker had already figured out that the two most important things, assuming the engine ran properly, were to keep the wings level with the horizon and to keep the nose of the aircraft from rising or falling. He did this for about five minutes, noticing to his dismay that the airspeed would fall off to 75 mph or climb to 105 as he tried to hold his altitude. He had no trouble keeping the wings level.

"Cripes," he said over the intercom. "I can't hold my altitude."

"Let go of the stick, I'll show you something," Travers said. "Notice the plane won't climb or dive by itself once you let go of it. I've trimmed it for this cruising airspeed. It's a stable platform. Watch this."

Travers suddenly shoved the stick forward several inches and released it. The little plane bobbed up and down, then leveled itself almost immediately. "Take control, Parker, only this time don't get such a death grip on the stick. Hold it lightly between your thumb and forefinger."

Parker did as he was told.

"Now ease the stick to the right. We'll enter the landing pattern. Push some right rudder, and get us on downwind," Travers said. "A little back pressure now, the nose is starting to drop. Good, that's it. Do as I say now and we'll land. I'll handle the throttle and follow through on the controls with you."

Parker had never felt so excited as he obeyed Travers's instructions in the pattern and down to five feet above the concrete surface of Runway 27 at Bien Hoa Air Base. The Bien Hoa Control Tower had squeezed them in between a landing A-1E prop job and two F-100's in formation, gear and flaps down, lights shining, on GCA final. "Get down and get off" is essentially what they told Copperhead 03.

"I've got it," Travers said. "Now you follow through on the controls with me."

Parker followed through as Travers landed the fang-mouthed 0-1E in a perfect three-point attitude and turned down a taxiway within the first 200 feet of the approach end of the runway. As they taxied in Parker said, "There seemed to be an awful lot of fast stick and rudder movement until we slowed down."

"Yeah," Travers said, "we had about a ten-knot crosswind from the right and there was a bit of jet wash on the runway from that last Hun that took off. Besides, there's a storm moving in. Here, you taxi this thing."

Oh God, this is great, Parker thought, manipulating the throttle and the rudders, trying to keep the plane straight on the taxiway. The chain connecting the handcuff on his left wrist to the briefcase on his lap hampered him only slightly as he moved the throttle. But the survival vest and bulky parachute he wore on his back cramped his space in the narrow backseat just as the shoulder harness cramped his mobility. He had had a difficult time attaching the shoulder harness to his lap belt, which was tangled over the .45 strapped to his hip and the flak vest he sat on. Travers had instructed him to sit on the thick vest because the parachute harness wouldn't fit over its bulk. "Besides," Travers had said, slapping the vest folded on the seat, "this will protect the family jewels."

Parker goosed the throttle. "Oops," he said as he lost it with a too sudden rudder movement. Travers corrected for him. "Keep your stick in the left rear corner to counteract the quartering left crosswind," he told the struggling backseater. Parker did that and managed credible but wobbly taxiing all the way up to the chocks by Travers's trailer on a remote parking revetment at the northern perimeter of the base. Travers shut down the engine.

In the silence when the propeller clicked to a stop, Travers said over his shoulder, "Come on in and have a beer, sport, you done good. You're rough as a cob, but you're doing what you're supposed to do. You make the airplane go where you want, not where it wants." They climbed out the right side and took off their helmets.

Travers had a wide mouth and light-red hair, slightly longer than the regs prescribed, now sweaty and matted. He stood a little under six feet, and had the faintest hint of a beer belly. Before coming to Vietnam as a FAC he had served as an Air Defense pilot flying F-106 interceptors out of Tyndall Air Force Base, Florida.

Parker helped him and the Bird Dog's crew chief push the O-1E inside the revetment under a lean-to of metal poles and a stretched canvas tarpaulin. The revetment, one of a series built by ARMCO, the American Rolling Mill Company, consisted of earth-filled corrugated steel bins twelve feet high and 5½ feet wide, built on three sides of a concrete hardstand to protect parked airplanes from attack. The trailer and the lean-to were each next to a wall. Sergeant Germaine asked how soon the airplane was needed.

"In about an hour, Mike," Travers said, looking at his Seiko. "Say twelve-thirty if the weather doesn't go sour on us. Full fuel and rockets."

Travers and Parker walked the thirty feet separating the O-1E and the Mason two-man trailer for which Travers had traded thirty-two VC Russian-built AK-47 assault rifles. A dented 375-gallon camouflaged F-100 drop tank full of water, heating in the sun, was mounted on a frame next to it. Under the frame was a shower head. A hose from the tank ran into the trailer through a hole punched in the wall.

Sergeant Germaine had the one-room, separate-entrance portion of the trailer. Travers used the rest for his operations board (a four-foot, acetate-overlayed map of South Vietnam), his mess hall (a two-burner hot plate and a small refrigerator), and his bachelor officer's quarters (the adjoining eight-by-six-foot bedroom with chair, chest of drawers, and a G.I.-cot with pillow and sheets).

Travers had also traded six VC home-built hand grenades for the 18,000 BTU GE CoolTone air conditioner strapped and propped in a front window. An eighteen-inch box fan he'd bought from the PX blew the cool air all the way through to the tiny bedroom.

There was a hand-cranked EE-8 field phone and a Prick 25 (a PRC-25 FM radio) on the homemade desk along with the map. Travers and Parker walked in, sweat-drenched. Travers pulled two cans of beer from the reefer, handed one to Parker, unzipped his front zipper to his crotch, stood in front of the air conditioner, and cranked up the field phone to ask for Weather.

"Hey, Stormy, Phil the FAC. What ya got in War Zone C and D and on up to Loc Ninh from now till dark?" Travers listened and took notes. "How about tomorrow by first light?" He took more notes, said thanks, and placed the black Bakelite field phone in its olive-drab canvas container. He turned to face Parker, hip resting on the desk, arms folded.

"No go, Parker. We got the usual afternoon line of thunder-bumpers north of here marching west to east till probably nine o'clock tonight. They're from the deck to fifty thou. Nothing flies up there, including choppers, till they swing through. We could maybe beat them in, but we'd never get back out."

"Can't we get a jeep or something and drive up?" Parker asked.

"How long you been in-country, boy?" Travers asked, eyebrows raised. "That Highway Thirteen doesn't belong to us, even with a nine hundred–man tank battalion driving on it. It's a ten-meter wide hardtop road, which means at any given time our front line is only ten meters across, and at that you got to have flankers on each side and a point man out in front to trip ambushes. This isn't like World War Two or Korea, where there were definite lines to defend or attack."

Parker nodded, beginning to understand. "Well, look," he said, "I got to call somebody, a Lieutenant Foure, a PI, and see if I can get rid of this stuff." He tapped the briefcase chained to his wrist.

Travers took another beer from the small fridge. "Don't sweat it. Foure's on his way. I asked the tower to call him on the land line and tell him to get over here."

"How did you know to do all that?" Parker asked.

"This isn't exactly the first time I've made this run, you know, I run classified stuff up to An Loc and Loc Ninh. Stuff like aerial photos of their local area in return for their ground observations and reports. Colonel Norman, the guy you work for at Seventh, has set this up as perhaps a better way to swap intel with the ground troops. In this case, the Special Forces. The local Special Forces A Team here at Bien Hoa is assisting a camp at Loc Ninh, and another A Team has the camp at Song Be. Both of them are in my TAOR—my Tactical Area of Responsibility." Travers took a long pull at the beer, wiped his mouth, and continued.

"There's over a hundred Special Forces fighting camps in Vietnam. Their missions range from border watchposts and intel gathering to interdicting and harassing the VC and NVA. Those snake eaters groove on that stuff," Travers said, the respect in his voice obvious.

He finished the beer, crumpled the can, and tossed it into a cardboard C-ration box already full of Coke and beer cans. "How come you didn't know any of this? How long you been with Norman's outfit, anyway?"

"Well, actually, ah, I only got here a few days ago. The guy who fitted me out this morning, Sergeant Miloyka, told me you were a good man, and would tell me all about the courier business. I just have the names and places of where I'm supposed to pick up and deliver stuff."

"Like I said," Travers began, "in between FAC jobs I fly the courier around. Sometimes we have an Immediate Request for air support that I have to divert to while going or coming from a delivery. That happens most of the time, in fact." He took out another beer. "You on any flight orders? You drawing flight pay?"

"Well, no, actually I'm not. Colonel Norman didn't say anything about that. I, uh, I thought maybe one or two runs was all I'd be set up to do," Parker said.

"Perhaps that's all you'll get, Parker. This is a new arrangement, and it may not prove out. I've only made ten runs so far." He heard brakes squealing and turned to look out the window in time to see a fatigue-clad USAF lieutenant wearing a steel pot climb out of a jeep and head for the trailer.

"Hey, Phil, you got it real cold in here," the lieutenant said as he came through the door. "You must be Parker," he said. The two lieutenants shook hands.

Parker rubbed his wrist after unlocking the handcuff and giving the case to Foure. "Sign here," he said to Foure, handing him a USAF Classified Movement form in triplicate. Foure signed the paper and left the trailer.

"How come you don't pick up and deliver the bag yourself, Phil?" Parker asked as Foure drove off.

"First off, it's hard to fly an airplane with that thing chained to my wrist," Travers said, pointing at Parker's attaché case, "and secondly, once in a while I'd have to spend time on the ground to go over some of that stuff when I should be up doing my FAC thing."

"Who did this before?" Parker asked.

"A guy named McAdoo, first john like you."

"Why isn't he doing this anymore?"

"He's in the Third Surgical Hospital down there at Saigon."

"Why, what happened to him?"

"Got himself full of mortar frags on the ground at Loc Ninh when the VC tried to overrun it one night last week."

1730 HOURS LOCAL, 20 DECEMBER 1965
ALPHA AIRLINES, TAN SON NHUT AIR BASE,
REPUBLIC OF VIETNAM

☆

Bubba Bates was chewing the skinny butt off Nguyen Tran, his chief of Vietnamese government liaison who also screened indigenous personnel (meaning Vietnamese) applying for work with the Alpha Airlines station at TSN; TSN was the station identifier for Tan Son Nhut. Alpha was soon to open another station up in I Corps at Da Nang for its DC-3 and DC-4 passenger and cargo route. Most Vietnamese workers preferred the TSN station because it was right in the lap of the delights of Saigon.

Bubba was pissed at Nguyen Tran because he was having a hard time recruiting shift bosses to go to Da Nang and set up the baggage-handling system, and he blamed Tran for not providing him with enough enthusiastic support. Tran tied to tell Bubba that the shift bosses who went to Da Nang, even if only for a few weeks, needed extra money—they were paid in Vietnamese piastres, called P– to pay someone to look after their families while they were gone.

"Tran, I don't *have* any extra money. You know that as well as I do. Tell 'em I'll give 'em double comp time when they get back. Okay?"

Ong Tran—Mr. Tran—who had received his baccalaureate in civil engineering from the Université de Saigon in the late fifties, told Bates that time off wasn't the answer.

"You must hire Nung guards, those Chinese mercenaries," Tran said, "at least one for each house. They don't cost much. Maybe a hundred P a day. And rice. You pay this, the men will go. You pay one hundred P and maybe ten more P each day for rice and the men go Da Nang. Go *to* Da Nang," Tran corrected.

"Why, for Chrissakes, the guards? They think VC overrun their hootch the minute they go? Or some Nguyen down the street come diddle the old lady?" Bates hawked a laugh at that one. He thought it pretty funny. The 110 P per day was about ninety-five cents in real money. That came to about thirty bucks a month for ten guys, which totaled three hundred dollars. Bates couldn't afford that from the slush fund or petty cash Alpha had set up for such contingencies because Bubba was all the way into the slush fund and petty cash to support his air-conditioned apartment in Saigon on Hai Ba Truong Street near the Saigon River, not to mention the greatly gorgeous Tui, his mistress.

"No, Mr. Bates, that is not the problem. The problem is Saigon cowboys. They come around houses and ask for money when they know people work for Americans. They think they have much money. They want some. If the man is gone, he must provide protection," Ong Tran said.

"Protection, hell. Sounds like extortion to me. They're trying to extort the money out of me." Bubba Bates wiped his face with his giant red bandanna. It came away soaked with sweat and grime from the construction. Ong Tran in his white shirt and black pants, on the other hand, looked unrumpled, dry, and clean. Bates didn't know why, but he rarely saw a gook with sweat on his brow. Just didn't work as hard as a white man, he would say when commenting to his fellow Americans about the tough life at TSN.

"Tell 'em fifty P, Tran, that's all the company can afford." When Ong Tran tried one last protest, Bates gave him a shove and told him to, goddammit, go deal with the problem. What the hell did he think he got paid for, anyhow. Shee-it, Bates said to himself, wiping his head and neck again, his black hair hanging wetly next to his florid face. If it isn't one thing, it's another. After yesterday's humiliation in the terminal in front of Joe and Al by that broad from Braniff, he was ready to kick the crap out of anybody who got in his way. As an equivalent to a General Schedule position 8(GS-8), Bubba Bates had Officer's Club privileges. He planned to stop by the O-Club each night on his way home, on the chance he'd find that dickhead lieutenant, Parker was the name on his tag, and teach him a thing or two.

At 1800 Bubba's replacement reported in for the midshift, freeing him until 1000 the next morning. Bubba briefed him on the day's input, on lost baggage, on the schedule of birds due in during his shift, and then signed out. He walked out of the western end of the Alpha Airlines Quonset hut into the parking lot, unlocked and opened all four doors of his company-furnished Quatre Chevel Renault to cool the 130-degree heat inside to the day's 92, then drove to the Officer's Club. He drank a shot in a beer, then left when he couldn't find that dickhead lieutenant.

As a U.S. government contract worker, Bubba Bates also had full

PX and—something the average G.I. didn't have—full commissary privileges, which he abused with great fervor. As he did about every fourth day, he drove to the big PX and Class VI store in Cholon to pick up six bottles of Jim Beam whisky, twelve cans of Revlon hair spray, and four cartons of Salem cigarettes. He waited in the longer line at Aisle 3 to be checked out by his special friend. When his turn came, he handed her thirty-eight dollars in Military Payment Certificates—also known as MPC, script, or funny money—and his ration card with an American-five dollar bill folded in it. The plump *Co* at the register, demonstrating great experience, palmed the green bill neatly and only pretended to punch Bubba's rat-card. Bubba nodded, hoisted his bags, and walked out, proud he was able to beat the rationing system so easily.

Tui met Bubba at the door of his third-floor apartment on Hai Ba Truong Street and took the two brown paper bags from him to the small table in the kitchen. She was barefoot and wore a white shift with a slit up the left side and no makeup. Her hair, more brown than black, hung in a smooth cascade down her back, just past her shoulder blades. Quite tall for a Vietnamese, she almost matched Bubba's five-foot-nine height. Her eyes were more dark blue than black, more wide-set and rounder than most Asian girls'.

She divided the goods from the heavy American commissary brown paper bags in half and transferred the whisky, hair spray, and cigarettes into two old hemp shopping bags. She stuffed Vietnamese newspaper around the bottles to muffle any clinking sound, then carefully folded the paper bags and added them to a stack under the sink.

As was the daily ritual, she took a frosted mug from the freezer section of the new refrigerator and a Budweiser beer from below, poured the beer into the mug, adjusting the foam, then added two fingers of Jim Beam from a bottle she took from a cabinet, and carried it on a rosewood tray to the balcony, which overlooked the Saigon River. Bubba sat in a papasan chair, bare feet crossed on the balcony railing.

The traffic noise was a buzzing hum of Honda scooters punctuated by beeps from the tiny blue-and-white Renault taxis. Yet the noise wasn't as bad as over on Tu Do Street, where most of the G.I. bars and shops were. The stink of castor-oil–laced gas from the scooters went unnoticed by Bubba. He was used to it. Tui set the tray on a wicker table and handed Bubba his drink. After he took a long swallow and wiped his mouth with the back of his hand, she bent over him from his right side, kissed him on the lips, ran her tongue around inside his right ear, then began to massage his neck and shoulders.

"Harder on the left side. That's it. Harder. Dig your fingers in. Ah, God that's good," Bubba sighed. He drank heavily from the frosted mug. "You're the best, Tui. The best." Then, after a pause of several minutes, during which he alternately sighed and groaned, he asked, "How did we do today?"

She left him for a moment and returned with a small neat package wrapped in newspaper. Bubba opened it and counted the MPC inside. The funny multicolored currency totaled $294, Bubba's return on yesterday's thirty-eight bucks worth of booze, hair spray, and butts. It would be forty percent less than if he were to be paid in green, American currency, but he accepted the funny money, which was as good as green once deposited in his account at the Saigon branch of the Chase Manhattan Bank. Another privilege the common G.I. did not have.

Via a scam with an Army finance clerk, Bubba was close to getting as much green as he wanted, so he could buy more MPC cheap from the Indians on the southern end of Tu Do Street. Here's how it worked. Legally, no American government worker—civilian or military—was allowed to have American money in his or her possession. It created inflation, so the reasoning went. As it was, Vietnamese shopkeepers, bar girls, black marketeers, and pimps, who preferred hard currency, would accept funny money from G.I.'s who had run out of piastres, the Vietnamese currency they were supposed to buy at 118 to the dollar—at a rate that screwed the G.I. out of about 50 percent of its value. To get rid of the funny money, which had no value on the local economy, they would sell it at a ratio of $1.40 MPC to $1 to whoever could come up with American greenbacks. This new and highly lucrative source of money for Bubba would be a welcome addition to his black marketeering, which was really small potatoes compared to some big-time operators. The situation in Vietnam was Curtis "Bubba" Bates's one shot at the brass ring and he intended to max it out.

Bubba handed the money to Tui, who stashed it in the grip in the closet. When she returned to the balcony she took Bubba's beer away, then sat on his lap. She placed his hands on her breasts, began to grind her hips slowly over his maleness, and leaned forward to dart her tongue around the inside of his mouth. In about three minutes, as was the ritual, Bubba picked her up and carried her to the bedroom. She had already turned up the air conditioner. The tiled floor was cool to his feet. The austere Vietnamese handmade double bed was covered with a taut white sheet. Two American pillows were under the sheet at the head of the bed, a folded sheet lengthwise at the foot.

Bubba stood next to the bed. Tui stepped out of her shift and, kneeling, undid his belt and his zipper, stripped off his pants and underwear, then his shirt, pushed him gently back on the bed, and straddled him. She had to work on his flaccidness a moment before guiding him into her. She rocked back and forth. It was over in seconds. As it always was.

Tui disengaged, stood up, and watched Bubba for a few moments. When it was clear he had gone to sleep, she pulled the sheet over him, turned down the air conditioner a notch, picked up her shift and left the room.

After her shower, during which she scrubbed with great attention, Tui put on a black-and-white *ao dai,* a white silk scarf to cover her less-than-black hair, picked up the two hemp shopping bags, put her small black purse into one of them, and left the apartment, making sure the door was safely locked behind her. In the vestibule she unlocked the chain holding a Honda scooter and, with the shopping bags stowed one in each saddle bag, wheeled to the Cercle Sportif on Hung Thap Tu Street, where she arrived at dusk.

Buey Dan, the second assistant tennis pro, who spoke fluent French and good American English, met her in his office, which overlooked the courts. Tui gave him the hemp bags. Without glancing into them, Buey Dan placed the bags in a locker from which he took an identical bag containing a folded hemp bag and $294 in military script wrapped in newspaper. He handed it to her and sat at the desk.

"What have you found, little sister?" he asked in Vietnamese.

Tui nervously licked her lips. "I have found he is the wrong man," she replied rapidly in the same language. "He knows nothing and never will."

She stood up, took the kerchief from her head, and shook out her hair as she walked to the window overlooking the courts. Except for one Caucasian, the six lighted courts were full of Vietnamese players dressed similarly in white polo shirts, white shorts, white wool knee-highs, and American high-top tennis shoes. There were no Vietnamese women players. Ball shaggers, called *bo doi,* in dark shorts and armless T-shirts, slouched or ran, depending on the prowess of their players. The commonplace scene calmed her.

"Have you found me another here, uncle?" she asked, watching the slim Caucasian skillfully returning the ball. She could tell from his elegant, energy-conserving *placer la balle* style that he was French, probably a *colon* planter from up north. When they played, the Amis seemed to squander energy as they raced around the courts.

"No, little sister. There are some Ami military here, but they are staff to *Dai-Thong* Westmoreland and are scared to ever do anything by themselves. There is one, a *thieu ta,* a major, who gets sometimes too drunk, but he does not show himself alone in this club. I had him followed to Tu Do Street. He takes girls in the bars there. It is reported he likes them very small. We have someone who might interest him," Buey Dan said. Tui was silent for a moment.

"Is the gossip bad? Could I return here to the Cercle Sportif to look for another?" she asked finally.

"You possibly could return, but we have other plans," Buey Dan said.

Tui turned from the window to look at him in the deepening shadows. He had yet to switch on the light.

"Then you already knew, uncle, I was unsuccessful," she said. "Do I go to the bars now to sell Saigon Tea?" Tui straightened her shoulders in a thin gesture of defiance.

Buey Dan leaned back to look up at her and said, "Little sister, we will not send you to the Tu Do Street bars or even the international nightclub. We have others for those places and for the American Embassy people. Instead, we want you to convince the *mui lo* long-nose to take you to the officer's club on their air base Tan Son Nhut. You will make it more and more obvious you are dissatisfied with him as you meet the men who go there. You will concentrate only on military officers. Supply us with as many names as you can. We will give you information on them. And we will give you names of officers to watch for. We will determine for you which one to target. Meanwhile, act American, pretend to drink a lot, wear miniskirts, dance by yourself to the machine music. Go to Chez Robert and see how the American embassy secretaries act when they drink. Imitate them. Become a round-eyed American beauty queen."

Actually, Tui thought to herself, it would be far more enjoyable visiting the Officer's Club than spending all day confined to the barbarian's apartment. She pictured the American officer's club as being like that of the French: quiet, dignified, elegant white linen on the tables, crystal, china, fine wines, a sommelier, a maitre d'hotel in attendance. "Yes, Uncle. I will do that. How soon?"

"Immediately," Buey Dan said, standing up. "Immediately."

Tui started for the door and paused. "Uncle, I know of your sorrow," she said, eyes downcast. Buey Dan's eyes flickered. "It was for the Liberation," he said in a voice that sounded like glass being cut. "For the liberation," he repeated after she went out the door, seeing again in his mind the bulky long-nose cutting down his son.

As Tui expertly wheeled her Honda through the now darkened Saigon streets, she thought about her past. She was a *métisse,* a Eurasian: Vietnamese mother, Caucasian father. He was a German who had joined the French Foreign Legion directly from a French prison camp in 1945. He had died a hero's death in 1954 at Dien Bien Phu. Tui had completed two years in the Sorbonne in Paris, on money from the modest estate her Legionnaire father had stolen as an SS officer in Holland.

Besides her classical Vietnamese, Tui, something of a prodigy, spoke fluent French and *Hochdeutsch* in such a soft, mellifluous manner that it didn't sound the least bit Teutonic. She also spoke quite correct British English, which she had learned when she worked as an au pair in the U.K. during the summers of '62 and '63 to supplement her income, and at the direction of Buey Dan, her party cadre boss of eight years. Through the years her trust in Buey Dan had slowly eroded into fear as she had seen him become more fanatic in his beliefs. She knew he was sometimes called the Lizard from Hanoi Lake, but she didn't know why.

Tui was nineteen but looked fourteen and was, if not a pure Marxist, at least a Vietnamese nationalist who truly believed that salvation for her beloved country lay with Ho Chi Minh, not the former air marshal who was now South Vietnam's prime minister, Nguyen Cao Ky, and American President Lyndon Baines Johnson.

Tui could erotically manipulate Curtis Bubba Bates in such a way as to reduce him to a quivering whimpering mass if he didn't do her small favors. She felt nauseated while doing it, but she did it, for "the Liberation" she told herself. Outside of getting her schedules for incoming cargo and G.I.'s on Alpha Airlines and other MAC contract flights, Bubba could perform no significant favors of any intelligence value.

Tui, who was a member of the Cercle Sportif, had mistaken Bubba Bates for an important American when, through a simple contrivance, she had met him by the pool late one afternoon. Bubba's loud manner, condescending attitude toward the waiters and pool boys, and extravagant handling of money had convinced her this was so. Only a general, a *dai tuong,* or a high state department official, a *dai su,* could act this way was Tui's reasoning. What Tui knew about American capitalists came from what Buey Dan had told her, and Bubba Bates fitted the description like the skin on the tamarind fruit. The membership committee of the exclusive athletic and social club had opened membership, albeit reluctantly, to Americans. Bubba, and a few pretentious others, had rushed to join. The rest had neither time nor inclination to join the club merely to hobnob with snobby French and Viets who, even if they knew how, would not speak a word of English nor understand the American's attempt to speak French. There were, however, two major exceptions: General Westmoreland, the COMUSMACV, and *Dai Su* Henry Cabot Lodge. They were welcomed and fawned over by all the French and the Viets.

It didn't take Tui long to realize her mistake, but she had already compromised herself by moving in with Bates at his Hai Ba Truong apartment. She would now use him to better advantage as an entry to the Officer's Club at Tan Son Nhut. She knew he could get her a temporary Alpha Airlines employee's pass to the giant air base. Maybe even a permanent one. She would soon find the right target. She would deal with Bates's objections when the time came. It would all depend on how much control she had over the long-nosed barbarian.

Bates was still asleep and snoring when she entered the third-floor apartment.

8

☆

Christmas in a combat zone is unlike Christmas anywhere else. In a combat zone one doesn't exactly celebrate Christmas, one endures it. The combatant wants to get through the days devoted to the holiday season as fast as possible. Mashed boxes of Christmas cookies and candy mailed to the APO number are turned over to hootch mates with nary a twinge. One must quickly get rid of the cookies that *she* baked, or one might want to save this crumbling evidence of a normal home life, which could lead to wet-eyed distraction and death.

Strangely enough, attending a church service in a combat zone on Christmas Day somehow seems normal and not painful. Probably because one doesn't "go to church" in the dress-up, drive-the-car, "now-you-kids-settle-down" sense of the word. In a war zone one merely attends a service in whatever one happens to be wearing, whether it's combat fatigues with matching rifle and steel pot, or sweaty, salt-encrusted flight suits, or greasy mechanic's coveralls, or outlandish Bermuda shorts.

By reverse—repulsive—psychology, AFVN helps one endure Christmas. The American Forces Vietnam Network broadcasts from Saigon and from repeater stations twenty-four hours a day to the troops in Vietnam. "Gooooood *morn*ing, Vietnam," booms the super cheerful announcer before he launches into the latest R&R information, what the current booby traps consist of, and other pertinent life-prolonging in-country information. Then, during all of the Christmas season, whether subconsciously or not, the DJ's play all the Christmas abominations. Thirty repetitions of "Rudolph the Red-Nosed Reindeer," twenty of "I Saw Mommy Kissing Santa Claus," ten of "Rockin' Around the Christmas Tree" cause even the most sentimental combatant to emit a Pavlovian response of disgust at the whole thing.

Bob Hope had been onstage that day at Long Binh with his long-time pal with the big mustache, Jerry Colonna. Also in the troupe were Charmaine the dancer, Miss World, two NFL football players, a magician, a six-member dance troop, and an eight-piece orchestra. "We're glad to be here today at Long Binh, where even the rats wear black pajamas" and "You know, Vietnam is the only place where you can get bombed without taking a drink" brought the troops to their feet. Nobody seemed to mind the elaborate cue-card and camera platforms erected to film the Hope show for the paying audience in the U.S.

Major Doctor Conrad D. Russell and Captain Courtland EdM. Bannister had had a long day. In keeping with Rawson's nasty-job threat, Court had spent his time helping the Form 5 clerk compile sortie logs and then cutting up flight maps into zone strips. Doc Russell had finally traced an unusual surge of jock itch to excess naptha in the soap used by the Vietnamese laundresses. After a couple of drinks at the Hawk Inn, they decided to hike the few blocks to the Bien Hoa Air Base Officer's Club.

The air was silent and heavy with mosquito spray, the sky clear, as they strode the freshly rolled asphalt road past officer and enlisted men's hootches that were as quiet as befits a working air base late at night. Noise from the O-Club became increasingly loud as the two men approached. As the laughter, hoots, and snatches of song, both live and recorded, increased in volume, the two men involuntarily increased their pace. They were ready for some fun.

Bannister had begun to regret being so open about his feelings with Doc Russell the other night. Russell, conversely, seemed perfectly happy to be informed of this man's life and motivations, and had decided to probe deeper.

"What is your deepest, darkest secret?" he asked lightly.

"Nothing other than that I want to be the first man on the moon. And, yeah, I like opera," Court said. "One Fine Day' from *Butterfly* makes my eyes water."

"You know what it all adds up to, don't you?" Russell said with alcoholic confidence. "You are a man far more complex and driven than anyone would suspect."

"What a crock, Doc," Court said disdainfully.

Russell knew that to all outward appearances, Bannister had it made. He stood six-foot-one, was thin but trim at 170 pounds, had a squarely handsome face with short-cropped brownish-blond hair bleached by the Asian sun, was a world traveler, and, because of his famous actor-father, was probably rich as hell. Devoted fighter pilot, Courtland Esclaremonde de Montségur Bannister would seem to be the envy of the working-class pilot. Indeed, he was envied by some. But most pilots in the squadrons he had flown with before Bien Hoa had accepted him as he was: an above-average stick and a hard worker who kept his mouth shut. Yet all had one unanimous opinion: He was aloof.

In a squadron, aloof was not what one should be, unless one had some great aerial reputation that had preceded one's arrival, which permitted such eccentricities. Reputation by birth or position or athletic achievements meant nothing after five minutes. The first item in the squadron's eyes was the amount of respect the new pilot, the FNG, earned between the moments he retracted and then extended his fighter's landing gear. Conversely, the few who were merely career-oriented considered all the factors that made up their individual squadron mates in terms of how they might be helpful at some future date. Some had decided that Court Bannister, via his father, would make a valuable friend. Used to being approached like this since his childhood in Hollywood, Bannister could spot those types at the drop of a syllable and the turn of an ingratiating smile. There weren't many like that in the USAF and that was one of the reasons Bannister appreciated service life. He knew he rose or fell on his merits as a fighter pilot, not on who his father was.

Nonetheless, Bannister paid a price for his background. While he was considered aloof, his squadron mates were equally if not more so. Bannister had to prove himself all over again. He had been out of fighters for the two years it had taken him to get his engineering degree, and except for Paul Austin, also an ASU grad, he knew no one in the squadron, and no one knew him except as the son of Silk Screen Sam Bannister. He admitted he hadn't tried very hard and that he did spend a lot of off-duty time with his Special Forces buddies in the nearby Mike Force. As far as the tight-knit 531st was concerned, most pilots thought Court's reputation as a fighter jock was yet to be established.

As far as Rawson, the ops officer, was concerned, Russell, who was more than a mere amateur psychiatrist, knew he suffered from lack of confidence in both his ability as a pilot and as a leader. Rawson was being pressed beyond his limits and it was beginning to show in his nervousness and erratic actions under pressure. Unfortunately, Russell knew, as long as Rawson was the acting commander, the squadron would suffer a morale loss that would affect both duty accomplishments and prestige among the other squadron pilots. Every pilot liked to say his ops officer was a tough SOB who could fly a tabletop and a fan, a guy you would fly wing on into hell if necessary. No one said that about Rawson.

A loud blatting quack, as if a giant duck had been punched in the stomach, sounded from above their heads as they approached the door of the wood-and-screen one-story Bien Hoa Officer's Club. There was movement and something shuffling on the slightly pitched corrugated roof. Then they saw a flight-suit–garbed figure with a flowing white beard burst from the shadows to run and flop flat on the roof, head down over the edge, holding what looked like a six-inch flute. The figure pointed the instrument into the top of a screened window and, from his upside down position, let go several flatulent eardrum-grating quacks. Immediately the Club's screen door banged open and two green-bagged pilots dashed out with fire extinguishers, which they aimed up in the general direction of the duck calls.

The two spray artists were Lieutenants Freeman and Fairchild. The duck-calling Santa Claus was Higgens the Homeless, a pilot banned from setting foot in the club for thirty days by the wing commander for "conduct unbecoming." A touring Congressman's wife who had decided Sunday morning at the O-Club was a good time to tell our dear boys about her hardworking husband had been asked by Higgens in a loud voice to "show us your tits."

"Gotcha, gotcha," the lieutenants yelled as they ran around the side of the structure in hot pursuit of the quacking Santa. Higgens let out another blast as he galloped, slipping and sliding, around the perimeter of the roof. Higgens the Homeless had taken the WingCo at his word. He did not set foot *in* the O-Club, only *on* it.

Bannister and Russell entered the Club and tried vainly to edge to the horseshoe bar. One half point less than total pandemonium reigned amidst the forty or so officers celebrating Christmas. Or was it another bombing halt? Some weren't sure. The standard USAF-issue red MERRY CHRISTMAS banner hung on nails behind the bar.

Two pilots, wearing white skivvies only, were riding bikes directly toward each other on top of the bar. Each carried a long bamboo rod as a jousting pole.

"Go! Go!" cheered a row of pilots prudently standing clear of where the inevitable crash would occur. The two riders wobbled and slammed into each other without even trying to jab with the poles. That would have been dangerous. Falling to the glass-covered floor was not so considered. The surrounding pilots surged in to catch them as they toppled sideways off the bar.

"Medic! Medic!" someone shrieked from the group. Before Bannister or Russell could respond to what they thought a hoax anyhow, a tall captain carrying an open can of beer climbed over the bar, grabbed a dish towel and threw himself into the melee, shouting he was a medic and would they please make room. He knelt and began earnestly pouring the beer over the two jousters while mopping sweat off his own face with the towel.

"You're no medic," one of the crashed lieutenants accused the tall captain.

"I am so," the captain replied.

"How could you be," the prone lieutenant persisted. "You don't even have a stretcha . . . stetcha . . . stethoscope."

"I do so too," the captain said, jumping to his feet, "and I can even piss through it." He snatched his zipper down from naval to crotch and started to piss on the boots of the man nearest, who promptly pulled out his own stethoscope and returned fire. The men on the floor rolled away from the splashing.

Bannister and Russell gave up trying to get a drink from the bar and wedged themselves into a corner near a beer tub. Booze was free and flowing, inside and out. New riders had salvaged the bikes and were circling the crowded floor banging into the unwary. Various groups were laughing, joking, talking, singing. One favorite song was an enthusiastic rendition of "Deck the Halls with Heads and Holly." Someone said he learned it from a Marine pilot out of Da Nang.

In one corner, several pilots from another squadron were trying to introduce their monkey mascot, Sir Pissalot, to a very interested Ramrod. Sir Pissalot rendered some heartbreaking screeches and broke loose to scamper up the walls to a high point, from where he absently dribbled over the crowd below.

Clearly the evening was controlled by the young lieutenants and junior captains. A few senior captains and one or two majors watched with great interest and enjoyment, but didn't really participate in what they loftily considered sophomoric activities more suited to college frat houses than an Officer's Club. The more senior officers, lieutenant colonels and full colonels, were gathered at one or two private get-togethers in their more spacious quarters or half sections of house trailers assigned to men of advanced rank. The wing commander rated a whole trailer with two bedrooms, one converted to an office.

Captain Jack Laird elbowed his way through to Bannister and motioned him to follow. Laird, the old head among the 531st, and among the entire 3rd Tac Fighter Wing for that matter, had nearly two thousand hours in the Hun. He was a narrow-hipped man with broad shoulders, dark-brown hair, high cheekbones, and the perpetually tanned face and squint lines of a man who has spent much of his life outdoors. He climbed on top of the bar, spread his arms and yelled at the pilots to shut up. They obeyed.

"Inasmuch as we want to welcome the man who 'had a situation,' the approach end engagement man who so recently availed himself of said facilities when he could have stepped over the side . . . but was probably too afraid. . . ." The crowd laughed, and Higgens the Homeless blew a double quack through the window. "Silence, silence," Laird went on, "we hereby welcome Court Bannister, *Crash* Bannister, to our great band of warriors. I hereby pronounce you an official member of the Third Tactical Fighter Wing and an official member in good standing of the 531st Tactical Fighter Squadron sent here by a grateful country to kill the beady-eyed Cong." More cheers, whistles, and applause.

Crash Bannister realized something was expected of him. He climbed up on the bar next to Jack Laird. Both men's flight suits were dark with sweat. They shook hands and slapped each other on the shoulder. Below, in the crowd, Bannister saw Jones, the flying safety officer, grinning broadly and next to him, laughing, was Doc Russell. Court waved a casual salute at them, then turned his attention to the raucous crowd of pilots.

"Men," Bannister's voice was clear, crisp, and commanding, and he knew it. As a kid, after much voice coaching, he had once played the role of a Winsockie cadet major. "Men," he repeated, thinking that although he might have a commanding voice, right now he didn't know what in hell to say with it. He felt his face flush. This is really dumb, he thought. Here I am in front of all these guys and I don't know what to say. He looked down and grinned.

"You guys are shit hot, you know that? I'm damn glad to be with you." He held his beer up and drank it down as a toast to his audience. And then, because he couldn't think of anything else to do and something frivolous seemed in order, he jumped from the bar, performed a perfect parachute landing fall on the bar-room floor, and rolled to his feet. The pilots crowded around to pat him on the back and cheer. Court shook hands with many of them as he edged through the crowd to join Russell and Jones at the beer tub, where they handed him a fresh one.

Laird pressed his way through and joined the three men. He and Bannister grinned at each other.

"Some 'situation.' You done good, bringing that bird in that way," Laird said.

Bannister nodded his thanks.

"I heard Rawson was a bit rough on you," Laird continued.

"Yeah. He took me off flight-lead status," Bannister replied.

"Damn, that's too bad," Jones said, "but we're on stand-down for another stupid bombing halt. Maybe when it's over he'll put you back on." He ducked as a foamy spray shot over the crowd from a pilot violently shaking a full beer can.

"Yeah, maybe." Court didn't think Rawson would. He had seemed too intensely interested in rescinding the orders. You had to be good to be a flight leader. To lead other pilots into combat required skill and experience. The position of trust meant a lot to him. To lose it to one man's capricious whim was not a pleasant experience.

"What in hell did you see up there at Loc Ninh that caused all the excitement over at Intel?" Jack Laird asked, raising his voice against the crowd noise.

"It's not so much what I saw as what I felt," Bannister replied. "There are some highly accurate gunners there that aren't afraid to shoot. I read the after-action report of the FAC, Copperhead Zero Three, and I talked to him later that day. He thinks there's something going on."

"Who is Zero Three? He flies out of here, doesn't he?" Jones asked.

"Yes, he does. It's Phil Travers. He bunks in that scrounged-up trailer of his in the revetment on the north side of runway 27. He took a couple hits also. He said that during six months and nearly five hundred hours of FAC-time he hasn't seen ground fire like that since the VC tried to overrun Plei Mei last October," Bannister said.

Doc Russell spoke up. "So what's going on? Is it a buildup or what? Is there a Special Forces camp up there at Loc Ninh they want to take?"

"Yeah," Laird said, "there's an SF fighting camp set up there to interdict VC and NVA activity from Cambodia. But the bad guys usually don't call much attention to themselves before an attack on a camp."

"I think it's a buildup," Bannister said, "and so does Phil Travers."

"I don't look at maps like you guys do," Russell said. "If they're building up, it has to be for an attack on something. If it's not the SF camp, what is it that's big enough to risk exposure like they have?"

"Right here, Bien Hoa, us," Bannister replied. Laird and Jones nodded assent. "Blasting this place would be a prestigious move. Uncle Ho would show the United States, and the world, for that matter, that he can hit wherever and whenever he wants. Even big important bases like Bien Hoa. And these bombing halts we put up with gives them a perfect chance to run in more troops and supplies from Cambodia."

The more he talked, the more Court Bannister surprised himself how much he was holding forth on what he surmised Ho Chi Minh could or would do. Particularly, he was amazed at how much credit he seemed to give Uncle Ho for managing world opinion.

Over in trailer 21B, Colonel Frank Darlington, the Director of Operations for the 3rd Tactical Fighter Wing, hosted his three fighter-squadron commanders for a little Christmas cheer. Since Lieutenant Colonel Peter Warton was still in the States on emergency leave, Major Harold Rawson represented the 531st. He only sipped his drink while the others were doing a good job of putting the booze away. The two squadron commanders, Dietzen, dynamic and exuberant, and Baldwin, dark and broody, felt at home with Darlington. The Wing Commander, Colonel Jake Friedlander, had retired to his quarters earlier. Darlington, Dietzen, and Baldwin were talking flying and the capabilities of their various pilots. Rawson had not contributed much beyond a head nod now and then.

Almost all the combat fighter pilots doing close air support work, they agreed, preferred weapons like the snakes, CBU, nape, and 20 mike-mike. A few, less hardy souls, really didn't want to get down in the weeds where those weapons could be delivered with great accuracy. They preferred to dive-bomb. Roll in from a comfortable height, say 13,000 feet or so, pickle at, oh, say, 6,000, then bottom out by 4,500, well above anything that might hurt or puncture the aircraft or the overly cautious pilot within. Never mind that one couldn't hit anything from those high altitudes except the ground.

But pinpoint accuracy was the name of the game in South Viet-

nam, because the biggest percentage of F-100 missions were flown
in support of U.S. or Vietnamese ground troops in contact with the
enemy. Under the expert direction of a FAC, who was in constant
contact by FM radio with the ground commander, the strike pilots
would carefully lay their ordnance in where directed. Sometimes the
desired impact point was quite close to the friendlies. The higher
above the ground the pilot released his ordnance, the greater chance
for an error that could cause friendly casualties.

Rawson was regarded as one of the "high school" boys. Odd, too,
since he had been flying fighters for most of his career. He had received his wings and commission when he had graduated from aviation cadet training in the late forties. He had spent most of his time
in fighters and had accrued a modest twenty missions flying an F-86
from Kimpo during the Korean War. But, as most knew, flying
fighter iron didn't make one a fighter pilot. It was a state of mind,
an attitude, fighter jocks agreed.

Most fighter pilots could name maybe two or three people who
had influenced their lives who weren't fighter pilots at all, but who
had the right attitude. The "Let's give it a try, why not try it this
way, I think I can do it" kind of attitude.

But Rawson wasn't that way, and the other men knew it. Rawson
considered himself a very safe pilot. He had never had an accident,
had never raised his pulse to an almost unbearable rate because he
was pushing an airplane—or himself—to see what he could see. The
top pilots did this. They needed to know the envelope of the airplane
and of themselves. They needed to know the limits to which they
could push themselves and their craft and still be in control. They
needed to know the precise point at which they or the airplane would
depart from stable and controlled flight.

So Rawson was now the commanding officer, albeit temporarily,
of a fighter squadron, a position to which he had always aspired. He
knew this temporary command slot could lead to his taking over the
squadron permanently. As a reserve officer who coveted a regular
commission that would assure him tenure beyond twenty years and
probably a shot at full colonel, he knew doing a good job as commanding officer would almost assure those goals. He certainly felt he
looked the part. He always kept his little peanut Smiling Jack mustache neat and trimmed exactly so above his thin lips. He always,
but always, managed to take at least thirty minutes each day to bask
in the sun and make sure his tan was in place. He carried a collapsible
pencil that expanded into a pointer. At briefings, when he was on
the platform in front of the squadron, he would pluck the metal

pen-pointer from his left sleeve pocket, expand it with a flourish, then tap the board or map or wherever it was he wanted the pilots to focus their attention.

Rawson's eyes flickered as he once again put out of his mind the bomb he knew he had dropped short of the target in IV Corps a few days ago. He refused to think of the angry shout that the FAC had given over the radio. All he knew was that the incident had never been reported.

"Harry," the DO addressed Rawson, "you haven't said much. What do you think?"

Rawson looked nonplussed and decidedly uneasy. Darlington pressed on.

"Is it all a bunch of manly malarkey or is there really something to this fighter-pilot mystique thing?"

Rawson was definitely uncomfortable. He indeed thought the attitude stuff a lot of malarkey, but this obviously wasn't the time or place to expound his theory that flying fighters was no different from flying cargo or bomber aircraft.

"Well, yes," he said, "I think you've got something there. Mmm-hmm, sure." He looked at his watch, started to fiddle with his mustache, thought better of it, and said it was time for him to hit the sack. Colonel Darlington saw him to the door and outside.

"How did it go when General Austin called?" Darlington asked.

Rawson thought for a moment. "It went all right," he said. "Actually I was quite surprised how nice he was. He told me he wondered why the Defense Department was listing Paul as Missing in Action, Presumed Dead, Body Not Recovered (MIA/PD, BNR). I told him I'd have Major Jones forward a copy of the 127-4 report and that if he wanted further details he should talk to Bannister. He said the report would be sufficient for the moment and that he saw no reason to bother Bannister, who had enough to do fighting the war right now."

Darlington nodded. "By the way," he asked confidentially, "what is it you've got against Bannister?"

Although Rawson had not told Darlington everything he had said to General Austin on the telephone, he decided maybe this was the time to air his theory about Bannister. "That Hollywood showboat is laughing at us, at all of us," Rawson said with a vehemence that surprised the DO. "He doesn't have to be doing this. He doesn't have to be in the Air Force and he knows it. He isn't a career man and never will be. He can quit and run home to his rich father any time he wants. He isn't like the rest of us. But I'll show him up."

"How's that?" the DO enquired.

"His Efficiency Report. The way I'll make his ER read, it won't even be submitted to the promotion board for Major."

"I see," the DO said, nodding, then added his goodnight. He closed the screen door and reentered the warm and boozy circle of companionship of the two squadron commanders.

Major Harold Rawson strode away, slamming his heels into the crushed gravel path as if he were on a parade ground. He reviewed the last thing he had said to General Austin about his son's death. He had surprised himself at how easily the concept had come to his mind.

"Maybe if Paul had had another wingman, he'd be alive today."

"What do you mean?" the general had demanded.

"Sir," he made up as he went along, "maybe Bannister didn't call out the ground fire like he should have." There had followed a long silence broken only by overlapping patches of conversations from other lines.

"That's interesting," General Austin had said, and broke the connection.

9

☆

He was from Texas, stood six-foot-three, weighed 210 pounds, and said he did not trust a man whose pecker he did not have in his pocket. He sat down for lunch with four others at an oval-shaped mahogany Duncan Phyfe table covered with a thick white linen tablecloth. A mural on the far wall depicted Cornwallis surrendering his sword at Yorktown. Enough bow-tied waiters were in attendance to ensure swift service. The luncheon was a Tuesday ritual that started at one o'clock in the family dining room on the second floor of the White House. He was the thirty-sixth President of the United States, but the first to select bombing targets at a weekly luncheon.

The guests always included the Secretaries of Defense and State, the President's press secretary, his closest adviser, and, occasionally, the Director of Central Intelligence (DCI). He rarely invited members of the military to his luncheon. In fact, he rarely saw members of the military at all. Since June 1965, he had met privately with the Chief of Staff of the Army only twice. He did meet privately with the USAF Chief of Staff once in a while, but always in his office, never at the Tuesday luncheon.

Therefore, it was to the surprise of many, the lively and quick-witted Chief of Staff of the Air Force, the CSAF, whose spectacles and gangly frame belied the fact that he was an experienced combat aviator, was invited to a Tuesday luncheon. To accompany him was the SecDef's personal target officer, USAF Major General Albert G. "Whitey" Whisenand, the Deputy Director of Ops and Planning (Detached). Considering what happened, the odds were good that Whitey would not be invited back.

Before moving into the semioval dining room, the luncheon guests met in the sitting room for drinks, which the two officers declined. The luncheon talk was banal and did not afford much opportunity for the two Air Force officers to contribute. After the table was cleared and the waiters dismissed, aides erected the portable briefing easels to hold the target information charts. The President stood and spread out on the table some highly detailed black-and-white target photos (taken at high cost by unarmed RF-101's). He bent over to inspect them. This particular stack of targets selected for his approval had been made up by Whitey from the JCS Target List. The list was a compendium of the most serious of the ninety-four military targets in North Vietnam, ranging from Petroleum Oil Lubrication (POL) storage areas to docking facilities in the Haiphong Harbor and the two rail lines running south out of Red China. Had they been swiftly and completely destroyed in 1964 or 1965, the JCS believed the war would have been stopped before it started. Barry Goldwater, a fighter pilot in the Air Force Reserves who had been running for President in 1964, had vowed to do just that. His opponent, LBJ, had won the election by vowing not only that he would *not* drop any bombs and thereby risk starting World War III, but that he would never let American boys go fight a war the Asian boys should be fighting.

Now, after due consideration and no little anxiety, a few JCS targets were being hit piecemeal. Each time one was authorized at the Tuesday lunch, the White House held its breath for fear that either the Soviets or the red Chinese would be provoked to retaliate. The Pentagon was about evenly divided on whether or not the two Communist powers would likely launch retaliatory attacks. The White House had apparently only one position: The Communists, China or Russia, would indeed respond—as China had in Korea—and World War III would most probably start. White House policy was based on that thesis.

There were other criteria to be examined before a JCS target strike was authorized. Each request presented to the President was on a single sheet of paper containing a four-point checklist:

1. The military advantage of striking the proposed target.
2. The risk to American pilots and aircraft in the raid.
3. The danger that the strike might widen the war by forcing other countries into the fighting.
4. The danger of heavy civilian casualties.

Once the target list reached the luncheon committee, Whitey and the CSAF, in fact the whole Joint Chiefs, were out of the loop. Knowing that, Whitey and the CSAF wondered why they hadn't been dismissed when lunch was finished. Must be this was a social luncheon and not a business session where the Air Force men would actually be asked to comment on Air Force matters. But it wasn't.

They watched the President and his men hunch over their own copies of the Number 1 request and its accompanying photo, which was to airdrop mines into Haiphong Harbor to prevent shipborne resupply of war materiel. It was an oft-repeated request of late, which made the negative answer predictable. Each man graded his copy of the checklist, and together they totaled and averaged their scores to sum up a collective "No." Although the Haiphong mining and the cutting of rail supply lines that ran southeast and southwest out of China into North Vietnam had great military value, it also had, as the Secretary of State put it, a "war-widening value"; and, furthermore, was a risk to aircrew.

Later, Target Number 7, the cement plant near Nam Dinh, was approved first time up. It had low military value, but then its war-widening risk was equally low. Using the same techniques, the President quickly disapproved fourteen more requests. On-scene commanders could process and approve air strike target requests in South Vietnam and in Route Pack One in the southern portion of North Vietnam, but not the rest of the North: that was the President's personal turf, and that was the area in which he was selecting targets today.

From half a world away, these men, politicians for the most part, would decide which targets would be struck and with what ordnance. On a case-by-case basis, they would labor over reccy photos and target information of railroad junctions, petroleum storage tanks, railroad bridges, factories, warehouses, airfields ("war-widening"), Antiaircraft Artillery and missile sites ("only if fired upon"), docks ("awful, just awful, lots of boats there with Quakers and Swedes, and Rooskies, too"), and truck depots ("probably civilian workers there").

Watching the President perform this activity, Whitey became bored and fell to musing over topics ranging from the overhaul needed soon for his cranky steam-heating furnace in his McLean, Virginia, home to the ambiguous reports surfacing concerning the buildup at Loc Ninh in South Vietnam. He was becoming more convinced that the VC and VNA were gathering men and materiel in that area north of Saigon in Binh Long province for some unusual purpose. Normally it was quiet up there.

He thought about Morgan and Tunner, his two staff assistants. Although both had extensive fighter experience in Korea and considerable command experience as well, neither had as yet taken a combat tour in Southeast Asia. Both had volunteered to do so, and they often talked about going. They had too much rank to be assigned as line fighter pilots, and would, in fact, be lucky if they were allowed to fly at all. Combat fighter flying in Vietnam was being done by lieutenants, a great number of captains and majors, and a handful of lieutenant colonels. The few colonels who were allowed to fly did so because they held command slots in flying units. Brigadiers and above weren't even allowed into cockpits by themselves. The Navy did it the same way, flying the hell out of their lieutenants and lieutenant commanders. It wasn't that the higher ranks didn't want to or couldn't fly. It was because they had too much rank and command position to be flying daily combat sorties. They had long since been promoted beyond the fun and relatively carefree duty (if you don't count getting shot at) of squadron fighter jocks.

Partway through the target request list, the President straightened up and stretched his back. He looked over to Major General Albert G. "Whitey" Whisenand and asked him, with obvious pride, but in a manner that would brook no abstaining, what he thought of his, the President's, ability to prosecute an airwar. Whitey looked at the surroundings for an instant, then back to the tall man from Texas. He had been dreading a question like that—and hoping for it at the same time. Well, here goes, he thought.

"Sir, respectfully, I must point out that as a target officer you are unschooled in basic Douhet principles—principles which clearly stipulate that piecemeal application of airpower is imprudent. Couple that lack with a use of airpower which lacks mass, surprise, and consistency, and you have a situation that wastes lives and money. This, in turn, fosters further contempt for this nonwar in the opinion of the American people, and that of the rest of the world, while accomplishing exactly nothing. Furthermore, you cannot use American pilots and planes to *send messages*."

There was shocked silence in the room. Those moving seemed to pause in midstride. The SecDef, black hair slicked back, gave Whitey a hard and thoughtful look. The President stared at him. They were about the same age, midfifties. The President knew Major General Albert G. Whisenand was a congressional favorite because he was from a wealthy and influential family that went back to the Mayflower, and he would always speak what he believed to be the truth, regardless of the consequences.

In 1954, in fact, Whitey had saved the U.S. from a near disastrous plan to add American airpower to that of France in Indochina. The then chairman of the Joint Chiefs of Staff, Admiral Arthur W. Radford, supported by Secretary of State John Foster Dulles, had proposed to President Eisenhower that furnishing American aid in the form of fighter-bombers and aerial resupply would save the beleaguered French garrison at Dien Bien Phu. Major General Whisenand, then Colonel Whisenand, had informed a Senate subcommittee that such a move was a clear-cut signal to the world at large that the United States supported colonial powers in a post–World War II era that abhorred such things. Further, Whisenand had said, the use of U.S. airplanes, which eventually would have to be based in French Indochina, as Vietnam and the neighboring countries of Laos and Cambodia were then called, would require the commitment of ground troops to maintain, supply, and protect the American airmen and their airplanes.

U.S. Army General Matthew Ridgeway had concurred and so informed President Eisenhower. Big Matt hadn't really needed Whitey's input, since both were members of the "Never Again Club," but he'd appreciated and needed Whitey's support in front of Congress. Both had served in Korea, and from his experience fighting the North Koreans and Chinese there, they knew that the U.S. should "never again" engage in an Asian land war.

The President stared steadily at Whitey, then finally threw back his head and gave a great yelp of laughter. The civilians breathed a collective sigh of relief; so did the CSAF. He had decided that it would do no good to echo Whitey's quite correct statements, because as the CSAF he could be of more benefit in these bad days by maintaining his own position. He believed that one of his more important duties was to serve as a buffer between the troops in the field and that combination of an intransigent and abusive Secretary of Defense and an equally domineering and dictatorial President of the United States.

"Whitey, you old fart, you don't back down an inch, do you?" the President guffawed. Whitey, wisely, remained silent while the room sprang back to life. Sprightly conversation picked up about everything except the President's use of Navy and USAF aircraft to send messages to Hanoi.

After a moment, the President looked straight at Whisenand and said, "Whitey, I'm going to tell you an old Texas story." The room fell silent again. "Back in the days of the Depression, back there by the Pedernales River"—he pronounced it "purden-alice"—"a new young teacher applied to the school board for a job. His papers were in order, but to test him, a member asked whether the world was flat or round. The young man thought for a moment and replied, 'I can teach it either way.' "

Whitey grinned at the humor of the story, but not the current situation. He thought he knew what was coming.

The President went up and put his arm across Whitey's shoulders. "I've got to teach it both ways," he said quietly and in a manner indicating he was taking Whitey into his innermost confidence. "You understand I have the duty to satisfy the American people at home yet protect their interests abroad. Do you know what that means? Do you know the heavy responsibility I carry?"

Without waiting for an answer, the President disengaged his arm, strode to the table, banged his fist on a photo of the Thanh Hoa Bridge, and said, "I've got to tell Ho Chi Minh that unless he stops his aggression in South Veet-nam, that I'm going to hammer hell out of him; and at the same time I've got to tell, to convince the American people, that I am not going to escalate this Veet-nam war."

The President glared at Whitey, and then at the CSAF. "Dammit, I'm teaching it both ways. I have to teach it both ways. Furthermore, I don't think you or anybody else over in that goddamn five-sided crap house knows that."

The CSAF took Whitey back to the Pentagon with him in his chauffeured Air Force–blue Plymouth sedan. They got out at the River entrance, mounted the eleven steps, and entered the far left one of the five tall, oaken double doors. Whitey automatically started to turn right. He planned to say goodbye then go down Stairwell 71 leading to his basement domain. The CSAF put his hand on his arm. "Come up and have some coffee. We need to talk." Whitey nodded and followed him up the escalator.

1415 HOURS LOCAL, 21 DECEMBER 1965
OFFICE OF THE CHIEF OF STAFF
UNITED STATES AIR FORCE,
THE PENTAGON, WASHINGTON, D.C.

☆

Christmas in the Pentagon is just the opposite from Christmas in a combat zone. For weeks ahead of the actual event, certain doors far away from the power corridors become decorated with large Santa posters, red and green crepe paper, shiny ribbons, and clever sayings such as YOU'D BETTER BE NAUGHTY written across the bottom of a picture showing a provocative girl in a revealing Santa costume. Inside these same rooms, miniature green or silver tin-and-plastic Christmas trees stand on desks, on filing cabinets, or in corners. Ropy tinsel becomes more evident as the actual holidays draw near. There is great anticipation of the office party. Will there be booze? Will the colonel come? Will it be like last year when Florence got so tipsy she threw her arms around Major Cruikshank and told him he was adorable, simply adorable? And don't forget Staff Sergeant Tine, who got more than tipsy, threw *his* arm around Major Cruikshank and told him what a shit he was.

Actual paid holiday time off at the Pentagon wasn't much, according to the majority of the lower-ranking GS workers and enlisted men, and what few lieutenants and captains there were in that five-sided building (they had heard what the President had called it). On the one hand, the senior GS employees, along with the senior NCO's and senior officers, dreaded the holiday season because it really cut into their tight schedule and work productivity. On the other hand, some welcomed it because it meant they could come in during the holidays and get a lot of nag jobs over and done with. These types, regardless of rank, were generally spoken of—not kindly—as workaholics by their peers. The CSAF was regarded as one.

The CSAF steered Whitey to the side of his large main office, where three burgundy-colored leather armchairs were placed around a coffee table in front of a matching couch. The table was covered with the latest editions of various defense journals and copies of the *Washington Post* and the *Washington Star*. The two men waited while the steward served coffee in huge plain ceramic mugs with the USAF logo.

"Whitey," the CSAF said, "do you think the SecDef will keep you on after what you said today?"

"No sir, I don't. And it doesn't matter. I was never really necessary in that position. No one was ever necessary there or is now or ever will be in the future. I think the original idea was to have one more military hand on the throttle, but it didn't work the way he, the SecDef, or they, the President and the SecDef, envisioned. The hand, my hand, tried to hold the throttle back or jam it all the way forward. Either stop the train or run it full steam to its destination. It is unwieldy enough to have target authorization requests come up from J-three Operations at MACV, in conjunction with Seventh Air Force, through CINCPAC, without being shunted off to a side office such as mine. It makes no difference what I or my people, Morgan and Tunner, say. The lunch group picks the shots on their terms of reference."

The CSAF took a long swallow, placed his mug on the coffee table, and leaned forward from his deep armchair. He shook his head, his glasses gleaming.

"Whitey, you're the oldest living active duty two-star, and you're so well supported that I can't fire you." He gave a fleeting smile. "Not that I would. All I can do is ask if you would consider retiring from active duty."

The CSAF leaned back in his chair; request made. He knew what Whitey would say, but he also knew he'd have to tell the SecDef he had asked Whitey to retire. The President might appreciate, albeit grudgingly, Whitey's candor, but not so the SecDef. He had fired senior officers for smiling at times the SecDef judged inappropriate. Since the SecDef himself never smiled, all times were inappropriate.

"No, sir, I'm not ready to retire." Whitey knew the game.

"Well, then," CSAF said, "where can I possibly put you out of harm's way?"

"Out of harm's way?" Whitey put his mug down and walked to the chief's window and looked out at the Potomac River. "I don't know what you mean by 'out of harm's way,' but I'll tell you what I would like. If you don't mind," Whitey added, almost as an afterthought.

Damn, the CSAF thought to himself, hoping Whitey didn't want command of an air division or some other operational slot. He's got the date of rank, but those jobs belong to younger men moving through to even higher positions of responsibility and authority.

"Tell me," the CSAF ordered.

"If I can't stop it, I might as well join it. How about chieftel at Tan Son Nhut?" Whitey asked. The CSAF glanced at Whitey, surprised. Actually, he thought, chief of intelligence at TSN, though a one-star slot, was fine. In fact, he mused, the extra horsepower of Whitey's second star wouldn't hurt, although the Army wheels in MACV would scream and most likely readjust upward the rank of *their* Intel chief. Another thought struck him: the farther away the better. Although he liked Whitey personally, as the Chief of Staff he could not afford to have a subordinate around who might cross the Secretary of Defense or the Commander in Chief out of hand.

"That might be arranged," the CSAF said.

"Chief," Whitey said, "if I transfer out I've got to take care of my boys. Would you look into this?" Whitey pulled out his notebook and scribbled out his suggested assignments for Morgan and Tunner. He handed the paper to the chief, who placed it in his blue-covered "To Do" folder.

He then thought of Whitey's Vietnam reconnaissance plans.

"What about your recce plans with the NRO? You were getting to the point of briefing the Joint Chiefs, weren't you?" the CSAF asked Whitey, alluding to his position on the board of the National Reconnaissance Organization and its attempt to set up intelligence gathering in hostile SEA areas with a combination of ground teams, drones at low altitudes, U-2's in the upper atmosphere, and satellites in space.

"Yes, sir," said Whitey, "we are. Lieutenant General Austin has, I believe, an appointment to brief the JCS in the tank next Tuesday at 1400." The tank was what senior military staff called their sequestered briefing room. Whitey continued, "I think you'll find the gaps, particularly those that apply to ground and drone recce, will be filled. My input is terminated."

"All right, Whitey," CSAF said standing up, a clear sign of dismissal, "in that case the slot at Seventh is yours as soon as it opens up."

Then, remembering, the CSAF snapped his fingers. "Tex Austin. His son just went KIA, didn't he?"

"Yes, damn shame. Young Paul Austin. He had no business in fighters. He could have, *should* have, stayed in MAC. I heard he had a good career going there." Whitey paused, then added, "Did you know his wingman was Sam Bannister's oldest son? He got shot up at the same time and barely made it back to the runway at Bien Hoa."

"You mean Silk Screen Sam, that randy actor's son, is an Air Force pilot at Bien Hoa?" The CSAF looked up with interest. "We need, correction, *I* need, to keep track of stuff like that. Remember when Dugan's kid, the F-84 squadron commander, blew his brains all over his squadron office ceiling with a service .45? The Chief of Staff didn't even know about it until the *Washington Post* called for comment."

"This is different, Chief," Whitey said.

"In what way?"

"The Dugan boy had an authentic, grade A, war hero dad whose exploits as a Navy fighter pilot in World War Two were legend. The movies of him are still on the late show. It all caught up with the son. Notice he didn't join the Navy to fly. He joined the Air Force. Wanted to forge his own identity, I suppose. Kind of reminds me of

Tex Austin's kid. Should have stayed in MAC. Each kid probably was out to prove something and it caught up with them."

"Using what you just said as a guide, don't you think Silk Screen Sam Bannister's son is the same way—out to prove something?"

"Maybe so. Aren't we all in one way or another? But the man's record is good. He slugged through an Air Force Institute of Technology engineering degree and has been accepted for the test pilot school at Edwards, as I recall," Whitey said. "At any rate, he never goes for publicity. Always plays it low and quiet."

"He didn't play it low and quiet at Las Vegas. He got in some brawl, didn't he?"

"Chief, some downtown punk pressed him too far at the Silver Screen Hotel one night about his dad, so young Bannister fed him his teeth. He's very protective of his father."

"What is his name? Silk Screen Sam like his Dad?"

"No. If anything, it's Quiet Court. His half brother is called Silky Shawn. He's a bit slick."

"Never heard of him. Wait a minute, isn't he that loudmouthed journalist?" Whitey nodded. "You mean that writer punk is a brother to one of our guys?" The CSAF seemed to take this as a personal affront to the untarnished name of the United States Air Force.

"Half brother. Same father, different mother. And Silky Shawn is not a full-fledged journalist. He's a stringer in Saigon for the *California Sun* magazine."

"How come you know all this, Whitey?" the CSAF asked, fixing Whitey with a squinty stare.

"I'm Shawn's godfather. Samuel Whisenand Bannister and I are cousins."

"Humph, I should have known," the CSAF said, ushering Whitey out a side door to the E-ring corridor.

Forty minutes after the Chief of Staff of the United States Air Force ushered Whitey out, the red phone on his desk buzzed once, indicating the Chairman of the Joint Chiefs of Staff wished to talk to him. That the Chairman's hotline buzzed only once instead of emitting a strident, continuous ring until picked up—which is what happened with an imperious predecessor—was a tribute to the gentlemanliness of the current CJCS, U.S. Army General Earle Wheeler.

"John," the Chairman said, "the President just called. He wants Whitey Whisenand assigned to the National Security Council, effective immediately. You were at the White House today with them. What's this all about?"

"General, I wish I knew. I was about to call and tell you about it. I thought Whitey bumped heads badly with the President about the President's ability, or lack of ability I should say, to select bombing targets in North Vietnam. Apparently the President thought Whitey's frankness refreshing and wants him to infuse some of the same into the NSC. I'll see that he gets the word."

"Do that," said Wheeler. "Like Methuselah, he'll be with us forever. I suppose we need people like him, although for the life of me I don't know why."

The chief of the Air Force restrained himself from comparing Whitey more to Diogenes than Methuselah and replying, "To keep us honest." Instead, he thought this a good time to get some power to back Whitey's request for Navy Captain Jim Tunner. Not that he was afraid to go to the Chief of Naval Operations himself, but it didn't hurt to ensure high-level interest for his request. Besides, with Whitey on the National Security Council at the President's request, he'd best keep on his good side.

"General," the Air Force chief began, "Whitey believes that the Navy captain who worked for him earned a good assignment and wants to help him get it." He told him about Captain Jim Tunner. They both knew the man had to be qualified and in line, because no service chief would submit to pressure from above to promote or position an unqualified man over his peers. The Chairman told him he would mention it to the CNO who would take it from there.

1500 HOURS LOCAL, 27 DECEMBER 1965
OFFICE OF MAJOR GENERAL ALBERT G. WHISENAND,
THE PENTAGON, WASHINGTON, D.C.

☆

Outside the Pentagon, the heavy gray air of low ceiling muffled the engine sounds of planes taking off from Washington National. Slush was on the streets. The forecast called for sleet. It was the Monday after the long Christmas weekend, a typically dark December late afternoon. All the lights were on in the Pentagon, where U.S. Air Force Colonel Ralph Morgan and U.S. Navy Captain Jim Tunner reported to Major General Whitey Whisenand as requested.

At forty-one, the five-foot, ten-inch Morgan could be described as pudgy, if not heavy. His face, already tending to jowls, was accented by a deep frown that had become almost permanent. Tunner, lean and tall, had a finely sculpted face and thin lips. Neither officer knew what the general had in mind. They did know that after his visit to the White House last week he had spent time with the CSAF, then sequestered himself in this very office making and receiving many phone calls, according to the information they had weaseled out of his secretary, Betty. She said even the White House switchboard had come through for him and wasn't that something.

The general served coffee. Morgan and Tunner sipped, as politely as possible, the acrid, black, steaming liquid from the Ansley bone-china mugs the general had supplied. Morgan and Tunner, no strangers to the general's Brenny coffee purportedly from the Isle of Man, had opined that since the Isle of Man grew no coffee beans they knew of, the noxious grains were probably from a cache of coffee beans full of one-hundred-year-old rat turds retrieved in the eighteenth century from a sunken sailing vessel, and thence left to rot in a potato cellar. Whitey Whisenand sipped a few sips, smacked his lips, then mouthed to the world at large his favorite double entendre, "Ahhh, *Man,* that's good coffee." Finished with the coffee ritual, he looked steadily at Morgan and Tunner.

"This office is dissolved as of midnight tonight. The President has requested I accept a position as a special advisor for air on the National Security Council."

"Great Scott," Tunner said, truly surprised. Both he and Morgan thought Whisenand would be involuntarily placed on the retirement list.

"Now, as to you two gentlemen. Ralph, you are going to spend some time upgrading into the F-105 at McConnell; Jim, you're going to spend about the same length of time going to every replacement air group the Navy has for fighter aircraft. Then you both go to command slots in Southeast Asia. Ralph, you've got the F-105 Wing at Tahkli, Thailand. Jim, you're to be the new Commander Air Group on the carrier *Coral Sea* in the South China Sea. Any questions?"

That night each of Whitey's officers took his wife out for a gourmet meal and plied her with wine and compliments. Somewhere between the entrée and the desert, both men, barely able to conceal their glee, told their wives of their new assignments. Later that night, each man made love to his spouse with more vigor, imagination, and ardor than usual. One wife was tearful and clinging. The other tried desperately to hide her joy at her husband's imminent departure. She thought she was successful.

0300 HOURS LOCAL, 28 DECEMBER 1965
BRANIFF INTERNATIONAL PARKING LOT,
LOS ANGELES INTERNATIONAL AIRPORT, CALIFORNIA

☆

After Braniff International Military Airlift Command contract flight number B2T5—the numbers were always odd flying east, even going west—deplaned its load of weary G.I's at the Los Angeles terminal, Mrs. Bradley L. Lewis, known better as Nancy, went to Braniff's employee parking lot, where she ground the battery dead after trying to start her old blue 1957 Chevy two-door. She closed her eyes and rested her head on the steering wheel. "Ah, Brad," she moaned. "Oh God, I never thought it would be like this." She'd had the Chevy since before she married Brad; she drove it to and from work to save the splendid Oldsmobile '88 convertible that they'd bought a few months before Brad went to Vietnam the preceding spring as an adviser. He had been assigned to Team 75 out of My Tho to the 7th ARVN Infantry Division in IV Corps, South Vietnam. As he'd left, from this terminal, she'd decided that she didn't want to put any more mileage on the beautiful convertible until he was home. She had driven it to their apartment in Marina del Rey and put it in storage the next day. Two months later, in July of 1965, she'd found out Brad would not be coming home at the end of his tour. His ARVN field force had been overrun and he was declared MIA. Nancy, Mrs. Bradley L. Lewis, had heard nothing from the Department of Defense since.

She climbed out of the expired Chevy and walked through the well-lighted, securely fenced lot to the gate guard's shack, where red and blue Christmas tree lights gaily framed one window. Braniff International knew car batteries could be unreliable when their employees were gone for weeks at a time over the Pacific.

Old Ramon pushed the battery cart to Nancy's Chevy and started it for her. He refused the dollar bill she tried to give him. As she drove the Chevy out of the lot, Ramon noticed her left taillight was out. He made a note to himself to buy one and fix it for her when she next came in. He was sixty-three and felt very fatherly toward the girls who flew so far out to sea. And he had met the brave Sergeant First Class Brad Lewis and felt particularly fatherly toward his beautiful amber-eyed wife.

10

☆

The Wolf, dressed in the camouflage fatigues known as Tiger suits and wearing his mashed and sweaty, sun-faded green beret for the first time legally in eight months was at the wheel of a jeep rumbling down a dusty road on Tan Son Nhut Air Base headed toward the O-Club to celebrate. He was happy. Thoughts of church bombs and nosy newsies were behind him, although he did remember, with a yearning ache, the cool green eyes of the girl, Charmaine. All told, he was happy. More than happy, ecstatic was the right word, he thought. Colonel Morton had arranged for the 5th Special Forces Group at Nha Trang to give him the transfer he had wanted for so long. Rather than function as an adviser out of My Tho in the Dinh Tung and Kien Thung provinces in the Mekong Delta area of IV Corps, he was assigned special duty to a Special Forces A Team: Detachment A-302, in III Corps. And not just any A Team: Detachment A-302 was a Mike Force team. That meant they were the mobile reaction force for all of III Corps.

Allowed to recruit two companies of Nung Chinese mercenaries and one company of Cambodians from jails and elsewhere, the mission of the III Corps Mike Force was to react to Special Forces camps in trouble, particularly those that served as watchposts along the Cambodian border, or to go out on small unit patrols to find Charley, as they called the VC—not to engage the larger units, just to call in some artillery, or air, or U.S. infantry units. They also performed bomb damage assessments, called BDA's, after B-52 strikes. Elite of the elite, the Mike Force team selected its own members from a long line of volunteers who had to have at least one tour at an SF camp under their belt to be considered.

The Wolf was assigned to the Mike Force for a few weeks to augment its intelligence-gathering and -assessment capabilities regarding a suspected buildup in War Zones C and D. He was delighted to throw away his tin pot and don the green beret he had worked so hard to earn many years before. He thought with disgust of the leadership of the 7th ARVN Infantry Division. The lower ranks, although eager, did not fight well, and as a puking adviser the Wolf couldn't do anything about it. You don't *advise* a man into combat, goddammit, you *lead* him. He had been caught, more than once, leading platoons from the 7th into heavy VC encampments.

Secretly, the J-3 Ops people at MACV were delighted with Wolf's assignment. Officially they had to get rid of the Wolf, since the 7th ARVN Infantry Division commander and both province chiefs wanted him out of their jurisdictions. He was not operating the war in a manner conducive to profit making for them. MACV, operating under the McNamara policy of "We are guests in Vietnam," complied and pulled the Wolf out. His old mentor, Army Colonel George Morton, heard about it and arranged his new job with the commander of the 5th Special Forces Group, who was only too happy to oblige.

Major Wolfgang "the Wolf" Lochert drove to the Tan Son Nhut Officer's Club in a MACV jeep signed out to him by a Motor Pool sergeant who was delighted to do this small favor—"Any time, major, any time"—in return for an authentic VC flag. The Wolf had purchased a dozen such flags from a street vendor in My Tho. That the flags were authentic VC was undisputed, since the vendor, who also sold black market cigarettes, liquor, and other items, was a known VC. He was allowed to run free because he never detected the local Viet police following him to his weekly clandestine meetings, thereby allowing the U.S.-sponsored South Vietnamese intelligence-gathering net to flourish.

Besides taxing the locals to raise funds for their National Liberation Front, the VC had a neat little business churning out the cheap cotton rags with the yellow star on a split blue-and-red background, Viet Cong heraldry, to hawk to American G.I.'s and newsmen on the street. The better fabric went into the VC line unit flags. The Motor Pool sergeant, in turn, would sell or trade the authentic VC flag to Saigon commandos for twenty dollars or items of comparable worth. He hoped to do more business with that rude and ugly Major Lochert.

The rude and ugly Major Lochert parked his jeep in the shade on the east side of the club. He removed the rotor, rigidly chained the steering wheel to the brake pedal, squared away his green beret, and headed for the club. He had things to celebrate before tomorrow, when he was to report in, first to the C Team near the village of Bien Hoa, then to the Mike Force A Team near the Bien Hoa Air Base. Nearing the club door, he noticed the cloud buildup, a sure prelude to the usual afternoon thunderstorm. Close behind him walked Bubba Bates, with Tui.

"I still don't understand why you keep wanting to come to the Officer's Club," Bubba Bates said to Tui. He was frowning. "You never asked before, now all of a sudden it's a big deal." Tui had been badgering Bates for weeks to take her to the club. She had finally succeeded and this was her first trip. She had not answered Bubba's petulant questions.

Bates was wearing his usual uniform of thin black pants and a short-sleeved white shirt open at the neck. Tui had on a simple white summer cotton frock with thin black vertical lines down the side, accentuating her curves. She carried a black leather purse that looked and opened like a business envelope. She had combed her brown-black hair back in wings on either side of her face and let the rest fall in a perfectly straight line down her back. She looked fourteen and virginal. It was slightly after 1800 hours in the early evening. To avoid the imminent rainstorm, they had dashed from Bates's parked Citroen to the club entrance. A cool and gusty breeze smelling of wet dust hinted at the downpour to come.

Walking in front, Bubba barged through the throng of Vietnamese and Americans, all in civilian clothes, gathered to play the slot machines. Tui was appalled at the informal—no, worse than informal, the sloppy—rough atmosphere. This was not like the carpeted French Officer's Clubs she had known that had high ceilings and quiet manners. This club was like the Texas roadhouse she had seen in an American movie. The smell of stale beer and old cigarettes assailed her nostrils. A low muttering of harsh conversation broken by clangs and whoops from the slot players assaulted her ears. Sweating, fatigue-clad men gathered at the bar in groups, in pairs, or alone, eyes roving. Other men sat at tables or stood in conversational clusters along the walls. Vietnamese waitresses scurried from group to group with trays of drinks and cans and bottles of beer. The lights flickered as a thunderclap shocked the air out of the club for a heartbeat. Rain began to crash on the tin roof.

Knowing why she had come, Tui followed Bubba Bates to a table in the farthest corner of the rapidly filling barroom. At first she kept her head down in the proper fashion of a Vietnamese *co*. Then, remembering the American women she had studied at Chez Robert's, she squared her shoulders, lifted her chin, and slowly glanced around as if to study every man in the club. Her heart was pounding and she really didn't register what she was seeing. But, in the timeless fashion of women everywhere, she knew every eye was focused on her. That gave her strength. By the time they reached the table, her pulse had slowed. Bubba sat without offering her a place or holding her chair. Tui remained standing, poised and erect, next to a vacant chair. Bubba was busy snapping his fingers at a trio of Vietnamese waitresses at their bar station.

"What the hell," Bubba said, turning to see Tui, still standing, tall and proud. "Siddown," he snapped. Tui's nerves almost broke. As she was about to dismantle the tableau she had staged by sitting down, a figure broke loose from the gawking men at the bar and dashed to her side.

"Geez, here, let me hold this for you," the man said as he pulled the chair into proper position. Tui looked full into his face, into his eyes, holding her glance that microsecond longer than necessary, giving the unmistakable signal of obvious interest: Here is all-woman looking for all-man.

"Thank you," she said, eyes dropping to the name on his fatigues. "Thank you, Lieutenant Parker. Would you care to join us?"

At that, Bubba, who recognized Parker as that dickhead lieutenant involved in the humiliating incident in the terminal, jumped to his feet, knocking his chair backward. He grabbed Parker's arm with his left hand to swing him around into a right cross.

"Oh, nuts," Parker breathed, at last recognizing the man with Tui. He ducked, causing Bates's swing to go wild. Tui jumped up and stood back. As Parker ducked he spotted a beer bottle on the table next to him. Coming up, he grabbed it by the neck with both hands and swung it like a baseball bat into Bubba Bates's face. Bates fell back, his hands going to his nose, which started to spurt blood, tripped over his fallen chair, sprawled backward, cracked his head on the floor, and lay there, all the fight gone out of him.

For an instant, Parker was aghast at what he had done in unthinking reflex. He thought that if Bates were to get up and come after him, he'd run out the door in a panic. As his pulse and adrenaline flow slowed, he realized he not only had survived an attack, but had won the encounter. He shook his head, smiling ruefully, as he realized the only two fights he'd had in his life had been with the same man over two different women. Vietnam, he thought, is one helluva place.

He looked over his shoulder to see Tui backed up against the wall, eyes wide. He stepped to her side, marveling at this wondrous creature who seemed so out of place. He was too intent to notice that behind him a civilian dressed like Bates walked from the bar toward the table. He was one of the two Alpha employees who had helped Bates from the terminal when he was doubled up from his encounter with Nancy Lewis. As he was about to grab Parker, an Army officer in a Tiger suit stepped in front of him and thumped a thick hand flat against the civilian's chest. Hearing the sound, Parker turned.

"Let it go, Mack," Wolf Lochert growled, lips pulled back in a menacing grimace that was, Parker thought, exactly how Cro-Magnon man about to spear a sabre-toothed tiger must have looked. "Get your buddy and get out of here." Lochert jerked his head toward the fallen Bates. "And we'll take the lady home." White-faced, the Alpha employee nodded and once again helped a defeated Bubba Bates from the *champs d'honneur*.

As the two Alpha employees withdrew, Lochert explained to the harassed club officer, who arrived too late to see anything, that the "ell tee here, was defending himself against that frapping sillyvilian, who shouldn't be allowed in here anyhow, and did the club officer desire to follow this incident up with any kind of a formal report, perhaps?" After a second's thoughtful deliberation, the club officer replied that no, he did not. He gave a surprisingly wide grin, and walked away. Lochert turned back to Toby and Tui. He pointed to his table.

"C'mere and siddown," he commanded. Tui and Parker sat, Parker first holding her chair.

"Parker," Lochert rasped, reading the name tag, "for a flyboy ell tee, you ain't doon too bad." Lochert had a look on his face, actually less a scowl than normal, that Parker thought was almost approving. "But you sure don't know how to finish a fight." Lochert did not refer to their earlier meeting on Toby's first night in Vietnam.

"Ah, colonel, I mean major," he said, "really, I'm not a flyboy. That is, I'm not a pilot. Or a navigator, for that matter." Parker cleared his throat. He really wanted to look at or talk to the girl he had apparently just won in combat fair. The dragon was, if not slain, at least vanquished temporarily. But he wanted to know what Lochert was talking about. "And, ah, what do you mean about 'finishing a fight'?"

"When he was down, you didn't kick him in the head a couple times to let him know you were serious. Now he'll be coming back at you. From behind," Lochert added.

Tui, no longer playing the femme fatale, demurely kept her head down to listen. She had to measure these two and find out what they could do for her and for the cadre. "Meet people, take names, we will do the rest," Buey Dan had instructed. A young *thiêu uy* and an older *thiêu tá*, a lieutenant and a major, didn't look all that promising, she thought, except as a way to meet others. She looked up.

"Please," she said, "may I have a martini?"

Lochert swung his head to stare at her for an instant then asked in rapid-fire Vietnamese, *"What do you know about martinis? Where are you from, little sister?"*

Flustered at hearing her own language, Tui stammered slightly as she said in English, "I have had martinis before. In England and in France. It is what I drink."

She spoke French-accented Vietnamese, Lochert noted. *"Est-ce que tu parles français?"* Wolf Lochert asked the Eurasian girl, deliberately using the familiar form as if she were a bar girl. Tui hesitated slightly before answering. This long-nose was probing. "Yes, I speak French," she said in English, deciding to concentrate on the younger man, who obviously wasn't as perceptive as the *thiêu tá*. "Of course I speak French. I lived there. And England, too." Trying to dismiss Lochert, she tilted her head back to look at Parker. She needed some estimate of his potential.

"Have you been here long, lieutenant?"

"Uh, no ma'am, only a month. And, please, my name is Toby."

"Yes, Tow-bye," Tui said, indicating she had trouble getting the pronunciation correct, "and do you like my country?"

"I haven't been here—or even off base—long enough to find out. You're the first—" He stopped in confusion. "Ah, you are Vietnamese, aren't you?"

"Yes, Tow-bye, I am Vietnamese. I am what one calls a *métisse*. My mother was Vietnamese." She paused for a moment to glance at Wolf Lochert. "My father was in the French Foreign Legion. He was killed fighting the Viet Minh when I was very young. He was a great hero." Her tongue flicked up for an instant to her upper lip in a movement Wolf thought was caused by nervousness.

Parker couldn't help staring at her. He had never seen nor imagined such rare and fragile beauty. Her high cheekbones, the smooth tanned skin, the way her mouth would curl when she showed perfectly white and even teeth in quick, nervous smiles, her French way of rolling her R's, all this captivated him. She would touch her tongue to her upper lip every so often, as if to taste of some hidden and exotic flavor.

"Where do you live?" Lochert asked in Vietnamese.

Tui flushed. She knew how she had to answer. "With Mr. Bates," she said in a low voice, hanging her head. Her hair on the left side swung forward, partially hiding her face. She made no move to brush it away. Parker felt his heart fill to near bursting.

"We'll get you out of there," he blurted, implicating Lochert without really knowing if he could even count on him.

"No." Tui's head swung up involuntarily. "I mean, you can't do that." She stammered slightly.

Lochert squinted at her and pulled his lips back, "Why not?" he barked.

"I have no other place to go. I have no home. My mother is dead. I have no family in France." Tui lowered her head and pulled a delicate white lace handkerchief from her bag to hold to her eyes.

Parker, nearly weeping with compassion, reached over to take her hand. "Hey," he said, "I mean it. We'll take care of you." He looked at Lochert. "Won't we, sir?"

Army Major Wolfgang "the Wolf" Lochert studied Air Force First Lieutenant Toby G. Parker for a long moment, then turned to look at Tui. His scowl receded, his face almost softened.

"Yeah," he growled, "we will."

2145 HOURS LOCAL, 17 JANUARY 1966
L'AUBERGE RESTAURANT,
SAIGON, REPUBLIC OF VIETNAM

☆

Later, Lochert and Parker sat with Tui long after they had finished their meal at Restaurant L'Auberge near the Hotel Catinat. Curfew was in one hour, at eleven o'clock. They were less than five blocks from Bubba Bates's apartment on Hai Ba Troung. No one had said much, though from time to time Toby Parker had asked Tui how to say a few polite things in Vietnamese. And he did brag a bit that he was flying the next day on an important mission. Toby wanted desperately to be cosmopolitan and witty and to lead sparkling conversation, but he found he was all but tongue-tied in the presence of this remarkable girl. Wolf Lochert had been silent yet purposeful as he ate, and seemed at his ease. So they had relaxed and let the happy accordion music of French village songs surround them and take the place of what could only be stilted conversation.

Tui looked at her tiny watch on a narrow black band of material matching her purse. Parker, who had stared unabashedly at her all through the meal, caught the glance.

"It's time, isn't it," he said.

"Yes," Tui replied.

Mumbling something, Lochert placed a stack of P on the silver plate with *l'addition* and motioned for the *garçon* to come get it.

"Cam on, Thiêu Tá Wolf. Thank you, Major Wolf," Tui said.

"Cam on, Too Tah Wolf," Parker echoed, grinning. The Wolf nodded in acknowledgement. As they stood up to go, a figure approached from the crowded bar area. It was Charmaine.

"Why, hello there, Major, ah"—she looked at his name tag— "Lochert. You didn't give us your name, you know." She grabbed for Lochert's hand to shake it. He reluctantly allowed her to do so, her warm fingers feeling delicate and moist in his big, knuckly paw.

"You do remember me, don't you? You ruined Shawn's film, then left us without a word." She searched his dark-brown eyes for some sign of recognition.

"Yes, I remember," the Wolf said in a low voice, wishing he could look away from the deep green of her eyes. He released her hand and cleared his throat. "Now it's your turn to remember. I do not like newsies," he articulated with crackling clear words. He wanted to reach out and touch her lush, mahogany-colored hair.

"I'm not a newsie, I'm a dancer, Major Lochert," Charmaine said.

Shawn Bannister appeared at her side. He nodded at the Wolf. "Major Lochert," he said, not trying to shake his hand. He glanced briefly at Parker and Tui, news antennae twitching, trying to place them and wondering what in hell they were doing with this green-beanie gorilla. He returned his attention to the Wolf, trying to decide the best way to approach him.

"I really want to do a story on you, you know," he said.

"Yeah, I'll bet you want to do a number on me," the Wolf said, turning to glare at Shawn Bannister. "I know that left wing rag of yours. I know what you wrote about the Americal Division's hatchets and I know what you'd write about me. 'Apelike Cretin Eats Babies in Vietnam,' that's what you'd write. I know your type."

Charmaine cringed at the exchange. Behind his fierce glare she saw the suppressed hurt in the Wolf's eyes. Somebody wrote something like that about him once, she said to herself.

"It's not like that," Shawn said. "I didn't write that piece about

Patton's son and the hatchets. Besides, this is different. You are a professional soldier and my readers want to know about professional soldiers: where they're from, what they do, why they—''

"Shawn, we're disturbing these people," Charmaine said, cutting him off. She turned to the Wolf and took up his hand with both of hers.

"Pay no attention to him, Major Lochert. He can find plenty of other people to write about." She squeezed the Wolf's hand. She liked and instinctively trusted this big fellow. Though he seemed so volatile in his words and actions, she perceived a great gentleness in him. She released his hand, noting he had returned a faint pressure.

"Shawn, sometimes you are a bore," she said, steering Bannister away. "Lets go back to the bar." The Wolf stared after them for a moment, then shook his whole body for a second, like a fur-bearing animal shaking off water. He looked back at Toby Parker and Tui and nodded his head toward the door.

They retrieved the jeep, installed the rotor, unchained the wheel, and drove away, Tui in front. Toby sat sideways on the jumpseat in the back, where he felt exposed in the open jeep on his first night in Saigon.

Wolf parked the jeep 200 meters from the apartment Tui had pointed out. He had never turned the lights on because the Vietnamese drove French-style, with only parking lights on in the city at night, or with no lights at all. "Wait here," he growled, then added something about a "recon" that Parker took to be army slang for reconnaissance. He was right. In a few minutes, unseen, the Wolf glided up noiselessly in the dark behind them and placed his hand on Parker's shoulder.

"HUP!" Parker blurted as his heart leaped in startled terror. "Stay alert and stay alive," Wolf repeated the first maxim a long-nose learns in Vietnam. "No one there," he added. He was lying. He had seen some activities but had judged them to be no immediate threat. That they were being watched he was sure.

"In America, the boy walks the girl to the door," Toby said to Tui after he vaulted out of the back to help her from the front seat.

"*Merci,*" Tui said with a lilt that made Parker's knees tremble, "but Tow-bye, Tow-*bee,*" she corrected, "you must not. Someone will see. I will be in trouble."

"I've got to see you again," Toby Parker said. "Do you have a phone?"

"Yes. No," she corrected herself. "The telephone is for Mr.

Bates's business. It is an Alpha Airlines telephone. You cannot call me."

"I'll come here," Parker said.

"No, no," Tui said quickly, "you must not." She looked at him intently. In the dark he couldn't see her eyes suddenly soften. "Meet me at the Restaurant My Canh two nights from now. At eight o'clock." She broke away from Toby Parker and ran, silent and doe-like, in the direction of the apartment until she disappeared in the darkness.

Toby Parker was mesmerized by the swing of her derriere as she ran from him.

Wolf Lochert's eyes squinted slightly as he watched.

"Come on, kid," he said after a moment, "you got to fly tomorrow, you said. Let's go home."

They drove down the near deserted street, jeep muffler rumbling nasally in sync with the shifting of the gears.

Silent as a wisp of smoke, Buey Dan broke cover from a recessed iron-grille doorway and caught up with Tui before she entered the apartment building.

"Little sister," he hissed, pushing her toward the door, "we must talk. Open the way to the courtyard."

Her eyes rolling with fright, Tui tried to settle herself. "Uncle, you know you must never come here," she said, trying to keep her voice steady. She unlocked the door to the courtyard.

"We have a change," Buey Dan said in a whisper as they stood under a stairwell. "But first, who is that man?"

"A mere *thiêu uy,* a first lieutenant of the Air Force. But he does carry things to Bien Hoa," she said, before she could stop herself.

"Bien Hoa," Buey Dan mused, rubbing his chin. "I meant the other man, the big one driving. Who is he?"

"*Thiêu Tá* Lochert of the *forces spéciales.* I think he too will go to Bien Hoa, to the Nung unit, I think."

Buey Dan was doubly grateful for the name and location of the man he must kill, but he had business of a more urgent nature.

"You must get me Bien Hoa information," he said to Tui. "It is necessary. Immediately."

"Yes, uncle," she replied, wondering how much Toby Parker knew. "But what kind? Order of battle, base defense, outer perimeter size and composition, defensive weaponry?" She had learned her trade well.

"No, no," Buey Dan replied impatiently. "We know all that.

And we have all the distances and aiming points for our rockets and mortars all staked out." He paused to look around. Night sounds from the apartments echoed faintly in the courtyard. The still air smelled of Vietnamese food.

"We need to know if the *mui lo* suspect an attack from the Loc Ninh area and if they plan to reinforce and reorganize their defenses before next Sunday."

Tui gave a start and hesitated briefly. "The *thiéu uy* also goes with things to Loc Ninh, this I know," she said, surprised at the feeling deep within her that she was betraying something. She came close to not telling Buey Dan this additional information about Toby Parker. Her heart began to pound.

"You must see him again," Buey Dan ordered. "Immediately. What arrangements did you make?"

Tui paused. "None," she said, "I cannot see him again."

Buey Dan stared at her in the dark, his eyes glistened. Quick as a snake, he grabbed her by the throat to pinch her voice box.

"Liar. Little sister slut, you lie. I heard you tell the *thiéu uy* you would see him in two days at the Restaurant My Canh." He pinched her throat nerve, sending hot wire pains into her jaw muscles. She whimpered deep in her throat.

"You are coming with me now," Buey Dan said. "You have no need ever to return upstairs." He nodded up at Bates's apartment. "You will stay with some members of the liberation in Cholon tonight. We will get you on to Tan Son Nhut tomorrow to see the *thiéu uy,* to bring him out so we can talk to him." Using a hypodermic needle, Buey Dan's men had abducted other Americans for interrogation. None were ever seen again.

"He flies," Tui squeaked through the pain. "He flys to places like Bien Hoa and Loch Ninh."

"Then meet him as planned when he returns. We will pick him up then. No one will miss a *thiéu uy.*"

Buey Dan grasped her arm and led her away, into the night.

11

1100 HOURS LOCAL, 18 JANUARY 1966
531ST TACTICAL FIGHTER SQUADRON,
BIEN HOA AIR BASE, REPUBLIC OF VIETNAM

☆

The bombing halt was long over. The North Vietnamese had used the respite to refurbish supply points, supply routes, and gun pits. Although the President had little trouble with Congress in increasing troop strength in Vietnam, the number of war protesters making their voices heard in rallies across the United States was also increasing. The 3rd Tac Fighter Wing was back in the war, mounting scores of sorties per day. In the 531st, Rawson had loaded Court Bannister with as many extra duties as he could find, including voting officer and post office liaison. Another was to deliver weekly briefings to the pilots of the 531st on a subject of Rawson's choice. Today Bannister was about to give a basic brief on the airplane and the weapons. Fourteen pilots, seated on folding chairs or lounging against the plywood walls, were assembled in the squadron map room.

"The F-100D can carry six thousand pounds of munitions on six under-wing hard points, three on each side, and one centerline station on the fuselage," Bannister began. He had taped bombing charts and photos to one wall, which he referred to as he spoke. "Usually we carry two 275-gallon fuel tanks, one on each of the intermediate or middle-wing stations, to extend our range, since we don't midair refuel here in South Vietnam."

The pilots were listening to Courtland Bannister tell them what they already knew, but never tired of hearing, because every pilot sincerely believed any information pertinent to fighter flying, particularly in combat, needed to be hashed and rehashed time and again so that selection and usage became as natural as an eye blink.

"We can carry four types of bombs, two types of napalm, two types of cluster bomb units, rockets nineteen to a pod, and 800 rounds of 20mm ammo for our four M-39 cannons. Delivery speed for all ordnance is 450 knots, which equates to 515 miles per hour. Dive angles range from zero for the CBU up to sixty degrees for dive-bombing. Release altitudes range from 300 feet for CBU, nape, and strafe, up to 4,500 feet for sixty-degree dive-bombing."

He pointed to a photo. "The bombs, all called GP for 'general purpose,' are the 250-pound Mark-81, the 500-pound Mark-82, the 1,000-pound Mark-83, and the 2,000-pound Mark 84. Using the Mark-904 nose fuse, they can be set to explode on contact or delay up to a second, allowing penetration of bunkers or tunnels before detonating. The Mark-82 500-pounder comes in both the high- and low-drag configuration. As a high-drag bomb, called a snake-eye, the basic bomb shape has a folding metal umbrella fitted to the rear that opens up, which increases drag when the bomb is released to slow its speed instantly, like our drag chute does when we land.

"This allows us to drop the bomb as low as 300 feet from a shallow fifteen-degree dive, yet escape the fragments, because it slows down and impacts well behind us. The bomb also has time to arm before impact, as the tiny propeller on the nose fuse revolves a predetermined number of times that, by screw action, lines up the firing pin in the detonator. Of course, the wire attached to the bomb rack holds the propeller in place until release, otherwise we'd be flying around with armed bombs the minute we took off and the airflow wound it down."

Bannister nodded at Freeman, who had raised his hand. "What's this I hear about using gas?" the lieutenant asked.

Bannister grinned. "Actually, that subject is supposed to be classified until the substance is used. But it would be difficult to brief its use on a scramble from alert. The Mark 94 container holds 500 pounds of DM or CN tear gas with a vomit kicker. It's only used in or north of the DMZ during a rescue attempt when bad guys are closing in on one of our guys who has been shot down. We do not use it flying this far south." Bannister saw another raised hand, a new lieutenant.

"What are those two-foot pipes I saw on the nose of some bombs?"

"Those are fuse extenders called daisy cutters for use against troops in the open. The pipe sticks out of the nose fuse and explodes the bomb two feet off the ground, scattering fragments in a lethal radius out to about seventy feet. Other antipersonnel weapons are the CBU's, the nape, and the 20 mike-mike strafe. The 2.75-inch folding-fin rockets don't hack it. They are World War Two vintage. Half the time the damned fins don't unfold evenly, and they wind up going all over the place.'' He slapped his hand on a photo of rocket pods. ''You'd cause more damage to the VC jettisoning the whole damned pod full of rockets on their heads than salvoing the rockets at them.

''The Special Forces particularly like CBU and nape because they are so accurate, and they are so accurate because we drop them so low. For nape, use a shallow fifteen-degree dive. To drop CBU, fly straight and level at 300 feet holding .72 Mach, which is about 465 knots or 500 miles per hour. The bomblets are grapefruit-sized. They dribble out from the rear of the canisters, one under each wing, and unfold narrow strips of metal that make them float down like winged maple seeds. There are two types of CBU, One and Three. CBU One explodes on contact, sending out 200 marble-sized pellets lethal to thirty-eight feet. CBU Three is white phosphorus, Willy Pete, the same stuff the FAC puts in his marking rockets. The guys up north use a whole different type for flak suppression that can be dropped from a higher altitude.'' Bannister pointed to another hand. It was Colonel Frank Darlington, the director of operations.

''Remember, gentlemen,'' the DO said, ''if you press in there and drop this stuff too low, it won't have time to arm. Charlie loves dud 500-pounders and CBU's. He cuts 'em up for mines and booby traps.''

''That's right,'' Bannister interjected, ''drop too high and you increase your chance of missing the target; too low and you give Charley more ammo.'' He stepped closer to the seated pilots. ''Remember also, gentlemen, you don't drop anything, not even a hint, without the forward air controller's permission. It makes no difference what your rank is, he's the boss down there. He can send colonels home. He knows the land, the people, the weather, the friendlies, the bad guys, and where the guns are. A ground troop wants air, he puts in a request through his net. If it's approved, he gets a FAC and the FAC gets us. The FAC talks to the ground guys on Fox Mike, then relays to us on our UHF. You must get permission to release ordnance on every pass, I say again, *every* pass. There is no blanket permission for a flight or for multiple passes. You get his clearance before each run-in, or you pull up high and dry. He may only have one percent of our horsepower and five percent of our weight, but he is one hundred percent in control.''

Another question was voiced, ''Why don't we have more 500- and 700-pound bombs, and why don't we have more armor-piercing incendiary and high-explosive incendiary 20 mike-mike? Using ball ammo doesn't do much.''

Bannister put his hands on his hips, glanced briefly at the DO, and said, ''Because, dammit, we are short of ammo. Not just here, but all over Vietnam. We know it's true for three reasons. First, the *Stars and Stripes* talks about it every day; second, the wing weapons officer confirmed it this morning as I was putting this brief together; and third is the most obvious. Look about. Who has been carrying a full load for the last three weeks? So, gentlemen, regardless of what the Secretary of Defense says to the contrary, we have a bomb shortage.'' Bannister paused as the pilots nodded and muttered to each other. As he was about to resume his brief about being able to strafe from any angle, but warning against target fixation and flying into the ground, he saw a lieutenant colonel from wing headquarters enter and whisper something in the DO's ear. They exchanged a few more words, then Colonel Darlington walked up to stand next to Bannister.

''Gentlemen,'' he said, ''the briefing is over. The frag shop has just called from Seventh. We are to surge and lay on extra sorties. The war is picking up. The VC, in numbers, are attacking various U.S. and Vietnamese camps and fire bases throughout South Vietnam. Colonel Demski here has the frag orders. Major Rawson, schedule your men as you see fit according to these targets and ordnance requirements.''

At this news, most of the pilots cheered and said words like ''Shit hot'' and ''Let's go get 'em.'' Others responded in a manner more pensive than pleased. Some wondered what in hell the VC thought they were doing. The remainder, a few, felt their scrotum tighten as they automatically speculated on the increased odds of pieces of metal puncturing their beloved pink bodies. Bannister, while glad soon to be back doing what he had told Doc Russell he wanted to do, was one of those who wondered what in hell the VC, who were so obviously being beaten, thought they were doing. Maybe some kind of a Vietnamese version of the Japanese banzai attack of World War II.

As the pilots began to leave the room, Darlington motioned Rawson to one side. ''I assume Bannister will fly today,'' he said.

''Well, yes,'' Rawson said, mustache twitching, ''he'll fly today.''

''Put him on my wing,'' the DO said.

☆

Two by two the heavily laden F-100 fighters took off in formation. Each flight lifted from the Bien Hoa runway, afterburners roaring and flaming like blast-furnace stacks. Once he had assembled his flight of four in fingertip formation, Colonel Frank Darlington, call sign Ramrod 20, called Paris Control for vector information to his FAC.

"Roger Ramrod Two Zero, vector 360. You will rendezvous with Copperhead Zero Nine on the 352-degree radial at 48 nautical miles off Bien Hoa's Channel 73 Tacan. Contact Copperhead on 253.4. You copy, Ramrod?"

"Roger, Paris. Ramrod copies Copperhead Zero Nine at 352 slash 48 off 73 on 253.4. Is that affirm?"

"Ramrod Two Zero. That's affirm. And Ramrod, be advised there are thunderstorms in and around the area. Paris out."

Ramrod Lead spent several minutes leading his formation up through the clouds. They broke into the clear at 15,000 and leveled off at 16,000 feet. He fishtailed his fighter, signaling Two, Three, and Four to spread out and fly in partially extended tactical fingertip formation, where each could view the other in addition to a selected segment of the sky and the ground. In position about 500 feet out and slightly aft of Darlington's left wing, Bannister flew as Number Two in the front seat of a two-seater F-100F. Rawson was in the back to give Bannister, as he said, "a no-notice check ride."

Equidistant out and aft on Darlington's right side, Captain Jack Laird flew the Number Three slot. As Four, Lieutenant Fairchild flew the same distance out and aft on Laird's right wing. Viewed from above, the four flight members were positioned like the fingers extended on the right hand, with the thumb tucked under the palm. Ramrod Lead positioned as the middle finger, Two the index finger, Three the next finger to the right of the middle, and Four situated as the little finger.

Darlington glanced to both sides, verifying the proper positioning of his flight. Satisfied, he transmitted the instructions "Ramrod go 253.4." Each flight member acknowledged in turn.

"Two," said Bannister.

"Three," said Laird.

C/S Ramrod 20 S/E 1245		TO 1300	TOT 1320
NO	PILOT	A/C NO	MISSION NO 6-2651
1	DARLINGTON	922	LOAD 8×82, 4×NAPE 4×CBU 3200×20MM
2	BANNISTER/RAWSON	215	TGT DESCR VC CAMP
3	LAIRD	641	RNDZV III CORPS
4	FAIRCHILD	332	RAD 352 NM 48 CHAN 73
			TGT CORDS XT 641 816
FAC COPPERHEAD 09 FREQ 253.4			RAD NM CHAN
REMARKS			

TAKEOFF DATA		LANDING	MISC
RT 95° PA +130' GW 34,200		LAND GW 30,500	BINGO 3500
LINE SP 126 ROTATE SP 150		FINAL A/S 165	MIG CLEMSON
REFUSAL SP 158 AT 4100		T-DOWN A/S 158	HAWK 60
T/O SP 175 AT 5600		NO CHUTE ROLL 4500	

—BNH FORM 16—

"Four," said Fairchild.

After their calls, all four pilots switched the knob on their AN/ARC-34 command radio to the FAC frequency. For a back-up frequency, all four flight members—like all pilots who flew—maintained a listening watch on 243.0 Guard Channel for emergency calls.

After checking in, each pilot shook his head and squirmed in his seat to relieve the kinks caused by the strain of close formation flying through the gathering thunderstorm clouds. Each relaxed, looked about to orient himself, then began to review in his mind the data he had entered on BNH Form 16, his mission card.

Each pilot also had a card on his clipboard listing all the AFVN repeater station frequencies and locations in South Vietnam. Tuning their AN/ARN-6 radio compasses to the proper station would allow the needle on the automatic direction finder unit to point to the station. Besides being a handy navigation device, the pilots could listen to the music being played on AFVN. Pilots called the card "music to strafe by." The two wingmen were tuned in to some Tijuana Brass. Court normally had his on, but refrained because of Rawson in the backseat.

After several minutes of holding the heading, Darlington called for his FAC. "Copperhead Zero Nine, Ramrod Two Zero." After thirty seconds with no answer he called again: "Copperhead Zero Nine, this is Ramrod Two Zero. How do you read?" This time he got an answer.

"Ah, roger, Ramrod, this is Copperhead Zero Three. Zero Nine had some problems. I'm replacing him. How do you read?"

"Loud and clear, Zero Three. Are you ready for my lineup?"

Captain Phil Travers said to go ahead, then told his new backseater, First Lieutenant Toby Parker, to copy Ramrod's lineup.

"Ramrod Two Zero, Mission Number Six dash 2651, four Fox One Hundreds with eight Mark-82 snake-eyes, four BLU-27 napalms, four CBU-1's, and 3,200 rounds of 20 mike-mike."

"Roger, Ramrod. Copperhead copies eight snakes, four napes, four CB's, and 3,200 times twenty mil. You got sparklers or balls?"

Travers explained to Parker that sparklers were the 20mm high-explosive incendiary, called HEI, that exploded in bright flashes, whereas balls were 20mm solid slugs. Darlington said they had some of each; every fifth round was a sparkler. Once in a while the airplanes carried armor-piercing incendiary, or API, but not unless they had to, because its destructive properties were useless in the jungle against soft targets.

"Listen up, Ramrods," Travers transmitted. "Here's what we got. Your target is near a small unit patrol that got bounced by a large force of Charlie and are pinned down. There is one canopy of jungle. Target elevation is fifty feet above sea level, wind is ten knots from 250 degrees, safe bail-out area is about ten miles northeast of us at the Loc Ninh SF camp. You copy?"

"Ramrod copies."

"And the weather is going to get delta sierra"—that meant dog shit. "You'll have to thread around the best you can. Copy?"

"Ramrod copies."

"We'll start with the snakes first to open things up, then nape and CBU, and if we have anything left we'll use the 20 mike-mike. Copy?"

"Zero Three, Ramrod copies. We're at the rendezvous point now. What's your position?"

"If you see the horseshoe bend in the river with the rice paddies to the north, I'm orbiting south at fifteen hundred."

"Tallyho, Zero Three," Darlington transmitted and began a left orbit over the FAC. He pumped his control stick fore and aft to make his F-100 bob up and down, the signal for his flight to go into trail formation, one behind the other, with about 500 feet between each airplane. When the FAC marked the target, the four ships would form a box pattern around it, each one rolling in after the other, spaced so as to keep their guns on the target while the F-100 in front pulled off. The pilots preferred to fly a wheel pattern where they could roll in from random headings to confuse the gunner's tracking solution; but with friendlies on the ground, precision was the word, even if it meant taking a round or two. Often the FAC told them what heading to use in a simple code.

"The FAC's rolling in Florida to New York to mark," Travers said.

"Roger, cleared. Set 'em up, Ramrod," Darlington transmitted.

Each pilot reached down to his armament control panel and set the switches: the BOMB switch to SINGLE RELEASE; BOMB ARMING to NOSE AND TAIL; RELEASE SIGNAL to MANUAL; and MASTER SWITCH to ON. The little button left of the trim switch on top of the pilot's control stick closed an electrical circuit each time the pilot pressed it to release whatever weapon was selected on the armament panel. Pilots called it the pickle button. The two wingmen lowered the volume of their AFVN music.

"Oh, yeah," Travers said, "Copperhead Zero Nine reported light to moderate ground fire but was unable to pinpoint the positions before he took a round in his engine and had to return to base."

Bannister tightened when he heard the guns were up. He could see the general area to the north where Austin had gone in. Austin's fireball flared and played just behind Bannister's eyes. Damn, he said into his mask, not at all certain he was ready to go up against the guns again. He arranged his switches and noted his fingers were trembling as he flicked up the MASTER ARM switch to ON.

12

☆

Travers had racked his little O-1E into a vertical bank, pulled it through a ninety-degree turn, rolled level, then shoved the control stick forward until the plane was pointed nearly straight down. To Parker, the noise of the wind through the struts rose alarmingly. He was flung forward when the engine was suddenly throttled back, and was pressed against his seat belt as Travers pushed over, applying more negative g-forces. Then Parker nearly leaped out of his skin when, with a thunderous sharp bang, the starboard 2.75-inch Willy Pete rocket ignited, and whooshed out from its tube under the wing. As Toby tried to follow its smoke trail, he was pressed heavily into his seat when Phil "the FAC" Travers jammed on the power—he had previously throttled back to prevent engine overspeed in the dive—and racked the tiny gray airplane upward, pointing its painted red mouth with lolling tongue skyward. They leveled at 1,500 feet. Parker, still not sure what had happened, looked down as the crisp, white smoke from the marking rocket drifted up through the jungle canopy.

"That's it, Copperhead," said a tinny voice on the FM. "We're about a hundred meters south. Hit the smoke and anyplace around it for fifty meters except south. Repeat, don't hit south. The bad guys are in the trees and on the ground but not dug in. You copy China Boy, Ramrod?"

"Roger, China Boy, I got a good copy. All around my smoke except south. I'm going up Uniform now and talk to the strike flight. Hold one. Copperhead listening out." Travers had confirmed on his FM radio the initial air strike plans of where to place the ordnance with the Mike Force ground commander Captain Tom Myers, call sign China Boy.

"Toby," Travers said on the intercom, "Uniform is the abbreviation for UHF. I've got one intercom and five radio-control heads up here. I talk to the ground guys on Fox Mike, and the strike flight on UHF. I listen to both at the same time, but can only talk to one at a time as I switch transmitters. I'm going back to Ramrod on Uniform."

"Ramrod, Copperhead," Travers transmitted, "you got my smoke?"

"Roger that, Copperhead," Darlington transmitted. "Ramrod flight, you got the smoke?" Each in turn acknowledged they saw the FAC's smoke: "Two," "Three," "Four."

"Okay, Ramrods. I want a left-hand box north of the target with runs at my smoke from California to Virginia. Hit in a half-circle arc from fifty meters short up to fifty meters toward Canada and fifty meters long. Don't unload south. Snake-eyes first, then the nape and CBU. You copy?"

"Lead."

"Two."

"Three."

"Four."

"You're cleared in hot, Lead. Call the FAC in sight."

"Just protecting myself," Travers hollered back at Toby.

As an experienced FAC, Travers knew this was a well-established routine, and every pilot's eyes took in the target, the other ships, the FAC, the guns, and the weather formations. Each kept a three-dimensional picture in his head stitched together with the time factor. After X seconds of looking *there,* a pilot would look back expecting to see the other planes *here.* It usually took a new pilot about twenty-five missions to feel comfortable on a four-ship close air-support mission. Up till then, they were usually too busy making sure they flew in the proper position and the switches were set up correctly. It was mighty embarrassing, if not dangerous, to fire a rocket when one meant to drop a bomb or vice versa. Few pilots screwed up that bad on switchology, but it did happen occasionally to pilots with little experience or aptitude.

Travers whipped his bird into a tight orbit south of the target at

1,500 feet, a FAC's normal altitude. It was perfectly all right for the FAC to fly over the friendlies, for the position not only kept him out of the fighter's strike pattern, but it also kept him away from the ground fire that could so easily reach a low and slow bird like the O-1E. And, of course, the FAC didn't carry anything to drop accidentally on the good guys.

Travers smiled to himself as he set up his orbit. He had all those strike pilots to worry about, plus five radios to juggle, in an airplane that flew slower than the stall speed of the big fighters. He loved it.

"Eeeee-hahhh," he whooped in Parker's headset.

"Eeeee-hahhh," Parker whooped back, genuinely pleased and thrilled to be doing what he was doing. He could see the bombs fall from the planes; see their metal umbrellas open up; hear the crack-*whoomp* of the explosion, and watch more jungle canopy strip away. He heard China Boy on the Fox Mike tell Copperhead to relay to the Ramrods they were doing a great job; and if they would now be so kind as to lay in some nape and CBU, they could wipe out the bad guys and all go back to the hootch for a cold brew.

"Super, Ramrods. You're putting 'em right in there. Let's go down with the soft stuff now. Get down there, and fry 'em up and punch 'em out. Hold the strafe until I clear you."

Lead rolled in with nape. Bannister, as Number 2, prepared to make his run barely above treetop level to put his cluster bomblets right across the area opened up by the bombs. He could see the smoke from the pitched ground battle drifting slightly east. He was mentally calculating his offset when Rawson started to speak on the intercom. Outside of grunts and groans from the g-pulling jinks coming off target on the dive-bomb runs, Rawson had been strangely quiet.

Then, without warning Bannister on the intercom, Rawson got on the radio.

"Ramrod Lead," he transmitted, "this is Two. We've got an engine-overheat condition and will have to abort."

"Overheat," Bannister said on the intercom, rapidly scanning the instruments, "we don't have an overheat. Do you have a warning light?"

"Roger, Two, you're cleared to return to base. Do you want an escort, Harry?" Darlington asked, recognizing Rawson's voice.

"Ah, hold one, Lead," Bannister cut in. "I, ah, think everything is okay." As he tried to continue lining up for his low-level CBU pass, the stick was suddenly yanked back and to the right, pulling the plane up and toward the friendly troops. Bannister hastily safed the MASTER ARM switch with his left hand, as he fought with his right on the stick to overpower the pressure from Rawson in the backseat. Although each stick activated 3,000 psi of hydraulic fluid to move the flight controls, they were mechanically tied together and moved in unison, subject only to the strongest input force.

Using both hands, Bannister quickly wrenched the stick from Rawson's grip so severely the plane banked to a near inverted position directly over the friendlies. Both men were panting over the intercom.

"The gauges are good," Bannister puffed, "and I don't have a fire warning light on."

"My tail pipe temperature is too high," Rawson said, "I order you to take us home."

"Two, what the hell is going on?" Darlington transmitted. "Have you got flight control problems? Get out of the pattern if you can't work. Get the hell away from the friendlies before you drop something." He watched in amazement as the tandem-seat F-100F pumped up and down, rolling first one way then the next.

Below, sixty meters to the northeast of China Boy's position, a two-man crew uncovered a 5-foot 2½-inch Degtyarev-Shpagin K-38 model (DshK–38)12.7mm (.51 cal) machine gun mounted on a high tripod formed by its trail legs for antiaircraft use. The Number 2 man fed a fifty-round metal-link belt of armor-piercing incendiary into the side of the MG. The weapon, of World War II vintage, was one of six recently brought with great care across Cambodia for use in South Vietnam by regular NVA troops.

The gunner took aim and began shooting the API, which exited the barrel at a muzzle velocity of 2,822 feet per second. He was experienced and did not need tracers to mark his bullet stream. From a side angle slant range of 300 feet, he positioned the barrel to lead perfectly the speeding airplane. The armor-piercing incendiary impacted squarely on the belly and right wing root of Ramrod Four, First Lieutenant Douglas T. Fairchild, a split second after he pickled off a 750-pound can of napalm B from a height of 200 feet above the surrounding terrain.

At first Fairchild thought the napalm can had somehow hung up on the ejector rack, and was making his F-100 fly canted. He changed his mind when his engine exploded with a grinding roar, every warning light on the panel lit up, the control stick went dead in his hands, and his airplane pitched straight up with a crushing load of eight g's.

Badly disoriented, Fairchild thought he was going in and wouldn't have time to eject. Hand still on the throttle, he punched the transmit button: "Four's hit bad!" he gasped, already feeling the g-forces slack off as the crippled jet lost airspeed. Fairchild raised his head, saw 2,500 feet on his altimeter, looked out and saw and felt the airplane in an uncontrollable roll to the right, "Bail out! Four, BAIL OUT!" he heard over his radio. His training took over as he fought his body to the proper bail-out position: head back against the headrest; feet pulled back into the footrests; elbows in; raise right armrest; squeeze trigger—

As the canopy exploded off the airplane, Fairchild saw himself looking up at a horizon crazily tilted ninety degrees from where it should be. The trees looked beautifully clear and green. He had a split second of regret that he hadn't punched the mike button and told somebody he was getting out. With an instant's giggling comprehension of great clarity, he heard the words of "Rudolph" over the ADF. The seat went with a bang that seemed far away to Fairchild.

"Four's out! Four's out!" Darlington yelled. He had pulled high, popped his speed boards, and throttled back to match the slow speed of the crippled airplane. From over Fairchild's now burning plane, Darlington had watched the entire ejection sequence. He pushed the throttle forward, brought his boards up, pushed the nose down on his nearly stalling F-100, and transmitted, "Zero Three, you got his chute?"

"Roger, Lead, he's got a good chute. He's right over the friendlies."

"Keep your eye on him," Travers yelled to Parker as he swung the airplane around facing where he knew the gun was positioned. He switched his transmitter to Fox Mike.

"China Boy, China Boy. We got a shoot-down. He's in his chute right over you. God damn, he's almost in the trees. You got him?"

"Oh hell, no, I don't have him. And Copperhead, you got to get that nape and CBU in here, that frapping Dash-K is shooting out our cover by the frapping roots."

"Roger, Roger, China Boy. I got the gun, you get that pilot, you copy?" Travers had already switched to Uniform strike frequency by the time China Boy said on FM he'd retrieve the pilot.

"Ramrod, hold high and dry for a sec. Try to call a chopper for your pal. I'll put two smokes in on that Dash-K, then you guys cream his ass," Travers transmitted. "Parker, keep your eye on that chute in the trees," Travers yelled as he pushed over into the gun from a slant range barely outside the 12.7's effective range. Parker groaned as he twisted in his harness and survival gear to keep sight of the white chute that had plumed over the jungle canopy. He lost it as Travers whipped the 0-1E around and down. The two Willy Petes went off with ear-shattering thunderclaps. In seconds Parker found the chute again. "I got it! I got it!" he yelled to Travers, scarcely able to breathe in his excitement, but aware he was performing admirably in this, his first combat mission, which he wasn't even supposed to be on.

"Ramrods, hit ten meters north of my smoke. That's the gun. Stay low on pull-off so he can't track you past the treetops. You're cleared in hot, whoever's first. Use everything you got."

"Ramrod Two," Darlington transmitted, "you're closest. Is your bird working or not? If it is, get in there and lay your CBU on 'em to keep their heads down, then Three, you take it out with your nape."

Darlington knew the CBU pellets probably wouldn't take the gun out, but they would totally distract the crew as the bomblets floated down *crack-cracking* toward them, while Jack Laird would zoom down and scrape his napalm off on the gun barrel. What the hell was the matter with Bannister, Darlington said to himself as he positioned for a strafe run.

"Roger, Lead," Laird, Number 3, said, "Two, are you in?"

In the front seat of the F-100F, Bannister drew his .38-caliber revolver from his survival vest. He took the stick in his left hand, held the plane straight and level, then turned to the left as far in the seat as his harness would let him. He pointed the gun back over his left shoulder in the general direction of Rawson's head, and spoke over the intercom.

"Touch that stick, and you're a dead man." Bannister tapped the gun barrel hard against the canopy. "Put your hands in your lap and shut up, major. I'm in front. We go by my gauges, and they read real good."

Bannister turned back, tucked the gun under his G-suit leg bladder, set up the switches for CBU, and called he was in as he positioned for his run. He pushed outboard on the throttle to ignite the afterburner to boost his airspeed to Mach .72, and headed for the deck. He had a few seconds to think, as he leveled and lined up, that this was how he had gotten shot up the last time. He lifted his gloved hand from the throttle and held it before his eyes. His fingers weren't trembling anymore. He exhaled sharply and concentrated on a perfect CBU run-in. He wasn't even aware how completely he had dismissed Rawson from his mind. He was ready.

"Two's in," Bannister transmitted.

Bannister's aircraft flashed over the Dash-K so fast and so close the gunner couldn't swing the barrel fast enough to track him as the roaring jet disappeared over the trees. The gunner heard the approaching *blam-Blam-BLAM* sound getting louder as Bannister's CBU's settled and exploded their marble-sized steel pellets into the 38-foot killing zone. The gunner told his assistant to duck on his command and they would rise together after the bomblets showered past them to fire at the next airplane.

They crouched under an overhang in the narrow gun pit as Bannister's CBU bomblets blasted by, sending hot pellets zinging harmlessly over their heads. Then, on command, they both jumped up to resume firing. The gunner spun and swung the barrel back. He barely had time to scream in sudden hot fear and rage as Jack Laird's shiny aluminum Blu-27 750-pound can of napalm B struck the ground twenty feet away, sending a 2,000-degree surf wave of flame curling up and over him.

"Goddamn, Copperhead, you got it," China Boy said on Fox Mike in an awed voice. "You earned your pay today. Yes, sir. You did more than only fry some rice. By the way, we got a pilot who just dropped in. Says he knows you. His eyes are kinda big, but outside of that he seems in good shape. You want we should send him home?"

"Yeah, Tom, send him home. All you guys come home. I just got the word on HF. The C Team has ordered the Snake Pit to send a couple Hueys for you guys, Slicks and Guns. Race you back to the barn. And say, get us some BDA." Travers switched back to Uniform.

"Ramrod flight," he called, "this is Copperhead; Four's okay, Hueys are coming to get everybody. You guys return to base. I'll wrap things up here. I got another flight coming in for top cover. You guys done good. See you at the hootch."

"Roger, Copperhead. Ramrod, close it up, look each other over for holes. We're going home," Darlington transmitted.

"Two."

"Three."

"All right, Harry, what happened?" Darlington asked two hours later when the four pilots were on the ground and debriefed. Darlington had pulled the ops officer off to one side as they walked out of the debriefing room. Laird and Bannister went back to the squadron PE room to clean their gear.

"I'm writing him up on charges," Rawson said, eyes chasing shadows.

"What are they?" Darlington asked, noting the rapid eye movements.

"Disobeying a direct order. Pulling a gun. Threatening a superior officer. Oh, I've got a lot on him. I've got him now." He pulled his shoulders back, and stared Frank Darlington right in the eye. "Yes, sir, I've got him now."

"Harry, I didn't see any smoke from your airplane. Did you have a fire warning light?"

"Well . . . no. But the TPT was high, quite high. The tail pipe temperature. It was . . . almost in the red."

Colonel Frank Darlington put his arm gently across the major's shoulders turning him toward the door. "Harry," he said, "we're going to see Doc Russell. He's going to give you a shot to let you sleep on this. You're going to take it easy for a while."

Rawson, mouth working, looked at Frank Darlington, the director of operations, with a quizzical expression, "Well, yes, colonel, if you think so, yes. But you'll see to it that Bannister gets what's coming to him, won't you."

"Yes, Harry," the DO said quietly, "I'll see to it that Bannister gets what's coming to him."

0800 HOURS LOCAL, 19 JANUARY 1966
531ST TACTICAL FIGHTER SQUADRON,
BIEN HOA AIR BASE, REPUBLIC OF VIETNAM
☆

The next morning, Court Bannister and Jack Laird returned from a mission in II Corps and walked into the Personal Equipment room, parachute and flight equipment jangling with each step.

"Christ," Laird said, "barely eight o'clock and already we're soaked." He hung up his helmet and ran his hands through hair glued to his head with sweat. "You know," he said, "we need some sort of an inner cap to soak up all this sweat. It's damn near impossible to get rid of it when it drips in your eyes from under a helmet." He wiped his head with a piece of towel. "I'll tell you, Court, we really got into it up there. I thought that FAC was going to kamikaze the camp when he said the bad guys were coming through the wire. Hell of a mission, wasn't it?" Laird faced Bannister. "You did a great job on the wing, Court, and some great bombing, too."

"Thanks, Jack. You're great to fly with," Bannister said smiling.

Major Derham, the assistant ops officer, stuck his head in. "Hey, Court, the DO wants to see you in his office. Pronto."

"Got it," Bannister said. Here it comes, he said to himself.

* * *

"Reporting as ordered, sir," Court Bannister said as he stood in front of Colonel Frank Darlington's desk and saluted. Both men wore flight suits. After the director of operations returned the salute, he indicated the chair next to his scratched gray steel desk and invited Court to have a seat and relax. Both men lit up after Darlington offered Court a Lucky Strike. Neither man smoked filter cigarettes.

Darlington was a quiet man, not given to excess words, which was one reason he had made full colonel rather late in his career. In fact, if his former wing commander hadn't recognized his natural leadership abilities and jockeyed him from job to job to get several top-block efficiency reports for the promotion board, he would be retiring now at age forty-six with twenty-five years service as a lieutenant colonel. If he didn't make any major errors, his present position as DO of the 3rd Tac Fighter Wing practically guaranteed him the slot of wing commander when Friedlander moved on. Darlington had thinning brown hair and brown eyes in a narrow face with fine squint lines drawn on his forehead and around his eyes. He was too slender for his height of six feet, and had been in the fighter business since P-51 Mustangs. The two men sat motionless for a moment as they listened to the ripping sound of F-100 afterburners on takeoff override the hum and hiss of a large window air conditioner.

Darlington leaned back in his chair, nodded at Bannister. "Well, Court, how're they hangin'?"

Caught unawares, Court couldn't help but smile as he chose one of the stock answers: "One in front of the other for speed, sir."

Darlington chuckled. "That was quite a day with Copperhead and the Mike Force, wasn't it?"

"Yes, sir, it was," Court said warily. He didn't know Darlington very well and wasn't sure where he was heading.

"Glad we got those guys out of there and picked up Fairchild. Too bad we lost a bird, wasn't it?"

"Yes, sir, it was."

"Harry Rawson is in the dispensary. Did you know he'll probably be med-evacked to Japan?"

"No, sir, I didn't."

"Not quite sure what's the matter with him. You got any ideas?"

Court was silent. He thought he knew exactly what was wrong with Rawson. He also thought it strange a colonel would ask a captain's opinion of a major. It didn't make much difference, though, for Court figured he was about to get it, right between the eyes. You just don't go around pulling guns on people, especially superior officers, and get away with it. He resisted an urge to shrug.

"Guess I can't expect you to answer," Darlington said. "I relieved him because he is in the wrong business." Darlington took a moment to let the implications of Rawson's cowardice sink in. He lit another cigarette, looked up at Bannister, and asked in words hard-cadenced like drumbeats, "Do you think you're in the wrong business, Bannister?"

Eyes widening, Bannister shot back, "No, sir." He paused. "Absolutely not," he added for emphasis and stood up. "I'm in the right business," he said, starting to get the panicky feeling he was about to be tossed out of fighters. A fighter pilot's biggest fear was not pain or death, but losing his fighter plane.

Darlington studied him for a moment. "Calm down," he said, "I happen to agree with you. You're in the right business and you're damn good at it. One of the Wing's best, in fact. So hang on. In a month or so there may be a job coming up you should take."

Bannister remained standing, astounded by the sudden words that all young fighter pilots yearn for. Then he remembered. "Sir, about that gun—"

Darlington interrupted, "Didn't say anything about a gun, did I? Extraordinary events call for extraordinary measures, don't they?" Darlington stood up. "Here's the lineup. Peter Warton isn't coming back, so Serge Demski from Wing is taking over as CO, and Bob Derham is the new ops officer. You weren't under Major Rawson long enough to get an ER, but I'm putting a favorable endorsement in your promotion file to cover the gap till Derham writes one on you. And you had best be getting to your squadron, you have a flight to lead at"—the DO checked his watch—"in two hours, at 1230."

"I've lost my flight-lead status," Bannister said.

"Not according to this, you haven't," the DO said handing him a freshly cut copy of orders.

DEPARTMENT OF THE AIR FORCE
HEADQUARTERS 3RD TACTICAL FIGHTER WING (TAC)
APO SF 96227

SPECIAL ORDER 51   19 JAN 1966
1. The following named officers, 531st Tac Ftr Sqdn (TAC), this stn, are designated as Flight Leader in the F-100D/F aircraft. Authority: Para 9-2B, TACM 55-100.

CAPT COURTLAND EdM. BANNISTER A03021953
CAPT LAURENCE M. DALTON 69040A
CAPT RICHARD F. FARRELL 69330A

FOR THE COMMANDER   DISTRIBUTION
                                                          "C"

JACK E. MINTON, 1STLT, USAF
Chief, Administrative Services

| 2100 HOURS LOCAL, 19 JANUARY 1966
OFFICER'S CLUB, BIEN HOA AIR BASE,
REPUBLIC OF VIETNAM |

☆

As flight lead, Court flew two more missions before the end of the day. That night in the O-Club he sat with Doc Russell at a small table off to one side. He had a Budweiser, the Doc was drinking scotch and water.

"I spent some time with Rawson," the Doc said. "I'm keeping him on Thorazine and Seconal to quiet him down. He talked a bit. Said you pulled a gun on him. That true?"

"Yes, it is."

"Why, Court?"

Court lit a cigarette with his rubber-band–covered Zippo and sank a drag deep into his lungs.

"Did he say where we were or what we were doing? Did he tell you he panicked in a low-threat situation when some of our guys were in trouble—Fairchild, for one? Or that the Mike Force was down there with a Dash-K chewing on them? Did he tell you about that?"

"No, he didn't. All he said was he tried to tell you the engine was overheating, and you pulled a gun on him."

"Look, Doc, there was a hell of a lot more to it than that. Nothing was wrong with our airplane, and the guys on the ground needed everything they could get. We still had two CBU's and all our twenty-mil." Bannister exhaled a strong puff of smoke, looking squarely at Russell.

"You think that's reason enough to kill a man?" Russell said, returning Bannister's gaze with steady eyes.

Bannister thought for a while. "I probably would not have pulled the trigger," he said finally, "in this case."

"Why not?"

Bannister took a pull at his beer. "Other airplanes were there with ordnance. I wasn't the only one that could help take out the gun pinning the Mike Force. Also, there was the possibility my shot could have gone wild and damaged the airplane, so we both would have had to punch out."

"What do you mean 'in this case'?"

"There were other people there. It wasn't a one-on-one situation."

"You mean if you were the only one with ordnance to take out that gun, you'd have killed to do it? You'd kill one man to save another?"

"Shit, Doc, isn't that what we try to do every day?"

"Look, Court, that's not how I meant it and you know it."

Bannister took another drag. "I suppose I do. But that's about as far as I can go with your corkscrew logic. I don't know where you're going with this, but I'm not going to try to stay up with you. Loc Ninh was what I considered a tight situation requiring something I could provide. I went the most direct route to provide it. Fortunately, things all worked out."

"Not quite. Rawson's been relieved of command and is in the hospital."

"Doc, with all due respect, that man has been coming apart for some time, and should never have kept the position he did." Court was silent for a moment watching Russell's eyes. "In fact, Doc, since you brought this mess up, isn't part of your job as squadron flight surgeon to keep an eye on us, on our mental well-being and all that?"

"Yes, it is," Russell said, "but I don't go around pulling guns on people to do it."

Bannister sat back. "Doc," he said, "the long and short of it is that my job is to take people apart, and yours is to put people together."

"True," Doc Russell said, "but the real long and short of it is my job is more satisfying because my craftsmanship results in life whereas yours results in death." The Doc delivered his words with strong conviction. Bannister looked away for a moment.

"Doc, you ever think maybe I'm saving lives? That in the long run the enemy I take out—"

Russell interrupted, "The people you kill, you mean. Say them, say the words *'people'* and *'kill.'* That's the trouble, Court, you use words like 'enemy' and 'bad guys' when you mean human beings, and words like 'take out' or 'waste' or 'blow away' when you mean 'kill.' " Doc Russell's face flushed.

"Hold on, Doc. I'm a professional. My job is to kill these people now before they—"

Russell interrupted again, "Yeah, yeah, I know: 'Before they are on the streets of San Francisco.' Right?"

"Something like that, Doc. Only closer, like, say, Saigon. Before they are on the streets of Saigon. Our whole job here is to push out the bad guys, *kill* them if you will, who are trying to take over South Vietnam and who kill those who resist them. What about that NVA outfit that took a flamethrower to the Montagnard village when the men were gone and torched two hundred women and children? Or the VC here in the south who decapitate and disembowel teachers and village mayors who wouldn't teach what they want or give them sanctuary? And you know about their stringing the guts of live G.I.'s they've captured down the trail so their buddies walk on them. What about that, Doctor Conrad Russell? And what's the matter with you, anyway? You didn't used to talk like this."

"Calm down, Court, for God's sake, or you'll need some of the same stuff I'm giving Rawson. I shouldn't be ragging you and I know it. I'm sorry. I'm getting fed up with this whole sorry scene, that's all. Politicians running a war. Hypocrisy. Euphemisms. The *War* Department is now the *Defense* Department. Bombs are weapons and airplanes are weapons platforms. At least in my business, a scalpel is still a scalpel." Russell held his glass up. "Here, a toast. In the words of the immortal beagle, the great Snoopy, FUCK WAR," the Doc boomed. Court Bannister grinned and clanged his beer off the Doc's glass. *"Fuck war,"* he echoed.

Two wing wienies at the bar looked over at them and shook their heads.

13

☆

"Were you scheduled for Bien Hoa, or did you trip trade?" Nancy's seatmate asked. Nancy Lewis looked pert and shiny as she sat with her crew in the Braniff International crew bus, which was headed from the LAX terminal to the Boeing 707 on the south ramp. It was cool that afternoon and slightly hazy.

Nancy turned from the window to look at the tall, blonde stewardess named Sally Churna. "I traded for it."

"Well, I think it's going to be a nice trip, what with a layover at Clark. Too bad we can't bid for trips on MAC like we do on domestic." Sally Churna smiled. "Do you have a lot of seniority?" she asked.

"Not much, four years," Nancy answered, and turned back to look out the window. She knew Sally would think her standoffish. Most of the girls did, ever since Brad had been declared MIA. Yet they all understood her moodiness and were protective. She did wish she were close enough to Sally Churna, or anyone else for that matter, to talk about how she felt. Someone to agree or disagree with her decisions. She felt so alone and only half functioning, as if a part of her thought processes had given up. But she coped, sometimes only minute to minute, sometimes day to day, but she coped.

She wanted Bien Hoa trips because of the Special Forces A and B Team camps near there. Somehow, she felt, she would be closer to Brad or people who knew Brad. Besides, being away from Saigon meant being away from Bubba Bates. Nancy had shared a warm Coke with him at the small and dirty Tan Son Nhut terminal bar one afternoon while waiting for her airplane to be turned around. She had felt sorry for him, he'd misunderstood and thought he had something going with her. She had been avoiding him ever since. She smiled as she thought of that young Air Force lieutenant so eager to save her. She wondered if he would write—what was his name, Parker?—and if he did, whether she would answer.

"The cleaning folks did a great job with this one," Sally said after they boarded and walked down the aisles to start passenger boarding preparation. Each girl was assigned specific duties to check equipment, food service, emergency apparatus, and the tiny bathrooms they called the blue rooms. The ultimate destination of the big jet was Bien Hoa Air Base, South Vietnam, where it would disgorge 165 American soldiers, most of whom would be in combat within days. To relieve congestion into Tan Son Nhut, Bien Hoa in the south and Da Nang and Cam Ranh air bases farther north had been outfitted to handle the surge of soldiers flown to and from combat in plush ways never dreamed of by World War II or Korean War veterans. The G.I.'s had started to call the returning civilian planes the "freedom bird" that would carry them to the "real world." That there were real, round-eyed girls on the freedom bird made the trip a fantasy almost impossible to bear.

"Good cleaning job, huh? Not like last time," a chunky little brunette named Tiffy Berg chirped. "They missed number two aft blue room. It was overfull, and well, eeecchh, simply stinky and all. The captain and the ground agent barely got them back in time to clean it out before the soldiers boarded. Said we're turning these airplanes around too fast or something."

Tiffy sighed and started checking the overheads for fire extinguishers. "I sure like flying G.I.'s," she added. "They're so much better than civilians because they never ask for anything. They're so quiet." She stopped, her eyes brimming. "But they're even *more* quiet coming back from Vietnam. Like they've seen the end of the world, and they're just kids," said Tiffy, herself barely older than the G.I.'s to whom she ministered.

An hour later the big jet, Braniff International MAC Flight B3T6, was airborne following the sun on the first leg of its 13,000-mile flight to Bien Hoa Air Base, RVN. Its first leg was to Hawaii, the second to Guam, the third to Clark Air Base in the Philippines, then to Vietnam. Given refueling, layovers, and crew changes, Nancy Lewis would be on the Bien Hoa Air Base in three days. There the plane would off-load its 165 G.I.'s at Detachment 5 of the 8th Aerial Port Squadron and be cleaned and reflued. Then it would on-load a batch of G.I.'s returning home, and fly back to Clark.

Inside, Nancy Lewis was all smiles and eager to give efficient service to the youngsters in their painfully new khaki uniforms.

> 1230 HOURS LOCAL, 22 JANUARY 1966
> LOC NINH, WAR ZONE C, III CORPS,
> REPUBLIC OF VIETNAM

☆

Over the intercom came a string of commands: "Hold it off; hold it off; a little more; get your rudder in there; that's it; pull your power off; now put it down, and stay on the rudder. That's not bad. Now add power; take it around and try it again." In the backseat of the 0-1E, Toby Parker did as he was told. He pushed the throttle up and pulled the airplane into the air from the dirt strip next to the Special Forces camp at Loc Ninh.

"Fine. Now bring it around and make a full stop. We got to make our pickup," Travers said. Parker flew the plane around the landing pattern and made a full-stop landing without too much help from Travers. Though he still had trouble with torque on takeoff and rudder control on landing, Parker was more than pleased with himself. He had done well on the big mission last week when a Ramrod had been shot down, and had proved of value again this morning helping Travers put in an airstrike as they headed for Loc Ninh.

They taxied to the end of the dirt strip, turned onto a hacked-out clearing, added power to spin the bird around, and shut down amidst blowing red dust stirred up by the propeller. The prop ticked to a stop and kicked back once. The engine and exhaust system popped and crackled as it cooled. Waiting for them were two SF troops wearing their standard uniform of tiger suits with green berets tilted slightly forward and to the right on skulls nearly shaven clean. Though neither wore rank insignia, each was a master sergeant. The shorter of the two, George Spears, held a briefcase. The taller and wider one was Jim Mahoney. They were both from the III Corps Mike Force team based at Bien Hoa, which was operational around the Loc Ninh area, probing VC and NVA units to establish their order of battle.

"Where's the *dai uy,* Captain Myers?" Travers said as he and Parker climbed out of the plane and stretched.

"Gone back to the Bien Hoa team house, sir," Spears said. "He said you put on a helluva show last week. He sent your shot-down F-100 pilot back with a piece of that gun as a souvenir." He swapped briefcases with Parker.

"There's some good photos in here," Parker said, tapping the case. "Colonel Norman is convinced the VC are massing for a major push. Maybe against you, maybe An Loc, maybe Bien Hoa."

"This will corroborate," Spears said. "We got agent reports and interrogations that nail down the increased capabilities of men and materiel, but no one knows their intentions. Definitely, there's a VC division in the area. We think it's the Ninth, but we haven't found it. That's what Captain Myers and the China Boys were out looking for when they found that Dash-K. By the way, Phil, he's got your BDA for you. Twelve VC killed by air and one Dash-K destroyed. He said their ass was grass, and the VC had the lawn mower until you guys took it out." He patted the painted mouth on the cowling of the 0-1E. "I know he plans on seeing you and the Ramrods at the team house. Tonight, probably." The SF sergeant turned toward Parker.

"Lieutenant, you still trying to fly, huh? Those landings looked lousy to me. You get to log one touchdown for each bounce, huh?"

"Up it, sergeant-of-the-green-beanie-army Spears, you beetle cruncher. You're just jealous," Parker was amazed how easy the repartee came to him and how at home he felt. Standing in the shade of the 0-1E's wing, stinking and sweaty, dirty with red dust, stomach and bowels ready to erupt at any moment from bad food, he'd never felt better. He thought of the vacuous, flat people with whom he had graduated from college. Lawyers now, accountants, stockbrokers, real estate men; he had visited and seen them at a reunion. He looked at the men around him. God, I'm lucky, he thought, to be meeting and working with people like this. For a moment he had the odd feeling he was playing a role in a World War II movie, yet at the same time viewing this tableau from off to one side. A breeze tousled his hair, rousing him from his reverie. He heard Spears tell Travers about a major from 5th Group coming in to study the buildup around Loc Ninh and Route 13. Travers asked who the major was.

"Wolf Lochert," Mahoney said, "He's right up there with Bull Simon, Charging Charley Beckwith, and Bear Gannon. He humps sixty pounds of rocks in the boonies just for a morning stroll. He won't admit it, but he's the guy who blew up the town hall in My Tho when he proved the council was all VC. He greased every one of them. Then he rifled the safe, and gave all the money to the Catholic orphanage."

"If he won't admit it, then how do you know all that, Sergeant Mahoney?" Travers asked.

"Hell, I was there. I'm demo, remember?" All SF men were specialists in three of five fields: demolition, communications, medical, intelligence, and logistics. Mahoney knew how to blow things up as cleanly as a sword stroke. Travers nodded.

"Time to go. Lets aviate," he said to Parker.

Two hours later, at 1830, Parker had divested himself of the briefcase at Colonel Norman's office, changed his clothes in his BOQ room, and was at the Tan Son Nhut main gate scrounging a ride to downtown Saigon. He had a date to see Tui at the Restaurant My Canh at eight o'clock.

2015 HOURS LOCAL, 22 JANUARY 1966
MY CANH RESTAURANT,
SAIGON, REPUBLIC OF VIETNAM

☆

"This place has a good reputation," Toby Parker explained to Tui as they sat at a linen-covered table for two on the river side of the Restaurant My Canh. A tall dripless candle graced the table; the pungent odor of burning mosquito repellent filled the air like incense gone sour. Most of the clientele was Western. Some wore fatigues even though they were not combatants. Fatigue-clad non-combatants were known derisively as Saigon commandos, and they ranged in rank from corporal to general.

"My friend, Phil Travers, said this restaurant enjoyed the reputation, among Americans anyhow, as being a good place to go. Travers told me this means it's clean, the food doesn't make you sick, they'll burn a steak anyway you want it, the whisky isn't watered, there are no bar girls here, they speak English, the price isn't . . ." Parker trailed off, concerned about the expression on Tui's face.

"Look," he said, "we only met here twenty minutes ago, yet you've been acting like you want to leave." He reached across to touch her hand. She pulled it away and glanced at the watch on her slender wrist.

"Tui, what is it? Before, you seemed happy to know me and to meet me here. Now, you look scared enough to run away. Is it Bates? Did he give you a hard time? Listen, I've met some guys that could have a short but intense talk with him." He thought of Spears and Mahoney.

Tui shook her head slowly. Her hair swung easily from side to side, one wing falling low over her left eye. "Tow-bye, Tow-bee, it is not Mr. Bates. I . . . I do not live with him any more."

Toby started to speak. Tui reached over and placed her fingertips on his mouth. He reached up to take her hand, kissing her fingers. She did not draw away.

"Please, do not ask questions. Let us eat. Order some wine. Let us enjoy this time. Look," she said brightly, turning to face the Saigon River, "the fish are jumping for, for . . . what do you call them? In French it is the *moustiques*."

"Mosquitoes," Toby said, "we call them mosquitoes."

"Yes, mow-sqwee-tohs," she parroted and laughed. Toby had never heard such an exquisite trill. A waiter poured the wine Toby had ordered.

"Tui, you are so beautiful," he said, still holding her hand.

"And you, *mon lieutenant,* are most handsome," she said. "Drink some wine, quickly. We will forget where we are." She smiled, even teeth flashing in the candlelight. They both drank deep draughts of the heavy burgundy. She covered her watch with her hand.

"I know," she said, "pretend this is the Seine, the river that loops through Paris, and we are in a *petit café* on the Left Bank. Do you know Paris?"

"No," he said.

"Oh, it is lovely," she said, her voice softening. "We will go there. On the Seine there are the *bateaux mouches,* the boats for us to go on the river, and to drink the wine and to see the lights at night."

She chattered on through the meal and wine. They danced several times on the tiny dance floor to the surprisingly good foxtrots played by a four-piece Filipino band. As Tui nestled close, her cheek tucked perfectly into the hollow of his neck. Toby felt the warm, smooth flesh of her back as he smelled the elusive fragrance of an unknown perfume in her hair. He was so overwhelmed by the wave of attraction he felt for this lovely woman that his knees nearly buckled.

When the dessert, an elegant baked custard called *flan,* was served, she fell silent.

"You've hardly eaten a bite," Toby said, pouring for them both from a second bottle of burgundy. Tui looked at him, then quickly looked away as her eyes began to fill.

"You will leave the Restaurant My Canh no later than thirty minutes after nine," Buey Dan had said. "We will be ready. Hail the blue taxi directly across the street, the one where the small boy is shining the left fender for the driver in a white shirt."

"Maybe I cannot get him out by exactly nine-thirty," Tui had said.

"You must, or you will both die," Buey Dan had responded. "Four kilos of plastique will be floated under the Restaurant My Canh, set to detonate at thirty-five minutes after the hour of nine."

She looked at her watch. It was ten past nine. The musicians had taken their first break of the evening. As a filler, the leader switched on a tape player with French songs and walked outside. Low and growly, with great clarity, the reverberating voice of Edith Piaf came perfectly over the sound system with the opening bars of *"Non, je ne regrette rien,"*—"No, I Regret Nothing."

Tui reacted, knowing she was almost out of control. Nothing had prepared her for this feeling. She felt swollen and moist and her head felt light. She had never, *never,* she repeated in wonder to herself, felt this way toward any boy, much less a *mui lo.* She had had no idea she ever could. She had always been so busy, there hadn't been time. The Liberation demanded everything; her time, her emotions, her life's blood, if need be.

"One more dance, Tow-bee, one more dance," she begged.

Toby Parker rose to his feet, held her chair, and escorted her to the floor. He was utterly lost in her closeness, and completely captivated by her femininity. My God, he thought, what is this? I'm falling in love. "No," he corrected himself out loud, "I *am* in love."

"What? What did you say," Tui murmured, her face buried in his neck as they danced.

"I said, 'I love you,' " Toby said, tipping his head and kissing her cheek.

"Mon amour, mon amour, embrasse-moi. Je t'aime, je t'aime," she whispered, grasping him tightly, tears falling onto his shoulder.

Piaf sang the haunting words in a voice of such timbre that Toby felt vibrations deep in his gut, Piaf's rolling R's echoed in his brain; *"No, I regret nothing, nothing. . . ."* Tui strained against him. We could be together, she thought, forever. Just hold each other like this for a few more minutes until forever begins.

Toby felt Tui strain against him and clasped her closer. No one else existed, only the two of them swaying, no longer dancing, to Piaf's magic spell. We are a world of two, Toby thought with exquisite wonder. Never in his life had he become so enraptured by a woman, and so quickly. No other girl had ever intoxicated all his senses at once. His chest ached and he began to shake with the intensity of his passion. He never dreamed he could be so affected. His eyes misted. Driven by a frenzy he couldn't identify, he knew he had to do something, and right away.

"Tui, I want to take you from here. I can find a place for you that Bates will never find. A place just for us," Toby found himself speaking louder to break through Piaf's words as she rolled into her ending crescendo.

"Just the two of us," the rapt and anxious Toby Parker said. "Now. Let's go." He tugged at her. "Just us." He felt his heart swelling, increasing the delicious pain in his chest. "Tui, Tui, I love you so much."

Tui reached up to hold Parker's face between her hands. He could see tears streaming down her face. "My lieutenant, I will love you forever." She stared into his eyes. "Forever," she repeated; then kissed him with parted lips for a long moment.

Suddenly, she released him. Surprised and off-balance, Toby stepped back. She looked at her watch. The plastique was due to detonate in seven minutes. "No-o-o," she moaned, "I cannot do that."

"Do what," Toby asked, "go with me?"

Tui looked at him. Her eyes narrowed with determination. "Yes," she said, "yes, I'll go with you. Anything you want. Now, this minute." She grabbed his hand and tugged him toward the door. "Now, quickly, quickly."

"Hey, wait," Toby said pulling her toward their table, "you need your purse and I need to pay the bill." He couldn't see any waiters around.

Tui pulled her hand free, swept past Toby to pick up her purse, and fling a handful of piastres on the table. "There, now we go." She again grasped his hand and half ran toward the door.

Outside, they saw two white taxis and a pedicab directly in front of the restaurant and one blue taxi across the street. A small boy was shining its left fender. The white-shirted driver stepped out to open the rear door. Tui moaned and pulled Toby into the taxi nearest the restaurant door, spewing a stream of rapid-fire Vietnamese at the driver, who started his engine and sped off, grinding his gears badly. As they pulled away, Buey Dan rushed from the shadows, a hypodermic needle kit in his hand, and jumped into the blue taxi, which made a U-turn, tires screeching, to follow Tui and Toby.

Tui leaned forward, touching the taxi driver's shoulder to point and emphasize her instructions. He made a few turns, scattered revelers on Tu Do, swerved around three G.I.'s crossing the street, arms around each other singing, and pulled up to the well-lighted red-and-white cement barriers at the entrance to Post 12 of the 716th Military Police Battalion, whose job it was to cruise Saigon keeping G.I.'s from getting into trouble, and to apprehend and book those who did.

Up to this point, the bewildered Toby Parker hadn't said a word. Two MP's from their guard post, M-16's at port arms, approached the taxi.

"Toby," Tui said, "you must get out here." She reached across him and opened the door.

"What in hell is going on?" Toby said. "Look, if it's Bates—"

"No, no," she interrupted, "it's not that pig." She looked out the rear window to see Buey Dan's taxi glide to a halt among the shadows across and back down the street. "Please, I love you, now get out, get out." She pushed him out and climbed out after him as the MP's split and took up positions, angled to each side, and looked at them with suspicion.

"Please," Tui said to them, "this is Lieutenant Parker. He is in danger. He is an important man, a courier. You must get him to Tan Son Nhut. The Viet Cong are following him."

One MP advanced under the cover of the other. "May I see your ID, sir?" As Toby pulled out his wallet, Tui leaned up to kiss him, pulled off a jade earring which she thrust into his hand, then whirled and ran toward the blue taxi in the shadows.

Toby started to follow her, but an MP blocked him. "Sir, you'd better stay right here," he said. They saw Tui slow to a walk, then slowly climb into the blue taxi. As it drove away, an enormous explosion and flash ripped the night in the direction of the river. Within seconds, the PRC-25 FM radio crackled to life from the guard shack.

"Sir, get inside." The first MP pointed toward the building with his rifle butt. "We'll get you to Tan Son Nhut." As Toby complied, he heard the second MP yell from the shack that Unit 4 said the My Canh had been blown up.

An hour later, Lieutenant Parker sat in the back of an MP four-by-four truck headed for Tan Son Nhut with two MP's going off duty. They were talking about the My Canh.

"They got the Claymore Café again."

"Yeah, I know."

"Eight dead so far, eleven wounded."

"Yeah, I know."

"All Americans. They said all the gooks split a half hour before, even the cooks."

"Yeah, I know."

"Except one, a broad. They said she hung around till the last minute, then *di-di mau'ed* with some G.I. They're looking for her." In Vietnamese slang, *di-di mau* meant "to go quickly."

"Oh, yeah?"

"Helluva way to fight a goddamn war."

"Yeah. Who says this is a war." He turned toward Toby. "Ain't that right, lootenant?"

1230 HOURS LOCAL, 24 JANUARY 1966
EXECUTIVE DINING ROOM,
THE PENTAGON, WASHINGTON, D.C.

☆

Colonel Ralph Morgan and Captain Jim Tunner met for lunch in the executive dining room on the fourth floor, A-ring, Corridor 10 of the Pentagon. It was two floors above and a world away from the hubbub of the plastic-and-chrome cafeterias on the second floor, second corridor up from the concourse. In the executive dining room, the linen and china, hostess and waiters, and paneled walls created a subdued atmosphere, gratefully appreciated by the officers and civilians constantly hammered by the hectic work pattern in the corridors outside.

Ralph Morgan ordered the diet special, consisting of lean hamburger and cottage cheese with peach slice. Tunner selected the club sandwich. Both men ordered black coffee, which was served immediately. Both men wore their service dress blues, each left chest covered with ribbons and badges.

"How's your clearance going?" Morgan asked.

"I've purged my files, turned over all classified stuff I signed for, and have turned in all my passes except the one for our office. Since our function doesn't exist anymore, I pitched about twenty pounds of directives, memos, regs, notes, things like that. How about you?"

"The same. Clearing the Pentagon isn't as bad as clearing the neighborhood. Audrey and the kids are going to live in Mason City with her parents, and she has to check out of more offices than we do. Church groups, PTA, local consumer action stuff, not to mention getting the house ready to show, while getting all our gear ready for packing. Are you going to give up your apartment?"

"No," Jim Tunner said, "we aren't. Babs wants to stay right here in Washington. She's thinking of a few courses at Georgetown University or maybe a job on the Hill as a secretary. Without kids we're pretty flexible."

Morgan made a face as he speared the last piece of lettuce on his plate.

"I'm sure tired of eating rabbit food."

"Hey, right. Why do you do it, then?"

"The Thud is a big bird, but I still want to lose another ten pounds before I strap in." He eyed Tunner's slim figure. "How can you eat those big sandwiches and still stay so trim?"

"I smoke more than you do," the Navy man replied. "But don't worry, once you get to Tahkli, you'll sweat it all off."

"I can't afford to wait that long. Those guys at Tahkli are fighting a tough war, and the last person they want to see taking over their wing is a pudgy Pentagon pencil pusher."

"I like the way you said 'their' wing."

"Well, it is. I'm merely an administrator who goes out and leads a mission once in a while," he said with great understatement. "My job is to keep their fighter wing the best in the United States Air Force while keeping the crap off their backs. I don't want them all tangled up with scratching perfectly good military plans for some civilian idea about sending messages with this on-again, off-again Rolling Thunder."

"Messages?" the Navy man echoed.

"Yeah, messages. The SecDef told us that stopping the strikes up North would send a message to Uncle Ho that we really were good guys who want nothing but peace, and here is a token of our all-American Christian good faith."

"What crap. They're Buddhists, what do they know about Christians?"

"About the same as the SecDef knows about Buddhists. Besides, they're Communists, not Buddhists." He paused, and looked at Tunner.

"Messages," he snorted. "If you want to send messages, use Western Union. Better yet, chalk it on the nose of a Mark-84 2,000-pound bomb!"

"Speaking of Mark-84's," Tunner said, "the Armaments guys at Tan Son Nhut are really crying for all kinds of ammo. They say the stuff is on a dozen or so boats in the Saigon Harbor, but they can't unload more than a ship or two every couple days because the dock facilities are so bad."

"I know," Morgan said, "and the SecDef says regardless of what the troops report, there is no bomb shortage in Vietnam."

"Hey, right," Tunner said, "the ammo is within the territorial waters of Vietnam, therefore it's *in* Vietnam. Damn, I wish I were smart enough to work figures like that."

"If you were, you could design an Edsel," Morgan said. He sat back and looked at Tunner with a bleak expression. "Not only do we have unloading problems, about one-third of what we do manage to put on the docks get swiped for the black market or for the VC." He shook his head. "Do you ever get the feeling we're maybe throwing this one away?"

Tunner looked thoughtful. "I don't know. I haven't been over. But I felt better back in '52 when I flew Panthers off the *Wasp*. Here, all we see are the number and type of targets we should be hitting and aren't. Juggle those figures with the pilot and plane losses and you get an unbalanced equation. That's up north." He paused. "Down south, we've got other problems. You know we're starting to lose more slow FAC's than fighters, yet the fighters fly ten times as many sorties. But I hear there's a classified study group called Commando Sabre looking into a solution on that."

"Yeah? Well, I hope so. When you send 0-1E's putt-putting around where the Dash-K's are popping up, you're going to lose 'em. Hell, at their low speeds and low altitudes, an AK can bring 'em down. They've got worse problems once they go out of South Vietnam. You just can't send those little buggers up to get sawed in half over the high-threat areas in North Vietnam and Laos."

"Shhh, Laos. That's a four-letter word. We're not supposed to be there," Tunner remarked.

"Tell that to the guys who've been shot down over that four-letter country. Maybe they can bow and say, 'Sorry 'bout that,' and come home," Morgan said. "Dammit," he said slamming his fist on the table, "does anybody know or care how many Air Force people we've lost in this screwed-up war? Somebody owes these guys something, and I—" Morgan broke off. He shook his head in apology toward Tunner. "I'm sorry, Jim. Your guys are taking losses just as heavy. Your job as Commander Air Group will be as demanding as mine."

"More so," Tunner replied. "Besides being top administrator and battle planner, I've got to fly every type aircraft on board, and outfly every young jock on the boat who thinks he can beat the old man. You Air Force guys only have to check out in one bird."

Morgan didn't pursue the old Navy–Air Force argument. There was little common ground, and he valued Jim Tunner as a friend more than as a parochial naval aviator.

"I just want to make sure I give those Thud drivers the best of what I've got," Ralph Morgan said.

14

☆

The Huey slick touched down at the Snake Pit helicopter pad next to the Bien Hoa runway. As the jet engine unwound and blade rotation slowed, Wolf Lochert jumped out holding his green beret on his head with one hand while reaching back with the other to get his battered mountain rucksack, left over from his days with the 10th Special Forces Group in Germany, and an M-2 carbine, left over from his more recent days as an ARVN adviser in the Delta, where M-16's and ammo were hard to come by. When he stepped out from under the blades he returned the salute of Captain Tom Myers, the leader of the III Corps Mike Force, who in addition to his green beret wore a thin red, white, and blue cotton scarf knotted at his neck. Both men wore the striped camouflage pants and jackets known as tiger suits. They climbed into a battered black jeep with no top, and Myers drove them to the main gate of the sprawling air base. Once out of the gate, they turned left, skirting the edge of the town of Bien Hoa.

"You want to go to the C Team first, major?" Myers asked.

"No. Take me to your team house. I don't have anything to talk about with the guys at C Team. They know why I'm here." Myers knew better than to chide the Wolf for not making a courtesy call on the lieutenant colonel who ran the Bien Hoa C Team, the team that had command responsibility for Detachment A-302, his team.

They drove down a narrow dirt road toward the team house. After driving through an open area they passed through the board and barbed-wire gate guarded by two Chinese Nung mercenaries. Bare feet shoved into open rubber sandals, the Nungs carried M-16's and wore combat harnesses with hand grenades. As did all the men in the compound, the Nungs wore tiger suits, but only the Americans wore green berets. The Nungs wore floppy jungle hats.

Past the gate, the black jeep putted down the sandy road and pulled up by the long, one-story team house. The walls were built of a close approximation of cinder blocks, the ceilings were vaulted corrugated tin over two-by-four's attached to steel beams. The interior was cooled by giant floor fans. Being less than a half mile north of the Bien Hoa runway, they heard the sound of roaring jet engines. The team was used to the sound and liked the "music," as they called it, of the birds they worked with so often and so successfully.

The two officers entered the front door that opened directly into a room made into a bar. Beyond the barroom, along the left wall, were fourteen sleeping cubicles: twelve for the team members and two for guests. An area to the right with stove and refrigerator had been set aside for eating and lounging. It also doubled as the team briefing room. One other large room housed weapons and other field gear. A smaller room was designated as the team leader's office. Beside the battered wooden desk was a heavy safe, from which the Nung and Cambodian fighters were paid.

Captain Myers directed the Wolf to their bar and handed him a beer. The hardwood bar was well built and included amenities that belied its primitive location. It had a real brass rail, comfortable bar stools, a high-fidelity sound system, running water, coolers, and scores of bottles of booze. Painted on the long mirror behind the bar was a replica of the Mike Force patch, a black-on-white Jolly Roger skull and crossbones. Hanging in the place of honor at the center of the wall facing the bar, amidst VC flags and captured Chicom SKS rifles, AK-47's, and other weapons, was a larger-than-life picture of film actress Martha Raye, known as Maggie to her beloved SF troops.

Maggie, a registered nurse and lieutenant colonel in the Army Reserve, had made many trips to Vietnam to be with her boys at her own expense. She was acknowledged as the SF's one true love, somewhat like Piaf and her songs for *la légion étrangère*. Wolf tipped his beer toward the picture, "To Maggie," he said. "To Maggie," the captain echoed. They drank. Wolf noticed some words painted in gold on the wall near the door. He walked over and read:

I see as the eagle, clear and from afar.
I listen as the deer, head cocked and alert.
I think as the snake, silent and unblinking.
I walk as the panther, lithe and sinuous.
I crouch as the lion, muscled and ready.
I kill as the mongoose, swift and silent.
I die like a man.
I am Mike Force.

Underneath was the author's dedication to the III Corps Mike Force and his name, COURT BANNISTER, FIGHTER PILOT.

"Hey, I know this guy," the Wolf said. "He went through jump school at Bad Tölz. He's an F-100 pilot here?"

"That's right," Myers said, "first one we've gotten to know personally. He linked up with Jim Taylor and Frenchy Marquis one night in Saigon. Since then we've logged a lot of time together in the air and on the ground. He went out on patrol with Edgell and Leon near Tay Ninh once. Kind of a hard-nose."

"Yeah, I know," the Wolf said. "Me and Medaris and Fafek were his instructors at Bad T. He was the only Air Force guy in the class. We ran his ass off, had him retching and barfing because he was always answering, 'I'm a fighter pilot, sergeant,' whenever Fafek would holler at the class and ask what they were. Everybody else did as they were told and yelled back they were straight-legs." The Wolf chuckled in approval and finished his beer. He absently crumpled the can in one hand, tossed it in the trash, and said he was ready to be briefed.

Myers took him to a table in the dining area and pulled the cover off an acetate-covered 1:50,000 map. It was set up with force positions and strengths drawn on it with grease pencil, blue for friendly and red for enemy. Taped to the top of the map was the Mike Force lineup in which he was listed as the team leader, then the executive officer—a lieutenant—and ten NCO's whose specialties ranged from medical and weapons to intelligence, engineering, and communications.

The twelve Americans commanded two companies of Nungs and one company of Cambodians. The mission of the Mike Force was purely reconnaissance and rapid reaction, designed to help SF camps in trouble by augmenting their firepower. They had successfully fought off MACV colonels from J-3 Operations who had on occasion wanted to use them as conventional infantry units.

"This time we have a fairly normal mission," Myers began. "Recon the Loc Ninh area in War Zone C, vicinity coordinates XT486689. We think the VC want to overrun some politically and militarily important places, because the South Vietnamese elections are coming up and the Communists want to show how badly the South is doing. My two Nung companies have been up there for the last two days scouting around. I'm keeping the Cambodes back here in reserve."

"I heard you had quite a fire fight up there yourself," Wolf said.

"Yes, sir, right about here." Myers held a finger on the map. "Four of us ran into about a company of what we think was NVA. We were doing good till they opened up with a hidden Soviet .51-caliber, Dash-K, they were really chewing us up. Shot down an F-100 in fact. We got the pilot, his buddies got the Dash-K. We exfilled with Huey gunships from the Snake Pit over at Bien Hoa."

Wolf nodded. Exfiltration was always tough. Especially so under fire.

Myers went on, "I'm glad you're here, because we'd like to show you what's happening so you can take the word back to convince MACV some heavy attacks are coming soon from the Loc Ninh area. I've got a gunship laid on to take us up there."

"I'm ready," the Wolf said. Both men folded and stuffed their green berets into a leg pocket, and put on floppy-brimmed jungle camouflage hats.

"Let's go, major," Myers said, moving toward the storeroom. "By the way, you want a real gun?" he said, pointing at the Wolf's M-2.

The Wolf nodded, reluctantly. "Dammit," he growled, shaking his M-2. "This was all we could get as advisers in the Delta." Myers handed him an M-16 and a preloaded pistol belt with nearly sixteen twenty-round magazines, four to a pouch, two full water canteens, a first-aid pouch, and some smoke grenades. They didn't take frag or Willy Pete grenades, because they knew they would be useless in the thick jungle. The Wolf didn't blink an eye as he strapped on the pounds, about double the weight of a basic load of ammunition. In addition to carrying his carbine in his right hand, he walked out with the M-16 slung over his back.

1315 HOURS LOCAL, 25 JANUARY 1966
UH-1H OVER WAR ZONE C, REPUBLIC OF VIETNAM

☆

Myers was on the radio in the Huey orbiting at 2,000 feet over the jungle of War Zone C, with China Boy 3, SFC George Spears. On request, Spears had popped purple smoke for the pilot and cleared them to touch down in a small clearing he had secured.

"China Boy Three, this is China Boy," Myers transmitted. "Understand you got two WIA to be med-evaced. Get ready to load as soon as we touch down."

Three minutes later in the clearing, Wolf and Myers jumped out and ran crouching under the blades to help load SFC's Jim Mahoney and Joe Meneuz into the Huey. Mahoney's right arm, wrapped in bloody bandages, was supported by a pistol belt slung around his neck. He had taken a round in his hand and forearm. The rear of Meneuz's pants were torn and soaked from his waist to his ankles. He had been shot in the buttocks. He groaned and moved in great pain, his brown face a pale grey.

"Gonna have a little trouble dumping a taco, Paco?" the Wolf said to him, leering.

"Yeah, Wolf, *cabron,* if I do, you can be the first to eat it." Meneuz groaned and tried to smile. The two men embraced, Wolf with extreme gentleness.

"Mahoney," the Wolf said, turning. "I'd shake your hand, but I'm afraid your fingers'd fall off."

The wounded men were strapped in and the machine started to lift off. "Up yours, Wolf," Mahoney yelled against the whining and whopping helicopter noise, using his good hand to hold up the bloody middle finger of the wounded hand. Wolf stepped back, looked up at the two wounded SFC's lifting away and gave them the salute he reserved only for men he respected. Then he crouched and ran after Myers, who wasn't surprised at the major's familiarity with his enlisted troops. He knew the Wolf was up from the ranks, was respected, and could do just about anything he wanted in the U.S. Army, except possibly get promoted beyond a major. As a West Point graduate, Tom Myers was too well programmed against getting so familiar, but he would make more rank. Down deep, he knew he preferred the comradeship to the rank.

The *whop-whop* faded rapidly as Spears led them to where he had positioned twelve more Nungs and the Prick 25 radio. The trees were between twenty and fifty feet high, forming a double light-filtering canopy. On the jungle floor, vines and bushes cut visibility to twenty feet. The group stopped next to a grove of *mai pha* bamboo clustered in an almost impenetrable thicket of wait-a-minute thorns. The utter silence of a jungle after the loud clatter of the departing helicopter caused the Wolf to whisper involuntarily, "I smell incense."

"You ever been around Nungs, major?" Spears asked. The Wolf shook his head.

"They burn joss sticks before a battle. Comes from the old days when they fought the Viet Minh with the French under their leader Phuc Po. They used to carry his picture, but now they burn joss for his good favor."

They stopped in the thicket where the Nungs with the Prick 25 had four sticks glowing. They expected bad times.

Spears squatted, Nung-style, and began to brief, using the field map he unfolded. The two officers crouched behind him.

"China Boy Two, Krocek, has the recon platoon here. China Boy Four, Haskell, is with him. They've had intermittent contact all afternoon. We are here, five klicks south, in the only clearing suitable for evacuation. They are trying to get here. They have about twenty percent casualties. The good news is all their radios work and they have plenty of ammo and water. The bad news is Krocek and Haskell think they're in the middle of the 273rd VC Regiment."

The Wolf looked up sharply. "How'd that happen?" he asked.

"About noon," Spears said. "Our guys, being their usual quiet selves, settled down for a break. Turned out it was in an area where the VC thought they were all alone. They came diddly-bopping down a trail, so Krocek and Haskell motioned their troops to hunker down. No joss, no talk. The VC spread out and bivouacked all around them. Jan checked in and told me what had happened. He had to whisper on the radio transmitter, they were so close. With his Czech accent, I hardly knew what in the hell he was saying. I think he said two of his Nungs knifed down a VC who had stumbled into them. They found a 273rd pay card on him, so that's how they know what unit they ran into. The regiment has been probing them for the last two hours, obviously trying to determine the size and composition of Jan's group. Anyhow, they've got to break out and get down here to exfil with the helicopters we set up at first light. It's damn near impossible to move at night, but they are going to have to do it. I've got a FAC due overhead in twenty minutes, with some fast movers carrying snake-eyes and napalm in thirty. We haven't much time, though. It'll be dark in just over an hour, and you know those fighter jocks can't work close in the dark."

"You going to have the fast movers cut a trail for them?" Myers asked.

"Yes sir, that's exactly what I had in mind. That's why I didn't ask for any CBU. The trees would set it off before it got to the ground," Spears answered. "And, if you agree, sir, I thought perhaps Major Lochert wouldn't mind staying here with a couple Nungs to hold the landing zone, while you and I head for the rendezvous point I set up with Krocek and Haskell. I figure we have four things to do: set up a secure point they can head for; create a diversion when the time is right; lay down covering fire as necessary; and lead them back here to the LZ, which is faster than they can find this place by themselves."

Sergeant First Class George Spears looked at Major Wolfgang Lochert and Captain Thomas Myers in turn, a questioning look on his thin face. Spears didn't stand over five-eight with his boots on, nor tip the scales over 140 in the same configuration, but he had the wiry and bunched muscles of a weightlifting flyweight.

The two officers nodded at each other. "It's your show," Myers said to Spears. Crooked smiles broke out on all three. They knew the Army would never approve a sergeant telling one, much less two, officers what to do. But this was Special Forces. Like two equally experienced fighter pilots switching lead, the man who knew the area best took command, quite simply and without formality.

They involuntarily looked up as the faraway drone of a light aircraft penetrated the jungle. Spears checked the prearranged frequency, picked up the handset of the Prick 25, and pressed the transmit button.

"FAC monitoring this frequency, do you read China Boy Three?"

"China Boy Three, roger, this is Copperhead Zero Three, read you loud and clear Fox Mike, how me?"

"Copperhead Zero Three, this is China Boy Three. I read you loud and clear. Authenticate Alpha Zulu, over."

After a slight pause, Copperhead Zero Three's "Tango Echo" crackled over the headset. Phil the FAC had set his code wheel to the shackle code of the day and easily found the opposing letters to answer the challenge. If they were not in enemy contact and had the time, they could use the same method to transmit coordinates and other pertinent information they did not want the listening enemy to understand. They knew that for every five Prick 25's the Americans had, the VC probably had two, making interception almost a certainty. Frequency hopping by simple codes such as "up a buck and a quarter" for a 1.25 increase in megacycles gave some respite from listeners and from the jammers.

"Phil, your friendly and fearless FAC, at your service, China Boy."
Toby Parker was in the backseat.

"Roger. You ready to copy coordinates?"

"Affirmative, China Boy, go ahead."

Spears read off three coordinates he had shacked up earlier. "The
first set," he told Zero Three, "is our location now at the Lima
Zulu. The second is the rendezvous point we want to make. The
third is the location for China Boy Two. You copy?"

"Roger, copy." He repeated the coded words.

"Zero Three, we're moving now. I'll give you one smoke to confirm our departure point." Myers gave his radio to Lochert as he
and Spears and six Nungs moved out. No one said goodbye. Wolf
Lochert popped a smoke grenade and tossed it to the edge of the
clearing.

"FAC has a purple," Copperhead Zero Three transmitted. The
Wolf clicked the transmit button twice, "Purple," he echoed.

Phil the FAC had Toby Parker fly the O-1E in lazy orbits several
miles off to the west with the sun at his back so as not to give away
the location of the Mike Force. Twenty minutes later he called China
Boy Three.

"My strike birds have checked in with snake-eyes and nape," he
said. "Where do you want me to start?"

"Stand by, Copperhead. Break, break. China Boy Two, this is
China Boy Three. You read?"

"Dis is Two, I hear you. Whad you want?" Krocek replied in his
thick Czech accent.

"Move out, move out," Spears said, "head towards the air strike.
Get ready to pop some smoke, acknowledge."

"Yah, we moving," Krocek replied.

"Copperhead, put your first strike on the rendezvous cords I gave
you. You'll see the river bend there. It looks like an upside down U
pointed north. Walk your stuff from the north end of that bend
straight north in the direction of China Boy Two's smoke. Copy?"

Phil Travers said he copied and repeated his instructions. Spears
called Krocek and told him to pop smoke for the FAC.

"China Boy Two," Travers called, "I got a red."

Krocek acknowledged he had released red smoke. If the color had
been mentioned beforehand, any VC monitoring the frequency could
as easily have sent up the same color smoke to confuse the FAC.

"China Boy Two," Travers said, "I'll start the snakes on the riv-
erbank and work toward you. We'll hold the nape and 20 mike-mike
for a bit to see if you make contact and need it. Otherwise, as the
strike flight gets low on fuel, they'll expend. You copy?"

"Yah, Cobberhud, I copy," China Boy Two, Krocek, said. "We alreddy getting shod ad, so I'll take the soft stuff after the bombs when you reddy."

"That's some accent," Toby commented.

"Yeah. Czech, I guess," Phil answered.

For the next twenty minutes, three F-100's streaked and dived to release one bomb per pass onto points in the jungle marked by the FAC. Their engine sounds grew alternately louder and softer as they dived and zoomed. At full power on the pullouts, the sound could vibrate guts. To Spears, though he was only two kilometers away, the boom of each bomb was muffled and dulled by the thick jungle. Up in the clear air, the FAC heard them distinctly above his engine roar and felt them as a concussive *crack-boom* as they exploded. The helmeted strike pilots sitting astride an engine roaring out 15,000 pounds of thrust never heard ordnance go off.

Krocek marked his position for Copperhead and had him lay the strike flight's soft ordnance, the nape and 20-mike-mike, almost all around his party as they advanced in a ring of fire. The nape would detonate high in the trees, then cascade to the ground as a flaming waterfall. Most of the 20-mike-mike cracked off in the trees before reaching the ground. The 500-pound snake-eyes had blasted a 100-meter path from the riverbanks north toward the Americans. The strike pilots thought they were on another monkey-killing mission, until Phil Travers told them on Uniform what was happening under the jungle canopy. "They're up and awake," Jan had said, "they found us, they mad." The pilots worked much harder then, trying to be accurate in the fast-fading light.

As Spears and Krocek made their way from opposite directions to the rendezvous point in the near dark under the trees, Copperhead put in two more strikes for Krocek and Haskell. After working the FAC, Krocek came up on the radio to Spears.

"Shina Boy Tree, this is Two. You listenink?"

"Roger Two, this is Three. I hear you, Jan. How's it going?" Spears had heard the *pop-crack*'s of small-arms fire in the background over Krocek's radio.

"Preddy bad. We got four more down and id's geddink dark. I say four-five hours before we make the river. Vat you tink, we ged a Spoogy, yah?"

"I copy, Jan," Spears said. "We'll be at our side of the river in one more hour. And yeah, the *dai uy* here will request a Spooky."

Spooky was the call-sign of the pre–World War II USAF C-47 or DC-3 aircraft outfitted with three side-firing 7.62mm gatling-style miniguns hosing off 18,000 rounds per minute. Since each fifth round was a tracer, the bullet stream looked like a curving tongue coming down to lick the earth. The moaning roar of the three guns spooked the VC, who'd first thought it a fire-breathing dragon. Spooky was also referred to as Puff, the magic dragon, or just plain Puff. Spooky carried 24,000 rounds of 7.62mm (30-caliber) ammunition, 45 flares of 200,000 candlepower, and enough fuel to shoot and illuminate for hours. No SF camp or hamlet protected by Spooky all night had ever been overrun. As an armed C-47, its designation was AC-47.

Myers called Copperhead Zero Three to request all-night Spooky coverage. Within minutes Travers put the request in with Pawnee Control, the air strike request center at Tan Son Nhut, on his HF radio. Pawnee said they'd get back to him. Travers and Toby Parker put the last strike in for Krocek. In the gloom the napalm lit up the sky like a sunrise, so that even Lochert back at the LZ saw the glow.

"I know you hurdink them," Krocek radioed, "I hear them scream. But we loose two more. Haskell, he okay. You god Spoogy yed?"

"Spooky is inbound," Travers told Krocek. "Listen up this frequency, he'll call you. I'm about out of fuel and going to RTB. See you tomorrow, China Boy. Copperhead Zero Three out."

An hour later, in pitch blackness, Myers and Spears reached the south banks of the Song Be. Although they couldn't see it, the river was nearly a hundred feet across. It smelled and gurgled like some vast wild thing as it swept around the bends on both sides of them. They deployed their remaining Nungs at ten-foot intervals facing the opposite bank. Spears and Myers stayed together. They could hear sporadic firing coming from beyond the far shore to the North. Periodic reports from Krocek said they would make the rendezvous in about three hours, but he'd damn well better have Spooky. Shortly after that transmission, Spooky checked in.

"China Boy, China Boy, this is Spooky Eight One with flares and minis. Please mark your position and that of the VC." The whole jungle seemed to hold its breath as the pulsing drone of the twin-engined AC-47 propeller plane began to fill the air.

"Spoogy, Spoogy, this is Shina Boy, Shina Boy. You make flare, yah?"

"Ah, China Boy, we want China Boy Two. Put the American on, please."

Spears and Myers collapsed in muffled mirth, banging the ground with their fists. The Spooky pilot thought an indidge, a Nung, was using the radio.

"*Gottamm. Mudderfug. I yam de Hamerigan,*" Krocek yelled back, overmodulating his radio badly. Myers and Spears had to bite grass.

Lochert, monitoring everything, barked. And then started a series of Hail Mary's to help Krocek.

"I read you, China Boy," an amused voice responded. "Give us a mark."

At Krocek's side, Haskell found an opening in the trees and fired a pen-gun flare that shot a narrow red streak up to 300 feet.

"Roger on the flare, China Boy. Where are the bad guys?"

"All around," Haskell said, shouldering the radio pack and taking over from the still sputtering Krocek. "Light the place up so we can move faster, then we'll tell you where to shoot. We're too strung out now to tell where everybody is. By the way, Spooky, you got open clearance to shoot?"

Before he could expend, a Spooky pilot had to have clearance from 7th Air Force, the regional U.S. army commander, the regional ARVN commander, and the local province chief, who might be out for dinner. Unless, of course, somebody was shooting at Spooky. In that case he could return fire.

"Normally we don't need that up here in War Zone C, but, ah, China Boy, just to be safe, I did see a tracer shot at us." Haskell caught on and fired another pen-gun flare in the general direction of the orbiting gunship.

"Yup, very definitely," the Spooky pilot said when he saw the red streak. "We're being shot at, so, yeah, we're cleared to fire anytime you want. And here comes the first flare." A crack sounded high in the night air behind the AC-47 as a 200,000-candlepower flare ignited under its parachute and started its slow drift earthward, trailing a thick white stream of smoke. The jungle canopy over Krocek and Haskell lit up in brilliant black and white as Spooky orbited and dropped three more flares. Light filtering through the canopy illuminated the area enough for them to mass their troops, gather up their wounded, and plunge forward without grace or stealth. VC fire was coming at them from the rear and both sides.

"We're in trouble," Haskell transmitted. "They're trying to set up a blocking force between us and the river."

"Where do you want me to shoot?" Spooky asked again.

Krocek and Haskell conferred as they ran through the brush. Haskell fired two pen-gun flares up and forward of their position, but both red streaks were absorbed by limbs and leaves.

"Spears," Haskell yelled into the transmitter, "fire some flares across the river toward us. Spooky, tell me when you see them." Haskell was starting to puff from the effort.

Spears did as he was told. "Tallyho the flares," Spooky said.

"Good," Haskell puffed, "Start shooting at the north edge of the river and work north slowly. I'll tell you when you're close. Then orbit and shoot at that point till I tell you to move south again in front of us toward the river." No time to shack it up, Haskell had to transmit the plans in the clear.

From their vantage point, Myers and Spears watched the great tongues of fire start at the opposite bank and work away from them. To save ammo as he worked north, Spooky fired his guns on half speed at 3,000 rounds per minute in three-second bursts. Each burst dispatched 450 rounds. Spooky carried enough ammo to fire 160 such bursts. The loud snapping of twigs and branches told Myers not only how many 7.62mm bullets were raining down, but how many were being absorbed by the trees. About 75 percent, Myers estimated, were wasted.

Myers, Spears, and the Nungs waited, crouched in their shallow dugouts, for their oncoming teammates. Being on the south bank at the top of the inverted U of the Song Be River, they neither saw nor heard the VC around each bend on either side of them swimming across the river with their weapons held out of the water.

Wolf Lochert, well to the rear, idled away his time following the battle and studying his map by shielded flashlight. He stared, musing, at the river bends. Suddenly, he realized the VC commander probably had the same maps, and had most likely been following the action just as he had.

He nodded to himself and grabbed his microphone. He hesitated. So far, he hadn't had to break radio silence. As far as the VC knew, there were no troops securing the LZ. The river crossers' orders were probably to flank Myers and Spears, form pincers behind them, then advance together and close the trap on this side of the river while the rest of their forces did the same to Krocek and Haskell on the other side. Both American units would be trapped across from each other with their backs to the river. Small comfort. The Wolf knew what he had to do.

He stripped off all his nonessential gear—the smoke grenades, the water canteens—after taking a long drink, his harness. He needed to move fast, silently, and lightly. He stroked up his face and hands with his camouflage stick. Checked his stiletto, put his Mauser in his pocket. He thought for a moment, then chose the old reliable M-2 carbine over the M-16, inserted a twenty-round magazine in it, and strapped it across his back. He muffled four other magazines with sweat rags and stuffed them into his back pockets. He decided he couldn't carry the radio. He put his hand on the Nung interpreter, Vong Man Quay.

"Take this," he said. "Stay on frequency, but don't talk unless you are attacked. Hold this LZ at all costs. We will all return before first light. If we don't have a radio, my signal that it's us will be two rounds, pause, two rounds. You understand?''

"Sure, boss. I hold. No radio. You shoot two times, you shoot two times, I welcome you, *thiếu tá.*" The Nung's brown and battered face split in a toothy grin. Wolf slapped him on the arm and disappeared into the night.

Heading in the direction of Spooky's flares was not easy. Wolf's sight angle was too low on the horizon and the jungle too thick for him to see anything except an occasional glimpse of something bright when the flare had just been released and was still high in the sky. The sound of Spooky's guns gave the Wolf his best bearing. The three 7.62 miniguns, each with five rotating barrels firing gatling-gun-style, detonated the cartridges so fast that the individual explosions overrode each other, producing a moaning roar that increased with intensity as the barrels got up to speed, then ceased abruptly as the pilot released the trigger. The barrel noise combined with the amplifying effect inside the fuselage of the internal gun noise made the overall effect sound to the distant Wolf like the hellish purr of an unearthly giant sky cat.

Between silent curses as he fought the clutching jungle vines and thorns, the Wolf grinned, thinking that whoever had coined the old saw about "ride to the sound of the guns" could never have envisioned this most basic ground movement, walking in a crouch, to the sound of the most modern death-dealing technology. He pushed on faster, realizing that for the moment, anyhow, he would have to sacrifice stealth for speed if he was to reach Spears and Myers before the VC closed the pincer this side of the river.

Forward of Wolf, beyond Spears and Myers, directly underneath Spooky's fiery tongue, some of the younger VC, the fifteen-year-olds, thought the intermittent roars were the moans of the death dragon. The older sergeants soon disabused them of that superstition as they goaded them to press and close with the flanks of the fleeing Krocek and Haskell, promising them that if they got as close as they wanted, they would be inside Spooky's protective umbrella. As it was, Spooky's flares helped them every bit as much as the men they were chasing and trying to kill. The creamy yellow light filtered through the jungle canopy as gray, setting a surrealist stage with greens turned black and white. On the stage, screams and shouts in English, Chinese, and Vietnamese were punctuated by frantic long and short bursts of automatic weapons fire at anything that moved.

Occasionally, single shots and rapidly fired groups of two or three indicated that the shooter might have a positive target.

The running battle continued for another hour, until the Americans had almost run underneath Spooky's withering fire. "Stop shooting. Spooky, stop shooting," Haskell yelled on the radio, still crashing through the jungle, Krocek at his heels, the Nungs scattered to hell and gone, but still fighting. Spooky's guns stopped immediately, leaving blackness behind. The top of the fiery tongue slid down the fiery trail like the end of a garden hose stream as its source is cut off.

Spooky's navigator, who was on his first mission, suspected the cease-fire order was a VC trick. "Authenticate Lima November," he cut in on the radio, asking Haskell to prove his identity.

"I can't," Haskell shot back. "What the hell you think"—Haskell had to pause for breath—"I'm doing down here?" Pause again. "Reading my code book?"

Then he recognized the calm and unhurried voice of the pilot, the man in the left seat sighting the guns and pushing the trigger button on his control column, who said, "No sweat, China Boy, we read you. We know who you are."

"How far to the river from your last burst?" Haskell asked. He had to hold the handset cord close so it wouldn't snag as he rushed through the brush trying to talk and run at the same time.

"About 150 or 200 meters," the Spooky copilot said.

"All right," Haskell said, "when I fire my pen-gun, you fire one last burst directly in front, then shoot the hell out of both flanks from the flare to the river. Make us road sides of cover fire. We gonna run like hell down that road. Got that?"

Spooky rogered. Haskell fired his pen-gun through the canopy in the direction of travel, then he and Krocek took off faster than before. Their interpreter translated and yelled to run like hell to the others.

"Haskell," Spears radioed from the far bank, "I saw your flare. You're close. You're doing great. Come on, come on. Follow the flare." Myers fired a pen-gun flare.

Under the urging of Krocek and Haskell, the beleaguered force made a massive effort and gained the north bank of the Song Be River. The two men conferred briefly and decided on a plan.

"Spooky, Spears, here's what we are going to do," Haskell radioed. "Jan is setting up a rearguard action while I get the guys in the river swimming to your position, George. When Jan is ready to jump into the water he'll tell us over the radio and fire a flare. At that point, Spooky, you hose down everything on the north side of the river." Haskell got an acknowledgement and handed the radio back to Krocek, who was lying prone, firing intermittent bursts with his M-16 back the way they had come. Haskell urged, pushed, cajoled and kicked the reluctant Nungs to drop all their equipment except their M-16's and take to the water. As the last one went in, he yelled back to Jan to disengage and follow. Haskell left his boots on, held his rifle high, and waded into the current.

Up over the edge of the bank, Krocek saw furtive movement and fired two quick bursts. He rolled over on his back and fired his pen-gun flare in the same direction. Then he jumped up, grabbed the radio, ran to the water's edge, and began to transmit as he waded out. When the water reached his waist, he stopped to keep the radio dry. He didn't see the rifleman crawl up to the edge of the embankment he had just left.

"Spoogy, Spoogy, shood, shood—" he said, then fell dead with a bullet in his skull. The radio pack pulled him down as the current rolled his body downstream. Haskell, looking back from midstream, saw everything by flare light. He hadn't had time to shout a warning.

Spooky's guns opened up on full fire, spraying the area with 300 slugs a second.

Hearing Spooky firing full out, Wolf Lochert guessed the men were swimming the river. He stopped to listen after a long burst, heard faint sounds in front of him, and slowly crept forward, his M-2 unslung, the safety off. He stopped again. Cocking his head he heard the sound of several men moving through the brush about ten meters in front of him. He estimated he was about 100 meters from Spears and Myers. Wolf slung his carbine and pulled out his stiletto. In five minutes he advanced thirty feet without making a sound. During another pause in firing, he heard enough to know he was close. He crouched and by looking to one side was able to discern the outline of a figure facing away from him and toward the position of Spears and Myers. He started stalking him until the next new flare yielded enough light to grab his mouth, pull him backward into an upraised knee, and reach around to slide the stiletto upwards through his belly into his heart. The man went down without a sound. As he crept forward, Wolf put away one more in the same manner. A third, off to one side, heard some noise and came to investigate. A distant but suddenly bright flare illumination revealed the two men to each other. The VC started firing immediately as the Wolf dropped his stiletto and dove into the closest thicket, trying frantically to unsling his carbine.

Myers had gathered everyone from the river and started south. They all went down when they heard the shots in front of them. But Wolf knew they needed to have more warning than merely some unexplained shots.

"*Ambush, ambush,*" he bellowed into the darkness. From under a thicket of thorns Wolf shot the figure in black pajamas looking for him. He retrieved his stiletto. "Hey, Tom. It's me, Lochert. There's some people here trying to schnitzel you guys. You hear me?"

"Yeah, we're right here." Myers's voice sounded close. After Spears had rounded up Haskell and all the Nungs on the south bank, he had resumed command for the treck south back to the LZ. He had heard Krocek's radio go dead and gotten the rest of the story from Haskell. There was no recourse. They couldn't recover Krocek's body, so Myers had painfully given the order to move south to the LZ. Thinking they were in the clear, he hadn't expected opposition until the Wolf yelled at him.

"Stay put, Wolf, we're moving to your location," Myers yelled back. His men unslung their guns but didn't need them as they advanced to meet Lochert. After a few words, they started south in the darkness. The Nungs rubbed phosphorescent moss on one another's backs to keep better visual contact. Spears worked the radio, keeping Spooky informed of their progress and where to shoot, but he didn't have definite targets because the situation remained strangely quiet as they drew close to the LZ. Finally, Spooky called down and said he had to RTB for ammo. Spears thanked him for all his help, gave him an estimated BDA, and cleared him outbound. As the party approached the LZ, Wolf got Vong Man Quay, the Nung he'd left in charge, to acknowledge they were inbound and would not shoot.

Once at the LZ, Myers deployed the Nungs, with Haskell and Spears as perimeter defense. Wolf forced himself not to take command, as he wasn't on the scene for that reason. He felt rather proud of himself. However, had he not agreed with Myers's plans, he would have taken command. Instantly.

Myers told him about Krocek. Though the Wolf said nothing, he was, in fact, saying a Latin prayer for the dead. The jungle was silent and black without Spooky. Myers noted it would be first light in less than two hours. The men took turns dozing.

Forty minutes later the VC sprang the perimeter defense alarms and attacked in force.

15

☆

That the 531st was designated the action squadron to cover developing events in War Zone C almost caused Sergeant First Class James P. Mahoney to blow Ramrod's head off. No one had remembered to tell him that 10 feet of inquisitive snake periodically hung from the rafters to check out visitors to the 531st squadron building. When the startled sergeant jumped sideways and swung his M-16 into position, Court Bannister barely had time to yell and grab the gun barrel. White-faced, Mahoney cursed, then laughed. Ramrod retracted himself back up, and silently went about his business cruising the rafters.

"It was on safety," Mahoney said, looking at his M-16. Fresh blood started to seep from under the bandages on his right arm.

"Oh hell, Jim," Bannister said. "I'm sorry. You want to go back to Long Binh and have someone look at that?"

"Nah," Mahoney said, "let's get on with it. Captain Myers and those guys are in deep kimchi. Are the radios all set up?"

"Yeah," Bannister said, leading him past the operations counter to the map room, where a Mark-128 radio pallet was set up on half of the big plywood plotting table. Power cables ran through the window to a generator in a small trailer attached to a Mark-151 commo jeep provided by Base Communications.

"Not bad," Mahoney said. "Considering you only had a few

hours to get ready." Mahoney himself had just been rousted out of the 3rd Surgical Hospital at Long Binh by the C Team commander and had been jeeped over to Bien Hoa Air Base.

The new ops officer of the 531st, Bob Derham, had gotten Court out of bed at five in the morning, saying there was an ops emergency involving the Mike Force up in War Zone C, and as their contact he'd better shag ass to the squadron and set up contingency plan War Zone Charley Three.

War Zone Charley Three was part of a new concept whereby each F-100 squadron had several Special Forces camps and areas assigned to them for special protection. The pilots were required to familiarize themselves with each camp from the air and, if feasible, on the ground. Which was precisely why Bannister had gone on patrol with the Mike Force. The object was to gain intimate knowledge of the camp and the surrounding terrain, enabling the strike pilots to provide air support under adverse conditions such as bad weather and loss of radio contact. If radio contact was lost, the SF men would light off a series of greasy rags stuffed in cans nailed to a ten-foot arrow set to swivel on a three-foot pole. They would point the flaming arrow at the heaviest enemy concentration. The F-100 pilots were trained to obliterate anything 100 meters beyond the camp in the direction the flaming arrow pointed. Because Bannister had run in the woods with the Mike Force, Rawson had made him project officer as an extra duty, thinking the whole scheme a waste of time. The new regime had seen no reason to change Rawson's orders.

An eight-by-ten-foot map composed of 1:250,000 aeronautical charts of South Vietnam was shellacked to one wall of the map room. Six pilots, each with a mug of coffee, most with a cigarette, were studying the grease-pencil marks at XT424680 where last contact had been made with the China Boys. Among them were Jack Laird, Doug Fairchild, and Bob Derham, out to see how the plan for his squadron would develop. K. L. Jones was down from Wing. Crowded into the room with them were representatives from weather, intelligence, maintenance, and armaments. Court began to brief.

"Good morning, gentlemen. Glad to see everybody looking so bright-eyed and bushy-tailed." The men groaned. "This is Sergeant Jim Mahoney, who was extracted out of the area last night. He is going to monitor the operation and provide liaison with the Army."

The pilots looked with unabashed awe at Mahoney, standing there in his freshly washed but faded tiger suit, green beret mashed down over one eye, arm in a sling, newly bloodied bandage. Almost as wide as he was tall, his close-cropped curly blond hair framed his map-of-Ireland face. Mahoney nodded and with a puckish grin made the sign of the cross, saying, "FAC, TAC, and napalm." The pilots grinned approval, and several gave him a thumbs-up. Outside, the roar of afterburners vibrated the room. Bannister glanced at his watch and waited until the noise subsided.

"It's ten past six," he said. "We go on War Zone Charley alert status at six-thirty. What you just heard were the primary alert birds. They'll be over the target area seconds before first light to meet up with Copperhead Zero Nine. He's been on station since Spooky left. It looks like a VC regiment has the China Boys surrounded. One of the four Americans is believed dead, body not recovered; and seventeen of the thirty-three Nungs are dead or wounded. We need to cover their exfiltration. To do it we have six dedicated birds with mixed hard and soft loads of MK-82 500-pound low-drags, high-drag snakes, CBU, napalm, and of course 800 rounds of 20-mike-mike each. Maintenance says they can turn the birds around in twenty minutes between sorties."

The maintenance officer nodded. "If you don't bring them back broke or full of holes," he said. Bannister continued.

"Some early-morning fog has burned off, and the weather looks good for the rest of the day. So far, no heavy ground fire has been reported. Isn't that right?" Bannister looked at the weather and intelligence officers.

"High scattered to broken at 25,000; visibility eight to ten in haze; temp 90 to 95; humidity the same; the usual late-afternoon thunderstorms. There is a stationary front out over the Gulf of Thailand, but it won't affect us today," the weather briefer said. The officer from the intelligence shop stepped up.

"Outside of that Dash-K that came up two days ago, we have no reports of anything heavier than small arms," he said. "But we think there are more of those Dash-K 12.7's in the area, so be on the lookout. By the way, if they use tracers, they are green. Friendly tracers are red or amber."

"It's pleasant to know whether your friends or enemies are shooting at you," Fairchild quipped.

"With the Mark-128 radio," Bannister said, pointing to the pallet, "we have five radios. Uniform for contact with the strike fighters, two Fox Mikes for FAC and ground troop contact, an HF with secure voice capability, and a VHF. Sergeant Mahoney will now bring you up to date as to the ground situation."

Mahoney pointed with his left hand to the 1:50,000 ground maps pinned up on the aeronautical charts and told the group what had taken place so far. Each pilot entered the details on his own maps and sketched out the LZ layout on the back of his mission card.

"The thing to watch for is our Huey gunships and Dustoffs orbiting around trying to lay down fire and get in the LZ. Hopefully the FAC will keep everything under control and we'll get everybody out and have a snake fry tonight, right?" Mahoney concluded his briefing. Bannister told the pilots of the incident at the door with Ramrod, then asked his boss, Major Derham, if he had any comments or questions. Derham said no. Bannister posted the flight lineup.

CALL SIGN	NAME	ACFT	LOAD	ALERT
RR 20	Laird	627	hi drag/nape	cockpit
RR 21	Fairchild	741	lo drag/cbu	cockpit
RR 25	Nabors	811	hi drag/nape	5 min
RR 26	Taylor	762	lo drag/cbu	5 min
RR 28	Derham	523	hi drag/nape	10 min
RR 29	Jones	398	lo drag/cbu	10 min

After filling out their mission cards, the pilots moved to the PE room to get their equipment: G-suits, survival vests, pistol belts, helmets, map bags, and backpack parachutes—over fifty pounds in all. Because of the heat they would not don their gear until after preflighting their airplane. Each stopped by the refrigerator, drank heavily from the water bottle, then took from the freezer his own two plastic baby bottles full of frozen water and placed them in small bags sewn to their parachute harnesses. The heat was such that the ice would melt by the time they got to the runway. Each pilot would drink one bottle before takeoff, the other sometime during the flight. Bladder control was no problem, since they sweated out far more than they took in. Doc Russell had calculated that from start to finish of a mission, the average pilot lost a quart of water, causing a weight loss of two pounds.

All six pilots went out to their airplanes. After performing their preflight inspection, Laird and Fairchild suited up and took their places in their F-100's parked side by side with umbrellas rigged to shield the cockpits from the sun. An aircraft skin temperature of 165° was enough to fry an egg. The five-minute alert pilots sat under one airplane in the shade. Derham and Jones returned to the briefing room in time to hear Copperhead Zero Nine calling.

"Ramrod Control, this is Copperhead Zero Nine, how do you read on Uniform?"

"Five by, Copperhead Zero Nine, this is Ramrod Control. How do you read us?" Bannister transmitted.

"Five by five, Ramrod. We have negative contact with China Boy since 0532 this morning, when they said they had heavy troops in contact and were about to be overrun. As a result of the TIC, I had no place to put in the alert birds, so I turned them over to Horn direct air support center for their use. You copy?"

"Roger, copy, go ahead," Bannister said.

"And we have a new situation up here," Zero Nine said. "There is an armored column, call sign Rover, from the First Infantry Division heading north on Route 13 about fifteen klicks east of China Boy. I think China Boy prematurely sprung the ambush the VC had set up for them, but the bad guys have attacked anyhow, in force. Also, nobody told me the First Division was sending anybody up here. Did you guys know about that?"

"Negative," Bannister transmitted. "I'll see what I can find out from MACV." He cut off to tell Mahoney to raise MACV on the HF radio. "Meanwhile, do you have a fix on the VC attacking the column?"

"Roger, they're all over the place, on both sides of the road. Copperhead Zero Three is on it. If I can't raise China Boy, I'd like to have your alert birds sent to him. Can you cut that?"

"What do you think?" Bannister asked Mahoney, who said sure, use the F-100's as long as China Boy wasn't on the air.

"Roger, Zero Nine, we'll send them to Zero Three, but you can have them back anytime you need them. Meantime you orbit China Boy's last position listening and looking for ground panels, or anything else they might signal with," Bannister said. Zero Nine rogered and said he'd be standing by on this frequency for future calls from Ramrod Control.

Mahoney found the command call sign for the 1st Infantry Division in the squadron codebook.

"Slingshot, Slingshot," he called on HF, "this is Ramrod Control. Do you read?"

Slingshot answered immediately and wanted to know exactly who Ramrod was, why they were on command frequency, and to preface their answer by authenticating Tango Zulu.

Mahoney authenticated and asked Slingshot if they could go secure voice on single-side band, known as SSB. Both stations went secure voice and Mahoney informed Slingshot that their armored column headed to Route 13 was in deep kimchi and he, Ramrod Control, had the TAC air to bail them out. Army Sergeant Mahoney was obviously relishing his position as an authoritative Air Force voice on an Army HF command net.

"Stand by, Ramrod," Slingshot said. Two minutes passed before the response came. "Ramrod, Slingshot. Roger, we will take all you've got. Have your FAC contact Rover on 48.35 on Fox Mike. And Ramrod, Slingshot Chief says not to worry. A couple hours ago he ordered the 195th Light Infantry Brigade to get some people into the China Boy LZ and get the Mike Force out. You concentrate on Rover. Copy?"

"Roger, Slingshot. Rover on 48.35 and 195th due in. What's their ETA?" Bannister responded, impressed that Slingshot Chief—Major General Dupuy in charge of the 1st Division—was taking a personal interest.

"Ramrod, the 195th is on four-hour alert status, they'll be in position any time now. Copy?"

Bannister said he copied and they both went off the air to maintain a listening watch on the Slingshot command frequency.

"Balls," Mahoney said. "I wish it was the 199th going in there. The 195th has got bad command problems."

By noon, Copperhead Zero Three and Zero Nine, spelling each other on station, had put in 18 sets of fighters, a total of 43 airplanes, for the armored column, Task Force Rover. The column, composed of Troops B and C of the 1st Squadron with M48A3 tanks, M132 flamethrowers, and various M113 tracks, was stretched out over a half mile of highway, cut into three segments like a chopped-up angleworm as elements of the 9th Viet Cong Division worked them over on Route 13.

The armored unit was there under a plan originated by the 1st Division to provoke an ambush at one of five suspected sites. By provoking an ambush, the tankers hoped to deplete both VC troops and the VC desire to mess further with traffic on the road. The idea was to keep Route 13 open from Saigon to Loc Ninh. That the Mike Force would spring the VC attack earlier than expected was not part of the contingencies listed in the basic Task Force Rover plan.

At the sound of the first B-40 round fired by the VC into his column, the commander of Task Force Rover, a lieutenant colonel, instantly gave the signal for his vehicles to button up, pivot, and face alternately outward in a herringbone pattern and shoot everything they could in a reflexive counteraction "mad minute" to shock the ambushing Charlie. The herringbone also afforded visual and weapon coverage of each vehicle's dead spots.

The 1st Platoon took the main thrust of the hasty area ambush. The commander of the lead tank was killed, the scout section was blasted out of action, and the platoon sergeant took over when the platoon leader was wounded. Canister round after canister round fired from the M48A3's 90mm guns tore into enemy positions, shredding as many tree limbs and branches as bodies. But the heavy fire kept Charlie's head down and made rising up to fire a rocket-propelled grenade a chancy thing. The lieutenant colonel looked over the situation, ordered Troop B into a better position to relieve the beleaguered 1st Platoon, and gave more air strike information to Copperhead Zero Nine.

Because no contact had been made with China Boy, Bannister released the War Zone Charley Three birds to fly two sorties each to support Task Force Rover. No one from the 195th had checked in, and repeated calls by Mahoney to Slingshot brought no news as to its whereabouts or how long it would be before they went to look for the overrun China Boys.

At 1230, Bob Derham entered the makeshift command post and pulled Bannister to one side.

"Court," he said, "do you have a relative named Shawn Bannister?"

"Yeah, he's a relative," Bannister responded, not really wanting to spell out the half-brother relationship. He knew Shawn was in-country but had made no attempt to see him. They had never gotten along.

"Well, the Wing public information officer called and said he's here on base with some high-powered credentials. Seems he got wind of the lost Mike Force troops and wants to do a story for the *California Sun* on how the Air Force participates in such a situation."

Bannister shrugged. "Sure, fine. But if he's got credentials, you don't need to check with me."

"That's just it. He wants to fly with you. The PIO at Seventh Air Force has General Momyer's enthusiastic approval. They think it would be great publicity."

Bannister, hands on hips, faced away from Derham and blew out an exasperated puff of air.

"Look," Derham said, "no pilot of mine has to fly with any

newsie if he doesn't want to, regardless of what Seventh Air Force says. Say the word, I'll tell the PIO to forget it."

Bannister knew if he refused to fly with Shawn, he'd be putting Bob Derham in an awkward position. "Send him down," he said. "I'll fly with him."

Bannister returned to Ramrod Control and the makeshift command post. For the next three hours, he and Mahoney were totally wrapped up in coordinating air support—adjusting weapons loading to the battle condition while monitoring the progress of the ground battle around the armored column. Flight after flight of F-100's from Bien Hoa and Tan Son Nhut had put in Mark-82's, CBU, and napalm against the VC trying to obliterate Rover. Some green tracer had been observed far to the west vainly reaching out for the attacking fighters. Two F-100's with snakes and nape shut it up.

"That Dash-K was firing from about the cords where Spears and Haskell ran into all that stuff," Mahoney said.

"Right," Bannister replied. "I think our guys screwed up the ambush timetable, so they couldn't get the gun in position in time. The VC showed damn poor discipline, firing so early. And with tracers at that. They're usually better."

"Yeah, well," Mahoney said, pointing at Bannister with the microphone in his hand, "Frying up a few of those gook motherfuckers teaches fire discipline in a big hurry."

The brilliant glare of a flashbulb filled the room as a voice said, "Excellent quote, sergeant. Where are you from?"

Both men turned to see Shawn Bannister in the doorway, down on one knee refocusing his Hasselblad 500EL. He wore a khaki safari suit and a floppy jungle hat with matches and what looked like marijuana roaches stuck in the band. Behind him stood the Wing PIO and his assistant. Next to them was Charmaine. Major Derham was off to one side. The flash unit went off again, galvanizing Mahoney into advancing on Shawn Bannister snarling something about seeing how far he could stuff that camera up his nose sideways.

Gasping and elbowing forward past Major Derham, the 3rd Tactical Fighter Wing public information officer, an older, rheumy lieutenant colonel, said to Mahoney, "Here, now. Don't you know who this is?"

The map of Ireland turned red as Mahoney's eyes bulged with fury. Clearly, he was en route to tear out the throat of the obstructing colonel to get at his tormentor with the flash camera, whose own face started to get a bit white.

"Oh, hell," Bannister said, half laughing as he slid in front of

Mahoney, "what the sergeant means is he's delighted to have this opportunity to converse with members of the great American press so he can tell them factually in a few words exactly what he thinks of this war."

Derham, hands on hips, wide grin on his face, spoke up. "Colonel, if you'll bring Mr. Shawn Bannister out here, we'll get this situation cleared up." The lieutenant colonel, apologizing profusely to Mr. Shawn Bannister, pushed him out of the map room with fluttering hands. Captain Correlli, the assistant PIO, a man with a pockmarked, street-wise face, winked at Court Bannister and Jim Mahoney as he followed. Major Derham said he'd see about getting Shawn suited up for the flight. Charmaine remained standing in the doorway. Her style of dress, a red linen miniskirt and a lightweight white cotton T-shirt, reflected the latest trend. It was obvious she did not wear a brassiere. On her feet were tan sandals with gold cords tied around her ankles.

"Hello, Court," she said. "I haven't seen you in a sweaty flight suit since we were stationed at Luke. How have you been?"

"This is Jim Mahoney," Court Bannister said to his former wife, ignoring her question, "and he likes to eat newsies. Or can't you tell?"

"You do know I'm not with the press, don't you?" she said to the Green Beret sergeant.

"Oh, yes, indeed, ma'am. You are definitely not one of those. No, indeed," Mahoney said, making a good attempt at a gallant bow while taking in her great legs and unfettered breasts. Charmaine extended her hand to shake his. For a minute Mahoney looked as if he was going to kiss it. He grinned, thought to hell with all these officers, and did exactly that.

Charmaine trilled a genuinely pleased laugh. "I'm so pleased to meet you, sergeant," she said. "Damn few gentlemen around here, wouldn't you say?"

"Damn few," Mahoney echoed, captivated.

A speaker crackled as one of the Copperheads called Ramrod Control requesting the arrival time of the next flight. Mahoney said he'd take it. Court escorted Charmaine to a corner in the ops room. Pilots walking to and from their airplanes, laden with flight gear, looked appreciatively at her from the corners of their eyes.

"I heard you were in-country with the Hope show." He pulled out a Lucky and lit it.

"Did you see it?"

"No time," he said.

"You quit smoking in Phoenix," she said. "When did you start again?"

"Here," he said, waving the cigarette in a circular motion.

"Do you still listen to opera?"

"Of course."

"And what happened to the test-pilot school? I heard from Sam you were accepted. He was so proud and happy. I thought you wanted to be an astronaut. Why did you turn it down?"

"I didn't turn it down, I merely put it off for a year."

"I don't understand. Why did you do that?" she asked.

"I did it so I could come here." He waved his cigarette in the all-encompassing circle.

Charmaine sighed, then assumed a bright expression on her face. "Court, you haven't asked, but yes, thank you, kind sir, I'm fine. Fine and dandy. My career is going again and I'm deliriously happy. Well, mostly happy." She swayed her hips. "I do miss you, you know. We were good together."

"In bed," he said.

"Yes, in bed." She frowned. "I guess that's all we remember, isn't it?"

Court stepped back. He felt a more than faint stirring in his loins. It had been a long, long time since he had bedded anything, and an erection in the standard USAF K-2B flight suit was about as concealable as a tent pole.

"Look," he said, "you're a good kid and all that, but I'm busy. Go find that newsie half bro of mine, and get on with your life."

"With him?" she said, deliberately misreading his statement, "not a chance."

"Why not? He'd be good for your career," he said with a derisive snort.

"Damn you. You used to be a lot nicer than that," she said.

"Didn't we all. Why are you running around with him, then?" he said.

"I'm not *running around* with him. He's showing me the war. I get to see and do things I never could with the Hope troupe. Besides, it's nearly impossible for a single girl to get around Vietnam without an escort."

"So okay," Court said, moving away. "Come with me." He checked the flying schedule, then brought her to PE, where the rheumy lieutenant colonel was watching Shawn get outfitted.

"We takeoff in one hour, at 1700," Court said to him. "Meet you in the map room as soon as you are finished here." He walked out as his half brother flashed his dazzling grin, more reminiscent of Silk Screen Sam Bannister than any smile Court could ever muster.

"At the ambush this morning, the armored column was cut into three sections," Court began the briefing. He showed Shawn the battle situation and explained the tactical plans for the elements to join up and fight their way out. Shawn took pictures of Court and his briefing map.

"I came here because of the missing SF troops," Shawn said, "not because of an attack on some tank heads."

"They're still missing," Court replied.

"Aren't they in the same general area as the armor?"

"Yes."

"Then why hasn't someone gone to get them, using your F-100's as cover?" Shawn asked.

"Someone is going."

"*Is* going? Who? When?" Shawn asked.

"The 195th Light Infantry Brigade, as soon as possible."

"I heard they were due there," Shawn looked at his watch, "four or five hours ago. Why the delay?"

"Let's fly," Court Bannister said to his half brother, well aware of the unacceptable delay. Court and Jim Mahoney had yet to get a response from Slingshot, but that was an in-house military problem, not something that he would share with a newsie. He led the way as they walked out of the squadron. Charmaine, who had followed them and listened to the exchange, remained behind with the PIO lieutenant colonel. The PIO captain went with the flyers.

Court assisted his crew chief in attaching the four seat straps, the G-suit hose, and radio wires to Shawn and his equipment in the backseat of the F-100F. He checked all the connections and had Shawn repeat the ejection and ground egress procedures one more time. A panicked passenger could sit and burn during a survivable ground incident if he didn't have the automatic reflexes necessary to unhook and unstrap from all his links to the cockpit. He then showed Shawn where to set his oxygen regulator, which could supply 100% oxygen to help stave off motion sickness, and how to press the button on the throttle to talk on the intercom. He made sure his half brother had a barf bag tucked under one leg.

"Don't touch anything else unless you want to eject," Court said.

"Just this," Shawn said, tapping his camera.

Court climbed in front, started the engine, got his wing man checked in, received clearance, and taxied from the revetment. Correlli watched them go. He had taken over forty black and whites of the two half brothers during the preflights.

"Here's the situation," Copperhead Zero Three radioed Court and his wingman, call signs Ramrod 43 and 44. "You can see down there, three elements have linked up and are closing with the fourth to the east. Once they are together, they will keep going east to the main highway as far as they can before dark."

Court had his two planes in orbit at 13,000 feet, Ramrod 44 in trail. Each carried bombs and napalm. They could see the curving road and its burned and blasted vehicles, some still smoking, mixed with tracks threading their way west, smoke spurting from barrels as they fought. Some time before the jungle forest had been cleared back from the road about a hundred feet on each side to expose ambush sites. That the VC attacked at this open spot instead of farther east, where the vegetation all but smothered the road, confirmed that the ambush had been prematurely sprung by Spears and Krocek. Small fires burned in and around that area on both sides from VC fighting positions that had been drenched by the M132 flamethrowers. Several bomb craters extended from the cleared areas into the jungle. The whole scene, as had others before, reminded Court of World War II movies. From over two miles high, he couldn't see any moving figures. He heard Copperhead transmit.

"Ramrods, I'll put some smoke in on each side of the clearing of the westernmost position. Each of you take a side and put your bombs in one at a time along the tree line. Then we'll do the same with nape in the clearing, only closer to the road. Make your runs New York to Oregon. Copy?"

"Roger, copy," Court said. "Set 'em up, Ramrod," he added, telling his wingman it was time to set up his armament switches. "You take the south side." Court had seen the wind from the south blow smoke over the road and into the treeline to the north. He allowed his less-experienced wingman to make his passes in the clear while he made his in the smoke-obscured north edge of the clearing.

Phil Travers had set up the overall pattern so the attacking aircraft would make their passes parallel to the friendlies, a Standard Operating Procedure designed to prevent long or short releases from impacting on friendly troops. He also had them pull west from their runs into the sun, blinding the gunners who came up to shoot as planes would pull off. The experienced gunners knew better than to shoot at the diving fighters, because the pilots zooming down head-on could quickly spot the muzzle flashes.

Travers had Parker from the backseat read off the wind direction and velocity, altimeter setting, target elevation, ground fire report, backup radio frequency, and safe bailout heading and distance. Parker had been along on every flight with the blessings of Colonel Norman, who knew the battle was joined and thought it good experience for his courier to see first-hand what was happening.

"Lead's in, New York to Seattle, FAC in sight," Court called, rolling in on his first bomb run from east to west. Travers cleared him, then his wingman. As they alternately made their passes, Shawn took pictures through the side of the canopy as Court would bottom out from his run. He thought he could see figures running around, jumping from hole to hole. He listened to the radio chatter. "Two's in . . . Clear . . . FAC in sight . . . Nice bomb . . . Lead, put your second on the gomers 50 meters east of your first bomb. . . ."

"Nicely done, gentlemen," Travers said after the flight had put in their bombs. "Hold high and dry for a spell while I talk to these Rover guys and see where they need the nape and CBU." In a few minutes he came back on.

"Listen up, Ramrods. They're ready to punch through and join up, but they've spotted a bunch of VC to the east they think are waiting for them. Put your nape right where I mark, Lead. Two, you hold your CBU till I see how lead does." Travers rolled in and marked. Court made his calls and rolled in from 5,000 feet. He concentrated on attaining the parameters for napalm delivery. He set up his switches, dialed 75 mils depression in his gunsight pipper, lowered the nose to achieve 10 degrees' dive angle as verified by his attitude indicator, adjusted his throttle to attain 400 knots indicated airspeed, cross-checked altitude as he approached release height, maintained a slight crosswind compensation that he would kick out at the last second, and watched his pipper drift up to the target. As he got lower he suddenly saw several black-pajama–clad figures jump from a bomb crater and start running parallel to the road as if to reach a better shelter from what they knew was coming.

"Got those gomers?" Travers yelled. "Get 'em."

Bannister didn't have time to answer as he concentrated on the figures growing larger in his view through the gunsight. In split seconds he rapidly crosschecked his parameters. When he couldn't look in the cockpit any more, and when he knew it was right and the figures were huge in his gunsight, he thumbed the pickle button, and felt the *chung-chung* under each wing as the release cartridges kicked the two 750-pound cans of napalm free of the airplane to tumble to the ragged earth and splash burning jellied gasoline over the running figures. The imprint stayed on Court's eyeballs as he climbed and jinked away. This was the closest Court had ever been to the enemy, and as he positioned himself according to Travers's orders for strafe, he kept seeing the running figures over and over again.

On his first strafe run between the VC position and the road, he pulled out low and saw the blackened figures tumbled and coiled amidst the lowering flames from the fire-soaked earth. He counted eleven. He was strangely thankful for the g-force and the wild rocking as he jinked extra hard to avoid whatever groundfire might remain. But he still saw the eleven running figures.

He strafed, pass after pass, cannons roaring, in tandem with his wingman, who had put his CBU in, strafing where Parker told them. Travers was getting second-to-second battle information from Rover, who had marshaled all his tracks and had indeed punched through to join up with his last cutoff element with all guns and tubes blazing in the gathering dusk. Everybody smelled blood and victory.

"Shit hot. Shit hot," Parker was shouting over the UHF to the fighter pilots as he monitored Travers's running conversation with the Troop's tank commander on FM. "They're linked up. Rover's all joined up."

Court and his wingman were fired out—Winchester, they called it. They orbited lower than normal, at 5,000 feet, to see the final flicker of flames and the eerie tongues of fire from the flame gun as Rover consolidated its position for the night. Copperhead Zero Three read off their bomb damage assessment—their BDA—and said that Rover was going to recover their dead and hold position for the night. Tomorrow they would punch out and rejoin their parent unit.

"Any word from China Boy?" Court asked.

"Negative," came the laconic reply.

Court now had time for his half brother in the backseat. Many times during the mission he had told Shawn to shut up when he tried to speak. He was aware that Shawn had become sick several passes back. Finally Court let him talk.

Sputtering and cursing, spitting into the barf bag, Court's half brother said, "Those were civilians. You just napalmed eleven civilians. I counted them. They must have been from an old bus I saw tumbled in the ditch. You killed civilians, you son of a bitch."

Court heard him as he looked down from his orbit. The sun, bloated and low on the horizon, sent reflecting rays into the smoke and dust, its golden spikes pinning burned-out vehicles to the road.

"Oh yeah? Well, let me show you something." Court said. He

told Travers and his wingman he was going to make a BDA pass, then savagely racked the F-100 into position for a dangerous low-altitude, low-airspeed pass. "Get your fucking camera ready, Shawn," Court said as he lined up to follow the road where the burned-out and holed American vehicles lay scattered about like toys in a sandbox. He flattened out from his dive, eased the throttle back to maintain 300 knots and followed the road, viciously banking the plane from side to side, saying "There" and "There" and "There," as he pointed a wing at the burned and punctured hulls of the American vehicles, many with blackened bodies and parts of bodies hanging from turrets and scattered on the ground.

"Here's your fucking bus," he said, dipping a wing over a crumpled M113 tracked vehicle modified to be a rolling command post. Blackened burn spots from where B-40 rocket-propelled grenades had holed the upper hull were spaced in a way that might appear as windows to the untrained eye. Shawn Bannister remained silent.

Court chandelled up from the carnage, signaled his wingman into position, checked out with Copperhead Zero Three, and headed home. Twenty minutes later, as last light faded, the two F-100's landed in perfect formation at Bien Hoa.

16

☆

Court taxied his F-100F into the revetment, obeying hand signals from his crew chief. The roar and hiss of the jet engine reverberated through the enclosed space as he swung the plane around to face outward. The scoop-nose bobbed as he braked the big fighter to a halt, stopcocked the throttle, and raised the canopy in quick-flowing motions resulting from long practice. Hearing returned to normal as the J-57 engine spooled down. The crew chief quickly slung two pairs of yellow wooden chocks around the main wheels, then hung a 10-foot ladder to the front cockpit ledge.

The flight line van used to transport pilots to and from their airplanes was parked outside. Charmaine and the two PIO officers stepped out and walked over to the F-100 containing the two Bannisters. The lieutenant colonel was smiling as the captain walked around pointing his camera up to the cockpit, snapping pictures. Both wore fatigues; Charmaine was still in her red mini and tee shirt. She noticed that Court, in the front cockpit, looked grim and remote as he handed his helmet to the crew chief on the ladder and started to dismount. Shawn, looking down at them from the height of his cockpit in the rear, removed his helmet and held his famous grin and a thumbs-up signal as the captain took several shots of the pose before the crew chief helped him unstrap. He climbed down and posed for several more pictures in his G-suit with his helmet cradled under his left arm, jaw set, legs spread aggressively, still wearing his survival vest, parachute, and webbed belt with pistol.

Court thought his half brother looked exactly as their father, Silk Screen Sam, had looked in a movie about Korean War fighter pilots. Even the PIO captain thought Shawn looked recruiting-poster perfect. Around the edges of the revetment, neighboring crew chiefs were gathered, busily shooting pictures of the event. They quickly dispersed as the line chief's blue flight-line van approached.

When he had a moment to himself, Shawn turned his body away to unzip his G-suit and tuck the well-used barf bag into a flight-suit pocket. Court, signing off the maintenance book for the crew chief, signifying the airplane had no mechanical problems, caught sight of Shawn's maneuver and grinned. Shawn flashed him a look of hatred as sharp as a muzzle flash from a rifle. Taken aback, Court handed the book to the crew chief and walked over to his half brother. His jaw had the same set as that of Shawn's earlier pose. Charmaine, sensing trouble, chattered to the others about her seeing the airplane. They were happy to accommodate her.

"Sorry about your getting sick, Shawn," Court said in a voice more angry than sorry. "That was a combat flight, and those were all standard maneuvers."

"Not that last part when you went rolling down the highway," Shawn said.

"That was to show you that what you thought was an overturned bus was actually a shot-up Army tracked vehicle, an M113."

"That was a bus, and it was shot up obviously by the Army, and those civilians you murdered were from that bus. I saw it. I know."

"Your pictures will show I'm right," Court said, jabbing his thumb at the camera hanging around Shawn's neck.

"I doubt if they'll turn out. It was too dark, it was a bad angle, and you were too fast."

"I was *too fast,*" Court all but shouted. "What on God's green earth are you thinking of? I had pulled it back, way back, almost too slow, just so you could see better."

"And I'm telling you," Shawn said, "I *saw* the civilians and I saw the *bus.* I don't think the pictures will turn out. But I tell you, you napalmed eleven civilians."

Court couldn't help reviewing the gunsight images of the 11 running figures on the screen just behind his eyes. With a jolt he remembered he hadn't seen any weapons, and if they did have any, they weren't shooting them at him. He had gotten them from behind.

"You don't know what the hell you're talking about," Court grated as he turned for the flight line van.

0215 HOURS LOCAL, 27 JANUARY 1966
531ST TACTICAL FIGHTER SQUADRON,
BIEN HOA AIR BASE, REPUBLIC OF VIETNAM

☆

At a few hours past midnight the air was cool and held the faint aroma of faraway flowers. The darkness was broken by isolated lightning flashes. The distant roar of a jet engine strapped down at the test stand huffed and chuffed as the mechanic slammed the throttle back and forth, checking for compressor stalls.

The squadron maintenance and ordnance men were still up, preparing their airplanes for predawn takeoffs. Three F-100's had holes, requiring several days' down time for the rapid aircraft maintenance team to repair them. Two had holes toward the aft section, easily patched by aluminite. One plane, the hangar queen, was still out for hydraulic leaks. Of the 18 airplanes owned by the squadron, the remaining 14 would be ready by 0500 hours. Crew chiefs in oil-stained T-shirts and faded fatigue pants snatched brief moments of sleep in their revetments alongside their airplanes, heads resting on field jackets scrunched against tool boxes.

Inside the squadron, Court, Jim Mahoney, Derham, and Lieutenant Colonel Serge Demski, the new CO, had finished planning tactics for the next day. Seventh Air Force had reaffirmed their standing frag order to provide on call whatever air they could as needed for the anticipated breakout by the armored column and to cover the search by the 195th for the missing China Boys.

Mahoney talked about what might have happened to his Mike Force team. He said the 195th had failed to make good their original time commitment from alert status, but would have search helicopters over the LZ at first light. Mahoney said that General Dupuy had personally fired the brigade commander because of the foul-up.

Besides the 531st being on alert for the coming activities in the War Zone C area, other USAF squadrons in South Vietnam would be tasked by the frag order, already being tapped out on secure teletype, to provide air at specified times. In accordance with this new method of supplying dedicated close air support, they had set up the flying schedule; who would lead, who would fly wing, what ordnance mix would be best, and what tactics to use if a Dash-K came up.

Finished, they sat back on folding chairs around the map table. A radio was tuned to the Spooky gunship channel as he orbited War Zone C, shooting as required for Troop A while listening for a possible call from the missing China Boy. The muted crackle of his voice talking to a Rover ground station they couldn't hear sounded in the loudspeaker from time to time. There was silence in the squadron. Cigarette smoke drifted slowly from overflowing ashtrays. None of the men had had a chance to clean up or shave and probably wouldn't before first light. Any more of this, Lieutenant Colonel Demski had said, and our flight suits can walk to the laundry by themselves. They didn't have anything more to do but were loath to leave the radio that might bring good news. Or bad. The single light over the map table left all four corners in darkness.

The sound of a jeep roused them from their reverie. Phil Travers walked in with Toby Parker in tow.

"Got a few things for you guys," he said as he rolled open a greasy khaki blanket, spilling assorted SKS rifles and AK-47 assault rifles on the floor. Mixed with them were torn pieces of black pajamas, some stained with blood. "Present from General Dupuy's A Troop guys for the good works you done today." The broad smile on Travers's face didn't mask his exhausted appearance; his red hair was dirty and matted to his head, and he had dark rings under his eyes.

"This is Toby Parker, a shit-hot FAC," he said, pointing to Parker, who didn't look any better. The upper portion of both men's clothes, Travers's flight suit and Parker's fatigues, were crusted white with dried sweat. Unlike the F-100, which had an air-conditioning system that could cool a three-room house, air conditioning in the tiny 0-1E consisted of whatever outside air was rammed through two small scoops.

Noticing the raised eyebrows, Travers continued, "Toby has been flying with me for the last six missions. Half the time you hear his voice taking your lineup or giving you your BDA. He was Seventh's courier to Loc Ninh, but that's on hold for a while."

Toby Parker shook hands all around. His infectious grin eked out a few return smiles and howdies. Mahoney grinned back, asking him if his landings had improved any since they had met at the dirt strip at the Loc Ninh SF camp a few days earlier.

"You bet they have," Travers answered for him. "And in about three hours he'll be making a backseat takeoff, because that's when we go back on station. And would you be so kind, Sergeant Mahoney, as to make us a sketch of the LZ that China Boy is trying to get to?'' Mahoney sketched it out for him and reaffirmed the coordinates on the map Travers held out.

"Thanks," Travers said, "and excuse us while we go to the trailer to log some Z's." He and Parker made a copy of the flying schedule, "Just to see who we'll be talking to," he said.

After they left, Demski and Derham said it was that time, told Court his relief would be in shortly and that, as the schedule showed, he wasn't flying until 1400 hours, so rack in late. The two senior officers, who had air-conditioned cubicles, seemed to have forgotten that captains and below slept in Bien Hoa huts so badly sun-heated in the morning that beyond nine o'clock, sleep was an impossible dream.

Shawn Bannister was in his small room in the trailer reserved for visiting field-grade officers. He sat hunched over a portable typewriter, chin on fists, as he studied the text in front of him. He wore only gold-colored silk briefs. In the pool of light from the desk lamp lay his notebook and a flask of brandy. Next to them smoke curled from a cigarette in an ashtray. The fan noise of the air conditioner had long since blended into the background. Moving finally, and making a sound deep in his throat, Shawn stabbed the cigarette out in short, angry strokes and resumed typing, banging the keys as if they were little round bugs that needed to be squashed. "Pandemonium Prevents Rescue," he titled his piece.

Charmaine, in the room next to his, was long since asleep. The VIP quarters had been provided by the 3rd Tac Fighter Wing PIO officer, the rheumy lieutenant colonel who, after making one desultory pass at Charmaine, had retired to his own quarters for the night. Charmaine and Shawn had spent the evening at the NCO Club, sipping weak drinks and talking with the troops. Charmaine had been extra engaging as she'd tried to get over her anger at Court's remaining in the squadron. She'd danced with practically every man in the club and done two solo numbers to the Tijuana Brass playing on the club's tape machine.

Shawn Bannister had been extra genial with the men as he'd tried to gather more behind-the-scenes information, particularly as pertained to his half brother. What he learned was that not much was known about Court, except he kept his peace, didn't give his crew chief a hard time (few pilots did), and what the hell did he want to know for, anyhow?

Court Bannister and Mahoney sacked out in the squadron. They didn't sleep well as radio speakers mumbled and crackled through the night with bleed-overs from frequencies carrying farther than normal in the night air over Vietnam. They heard snatches of calls to and from Hillsboro, Paddy, and Peacock. Spooky's call to the missing men repeated every half hour was particularly poignant, "China Boy, China Boy, if you read come up Fox Mike."

1000 HOURS LOCAL, 27 JANUARY 1966
TRAILER OF CAPTAIN PHILIP TRAVERS,
BIEN HOA AIR BASE, REPUBLIC OF VIETNAM

☆

By 10 in the morning, the full heat of the sun was starting to press down on the flight line. Already, the Wing had launched and recovered 28 F-100 sorties. Some had been preplanned for support down in the Delta, but most were for the anticipated linkup of the Rover armored column. Travers and Parker had flown one mission, and were on the ground getting a late breakfast of C Rations at Travers's trailer before launching for their second go at War Zone C at 1200. Travers explained to Parker his takeoffs that morning had really been bad, but safe. Privately he was even more impressed with the lieutenant's innate ability to control an airplane. Maybe he had once sailed boats or rode horses or something, he mused.

"Hey, Parker, you ever sail boats or jump horses or anything like that?"

Parker looked surprised. "Yeah, both."

"A lot? Did you do it a lot?"

"Well, yeah, I did. More horses than boats, though." Toby Parker didn't want to come right out and say that he had cleaned up in all Star Class boats when he was ten, or that he had ridden with the Woodsford Hunt in Virginia, where he grew up. He remembered how proud he had been the day he turned eighteen and received his colors and was able to don the scarlet coat and top hat to ride as a full member, not a junior anymore, with the hunt.

Sergeant Vivoda came in and handed Travers a package wrapped in Vietnamese newspaper.

"Thanks for picking that up for me, Frank." He flipped it to Parker.

"Here, you might as well suit up proper."

Toby unwrapped the package and held up a tailored flight suit. On the nametag was printed his name, rank, and the words "Super FAC."

"Just a little something I had made up for you in downtown Bien

Hoa. You've earned it." Travers bit down on a C-rat cracker. Sergeant Vivoda went out to prep the 0-1E with the lagging tongue with fuel and Willy Pete marking rockets for the next sortie. Toby Parker was without words.

Bannister and Mahoney munched C-rats in the squadron. They had splashed water on their faces to wake up and gone without shaves after finally giving up trying to sleep at 0530 hours. The F-100 pilots assigned to War Zone Charley Three made several nose-holding, pee-yew, remarks as they were briefed by the two men.

With the exception of the subject of China Boy, the briefing was good news. Rover had recovered their dead, salvaged what parts they could from wrecked tracks, and were roaring and clanking along Route 13, estimating linkup with the main unit at about noon. Mahoney overheard Slingshot Chief himself orbiting the site, wisely letting the ground commanders make the battle decisions, and reporting the good news to Slingshot Base. The 195th had observation helicopters up searching for China Boy, while gunships and troop ships were on ground alert, minutes away at the Snake Pit in Bien Hoa. This arrangement had been made by the new brigade commander the minute he'd received General Dupuy's affirmation of his appointment the night before.

By 1400 hours it was all over. Task Force Rover of the 1st Division had all its tracks together and was churning south back to base camp escorted by Copperhead Zero Nine, flying lazy figure eights overhead. Travers and Parker, low on fuel, made one final pass over the battle site, confirming BDA for the last flight of F-100's they had controlled. They still had one Willy Pete in its rack.

"Ramrod," Travers transmitted, "you got a hundred percent ordnance within 60 meters, 50 percent ordnance within 20 meters. Good job, guys."

"What the hell kind of a BDA was that?" Parker asked from the backseat, holding the airplane in a neat orbit at 1,500 feet.

"That's when there was nothing to hit anymore, but you gotta X in the squares. The guys had to expend because they were low on fuel and didn't want to drop dumb over the jettison area. They can't land with all that crap hanging under their wings, it might come off and ruin somebody's day," Travers said. "Let's make a run on the China Boy LZ on our way back to base. It's not that far out of our way."

"Okay," Parker agreed and turned to the heading. He started to say something about the low fuel level, but thought better of it. They had a 20-minute reserve and the weather didn't look too bad.

17

☆

Parker yawned and squirmed in his seat. He had flown so much with Travers in the last few days that he felt like a permanent part of the airplane. He had found it hard to tell Travers how much the flight suit meant to him. Up front he saw Travers pull out Mahoney's sketch and compare it to the terrain features sliding underneath. Travers nodded.

"Okay, Toby," Travers said over the intercom, "that's it." He pointed down at the clearing. "That's the China Boy LZ. I've got it." He waggled the stick to show he had control.

Parker transmitted the search call on 30.2, the Mike Force emergency frequency. "China Boy, China Boy, if you read, come up Fox Mike." Everybody knew the call was usually pointless. Of course, China Boy would be all over the Fox Mike if they heard an airplane. But sometime, so the reasoning went, a survivor might be hidden and not hear the sound of the searcher's engine. The survivor might be listening constantly but not transmitting—to save his battery, because the power required to put out a voice signal was many times that used by merely listening. So he wouldn't push the transmit button until he definitely had someone to talk to.

"China Boy, China Boy, this is Copperhead Zero Three. If you read, come up Fox Mike." Parker heard only random static rush in his headset.

Travers held the plane in a pylon turn at 1,500 feet directly over the LZ as both men stared straight down.

"Hey," the red-haired pilot said, "I think I see something." He tilted the little plane into a steeper bank and dropped down to 1,000 feet. "Look ten meters to the west from the northeast corner of the LZ at the base of the tree line. See that clump of bamboo that juts to the south?" Parker said he saw the bamboo grove. It was a thick clump, maybe 10 feet across, of tall, green bamboo stems soaring up to twenty feet or so, topped by thick clusters of green leaves. "Just at the south end of the grove, what do you see?" Travers asked.

"Something dark and moving," Parker answered, looking at a moving dot of color that did not match the green of the bamboo or the brown-green of the elephant grass that covered the entire LZ.

"Let's get closer," Travers said, dropping down to 500 feet. He kept the engine rpm up and had the airplane flying just over the redline speed of 128 knots. The controls were stiff and quick and the air rushing past the struts and through the three open rocket tubes sounded like a waterfall.

"Jeez, I dunno," Parker said, "that dark color does look out of place and, hey, I think it's moving."

"By Christ, we'll find out," Travers said between gritted teeth as he rolled the tiny airplane on its back and pulled through what looked like the second half of a loop in what pilots call a split-S. Travers deliberately left the throttle up, causing the engine to scream and the plane to vibrate badly as the airspeed needle crept 20 knots past the redline to quiver at 148. He flattened out 10 feet above the saw grass, headed north toward the bamboo clump. Their hearts beating wildly, both men stared straight ahead intently, Parker peering over Travers's shoulder. The plane was such a part of Travers that he didn't have to give any conscious thought to controlling it. As with all good pilots, he willed it to be where he wanted, and it happened. They were headed straight toward the bamboo grove, well below their tops.

"Toby," he yelled to Parker over the wind noise, not using the intercom, "I'm going to pull up and bank left. Look straight—*aaahhhhfff.*" Travers belched out air and slumped forward over the stick, forcing the plane down as a cluster of 7.62mm slugs from an AK-47 tore into the Plexiglas windshield and doors.

For an instant Parker was frozen as the wheels of the 0-1E dipped into the six-foot-high saw grass. Then, hardly aware he was doing so, he grabbed Travers by his collar with his left hand while trying to pull back on the control stick with his right. The 0-1E went down in the grass and the wheels slammed into the ground as Parker simultaneously pulled on Travers, worked the control stick, and fiercely punched the rudder pedals first one way then the other, trying to maintain lateral control and still get the airplane back into the air.

The plane wobbled and bucked and slewed left and right with each wild turn, the wings dragging first left, then right just on the edge of a ground loop, Parker acting instinctively, employing skills and strengths from an internal reservoir never before tapped. But he knew it was all over when two black-clad figures aiming AK-47's popped up in the grass slightly forward and to his left, their muzzle flashes beginning even before they assumed their shooting stance. Parker's heart gave violent thumps that he hardly noticed as he confronted death from the grass winking at him from two flashing fiery eyes.

After a split second of wild throat-clutching panic when his mouth filled with an incredible taste of copper, time stopped and he saw with great clarity of detail the two men in black pajamas shooting at him and, with hands still clutching Travers and the stick, throttle at full scream, he ruddered the stricken craft straight at the two men to kill them and die himself—but the two men crumpled suddenly, one firing wildly in the air as they were ripped by bullets from behind.

In the split second it took place, Parker realized that in setting up his death drive at the two men, he had regained control of the aircraft and was almost at flying speed. He eased back on the stick, still holding Travers, wondering why the engine didn't quit. The wheels cleared the grass and Parker looked down to frame a picture of four tiger-suited men: two crouching, two standing and shooting. He laughed insanely to himself and looked up to see he was below the approaching tree line. He horsed back on the stick in violent reflex, wheels brushing leaves, and felt the first nibbling shudders of a stall as the tiny plane traded what little airspeed it had for barely enough altitude to keep from crashing into the tree tops. Parker held it two feet above the trees as the engine pulled the 0-1E beyond stall to flying speed.

Realization flooded Parker that he was still alive and had a lot to do. As the airspeed built up he slowly climbed, heading away from the LZ until he reached a safe altitude. He let go of the stick and pulled Travers full back in the front seat, reaching down to move the knob that locked his shoulder harness while holding him upright off the stick, though Travers's head rolled from side to side on his chest. With all of Parker's senses concentrated on the task at hand, he didn't smell the blood and excrement soaked into Travers's flight suit and around his ankles to drip on the floor boards.

Parker circled back to the LZ in time to see the tiger-suited Mike Force team in a shoot-out with black figures advancing on the hidden position the Americans had given away when they brought down the two VC shooting at the 0-1E. Without hesitation Parker pushed the nose down into a screaming dive, wondering fearfully if the airplane would hang together as he reached over Travers and fired the remaining rocket at the black figures. He pulled up and switched to UHF Guard Channel.

"Mayday, Mayday, Mayday. This is Copperhead Zero Three at the 320 radial for 42 miles off the Bien Hoa Tacan. I found China Boy and I need all kinds of stuff; F-100's, chopper gunships, and a Dustoff to pick 'em up. They're under attack and wounded. I say again Mayday, Mayday. Anybody copy?" His voice was high-pitched and frantic.

Instantly the air was full of transmissions, squealing and blocking each other out. Realizing what had happened, they all shut up. One voice took over.

"Copperhead Zero Three, this is Ramrod Control on Guard. We got you. Go 273.4." Parker rogered and switched his UHF to the new frequency to clear Guard Channel.

Back at the 531st, Lieutenant Colonel Demski was running the map room command post. Bannister and Mahoney, airborne in an F-100F—call sign Ramrod Three Three—heard the Mayday and headed for the China Boy LZ just minutes away. Demski told his assistant, Major Bob Derham, to make the necessary calls to Slingshot on HF to get the rescue underway, then he transmitted to Parker.

"Zero Three, Ramrod Control. You'll get all we got. Break, break, Ramrod Three Three, you up this freq?"

"Roger Control, Three Three. We're at the LZ at 20 thou. We got the FAC in sight. Break, break. Copperhead Zero Three, do you read?"

"Yeah," Parker burst on the radio, his voice higher-pitched now as the enormity of the situation sank in. "Yeah, get down here. The bad guys are closing in, but I'm out of Willy Pete to mark for you. Wait a minute," he said.

He knew Travers kept some smoke canisters for such a situation. He edged forward and fumbled over Travers's shoulder to grab the canisters clipped to the map case. Travers moaned and clutched at Parker's arm.

"*Aaahhhh, God,*" he screamed, "Help me. I'm hit. I'm dying. Help me, Toby. Help me." In his delirium Travers began to thrash and jam the stick. Parker hastily disengaged from his clutching hands, snatched a smoke canister, pulled the pin, and dropped it out the right window. He had to grab the stick quickly to level the wings as Travers savagely writhed and flung his arms about, hitting the stick and nudging the throttle back. Parker jammed it forward. The canister fell to one side of the clearing, sending up billowing clouds of white smoke.

"China Boy is in the bamboo fifty meters northwest of the smoke. The VC are due west headed north. No bombs, they're too close to the friendlies. Quick, get some 20-mike-mike down to hold 'em up," Parker transmitted.

Bannister, who had been letting down at top speed, throttle back, boards out, instantly rolled in off-heading, at wrong airspeed and with switches not set yet but knowing he could correct it all as he got closer.

Parker could see that Bannister's first pass would make the VC stop for a minute or two, but then they would fan out to flank the China Boy team. Travers thrashed more, and screamed. Parker fought the stick and hollered on Fox Mike for any Slingshot helicopter. "Slingshot, Slingshot, where are you?"

Still listening on FM, he switched to Ramrod Control. "Where the hell are those choppers? Phil is full of holes and I've got to get him home."

"Take it easy," Ramrod Control said, "we—"

"All right Copperhead," a loud voice cut in, "Slingshot Delta's up. You read?"

Parker ignored Ramrod and switched to take Slingshot Delta's call. "How far out are you?" he demanded of Slingshot.

"Five minutes, five minutes, Copperhead, we've got three gunships and two slicks. Five minutes." Parker rogered and switched back to Uniform. He could see the VC's flanking move and had to correct Bannister's next pass. Travers screamed and thrashed, almost dumping the plane upside down.

"Phil, Phil," Parker sobbed, trying to fly the plane and pat the delirious man's shoulder, "it's all right. We're going home soon. Just another pass. Hold on, hold on. I'll get you home." Travers was becoming uncontrollable. His wild and terribly strong attempts were now focused blindly at the stick. He thought Parker was wounded and needed saving. "I'll get you home," he mumbled, head slumped on his chest, eyes trying to focus on the control stick as he grabbed it in a choke hold with both hands and snatched the plane straight up into a stall.

"Oh God, Phil, no, no-o-o-o," Parker yelled. He grunted as he fumbled at his holster and brought forth his .45 and clumsily hit Travers on the back of the head. "Forgive me, forgive me," he sobbed. He saw his first blow was ineffectual. He tried once more, then slammed him as hard as he could. Travers slumped, releasing the stick, the back of his head bloody.

Parker recovered the aircraft from the first wing dip of a spin, then quietly told Bannister where to drop his nape and that Slingshot Delta was due in five minutes. He orbited the plane at 1,000 feet to see better where the VC were mounting their attack from. After knocking out Travers, some inner mechanism completely dissociated Toby Parker's mind from the man in the front seat. He noted with complete detachment that he was operating in a completely automatic mode, for the moment, anyhow. Bannister had put in his last napalm when the pickup helicopters called in on Fox Mike.

"Ah, Copperhead, this is Slingshot Delta. We're ready to go to work. We got frogs, hogs, and chunkers to prep the LZ, and high and low Dustoffs to make the pickup. You copy?"

Parker knew from previous conversations with Travers that frogs and hogs were Huey helicopter gunships with various mixtures of miniguns and 2.75-inch rockets, while a Chunker mounted an M-79 grenade launcher.

"Roger, Slingshot," he transmitted, "set up your pattern and get to work. I've got an F-100 orbiting for whenever you need him. And go 273.4 on Uniform so we're all on the same freq, acknowledge."

"Acknowledged. Slingshots go 273.4."

"Ramrod," Parker said after switching to UHF, "hold high and dry. Slingshot will pick them up. Break, break, Slingshot, you got the bamboo clump on the north edge?"

"Roger."

"Right at the southern base are four of our guys and the Nungs. We have no radio contact. The VC are on all three sides and closing. You control your own pickup, I'll stand by with the Hun if you need—oh my God, my engine quit. I'm going in."

The little plane, in a steep bank at low airspeed, immediately stalled as the last drop of gas exploded in the cylinders.

"Roll level, get your nose down," he heard Bannister shout over the UHF. "Put it down in the grass. Slingshot, cover him on each side. I'll strafe in front of him."

Parker righted the plane and concentrated on recovering flying speed as Bannister slammed his F-100 into a wrenching turn, dove past the struggling 0-1E, and started firing into the tiny area directly ahead of Parker. The Slingshots whopped into position and started working over both sides of Parker's intended landing path.

In seconds the air was full of smoke and flames as rocket after rocket sped to the ground exploding and setting fires, the 7.62mm miniguns saturating the saw grass, the M-79 blooping 40mm grenades into pockets of advancing VC, as Parker flopped the 0-1E onto the ground between the advancing figures and the stranded Mike Force.

The right wheel hit a hummock buried in the grass and folded back, dropping the right wing, which dug in and spun the plane into a half circle before coming to rest, propeller bent back. The painted mouth looked like it was biting into the earth. Slingshot leader hovered directly over the broken airplane as Dustoff landed 100 feet away, next to the Mike Force team. Parker barely noted all the shooting and explosions of battle as he flicked open his seat belt and tumbled out the sprung right door into the space formed by the folded wheel and the broken right wing, which came down over his head like a lean-to shack.

He flipped over on his back and pulled his tangled feet out, then rolled onto his knees, still crouched under the wing, to reach the door panel next to Travers. The panel was bent back on itself where the wheel strut had collapsed against it. Parker pulled the hinge pins and wrenched the door from its sockets. He didn't even look for Travers's pulse, but started wrenching at the fastener to free his seat belt.

His world had narrowed into this small sweaty place under the wing in the crushed grass. Battle sounds faded and he felt he had all the time in the world. He fumbled and tugged at the metal fastener. It was covered with slippery red blood and had been fused shut by the slugs that had tumbled into Travers's stomach. Toby Parker didn't know he was making keening sounds in the back of his throat.

The Dustoff helicopter flattened the tall saw grass like wheat in a windstorm as it flopped to the earth between the crashed plane and the bamboo clump. Asian men in tiger suits rose from the tall grass to run to the landing bird, nearly giving the pilot heart failure until he realized these were the friendlies. Wolf Lochert and Myers yelled at Spears and Haskell to cover them while they ran in the direction of the crashed 0-1E. Flames from grass fires set by Bannister's napalm and Slingshot's rockets cracked all around while advancing toward the American position. Acrid smoke swirled out in rolling whirls from the rotating helicopter blades, which would keep the fire at bay until liftoff. The VC crept and knelt and fired from spots as they fought to get through the flames to overrun the Americans.

Crouching low, carrying their weapons, Lochert and Myers reached the crashed 0-1E and took in the scene instantly. Lochert bent and jammed himself under the broken right wing, then straightened his body, lifting the wing on his back while Myers, seeing Parker's problem, slid his K-Bar knife out and slit Travers's shoulder harness and lap belt.

"I'll get him," Parker said. He pulled Travers out by his arms and with Myers's help slid him over his back into a fireman's carry and walked on his knees clear of the wing. Myers scrambled after him. Lochert ducked out and let the wing and airplane crash back onto the ground. Flames had already started biting into the tail section. The grass-fire smoke was a dirty gray wall around the airplane.

"Which way?" Parker coughed.

"This way," Myers yelled, heading for the helicopter. Lochert pushed Parker along behind the running captain, then turned to fire long bursts into the smoke wall in the direction from which he knew the VC were coming. He heard the battle sounds with perfect clarity and, as did Myers, was able to determine exactly who was firing what weapon from where and whether the shooter was excited or calm.

Myers, in the lead, running through the smoke, shot two VC from the rear as he swept over their position. Parker with Travers on his back and Lochert following leaped over the bodies. The three men suddenly popped through the smoke into the fifty-foot-diameter clear arena formed by the Dustoff's downwash. Spears and Haskell, standing on each side of the helicopter, firing into the smoke at shifting figures, retreated backward to the doorways. On their command the Nungs did likewise. It was far too late to get the second Dustoff in. This one would have to lift off with thirteen men on board.

Slingshot Delta had been directing Court's strafe pattern in concert with his gunships, but they had to stop as the visibility in the LZ fell to nearly zero. As willing Nung hands pulled Phil Travers from his back, Parker bent forward onto the helicopter deck. He and Myers scrambled on board. Spears cried out, and spun to the ground, spasmodically flinging his weapon almost as high as the whirling blades. The pilot was pulling up on the collective to lighten the bird. He knew it would be a difficult takeoff since the tall grass would absorb most of his ground cushion. Lochert scooped up Spears and tossed him through the door, then jumped in behind him. All the men inside stood or crouched in both side doors, firing outward as Haskell took a running dive at the door. A potato-masher grenade arced through the open spot between the men in the door and lodged in the rear bulkhead seat webbing in front of Haskell's eyes as he lay on the floor. The helicopter was lifting off.

Yelling "Grenade, grenade"—which caused a Nung to jump out

and scream as three bullets ripped into him before he hit the ground—Haskell snatched at the smoking wooden handle, intending to toss the explosive overboard. It was too tangled. He paused, then hitched himself forward and up on his knees to cup the grenade into his belly and fold his body over it.

The Dustoff, nose down, was ten feet in the air, gaining momentum as the pilot fed forward cyclic as fast as the helicopter could take it. The men inside were still shooting downward. Only Parker, lying on the floor cradling Travers's head in his arms, saw Haskell's tuck. They were staring straight into each other's eyes as the grenade exploded.

The homemade cast-iron grenade fragmented into thirteen pieces as the low order explosive detonated. The splinters from the wooden handle and most of the fragments entered Haskell's belly, thighs, and chest. The remaining fragments tore away his hands and punctured the rear bulkhead and the flooring. One Nung, Lochert, and Parker each received fragments into the fleshy parts of their bodies, causing superficial wounds.

The roar and concussion of the explosion deafened and stunned the twelve men so badly that the pilot momentarily lost control and the helicopter started a torque rotation. The wind whipped the smoke out as fast as it appeared. The pilot regained control, and set the ship on course for the landing pad at the 3rd Surgical Hospital at Long Binh across the road from Bien Hoa. The remaining Slingshots formed up to escort the Dustoff. Bannister made one last strafe pass into the flaming LZ, agreeing with Mahoney, who said quietly from the backseat that it had been a helluva day, and exited the target area in time to hear Slingshot calling him.

"Ramrod, this is Dustoff. We just got the word. Long Binh's socked in. We have to recover at Bien Hoa. Can you get the hospital folks to have some ambulances ready? We got two Kilo India Alpha, six Whisky India Alpha."

"Roger, Dustoff. Wilco. Great job, man." Bannister switched to Ramrod Control and told them what was happening. Demski said he'd take care of everything.

Leading the arrow formation of protective helicopters, the Dustoff flew at its top speed of 115 miles per hour. It wasn't the first time the pilot had pushed the Lycoming T53 turbine engine to its maximum performance. The slipstream whipped in at the doors, drying blood and cooling the battle-weary men. Lochert, finished with bandaging Spears, sat strapped into a side seat, staring out the open door down at the green ridges and jungle canopy, reviewing in his mind the battle scene they had just departed.

Myers, next to him with his head back against the webbing and his eyes closed, also saw the battle and heard the explosions.

Spears, strapped between two impassive Nungs, was passing in and out of consciousness. The Nungs sat with folded arms, intoning silent prayers of thankfulness to Phuc Po. Parker sat on the floor, his back against Myers's legs, cradling Travers's head in his lap, trying from time to time to smooth Travers's wind-whipped hair.

Bannister and Mahoney beat the Dustoff by ten minutes. Doc Russell was waiting with three ambulances, four attendants, and the male nurse in the USAF hospital. The 3rd Surgical Unit at Long Binh had a medical crew due in 30 minutes. The helicopter touched down just ahead of a rain squall.

Russell got in before it had fully settled on its skids. Dried gore and blood made the interior look like a sloppy abattoir. The walking wounded eased out into the many waiting hands. Dazed and bloody, white-faced, Spears shook off offers of help as he stepped down and promptly collapsed into the arms of the nurse, who eased him down onto a stretcher. The Nungs looked with ragged suspicion at all the white faces gathered in a circle around the Dustoff. The crowd of curious dispersed as the rain whipped torrents of water on them.

Inside, Doc Russell turned from the shredded body of Haskell to kneel and examine Travers. He found a pulse and signaled an attendant to hand him the material to start an immediate plasma i.v. He plunged into his medical kit to extract a needle and gave Phil Travers one intramuscular shot of a quarter grain of morphine and one of antibiotics. Parker remained with Travers, holding his hand as Doc Russell worked over him. Parker's face was black with soot, his left cheek was torn, his hands were covered with dried blood, his new flight suit was bloody and torn. He had a small skin puncture from a grenade fragment in his left thigh from which he had yet to feel the pain.

Outside the helicopter, Lochert and Myers sat in an ambulance being swabbed and cleaned up by attendants looking for wounds. Rain drummed on the roof. In moments all three vehicles were en route to the hospital with an Air Police jeep escort, sirens screaming and lights flashing.

Though the Bien Hoa Air Base hospital was not used to treating wounded soldiers bloody and dirty, directly from the battlefield, their experience with the ruination caused by aircraft accidents and torn bodies from automobile crashes had helped them to prepare for the task at hand. Triage was performed in the emergency room and patients apportioned out according to the severity of their wounds.

The Nungs drew respectful stares as they stoically endured cleaning and stitching of wounds far deeper than originally thought. Phil Travers and George Spears were taken into the operating room for immediate surgery, to be performed by Dr. Conrad Russell and Dr. Robert Conley. The team from the 3rd Surge at Long Binh arrived to assist with their highly honed proficiency at treating gunshot wounds.

Within an hour the rainstorm had blown over. Parker, Lochert, Myers, and the Nungs had been cleaned up and released. Mahoney came along in a six-by to pick up the Nungs and Lochert. Parker and Myers remained, sitting in the hall outside the operating room.

On his way out, Lochert had put his arms around Parker's shoulders and said what a great job he had done. Parker merely nodded.

Soon, pale and unconscious, Spears was wheeled out on a gurney. The surgeon from Long Binh said he had lost a lot of muscle and tendon from his right arm but would be just fine. Myers, patting Parker's shoulder, left to accompany Spears to his bed.

Parker alternately paced and sat slumped in a plastic chair. At one point he asked a passing orderly for a cigarette and smoked the first one he had ever had in his life. After a few coughs, he dragged the smoke deep into his lungs with each inhale. He kept seeing visions of Travers laughing as he related some anecdote, then crumpling and crying out for help as Parker hit him with the butt end of his .45.

The orderly passed by and gave him more cigarettes. Parker paced and smoked, and sat once again. Once he dozed slightly, then jumped up when heard Travers scream for help. He looked around wild-eyed before realizing he had imagined the cry.

Another hour crept by before the door of the operating room suddenly swung open. The Long Binh team, pulling off gloves and hats, exited away from Parker, talking among themselves. Parker got to his feet to go after them just as Doc Russell walked through the door, with his sterile garb bloody and stained and his eyes red-rimmed and ancient. Staring at him, Parker knew the exact words Russell would say. And Russell said them.

"He's gone."

18

☆

Two days after the battle, the final and most formal debriefing of War Zone Charley Three was held at the 3rd Tactical Fighter Wing headquarters. In attendance to hear the tactical air support side of the story were two MACV brigadiers, one from J-2 Intelligence and the other from J-3 Operations; the lieutenant colonel from the 1st Infantry Division who had been in command of Task Force Rover; and Colonel Leonard Norman of USAF Intelligence.

The Army representatives had already met with the commanding officer, 5th Special Forces Group, at the C Team facility in Bien Hoa. As Wolf Lochert was their representative, the men from 5th were particularly interested in his report.

Lochert had already read Myers's after-action report before the briefing. After he listened to Myers orally debrief and answer questions from the MACV people, Lochert said he had nothing to add, except that Myers and Detachment A-302 of the 5th Special Forces Group were the best unit he had ever been in the field with, and he, Major Wolfgang Lochert, hereby notified the assembled officers that he was putting the Mike Force Team in for a unit citation and submitting SFC Charles Haskell, better known as Snake, for the Medal of Honor. The SF people and the armor lieutenant colonel nodded in agreement. MACV J-3 Ops immediately concurred. MACV J-2 Intel coughed and said he'd decide each case on its own merits. "I'm sure," said MACV J-3 Ops, looking MACV J-2 Intel straight in the eye, "that COMUSMACV will favorably endorse both recommendations without requiring extraneous counsel."

On that note the session was recessed, to be reconvened at the Bien Hoa Air Base. Along the way, Lochert and Myers stopped by the team house to pick up Mahoney.

The commander of the 3rd Tac Fighter Wing, Colonel Jake Friedlander, welcomed the group to the wing's main debriefing room, where he gave them a quick show-and-tell of the USAF participation in the relief of the Task Force Rover armored column as well as the support for the Mike Force rescue. He explained his first chart which depicted Bien Hoa F-100's flying 121 sorties and dropping fifty tons of ordnance over the three-day battle. His second chart displayed the sortie count from supporting USAF bases that had supplied fragged close air support, and air support diverted from other missions with a lesser or expired priority. He was also pleased to report the 3rd Tac Fighter Wing maintenance people had put forth such a fine effort that all squadrons were able to report a 92 percent in-commission rate for their F-100's. Finally, he compared response time from the moment the request was made by the ground commander to the arrival of air support overhead.

"It is clear," he said, "that the request from a ground unit via an overhead FAC relaying directly to a squadron for immediate air support is fast. Faster than putting the request through the Direct Air Support Center, who, if he can't fill it from airborne diverts, passes it up the line to the TACC, to the Tactical Air Control Center.

"At the TACC the request must compete with others from units calling for air support. In comparison, the dedicated squadron approach, at least in our battle, was faster by about 25 percent. In actuality, that meant a saving of seven minutes. Furthermore, our dedicated F-100's carried ordnance exactly appropriate to the field requirement."

Though outwardly enthusiastic in presenting the figures to the Army officers, Friedlander privately thought the new system cumbersome and redundant. But 7th Air Force wanted it tried out in III and IV Corps for at least a month, or five operations, whichever came first. At the end of that period, an impartial evaluation would be performed which would decide whether or not to continue the rapid response plan, or RRP, as it was called.

What no one in the assemblage knew, in fact what no one outside of the 7th Air Force staff knew, was that this RRP was the brainchild of a USAF lieutenant colonel working in the strike plans branch of the TACC. He was bucking for full bird in the best way he knew how—make a change, any kind of change, and get it reflected in his OER, officially AF Form 707, Field Grade Officers Effectiveness Form.

On his ninth F-105 mission into Route Pack 6 over downtown Hanoi, the lieutenant colonel had decided he could better serve his country in the headquarters at Tan Son Nhut and had volunteered to fill one of the many staff requirements that 7th was always levying upon the fighter wings for combat-experienced people. Once in position, the LC had been assigned to tally and post USAF sorties, weapon expenditures, and BDA's for the entire air war being fought over North Vietnam, South Vietnam, and Laos.

About 390 words of pica type written on the back of the LC's upcoming OER were required to support his hoped-for "outstanding" rating in the right-hand blocks, which might lead to promotion. These justifying words as required by Air Force Manual 36-10 under the heading "Facts and Specific Achievements" must identify exactly how advanced the ratee's strategic and tactical thinking were.

Since arranging what color grease pencil to use to display today's data doesn't necessarily ensure promotion to full colonel—lieutenant colonels are expected to know what color to use—the LC had made up the RRP, which had gotten sold to the director of operations for 7th Air Force by the LC's boss—who had every intention of claiming credit, should it work out successfully.

Unaware of the exact behind-the-scenes cabal, but suspecting something of the sort because 7th was always sending down idiot plans and bean-counting requirements, Friedlander pressed on with the task at hand.

"Gentlemen," he said finally, "this concludes my portion of the briefing. I introduce to you Lieutenant Colonel Serge Demski, commander of the 531st, who will continue the briefing from the squadron's-eye view."

Demski wasted no time introducing Court Bannister as the most knowledgeable member of the squadron because he had both coordinated air support from the Ramrod command post and had flown strike missions.

Bannister stood and added minor details to Friedlander's report. He praised Mahoney's effectiveness, though wounded, in the Command Post. Steering clear of the initial poor performance of the 195th Light Infantry Brigade, Bannister complimented their helicopter crewmen as being both skillful and courageous.

Lochert and Myers nodded agreement.

Mahoney was about to interrupt and deliver a thousand well-chosen words about what he thought of the abilities of the 195th

Light Infantry Brigade when, upon reflection, he decided this was neither the time nor the place for a sergeant first class to voice his opinions
on a subject already well known and appreciated. A grin crossed his face
as he congratulated himself on what he considered a mature and responsible decision. Bannister noticed the grin and nodded.

"The main problem we had was communications," Bannister said,
concluding his briefing. That was the last Bannister could say on the
195th problem. MACV J-3 Ops turned to Friedlander.

"Your FAC's, your AC-47 Spooky gunships and your A-1 aircraft
have FM radios so they can talk to the ground commanders. When
will your fighters get FM?"

"Probably never, sir," the Air Force colonel said to the Army
general. "The reason being, our fighters are designed and constructed primarily for air-to-air work and secondarily for air-to-ground
work. Further, the whole worldwide communications system is
geared to UHF operation. Ground Control Intercept sites, radar sites,
control towers, and foreign air forces have all chosen UHF for its
range and clarity of voice. Fox Mike, as you know well, sir, is limited
in range and power, since it's in the lower frequencies as opposed to
UHF, and is more subject to atmospheric disturbances."

He continued. "Close air support is merely one facet of the air-
to-ground mission. In addition to close air support, there is direct
air support and interdiction, neither of which requires contact with
ground troops, because ground troops are not present. Since close
air support is in response to the immediate needs of troops in contact
with the enemy, it is the only mission requiring FM radio. Here in
Vietnam, the USAF flies over 400 sorties per day in support of
ground troops. I'd say that, USAF-wide, taking into account SAC,
recce, air lift, and training, the close air support mission only ac-
counts for about fifteen or twenty percent of all sorties flown.

"That percentage, gentlemen," Friedlander waved his smoldering
cigar, "is thought by the powers that be at TAC headquarters and
in the Pentagon not to be enough justification for the added weight,
cockpit volume, and expense to mount Fox Mike in our fighters.
Meanwhile, we use an airborne forward air controller, the FAC. He
not only bridges the communications gap between the ground troops
and the strike pilot, but he also knows the tactical area of responsibility like the back of his hand and flies low and slow enough to spot
any changes. Strike pilots, who must go anywhere in Vietnam or
Laos, will never get that intimate and current knowledge. I have
heard, though, that we are buying some Navy F-8 Crusaders, which
we will call the A-7, which will be a dedicated air-to-ground bird
that will probably carry Fox Mike." Friedlander took a drag on his

cigar. "I also understand we will be getting the bigger and faster O-2's and OV-10 twin-engine aircraft for our FAC's to fly."

"I suppose I understand," MACV J-3 Ops said. "Except for our Tactical Air Control Parties and their special UHF-equipped Mark-151 jeeps, I know we in the Army sure as hell aren't going to hump the heavy equipment it takes to transmit and receive on UHF. And you can't operate wide-area UHF on battery like you can Fox Mike. What it boils down to, you can't run around the boondocks with a UHF on your back like you can with the Prick 25 Fox Mike."

Thus concluded the discussion that higher-ranking men had been fighting for years in the Pentagon. What MACV J-3 Ops had politely refrained from stating in mixed company was that, radio communications aside, the United States Army really wanted to control all air below 10,000 feet. Not only *control*, but *own* all the air below that altitude to include close air support, transports for aerial resupply—be it by landing or by parachute—and reconnaissance. Ever since the USAF became a separate service in 1947, the Army had wanted to take back the missions the Army Air Force had performed below 10,000 feet. Let the USAF keep the air-superiority mission and the strategic-bombing mission and high-altitude reconnaissance mission, the Army ground commander wanted immediate and complete control over the air power that supported his troops.

By creeping up on the one method of aerial transportation the USAF hadn't really considered as a gun platform, the Army had developed a rotary-wing contingent that was successful beyond their wildest dreams. They developed and put into service over 5,000 helicopters performing airborne assault, troop carry, med-evac, command and control, recce, and heavy-lift operations, all below 10,000 feet. Nearly 100 percent of the pilots were nineteen- and twenty-year-old warrant officers who flew in the best scarf-in-the-breeze tradition. These army helicopters carried UHF and VHF, a lower-frequency radio with limited use, in addition to their FM radios, and hence had no difficulty talking with air or ground forces.

If the truth be known about the chicanery of the Army–Air Force squabble over who owned what airplanes of what weight in the fixed-wing category, it would reveal that the United States Army had bought a bunch of Caribous, a Canadian-made twin-engine de Havilland short-takeoff and landing, or STOL, aircraft they first called the AC-1B and, later, the CV-2B. They said they needed the high-wing light transport in Vietnam for small-unit resupply.

The Caribou brouhaha had come to a head when the Army had been forced to request USAF tactical airlift support in the form of C-123 and C-130 transports when their Caribous couldn't resupply the airmobile troops in the Ia Drang valley fast enough to sustain their drive. A year and a half later, the Chief of the Air Force and the Chief of the Army, Generals McConnell and Johnson, respectively, negotiated an agreement whereby the USAF, responsible for airlift, would take over the Caribous. They did, and promptly redesignated them the C-7A. The bird still supported Special Forces camps and remote outposts as part of the centralized USAF airlift system set up by Military Airlift Command in Vietnam.

The USAF was deeply embarrassed during its first weeks of operating the Caribou. Its pilots had so many hard landings with heavy loads on short fields, they had to ask the Army to send along their warrant officer pilots with the USAF officers to retrain them in how to really fly the Caribou. Conversely, the Army was deeply embarrassed when the USAF showed how poorly the Caribous had been maintained.

MACV J-2 Intel cocked an eyebrow at USAF Colonel Friedlander. "I understand your FAC was not a pilot," he said.

"You understand incorrectly." MACV J-3 Ops interjected. "The FAC was a highly experienced pilot who was badly wounded. He later died. His nonrated observer in the backseat, a lieutenant named Parker, I believe, took over and put in the air strikes that effected the rescue of our men. I'm recommending him for the Air Force Cross, which, if you did not know, is identical in stature to our Distinguished Service Cross," MACV J-3 Ops concluded, with a grim-faced nod at J-2 Intel.

It wasn't that MACV J-2 Intelligence was dense or antihero. Not at all. He was, in fact, a brigadier who had served with distinction in the latter part of World War II and Korea in leg outfits, then had gravitated to intelligence. Since being removed from the grime and gore of combat, he had become a bit pedantic. Though not exactly classified as a bean counter, his body count figures were in great demand by the SecDef in Washington because they represented quantifiable progress that could be posted and admired. Since the war in Vietnam was not fought to push anybody anyplace or to hold captured terrain, charts of statistics had come to replace the battle maps of World War II, which had easily depicted front lines charging ever deeper into enemy territory.

MACV J-2 Intel and MACV J-3 Ops were not enemies, as it might appear. On the contrary, the two general officers frequently shared bottles of Vat 69 scotch together, each lecturing the other about duties and responsibilities. Public display notwithstanding, it was an amiable relationship. Besides, they were West Point classmates.

Jibes at his fellow staff officer aside, MACV J-3 Operations was not a sarcastic man who enjoyed pillorying his peers. Rather, he was a gentle man, given to jumping out of airplanes, who had earned a Distinguished Service Cross at Pusan in Korea.

He knew there wasn't much beyond the bits of ribbon and metal with which to reward young men for risking their lives in ungodly conditions. He knew also that his recommendation for a decoration second only to the Medal of Honor for an Air Force man would go a long way toward keeping the joint service cooperation skids greased. That Parker had earned the right to be considered for the decoration was unquestioned, but the very fact that an Army man put forth the recommendation was a gesture sure to be duly noted with good feeling by 7th Air Force.

Hopefully, this good feeling between the air and ground forces would trickle down to field level, thus leading to even greater efforts by the Air Force to come to the aid of the United States Army in its hour of need for close air support.

Colonel Leonard Norman, following the news of Parker's imminent award recommendation with avid attention, said he appreciated the general's interest in the lieutenant. He did not thank the general, for one does not thank a higher-ranking officer for any award or superior efficiency report because that implies the ranking officer is *giving* the award or efficiency report to the individual who has, in fact, *earned* it. Privately, on a personal basis, it would not be out of line for Norman, as Parker's boss, to thank the general for his thoughtfulness and efforts to secure the award.

When Norman had seen his courier lieutenant earlier, he had been struck at how melancholy and aged Parker had become in such a short period of time. He had told Doc Russell of his plan to leave young Parker on detached duty at Bien Hoa for a few days, where he would be in the company of the men he had come to know so well, to see if he might come around.

MACV J-3 Ops turned to Bannister. "Although you ran Ramrod Control and you flew as a strike pilot, you did not give us your views in your briefing as to the efficiency of this new system. Give us your opinion, please," the brigadier commanded.

Bannister, already standing at the briefing board, cocked his head and made a swallowing gesture. Looking straight at the Army general he said, "Sir, in perspective of the overall picture of supplying close air support for the Army throughout South Vietnam, I do not think this method is efficient for two main reasons."

The briefing room became deathly quiet. Lochert, Myers, and Mahoney looked amused. An afterburner boomed in the distance as an F-100 took off from the far runway. The general nodded, his face expressionless. "Continue," he said.

"First off," Bannister said, "you'll note we at Ramrod Control made a local decision to take the air dedicated to the Mike Force team problem and apply it to the Task Force Rover problem. Granted, the Rover convoy was nearby and even fighting the 273rd VC Regiment, which was attacking the Mike Force, but those airplanes did not belong to Task Force Rover. They belonged, were dedicated to, the Mike Force.

"Suppose the armor had run into trouble farther away, too far for us to risk sending the Mike Force F-100's to them. Other USAF assets would then have had to take their place, which in turn might have depleted someone else down the line. My point here is, we knew of the Rover problem because our FAC told us. But, in our small world, we would not have known of Rover had he been thirty klicks farther away talking to another FAC.

"That would have resulted in our alert birds remaining on the ground, of no use to anyone. But someone looking at the big picture would see problems like that, and direct what birds go where and when, which, of course, is what the entire Tactical Air Control System already does."

"And your second point?" the general asked.

"Sir, my second point is a continuation of the first. The response time saved by our dedicated birds was not much different from what it would have been using our normal alert birds. And, of course, diversion of tactical aircraft en route to lesser targets in the immediate target area would provide air support even faster. In conclusion, sir, I don't think the system of tying up dedicated aircraft is efficient, although this particular battle went well." Bannister stopped talking. Derham caught his eye with a see-you-at-the-hanging grin.

"Very interesting, Captain, ah"—MACV J-3 Ops peered at Bannister's name tag—"Captain Bannister. I too think the, as you call it, the 'dedicated bird' method used to support the effort in War Zone Charley went well indeed," he said, "but before I left MACV headquarters, the Deputy of Operations, Seventh Air Force, asked me if the fast response for emergency ground situations truly required dedicated alert aircraft. He wanted me to assess if the so-called rapid response plan was justified, or if we could live with the existing request net and current method of scrambling air support from ground alert status."

The assemblage looked at the general with some interest. This early evaluation of RRP was news to them. USAF Colonel Friedlander, with a glance at Bannister, looked wryly amused.

"The existing request net, as you all know," the general swept them with a wave of his hand, "is from a ground unit to the Corps Direct Air Support Center through the Tactical Air Control Center to Seventh for allocation of USAF aircraft for preplanned missions, divert missions, or aircraft scrambled from alert status. I've checked the response times versus the urgency of the requirements.

"Further, I've checked the nature of the urgency of two dozen ground-troop tactical emergencies.

"My conclusion is that it would be difficult enough to rank-order in priority any given ground-troop emergency over any other at the same time. Also, if a third or fourth emergency cropped up of an even more urgent nature, we could conceivably run out of local-sector air because it is tied up on the ground waiting to be used for lesser priorities. What we would have is a double or even triple aircraft alert system that would not make efficient use of existing resources."

MACV J-3 Ops stood up, causing the others to spring to their feet. "Therefore," he said, "I am telling Director of Operations, Seventh Air Force, that, as well as this situation has concluded, we do not wish to continue this dedicated RRP alert business any longer. Most assuredly, however, the pilots must continue to familiarize themselves by direct ground observation with the areas and Special Forces camps that may go into Flaming Arrow."

The general looked at Friedlander and shook his hand.

"Superb job," he said and moved to do the same down the line with Demski and Derham. Generals do not normally do this at a briefing, but MACV J-3 Ops knew well the value of keeping the Air Force happy and appreciated. As he shook Bannister's hand he said, "Young man, whenever you want a job as an air liaison officer with one of my units, let me know." Bannister grinned and thanked the general, knowing full well he would never take the good general up on his offer. An ALO slot with an Army unit was not a flying job.

The high-powered MACV entourage departed the briefing room, boarded helicopters for Tan Son Nhut and were swept away from the USAF officers and Special Forces men who saw them off from the flight line ramp. Once airborne, MACV J-3 Ops turned to USAF Colonel Norman and asked, "Was that captain really Silk Screen Sam Bannister's kid?"

Norman assured him he was. "Amazing," said the general, "for a Hollywood type he seems to be a real warrior."

Back on the ramp, before Lochert and Myers left in Mahoney's jeep, they told Bannister they'd come over to the Bien Hoa O-Club that night around nine p.m. to hunt up Toby Parker. They had something to give him that might raise his spirits.

After they drove away, Colonel Friedlander offered Bannister a ride to the squadron. He barely had time to tell Bannister he'd appreciated his candor about the dedicated bird situation, when a voice from the radio in his command jeep said a MAC airliner was on final approach with an engine out.

19

☆

Braniff International flight B3T6, a MAC Contract Boeing 707 en route from Clark Air Base in the Philippines, had ingested a two-pound bird in its left inboard engine as it entered the traffic pattern at Bien Hoa. Sucked into the Pratt & Whitney JT3D turbofan at 200 miles per hour, the bones and guts of the shredded bird had set up an overheat condition requiring the captain to shut down the engine. It was no emergency, the big 707 flew perfectly well on three engines. Since it was inboard, the loss of thrust didn't require much rudder offset to maintain a straight heading. The fifty-four-year-old pilot, with 24,000 hours of flying time, merely informed his roly-poly fifty-six-year-old flight engineer to shut off the fuel to the engine as he pulled the throttle back to the stopcock position. He told his copilot, a trim thirty-four-year-old ex-Navy jock, to inform Bien Hoa tower of the shutdown and tell them a crash crew was not required.

The senior controller in the tower, smart enough to know better than to take any pilot's word about whether the loss of an engine was an emergency or not, promptly punched the crash alarm.

He also knew full well that the engine problem the copilot described meant there was no way MAC Contract B3T6 was ever going to depart the Bien Hoa runway that day, which meant that the stewardesses would have to stay overnight. The knowledge that there would be real, live, round-eyed, American girls on the base caused his rugged countenance to dissolve into a colossal grin.

"Yahoo!" he belted out in the tower—not on the air, of course. His perplexed subordinates stared in wonder until he told them his deduction.

"Yahoo!" the subordinates echoed as they reached for telephones to tell their buddies to *di-di mau* down to base Ops ASAP if they wanted to see some real American stuff. Normally the stews never even deplaned when off-loading their G.I. passengers at Bien Hoa.

Procedures required that after the crash alarm was punched, the controller must notify base hospital, the Wing Commander, and the duty chaplain. However, owing to the impassioned personal interest emanating from the control tower, 20 airmen knew what was inbound before the Wing Commander, 32 before the duty chaplain. By the time the big airliner stopped in front of Detachment 5 of the 8th Aerial Port Squadron, 51 USAF personnel were waiting. Their Wing Commander, Colonel Jake Friedlander, had to use his command jeep's siren to make his way to the air stairs of the big airliner.

Confusion was rampant. The fighter pilots, a little late to get the word, had grabbed whatever transportation was available. Their bikes, jeeps, and crew vans edged up to the circle. Air Police security guards deployed to hold the panting crowd at bay. The doors of the airliner opened and the new G.I. arrivals started down the stairs. They were bewildered by the scattered boos they received. A stern command from a senior NCO put a stop to the outburst.

The last G.I. down the steps cast oblong shadows in the late evening sun. Then came a pause, an expectant hush, a straining. Lips were licked in anticipation. There was a stir at the cabin door, there was movement inside. The crowd leaned forward, breaths were held— then expelled, as first the roly-poly fifty-six-year-old flight engineer stepped out, followed by the first officer, as copilots are called in airline parlance. Knowing exactly what was going on, the two men assumed positions on each side of the platform, whence they made flourishing movements with their hands toward the open door from which the first stew stepped out and looked at the crowd.

"Oh, shit, you guys, did you really have to do this?" Sally Churna said to her fellow crew members from between clenched teeth framed by a wide smile. Blonde and rumpled, Sally maintained her dazzling smile as she began waving to the troops. The other four girls emerged. The crowd, including the senior NCO's, broke into cheers and whistles that even Bob Hope had never been accorded. Correlli from the Public Information Office elbowed his way through the crowd as he recorded the momentous event with his big Graflex cut-film camera.

As protocol dictated, the crew of the visiting aircraft waited for the captain to walk out, then followed him down the stairs. The captain was greeted by Colonel Jake Friedlander and two of his three squadron commanders. Dietzen was flying, as was Darlington, the Director of Operations. The duty chaplain, a married Methodist, stood behind Friedlander. Doc Russell had sent his ambulance back to the hospital and stood toward the rear of the crowd with Court Bannister. Until the girls appeared, they had been chatting about Toby Parker's depression.

Friedlander and the captain introduced themselves at the foot of the air stairs. The captain turned to his crew. "Colonel, may I present the cabin crew of Braniff MAC contract flight B3T6." He introduced each of the five girls to the Wing Commander personally and to the gathered crowd generally. The only names Friedlander really caught were Tiffy Berg, Sally Churna, and Nancy Lewis.

Following their introduction to the colonel, the girls turned to look out over a sea of smiling airmen. The closest men, with face-splitting grins, doffed their hats and nodded. The girls positively lit up. The lines of exhaustion in their faces gave way to smiles that were both broad and genuine. Each girl melted a bit in her heart as she saw, here in this faraway war zone, the face of every boy she had ever known.

The captain explained there was no way they could take off that night, and that a relief airplane with engine mechanics would not arrive until late the next morning. He had arranged all this on company HF with Saigon while the G.I.'s were getting off. Jake Friedlander shifted his cigar and waved the Methodist chaplain over.

"Padre," he said, "you are in charge of these lovely ladies. Get them VIP quarters from Billeting and divvy 'em up for dinner at the NCO Club and the Officer's Club." Friedlander then motioned to Master Sergeant Booker Washington Smith, the Operations sergeant of the 3rd Tac Fighter Wing Air Police Squadron. "Smitty," he said, "fix things up at the NCO Club."

The PIO lieutenant colonel, overjoyed at prospects for favorable USAF publicity, had shown up. Friedlander told him to have at it. Friedlander then gave a few more instructions to other staff members regarding maintenance, security, and communications. He spoke for several moments into the ear of the transportation officer from the motor pool. He motioned the Officer's Club manager over to give him detailed instructions regarding a dining-in to be held this evening. Then he turned to the three male crew members. "We'll fix you guys up with bunks over at the command trailers."

Master Sergeant Smith caught his colonel's eye. Friedlander nodded assent at the unspoken request on the face of the sergeant, who then quietly motioned his air police to let the airmen crowd around the girls. Friedlander, his staff, and the male crew members stood to one side as the girls, radiating genuine charm, happily greeted the young airmen with a "Hi, there" and "Where are you from?" There was much joyous banter and hellos. The girls couldn't believe they were giving so much enjoyment by merely talking and chatting with the young men. They shook hands and tried to talk to all of them.

They were interrupted as loud sirens and honking drew everyone's attention to the roadway leading to the ramp. Led by an Air Police jeep with red lights flashing and the siren on, was an open six-by-six truck festooned with colored paper and an American flag held proudly aloft by an airman riding in the front seat. The motor pool officer waved to the girls, indicating they were to climb aboard. Eager airmen helped them up the back of the truck, where they stood on the side seats facing out to wave to the crowd. Splitting the civilian crewmen between his jeep and that of his staff, Colonel Friedlander led the impromptu motorcade on a tour of Bien Hoa Air Base, allowing the men on duty to see what good luck had materialized. After thirty minutes of joyful parading, the girls were deposited at their quarters at dusk as giant cumulus cloud formations radiated red gold from the setting sun.

That evening, after refreshing themselves, the flight deck and cabin crew members divided up and accepted dinner invitations at the NCO Club and the Officer's Club. The captain, two girls, and the portly flight engineer went to the NCO Club, escorted by Master Sergeant Smith. Colonel Friedlander had said he would stop over for a quick drink later. The ex-Navy jock first officer, in company with Tiffy Berg, Sally Churna, and Nancy Lewis, was escorted to the Officer's Club by the married Methodist chaplain, a thirty-two-year-old captain who swallowed frequently.

By eight p.m. the club was packed. At first the drinking and the noise level were held to a minimum. There were no bicycle jousts, carrier landings, or dirty songs. Long tables with fresh sheets spread over them were hastily arranged, candles and wine magically appeared. Then it was time for the formalities.

Colonel Jacob Friedlander officially welcomed the crew of Braniff International flight B3T6 as guests to the very first 3rd Tactical Fighter Wing dining-in. As an aside, he explained that the dining-in tradition, borrowed from the Royal Air Force back in the big war, had been introduced into the USAF by General Hap Arnold, who had become quite famous for his wingdings. The dining-in was a ritualized, formal stag affair whose purpose was to raise morale and foster *esprit de corps*. They usually became RAF-style drunken brawls soon after the smoking lamp was lit. When spouses attended, the title was changed to dining-out and no drunken brawls ensued. Since in the true sense of the word the ladies present were not spouses of any of the men present, and since they were aircrew, Colonel Friedlander decided this function was a dining-in.

After the chaplain made the invocation, the Colonel, as President of the Mess, made the proper toasts to the President, the Chief of Staff, and so on down the line to the Commander, 7th Air Force. He then introduced Mr. Vice, by tradition the lowest-ranking lieutenant on the base, whose job it was to keep the dining-in proceeding in accordance with the rules.

Then Friedlander looked around and asked for one First Lieutenant Toby Parker to stand and be recognized. There was an embarrassed hum of questions until finally Court Bannister asked for and was granted recognition by Mr. Vice.

"Sir," he said, addressing the President of the Mess, "I believe the lieutenant in question is in the excellent hands of the Three Corps Mike Force, specifically those of Major Wolfgang 'the Wolf' Lochert. I don't believe he got the word about our guests or the dining-in." Bannister sat down.

Mr. Vice pounded his gavel, a hammer, on the table and said that Captain Bannister was fined one glass of wine in that he had not asked permission of the President of the Mess to be seated.

Bannister stood and drank his fine. He remained standing.

"I note your report, Captain Bannister," Colonel Friedlander said. "Tell the lieutenant to report to me when he arrives. I have some good news for him. You may be seated." Bannister sat. The hastily devised dining-in was in full swing.

There was no linen or crystal or well-served steaks. Diners ordered the standard menu fare of hamburgers or Salisbury steak and rice from the three Vietnamese waitresses, who seemed nervous and preoccupied. The fact that no one wore the prescribed formal mess dress meant nothing. Sweaty flight suits, fatigues, and khaki 1505's were definitely in order this night.

No one wore civilian clothes. Even the airline crew wore their uniforms, the men in short-sleeved white shirts with epaulets and tie, the girls in the uniform variation that permitted slacks in the tropics. As the meal progressed, the wine flowed faster than anticipated, thus depleting the supply. A hasty trip by a junior officer to the NCO Club took care of that problem. Meanwhile, whisky bottles and beer cans in profusion joined the wine bottles littering the tables.

The formal portion of the meal ended. After the President of the Mess announced the smoking lamp was lit, the impromptu entertainment began. Several F-100 pilots, virtuosos with guitars and ukes, sang the few clean fighter pilot songs they knew. Then the husky motor pool officer stunned the gathering by coaxing a beautiful rendition of the Moonlight Sonata from an old upright piano that looked as if its coat of white paint had been applied with a broom. He graciously consented to play requests and just as graciously agreed to play "Fleur de Lys" at Sally Churna's suggestion. Instead he delivered up another beautifully rendered Moonlight Sonata. When he struck the opening chords of the Moonlight Sonata for the third time in response to Colonel Friedlander's request for "Roll Out the Barrel," it became obvious the one-song pianist was shitfaced.

Before appropriate measures could be taken, a horrendous, flatulent quack stunned the participants as the forgotten Higgens the Homeless announced his presence from the top of a screened window. Lying on the roof and hanging his head and arms down from his vantage spot, he peered through the screen to announce further, now that he had their attention, that he personally had trained that bird, a Peking duck as a matter of fact, to vector into the engine at the proper moment to sacrifice itself for the express purpose of bringing joy and happiness to the officers and men of the 3rd Tac Fighter Wing. Higgens stopped talking and looked at the girls from his inverted position. They looked back at the apparition with dazed smiles. Tiffy waved. Higgens waved back. A collective sigh of relief was breathed by those who knew Higgens, when he did not yell the demand at the girls to *"show us your tits,"* as was his wont. "Higgens, front and center," Colonel Friedlander bellowed, clearly pleased by Higgens's restraint.

For once, Higgens the Homeless was speechless. "You mean *now,* sir?" he asked in a suddenly plaintive voice from his upside-down position behind the screen.

"Now," the colonel thundered. Higgens's face disappeared as he hastened to comply. The club fell silent as he entered and reported to the Wing Commander.

"Sir, Lieutenant Higgens reporting as ordered, sir," he said tossing off a snappy salute. The colonel stood up and took the cigar from his mouth.

"For the conspicuous bombastic and flatulent duck interludes you have provided this club and in honor of the fair guests we have tonight," the colonel waved his cigar at the girls, "and in honor of that kamikaze duck of yours that brought them here, you are hereby absolved of previous misdeeds and are formally invited to rejoin the Bien Hoa Air Base Officer's Open Mess. Ladies, gentlemen, I present Lieutenant Smiggens."

Thus it became obvious the colonel was shitfaced, and so began the real party led off by Smiggenhiggens, as he was to be forever known, singing a rousing "Be Kind to Your Web-Footed Friends," accompanying himself with appropriate quacks on his battered but perfectly tuned duck call.

Caught up in the spirit of good fellowship, Fairchild, the snake control officer, went to the squadron snake cage and placed Ramrod around his neck to introduce him to the Braniff crew. "What the hell," Tiffy said, and posed for a picture with Ramrod around her neck.

Court Bannister and Doc Russell sat to one side, drinking and watching the festivities. As usual, Court had beer and the Doc was on scotch, straight up. At 20 past nine, wearing tiger suits with red, white, and blue scarfs knotted at their necks, Lochert and Myers walked in with a stony-faced Parker in tow. Parker wore fatigues. He hadn't known quite what to do with his new flight suit, now torn and stained with Phil Travers's blood. The torn skin of his left cheek had been pulled together with three small stitches.

The two Mike Force men put their M-16's and pistol belts on the gray metal coat rack next to the door. Myers carried a small flat package wrapped in brown paper. In response to Court's wave, they edged their way toward his table. Before they could get there, the pilots spotted the tiger suits and set up a great cheer. Several pressed drinks into their hands. Parker gave a fleeting smile. He looked surprised when Freeman told him he had best report to Colonel Friedlander right away. Friedlander arose as Parker approached. The crowd grew silent.

"I should chew you out," the colonel began, "for being the two percent that doesn't get the word about the dining-in." He waved his cigar at the tables. "Instead, I have some news for you." He puffed his cigar. "I have it on good authority you are recommended for, and in all probability will receive, a high decoration for your deeds at Loc Ninh." Great clouds of smoke from the cigar. "Furthermore, I have it on good authority that, provided you can pass the physical, you may enter a pilot training class at the end of this tour." He paused while the crowd cheered. "Finally," he said, "because of your great FAC abilities, you are being released by Seventh

Air Force, one each Colonel Norman to be exact, to be reassigned
to the new FAC school at Phan Rang, where you will serve as executive officer to the commander.''

More cheers as the pilots slapped Parker on the back. He seemed
dazed by the proceedings and somewhat detached. Friedlander ordered Parker and the two Special Forces officers to come to his table
and meet some people from the real world.

As he made the introductions, Toby Parker found himself staring
into the amber eyes of Nancy Lewis, who did not recognize his
ravaged face. She looked right through him at Wolf Lochert and
Tom Myers, because she recognized the tiger suits as those worn
only by men from Special Forces.

She held her questions until Colonel Friedlander made the introductions, then she asked Lochert and Myers if she might speak to
them. They said of course, and, to the envy of the main table, led
her to where Bannister and Doc Russell were sitting. Toby Parker
tagged along, slightly uncomfortable with how far back in his mind
he had pushed the memory of his encounter with her and Bubba
Bates. Russell and Bannister stood up, Lochert held her chair, and
they sat down. She asked her well-memorized question without pre-
amble.

''Did you know Sergeant First Class Bradley L. Lewis, an adviser
on Team 75 out of My Tho to the Seventh ARVN Division?''

Lochert and Myers exchanged glances.

''I'm his wife,'' Nancy Lewis said, before they could ask. ''He
was reported missing months ago,'' she added.

''You bet I knew him,'' said Wolf Lochert. ''And a better soldier
never humped the boonies.''

''*Knew* him, major?''

''Well, ah, yes, ma'am. I don't, ah, know exactly what the Department of the Army said about his being missing, but the circumstances under which Brad disappeared don't leave much hope for his
survival,'' Lochert said with obvious reluctance. Nancy Lewis caught
at his burly arm.

''Tell me,'' she commanded, ''tell me all you know. You're the
first person I've found who knows anything about Brad.''

The table was quiet as Wolf began.

''There really isn't much to tell. He was out in the Delta when
the Vietnamese platoon he was with got backed against a canal by
the VC. I had contact with him on the radio net from the Division
Command Post. We got some Tac air diverted to him, but the
weather was going sour.

"A Beaver FAC could barely put in the air, because the visibility was lousy in the rain. The ceiling was so low they couldn't drop bombs, and could barely see to drop low-level stuff like napalm and CBU. The flight leader told the FAC he couldn't risk hitting friend-lies.

"I heard Brad tell the FAC they were taking heavy fire and were down to about twenty effectives. He said to tell the pilots to come right on in and hit whatever they could. I had the feeling that even though he was supposed to merely advise, he had actually taken charge." Lochert paused to take a swallow from a beer Bannister handed him.

"After a while, we heard him tell the FAC the fighters were doing good, even if he was taking a few short rounds, because they were dead without them. Then his radio went out during a fighter pass." Lochert wet his lips and took Nancy Lewis's hand between his knuckly paws.

"Twelve Viets out of a platoon of forty straggled back to My Tho that night. They were in bad shape. One was the best of the three squad leaders. He said the platoon leader, a lieutenant, and the pla-toon sergeant were killed along with Brad when some napalm splashed over on them." Lochert took a deep breath. "The next day, we got a few minutes on the ground from a helicopter. There had been a lot of, ah, damage done to the bodies. We brought out what we could, but we were not able to make individual identifica-tion. In accounting for those alive and the remains, we came up with three missing. So, well, we reported Brad as missing, but presumed dead." He squeezed Nancy's hand. "I'm sorry," he said. "He was a good soldier." Myers nodded in agreement.

None of the men at the table could think of anything else to say. One simply doesn't run into surviving spouses in Vietnam and have to tell them what happened to their husbands. Via letter, yes, from the commander; maybe even a visit once stateside for a particularly good buddy, but face to face in Vietnam, never.

Nancy Lewis could see the men were plainly uncomfortable. She didn't know how to tell them that somehow she felt Brad was dead.

"Thank you," she said looking from Lochert to Myers. "Let's have a drink."

Doc Russell sprang to the bar. He used his bulk and inoffensive manner to procure scotch doubles all around. He returned to the table in time to hear Nancy Lewis say she felt better, much better, thanks to their words and obvious esteem for her husband. Inside, she felt empty and just wanted to curl up and cry herself to death;

but, by God, these were Brad's people and she sure as hell was going to perform her role in the grand tradition.

"To my soldier, Brad Lewis," she said, rising and holding up her glass of scotch. The men rose. "Here, here," they intoned and drank. As there were no fireplaces or even room in the crowded club to throw a glass against the wall, they smashed their glasses on the floor, never to be sullied by a lesser purpose. Startled, but without missing a beat, Nancy Lewis did the same. Doc Russell went off for another round. Nancy decided it was up to her to change the subject.

"What was your name again?" she said, looking at Parker. She spotted his name tag. "Oh, sure, I remember you. You took on Bubba Bates at the Tan Son Nhut terminal last December. I'll never forget how sweet you were to come to my rescue," she said, making no reference to her wristlock on Bubba Bates or that Toby had been slammed to the deck twice.

"Bates, huh. When did all this take place?" Lochert asked of Parker, who was beginning to perk up.

"The same day I first met you, major," Parker responded.

"Call me Wolf," Lochert said, punching Parker's arm and turning to the amber-eyed girl.

"This man," the Wolf boomed, "laid out the same Mr. Bates at the Tan Son Nhut Officer's Club a short time back, and ran off with his girl," he finished up proudly. "Then, this week," the Wolf bored on, "this week he saved the collective asses of me and Tom here and some other people." Lochert stood up.

"A toast!" he bellowed to the club at large. Not satisfied with the latent response, he shouted in a voice that could crack steel, "A TOAST." The huge Special Forces major got his way. The club paused in their ever intensifying merriment and watched Lochert shoulder his way to the bar and climb up. Myers walked over, ripped open the package he was carrying, and handed him two red, white, and blue scarfs, identical to the ones they had at their throats.

"Out crawling in the jungle, you air force pukes couldn't find your"—he looked at Nancy Lewis—"couldn't find your nose with both hands. But in the air, in the air you are magnificent. And the best of all you pukes doesn't even wear wings." He leaned forward to point out Toby Parker, who was thinking this was worse than the face-off he had had with Lochert when he'd first met him. Myers pushed Parker up onto the bar, where Lochert knotted the coveted III Corps Mike Force scarf about his neck, then kissed him, French-style, on both cheeks which, by now, were flaming red.

"Toby Parker," Lochert thundered.

"Here, here," the crowd yelled.

After appropriate words, Myers tied the second scarf around the neck of Court Bannister for his air support on the two Mike Force operations and his ode on the team house wall. He did not kiss Court's cheeks.

Court steadied himself and held his scotch glass high. "The Mike Force," he toasted.

"Here, here! Shit hot! Yay!" the crowd cheered, tossing down whatever booze was at hand.

The party was now in full swing. The momentum began to feed upon itself and boosted even the most laggard of spirits. A drifting rain had cleansed and cooled the air. The new tape recorder was cracking out the trumpets and drums of the Tijuana Brass; real American girls graced the scene; all was well at the Bien Hoa Air Base Officer's Club.

Things were more decorous in the NCO Club because Master Sergeant Booker Washington Smith said he would pure beat the living crap out of any man who dared raise his voice or in any way sully the reputation of Air Force NCO's while the girls were there. In both clubs, surprisingly, members had to get behind the bar and help serve drinks, as the Vietnamese help seemed to be dogging their jobs. At the Officer's Club, Doc Russell remarked that it seemed there weren't as many on duty as when they'd first arrived.

Tiffy Berg had fallen in love with Ramrod. Totally oblivious to any Freudian phallic interpretation, she had wound the compliant rock python around her body in as many ways as she could think of while shadowboxing solo versions of the frug and watusi within a clapping and cheering circle of bug-eyed pilots.

The poised, statuesque, blonde Sally Churna only sipped the drinks that kept appearing magically at her elbow. She held another crowd of pilots spellbound as she played strip liar's dice with Jack Laird and Bob Derham. So far she had lost nothing, while the hapless pilots were already barefoot and nervously fingering their flight-suit zippers.

Lieutenant Donny Higgens, no longer homeless, was sitting next to Sally, staring at her in rapt adoration, absently tapping his duck call on his knee. He drank little and seemed to be trying to gather up courage to ask her an important question. In due time, Sally said to herself, she would pay attention to this shy lieutenant who was so obviously smitten.

Over toward the bar, Tom Myers excused himself, saying he had to get back to the team house. Nancy Lewis hugged the rugged captain goodbye. He made his way to the coatrack, picked up his M-16 and pistol belt, and headed out the door. In tiger suit with weapons, he looked lethal and competent and quite out of place among the partying pilots.

Nancy turned back to the table and thought she caught Toby staring at her. As she sat down, she realized he was detached and unfocused. He wasn't staring at her, he was staring through her. He was inexpertly and absently smoking a cigarette. She decided to concentrate on this sorrowful young man in hopes it would take her mind off her pain.

"You never wrote," she said.

"What?" Parker said. "What did you say?"

She touched his wrist. "Hey, Toby Parker, it's me. The terminal at Tan Son Nhut, Bubba Bates, remember?" As she spoke she realized Parker's face had lost all the eager and youthful enthusiasm she had seen on his first day in Vietnam.

"Oh, sure, I remember," Parker said, again surprised at how long ago and remote that day seemed. He thumbed Tui's jade earring back and forth in his palm.

"Those Special Forces men think a lot of you," Nancy said when she realized he wasn't going to say anything more. "What exactly did you do?"

After a second Parker focused on her. He looked deep into her eyes. They were wide and clear, and the amber color, more than anything else, reminded him of his first day in Vietnam and of his life before that day. She sensed he wanted to speak and pressed his hand.

At first his words were wooden and bare of description, and did not convey his feelings or concern. He spoke more as a chronicler of the events than a participant. He hadn't told the story of Tui or Phil Travers to anybody, so he had to search for the right words. As he continued deeper into the story of the two people who meant so much to him, he again heard Piaf sing, and, later, the thump and whine and crash of battle.

He relived hitting Travers and he saw Haskell's eyes as he died. Then he heard Doctor Russell telling him at the hospital that Travers was gone. He told her of the flight suit Travers had given him and how the first mission he had worn it, Travers was killed. He barely mentioned his role in any of the events. He told how Tui saved him at the My Canh, but not how he saved the Mike Force troops. He concentrated, morbidly she thought, on Travers's death. Then she saw the hard lines leave his face and his eyes well. The torn line in his cheek looked red and puckered.

Finally, his voice was husky and the words came tumbling out, as if he were trying to purge himself of memories too painful to retain. As he talked, she felt better inside. Her own recent pain subsided as she saw the haunted look slowly leave Parker's face. When he was finished, his thoughts swung back to Tui.

"This is what she gave me," he said, taking out the jade earring the *métisse* girl had given him before she disappeared that last night. Nancy looked at it and knew then that Parker had no more romantic illusions about her. She glanced at his face and saw him starting to retreat back to his vacant expression. She decided to see what she could do to make him smile again.

"C'mon," she said, grabbing his hand to tug him up from table, "let's go see what's going on."

They joined the crowd that was watching pilots run, then jump and slide on their bellies on beer-covered tables. They were making carrier landings as taught by a real Navy jock, the Braniff first officer. He was currently instructing them how to do night carrier landings during which they had to wear a blindfold and have the Landing Signal Officer talk them around the pattern and onto the beer-slick table. They weren't catching on well. Several, including Lieutenant Dan Freeman, crashed as table edges slammed into their stomachs. Watching from nearby was Freeman's buddy, Doug Fairchild, who was escorting a young Aussie nurse he had met from the Bien Hoa City Hospital. Her name was Fiona.

Sally Churna decided the liar's dice game had gone far enough when she saw Derham quite prepared, almost eager, to take his flight suit off. Besides his shoes and sox, he had already lost everything from his pockets. To Derham's and Laird's disappointment, Sally put down the dice, calling the game a tie. She sat back and turned to the shy young Lieutenant Higgens, sitting clutching his duck call to his chest as if afraid someone would steal it. He seemed finally to have gotten up enough courage to ask her his burning question. Probably to dance, Sally thought, looking with dismay at the crowded club. No one else was dancing. Tiffy Berg had retired with Ramrod to the bar and was in earnest conversation with several pilots. From the corner of her eye she saw Colonel Friedlander.

"Well, Donny Higgens," she said brightly to the young lieutenant, "what can I do for you?"

"Ah, would you, ah—"

"Like to dance?" she interrupted.

"Ah, why no. But thank you. Gosh, that was nice of you to ask," he said.

How cute, Sally thought, he's actually blushing.

"What I wanted to ask was, ah"—he wistfully twisted his duck call—"would you care to sit on my face?"

Sally Churna's full roundhouse slap knocked the lieutenant backward off his chair to sprawl at the feet of Colonel Friedlander, who had arrived in time to hear the query. He instantly exiled Higgens to his homeless status for another month. Friedlander, joined by Laird and Derham, apologized profusely. Sally managed a weak smile and allowed as how the wistful lieutenant was the first real card-carrying sex maniac she had ever met.

Across the room, at a table with Court Bannister and Wolf Lochert, Doc Russell looked over at the door to the club. "Well, I'll be damned," he said, calling their attention to the Wing PIO officer walking in with Shawn Bannister and Charmaine.

Obviously proud of his visitors, the rheumy PIO lieutenant colonel steered his guests to the head table to make sure his boss, Colonel Friedlander, had a drink with them. Charmaine caught Court's eye and smiled. After a drink and a few words with the colonel, she disengaged from the group to go to the table where her ex-husband sat. The three men stood up as she approached.

"Charmaine," Court said, starting to make the introductions, "this is—"

"Hello, Major Lochert," Charmaine interrupted, extending her hand to the Special Forces major, "how good to see you again."

The Wolf, well down the road to being smashed, was stunned. Many times he had thought of this girl with the green eyes and fabulous figure. Uncontrollably, as if his lips had a life of their own, his mouth formed probably the most simpering grin of his life. He tried to speak.

"Unnh, ah, ma'am, ah, miss," the Wolf said in a voice so low it astounded his drinking pals. He cursed himself for feeling so tongue-tied and drunk. He made a great and noble effort to coordinate his thoughts and speech. "It is good to shee, see you," he articulated carefully.

Charmaine flashed Wolf a dazzling smile. Then Court introduced Doc Russell, whose euphoric expression showed he too was in awe of the great dancer and singer. Being a specialist in bodies, the Doc appreciated hers. Her pectoralis major muscles particularly intrigued him. They curved smoothly down to join with her mammary glands, which looked to the Doc like two tight, cute half-cantaloupes that would just fit in his mouth. With this vision, good old Baby Huey knew he, too, had a ganglion or two separated by John Barleycorn.

"I am positively pleased to meet you," the Doc told Charmaine, succeeding with masterful willpower at keeping his eyes on her face and not on her chest. She acknowledged his greeting and, as if in appreciation of his gentlemanly restraint, gave his hand an extra squeeze.

Court, expecting some sort of a blast from his ex-wife, was pleasantly surprised when she took up conversation with Wolf Lochert, whose simpering grin had grown to painful proportions. Looking at him, Court thought to himself this was the perfect time for his dad's friend Benjamin Kubelsky, better known as Jack Benny, to play his screechy violin solo "Love in Bloom" for Wolf. When he started imagining the Wolf cavorting about in a ballet costume flinging flowers, he knew he was really crocked and started laughing out loud at himself.

"Where are you from, major?" Charmaine asked Wolf.

"Unh, call me Wolfgang," he said.

"I like Wolf better. Where are you from, Wolf?"

"Minninniapp . . . ah, Minnennapp—"

"Minneapolis?" she finished for him.

"Yes," he said, regaining his tongue. "That's in Minnesota, you know."

Afraid the sparkling repartee would be more than they could keep up with, Court and the Doc excused themselves.

"My God," the Doc said as they pushed through the crowd, "I do believe it's love at first sight."

"Beauty and the beast," Court said.

"How uncharitable," the Doc responded, "she's no beast."

They had another round of drinks at the bar. Court lit a cigarette and looked around. "Damn," he breathed as he saw the two PIO officers making their way over to them. The lieutenant colonel, about the only sober man in the club, looked distraught. The PIO captain with him looked noncommittal. Behind them, at the head table, Court saw his half brother watching them with a crooked smile on his face.

"Captain Bannister," the LC said, "your brother, Shawn, said that in about two days the *California Sun* will be printing an article he wrote about his flight with you. He won't exactly tell me what it's about, but he said the wire services are starting to show some interest in what is rumored to be a big story. Do you know anything about it?" The rheumy LC looked decidedly uneasy.

"First off, he's not my brother. Not my full brother, anyway," Court began. "Secondly, I don't have any idea what is in the article. Aside from the fact that he got sick in the airplane, and didn't like what we were doing, I don't know what he wrote."

"Can't you talk to him? Can't you find out?"

Court thought about it for a minute. Remembering Shawn's hateful look after they'd flown, he said, "No, sir, I can't."

"You mean you *won't*," the LC said. Court shrugged, thinking the LC looked about to plead his case. Instead, he glared at Court and went back to the head table. The PIO captain remained behind. Up close, his streetwise face looked resourceful, his black eyes canny. Tiny pockmarks accentuated his rugged good looks.

"Hi," he said, "I'm Angelo Correlli. I know what he wrote, and it ain't good." The two men shook hands.

"I didn't want to tell my boss," he indicated the departing LC, "until I talked to you. Besides, he probably wouldn't approve of my methods. My contacts in the billeting office told me Shawn was up late pounding the typewriter the other night. I sort of eased over the next day while he was out and read his draft copy. The title is 'Pandemonium Prevents Rescue.' In it, he says not only was the whole show fouled up, but you shot up a bus and napalmed the passengers when they tried to escape."

"Well, hell," Court said. "None of that is true, so what difference does it make?"

"A lot of difference," Correlli said. "There's an antiwar wave in the States. Even if they use the word 'alleged,' it'll be buried deep in the text while the headline booms out something like 'USAF Pilot Murders Civilians.' The old bit about only believing half of what you see and none of what you read no longer applies. 'It has to be true otherwise they wouldn't print it?' Right?" Correlli nodded his head to answer his own question. "Something else," he continued. "Shawn said as painful as it was to indict his beloved brother, he felt morally obligated in the interest of world peace to do just that."

" 'Morally obligated,' " Court snorted.

"All right, then," Correlli said, "so what actually did happen on that flight? Maybe we can figure out a way to head this off."

Court went through the F-100F flight with Shawn from start to finish. He told Correlli about how Shawn's untrained eye had mistaken the holed hull of the M113 command vehicle for a bus and the VC in the open for the passengers.

"What about the FAC?" Correlli asked, "He'd corroborate your story."

"He's dead," Court said, and told him that though Parker had been in the backseat, his word probably wouldn't be taken because he wasn't a trained FAC. "How about the word of the task force commander?" Court said.

"Probably not. They'd expect you two guys to back each other up." Correlli thought for a moment. "The pictures," he said, "would they prove your innocence?"

"Sure, but Shawn said the light was bad."

"I saw a Hasselblad 500EL in his room," Correlli said. "Was that what he used?" Court nodded. Correlli looked over his shoulder for a second to where Shawn Bannister now sat deep in conversation with a young pilot while the older PIO officer hovered nearby. The PIO captain turned back to Court and smiled, his eyes lively.

"I think I'll go for a walk," he said, and strolled out of the club.

Court watched him go, then turned and saw that Doc Russell had wandered off. He pushed through the throng to where Nancy Lewis and Toby Parker were in the center of some beer-soaked pilots, led by Lieutenant Freeman, who were teaching them the words to "There Are No Fighter Pilots Down in Hell." Spotting Court, Nancy disengaged, leaving a laughing Toby Parker behind.

"I don't know how you did it," Court said to her, "but that's the happiest Toby has been since . . . well, you know." He didn't want to say, "Since Phil Travers was killed."

"Just having him talk did a lot for me, too," she said. "I guess I thought I was the only one in pain."

Nancy tried hard not to stare at Court, thinking she had revealed too much and was unsure of what to say next. Damn, she thought, he looks terribly tall and handsome in his flight suit. I remember him from those terrible cowboy movies.

"You know," Court said, "you have the nicest eyes I have ever seen." The unexpected compliment further upset her balance.

"So do you," she blurted, looking into his grey-blue eyes. "I remember you from those cowboy movies," she said, inwardly kicking herself for such an inane remark.

"Weren't they awful," Court said.

"Now that you mention it, yes," she said with a grateful laugh.

"How about another drink?" he asked.

"Sure," she said, "as long as it doesn't have any alcohol in it. I'm up to here."

Court took her elbow to guide her through the throng of pilots toward the bar. The touch of her skin and the feel of her arm gave him an electrifying thrill that shot directly to his loins in a rushing swell of arousal that nearly unhinged his knees. He kept slightly behind her as they walked, hoping she wouldn't notice. Nearing the bar, he was jostled against her. He quickly put his hands out to hold her arms and steer her away from his lower body, but he was jostled again, forcing his engorged maleness to poke her from behind. She stiffened.

"Sorry," Court said, dreadfully embarrassed, but unable to keep a stupid grin from his face.

Nancy said nothing, not trusting herself to speak. My God, she thought, it's been so long. She could feel her legs trembling and grow weak. Then thoughts of Brad flooded her consciousness and she felt ashamed, yet earthy and restless.

She was grateful for the interruption as the first officer and Colonel Friedlander came by to say they were going over to the NCO Club to say hello to the other girls and have a drink with the troops.

"The captain sent word over," the first officer said, not slurring his words too badly. "We're to meet here in the club at eight tomorrow morning." He looked at his watch; it was barely past midnight. "The colonel has arranged ground transportation to Tan Son Nhut. From there, we'll deadhead out on the Okinawa flight. Make sure Tiffy and Sally get the word."

The two men excused themselves, then joined up with the commander of the Air Police squadron and left for the NCO Club. At the last minute, Shawn Bannister, saying he'd had enough of officers, went with them. At no time had he spoken to Court.

When they were gone, Nancy tried to lessen her feelings toward Court. They edged their way to a corner and spoke of the weather and her flying and what a hell of a guy Parker was. Relieved to have something safe to talk about, she told him the Toby Parker and Bubba Bates story.

"And you know, the funny thing is," she concluded, "I really thought he would write. I was kind of disappointed he didn't."

Court had decided to steer the conversation into something a bit more intimate, when they both noticed a hush spreading over the club. They turned to see pilots nudging each other and motioning with their heads toward the main door of the club.

Standing there, pale and hesitant in a freshly pressed flight suit, was Major Harold Rawson. His black hair was combed neatly back and his peanut mustache twitched like a rabbit's nose sampling the air as his eyes ranged over the crowd in wavering jerks.

20

☆

Over at the NCO Club, after Colonel Friedlander had arrived, Master Sergeant Booker Washington Smith stepped outside to confer with his boss, Lieutenant Colonel Fox H. Bernard, commander of the 3rd Air Police Squadron. They both had been edgy and uneasy. Counterintelligence from local sources had reported VC recce teams nosing around the area all week. Their assigned external base defender, the 173rd Airborne Brigade, was off on a search-and-destroy mission, leaving the area beyond the outer base defense perimeter guarded only by regional Vietnamese forces under the command of the Vietnamese Air Force.

"What do you think, Smitty?" Bernard asked.

"I think something's up, sir, and tonight might be the night. You know, some of our Viet people at the NCO Club walked out early tonight."

Bernard's head swiveled sharply to look at his sergeant. "So did those at the O-Club. Let's go look around."

Smith at the wheel, they sped off in one of their "self-help" vehicles, a camouflaged M-151 jeep with a pedestal-mounted M2 .50-calibre machine gun. The name Bertha Baby was stenciled in black letters on the front bumper.

Owing to a devastating lack of appropriate weapons and vehicles, somebody in the USAF had dreamed up the "Self-Help" program for the air police squadrons charged with internal base security in Vietnam.

The program, suggesting a spartan can-do attitude, was in effect because the air police had screw-all in the way of heavy weapons, off-road vehicles, or even adequate training to go to war and repulse enemy ground attacks. Thanks to an idiot order in the late '50's, thought to be from a certain Strategic Air Command general who believed himself a fighter pilot, the USAF had purged all heavy weapons from the air police inventory, leaving them with little else than the .30-caliber carbine and the .38-caliber revolver. On top of that, Dodge pickup trucks and International Scouts, even with the doors removed for ease of entry and exit, didn't even come close to providing the type of armored and armed transportation required to relieve guard posts at a defensive perimeter in a fire fight. Unable to correct the situation promptly, "Self-Help" was in operation, telling the USAF air police in Vietnam, in effect, "You're on your own, baby."

Bernard and Smith had studied both airpower usage and counter-insurgency. In drawing upon the lessons learned from studying Sun Tzu's *Art of War,* written 2,500 years ago, they had decided that a 20th-century variation of Sun Tzu and of air strategist Douhet's dictum could be perfectly applied to meet the conditions of modern warfare in that it would be easier to destroy the enemy's aerial power on the ground than in the air.

They also knew that, regardless of the proclamations of their Commander in Chief, President Lyndon Baines Johnson, American troops were moving out on more and more offensive maneuvers. They were not defensively hanging around to protect USAF bases. Ergo, VC attacks were ominously probable, so they had best prepare for them.

So, if "Self-Help" was the name, then self-help would be the game, and by God they would play it their way.

Using Military Interservice Procurement Requests—MIPR's—bartering, hoaxes, cons, and just plain midnight supply channels with the United States Army, Smith and Bernard, along with other selected air policemen, had amassed an impressive collection of weaponry. Their unauthorized inventory boasted M-60 machine guns, M-16 rifles, M-79 grenade launchers, several M18A1 Claymore anti-personnel mines, which threw 700 steel balls ahead of them in a sixty-degree arc, and were lethal to fifty meters, and two M-151 jeeps named Bertha Baby and Big Bertha, which mounted an M67 90mm recoilless rifle. They were particularly proud of these gun-toting vehicles because Smith had won them in a poker game from an Army warrant officer at the supply depot at Long Binh. Playing a hand of high-low split, he had bet two VNAF A-1 aircraft engines. No one doubted Smith could produce the 3,350 horsepower engines upon demand.

Yet, heavier vehicles were necessary, so Bernard and Smith had set up a "maverick" hunt, whereby all vehicles on or coming onto Bien Hoa Air Base without proper paperwork were "impounded." Though the maverick hunt had netted a six-by-six, so far no one had been able to turn up an M113 armored personnel carrier.

Parts for what vehicles and weapons the 3rd Air Police did have were always in short supply. As Lieutenant Colonel Bernard wrote to his boss at Tan Son Nhut in a scathing indictment of the system, "A 601B Supply Request Form won't stop Charlie at the fence, no matter how vigorously the sentry waves it."

And people were in short supply, too. Bernard and Smith had recruited several would-be cops, augmentees they called them, from base units such as food service, administration, and the postal squadron. Over 30 augmentees had been trained and assigned to report to designated internal positions, should the base come under attack.

In addition to their purloined weaponry, Bernard and Smith had rigged up a few unique surprises to defend the air base against ground attack. They called them Totem Pole and Fire Drum.

Totem Pole was a creation for high-intensity lighting of the base perimeter, using "rejected" and "surplus" aerial flares set in concave reflectors facing outward from the tops of tall poles. The triggering devices for these lights had been installed at the guard posts. That an unusual number of flares had been declared rejected or surplus didn't seem to bother a certain supply sergeant who was one of the top augmentees.

Fire Drum, in particular, had the 3rd AP's cackling and giggling to themselves. Someone with a particular talent for this sort of thing—a record search would reveal no name—had discovered that napalm and white phosphorous made a marvelously deadly mixture. The AP's called it phougas and poured it into metal containers remarkably similar to those used by the Army to ship 175mm propellant charges, which they stuck into the ground at an outward angle. They covered the open end with a weather-proof plastic membrane. An electrical circuit touched off an explosive charge under a plunger at the bottom of the drum, instantly expelling the phougas, which was then ignited by a phosphorous grenade. The burning material could fly out to 120 meters in front with a side coverage of 60 meters. So far, there had been no opportunity to use Fire Drum, and the AP's had been so secretive about it that not even the VC, much less higher headquarters, knew about it.

The air policemen were ready and eager to activate Fire Drum. They remembered their two men who had been garrotted during a VC night probe and the three dogs that had been poisoned. The suggestion from one of the handlers, whose dog had been poisoned, to use a Claymore mine as the propelling charge had been joyously implemented. Fire Drum now had steel balls, they said to each other.

After Bernard and Smith had checked in with AP operations on the jeep radio, they headed off base to check the surrounding Vietnamese guard posts. The results were not good. The first two posts had only one VNAF guard each. In pidgin Viet, Smith found out that the four additional regional forces due on duty in each post that night had never showed up. On hearing that bit of ominous intelligence, Bernard got on the radio to AP operations.

"Go Security Alert Condition Yellow," he commanded. The two men sped back on base, turned Bertha Baby over to its regular driver-gunner crew, and dashed into AP ops.

"Sir," the desk sergeant said immediately, "the dogs on the east perimeter are raising hell."

"Go SACON Red One. Put the word out," Bernard ordered, "safeties off, blast anything that moves."

"Does that include Totem Pole and Fire Drum?" Master Sergeant Smith checked to make sure.

"Damn right, Smitty." Smitty corroborated the word on the radio net. Instantly two Totem Poles lit up on the eastern perimeter. Ten seconds later the radio from Post Three, one of four out there, was heard from.

"They're on the wire," the operator screamed.

"Sound SACON Red Two," Lieutenant Colonel Fox Bernard ordered.

At the Officer's Club, Rawson stood deathly still in the doorway. Before anyone could move or say a word, and as if sparked by Rawson's presence, the base siren began moaning up to speed, signaling with its peculiar warble that Bien Hoa Air Base was now on SACON Red II, Security Alert Condition Red Option II, meaning a ground attack was imminent if not actually under way. As the siren wound up, a series of heavy explosions started in the distance, and in seconds ever louder ear-shattering blasts rippled directly toward the packed Officer's Club. The concussions caused dust to puff from joints in the wooden walls.

"Incoming," someone shouted.

"You don't say," someone else replied.

The pilots broke for the doors and windows to get to the bunkers. Doc Russell took off for the hospital. A blast close to the wooden Officer's Club sent small fragments ripping through the wall in back of the bar. Nancy Lewis felt something hot sting her left leg. She looked down in amazement at the widening red spot staining her slacks. Court put his arms around her, scooped her up, and ran out the door toward a bunker. He saw Wolf Lochert shielding Charmaine with his body as he ran in the entrance with her. Reaching it, he ducked to enter the dank sandbagged hole behind Toby Parker, Sally Churna, and a dozen or so others unidentifiable in the dark.

The bunkers on Bien Hoa Air Base were uniformly constructed over ten-by-twenty-foot rectangles dug to a depth of four feet. Cement covered the floor and formed walls to ground level. Sandbags piled on shelves of pierced steel planking, called PSP, rose four feet above ground to support the roof composed of timbers and sandbags. A few jagged corners of the PSP protruded into the blackness, cutting into those unfortunate enough to brush against them. There were no lights or supplies in the bunkers. In fact, a previous base commander had almost ordered them torn down during a base beautification plan he had originated. His boss, the wing commander, had halted that nonsense, along with the rock painting plan, in a torrent of verbal abuse that gave the base commander the trots for a week.

Sounding in the night sky over the sound of the whooshes and cracks of rockets and mortar shells, the base siren shrieked and warbled the note signaling, in case one was in doubt, that Bien Hoa Air Base was now officially in SACON Red II, signifying that enemy forces were actually attacking the installation.

After hustling Charmaine into the bunker, Wolf Lochert climbed on top of it. Facing east, he lay prone with the M-16 he had retrieved from the club along with his pistol belt. His 7.63mm Mauser and his stiletto were still strapped to his ankles. Stepping on the sandbags while climbing to the top, Wolf Lochert noticed the small wooden sign saying he was at Bunker 6.

21

☆

As the preliminary mortar and rocket attack began, Buey Dan, dressed in black pajamas, lay in the tranh grass a few meters outside the eastern perimeter of Bien Hoa Air Base. Once a year or less, Buey Dan would leave Saigon and join the field VC for a few weeks to train and participate in raids. At those times he used his field name, *Thán Lán*—the Lizard. The work revitalized him and kept him alert to what information the fighting front needed.

Next to Buey Dan, also in black pajamas, lay Tui. Her face was defeated and dull and without emotion. Strapped to her back was a khaki-colored satchel containing an explosive charge. Spread out on both sides of them was the sixteen-man assault team Buey Dan controlled for this raid. The team was one of three from the C-238 sapper company. Each team was composed of four cells: a four-man penetration cell with bangalore torpedoes, two five-man assault cells with satchel charges, and a two-man fire support team with B-40 grenade launchers and AK-47 rifles. The penetration and assault teams also carried AK-47's and hand grenades. They were all dressed in black pajamas and soft, floppy camouflage hats, and wore black rubber sandals cut from old tires. Knowing the 3rd Air Police Squadron at Bien Hoa had sentry dogs, each man smelled of *toi,* the garliclike herb they had rubbed on themselves to confuse the dogs' sense of smell. Each of the ten assault cell members had a faded khaki-colored canvas satchel strapped to his back. Each sack contained four kilograms, about eight pounds, of explosive that could be detonated by a six-inch cord with a small wooden ball at the exposed end.

The handmade lanyard was taped to the left side of the sack, where it could easily be pulled by the wearer's left or right hand but was not so loose as to catch on any protrusions. The carrier had his choice of unslinging the sack, pulling the cord, and tossing the sack at a target or of pulling the cord and making himself into a human bomb on a suicide mission. Although it was supposed to explode in eight seconds, the crude timer device would detonate the satchel charge anywhere from five to ten seconds after being actuated. The sappers were also trained to pull the lanyard on any downed comrade.

For the last three days, Buey Dan, as the Lizard, had supervised the extraction of last-minute information from the hootch maids and waitresses and other female and male workers on the air base. Family members of five workers had to be threatened and sliced before they would give the desired cooperation. Buey Dan had added the information he gained to that which had been collected by the prestrike reconnaissance team that had been in the area for several weeks. The team had sounded out external security measures and determined the internal layout and positions of defenses, ammo storage, airplane positioning, and officer bunkers in order to determine where to place the aiming stakes and position the rockets and mortars. They had noted that the 173rd Airborne Brigade was out on operations and that only weak, easily unnerved Vietnamese regional forces were on duty.

Buey Dan's Number 2 man had carefully depicted all of the air base information in a sandbox he had constructed in the huge underground complex east of Bien Hoa. Buey Dan would have preferred a full-sized stake-and-string replica, but space did not permit such luxury. Nonetheless, every team member had become totally familiar with the layout and knew exactly where he had to go by memorizing how many steps and how many turns in what direction were required to reach his target. At the signal, after selected sectors of the 122mm Katyusha rocket and 82mm mortar barrage were lifted at specified times, the sappers would rush in. Working with them were riflemen who would shoot and throw grenades at defensive positions. In this manner, something would always be impacting or blowing up somewhere on the base while the infiltrators were rushing to their appointed tasks in the barrage-free zones.

Buey Dan was using the tried-and-true VC tactical doctrine of four fast, one slow; fast advance, fast assault, fast battlefield clearance, and fast withdrawal are based on slow preparation.

The lead men in Buey Dan's sector had already penetrated the first coils of barbed wire and had placed their command-detonated bangalore torpedoes. The long, tube-shaped bangalores would blast a path through the wire when Buey Dan pushed the plunger on his Chicom LA-2B generator. The men had crept up to the second wire from which they would move when Buey Dan blew his whistle. He was prepared to do so in thirty seconds, when the barrage was due to lift in their sector.

Buey Dan, a satchel charge on his back as well, edged closer to Tui. He had had a hard time explaining to the sapper battalion commander why this particular woman should be on this raid. The commander had relented when Buey Dan had said she was making atonement for a grievous crime against the Liberation, and that he would assume total responsibility for her actions.

Buey Dan put his mouth close to Tui's ear.

"You know where to go," he whispered in tonal syllables.

"Yes," she whispered back after a brief pause, "Bunker Seven, near the Officer's Club." She repeated like a mantra to herself the number of steps and turns she had to make in the practiced path to her target. There were no memorized steps for a return path. She had no feelings or reactions in her mind other than the mechanics of what she was to do that night. Her reindoctrination and self-criticism periods hadn't taken well during the previous week, requiring Buey Dan to push a needle into the vein in her left arm twice a day to inject 60 mg of *bao ché,* a phenobarbital derivative, to keep her in the docile state he desired.

"Understand, little sister," he said in a smoothing whisper, "your life is your gift to the Liberation. Your memory will live forever as a glorious example for killing so many *mui lo* officers. You will die splendidly." Buey Dan knew that if Tui scrupulously followed her plan and there were no new base defenses, she had one chance in three of making it into Bunker 7.

In Bunker 6 Court flicked on his Zippo lighter to see Nancy's wound. He crouched over her as she sat with her back against the sandbag wall. The wound was in her outer left thigh about halfway between her hip and her knee; her slacks were now soggy with blood. Sally Churna pushed over to help.

"Where's your flight surgeon?" she asked.

"He took off for the hospital," a voice said.

Sally looked at Nancy's bloody slacks.

"Somebody give me a knife," she said. An opened penknife appeared out of the darkness to be placed in her hand. Someone lit another lighter as Court's flickered low. Someone else began ripping up pieces of paper to feed a small fire that lit the bunker with a weak and flickering flame.

Sally slit Nancy's slacks from the beltline to the ankle and peeled the soaked fabric back from where the fragment had sliced the skin. The wound was meaty-looking but appeared to be superficial; it was no longer bleeding heavily, which was a good indication that no veins or arteries had been punctured. Nancy, white around her mouth, looked on with fascination.

"Tear some strips for me," Sally ordered. Court tore strips from the slacks.

"Anybody bring a bottle of whisky?" he asked into the flickering light.

"As a matter of fact, yes," Lieutenant Fairchild said, appearing out of the gloom to produce a half-full bottle of scotch he had snatched on the way out of the club. The air reeked as Court poured some into the open wound. Nancy drew her breath in sharply.

"Damn," she said, "in survival training they told us this was not a good antiseptic. That it sometimes was of more value inside than out."

"It's what they do in the movies," Court said, handing her the bottle.

"Here's to a painkiller," Nancy said, taking a swig while Sally bound and knotted torn strips over the wound.

When the barrage in his sector lifted, Buey Dan pushed the plunger into the hand generator detonating the bangalores and blew the attack signal on his whistle while the crack of the wire-destroying charges still echoed in the air. The men of the assault teams rose and plunged forward, bending low to the ground and breathing easily as they ran, counting paces. After a momentary hesitation due more to confusion than fear, Tui rose, started her mantra, and plunged ahead. Buey Dan nodded with satisfaction as he ran after her and his teams.

At first the going was easy. Crouching low and running behind Tui, Buey Dan followed her through the path blasted in the wire. He inhaled the yellowish wisps of smoke containing the bitter smell of the picric acid used in the bangalore torpedo explosive mixture. For a few seconds, Tui and the advancing members of his sapper teams were outlined against the lights and reflected glow from the air base.

Buey Dan heard the sirens sounding SACON Red II and saw portions of the base black out as base engineering forces began pulling the main electrical circuit breakers to cut out all nonessential circuits. The smaller lights winked out, but the big floods on the flight line remained on, as did all floods that illuminated portions of the outer perimeter. Then Buey Dan heard the sound of scattered emergency generators starting as their solenoids sensed power failure, and clicked shut, feeding battery power to their starters. He knew the generators would feed priority air base communications and certain dispensary circuits. Each generator was targeted for a satchel charge.

After they breached the outer wire, Buey Dan saw his teams split into the smaller groups and head for fuel areas, ammo dumps, and the flight line. No team was to try for the airplanes in the protected rosettes, since they were easily guarded and difficult to get at. Instead, a group was to destroy targets of opportunity, such as airplanes diverted in for the night that were parked on the big ramp in front of the control tower. A grenade tossed into a rosette as you sped by was authorized, but the big satchel charges were earmarked for specific targets.

Buey Dan ran close to Tui. The five-man assault cells had split into individual attackers. Behind him, Buey Dan heard the AK-47 fire and B-40 blasts of the fire support teams, while ahead he heard sporadic M-16 fire as the defending security police probed by fire, shooting into areas they thought might contain advancing sappers. A man ahead and to Tui's left hit a trip wire, which pulled a flare, instantly illuminating his area. Looking away to protect his night vision, Buey Dan pulled Tui to the ground as a hail of fire swept the area from an observation tower. He heard the scream and gurgle of the sapper who'd tripped the flare, as the defenders poured a volume of fire at what was, finally, a visible target.

"Off this way," Buey Dan said, pushing Tui to crawl away from the light. Once out of the circle of flare light, he stood and pulled her up. "Hurry. Run." Tui looked confused. She had lost her count.

"Bunker Seven," Buey Dan said, punching her arm, then pointing. "That way." Tui started again, looking wobbly and frail.

Two sappers in front of her were appointed to blast a path in the secondary defense zone. She had fallen behind, which saved her when one sapper tripped a Fire Drum. It coughed and belched a horrendous shower of flaming detritus through the air, covering several sappers, while the 700 steel balls from the Claymore whistled low and deadly, scything down two VC outside the flaming arc. The screams of the burning men subsided quickly as the flaming material was sucked into their throats and lungs. Tui and Buey Dan ran through the low flames over the wounded and dead.

Tui dodged and feinted, her mantra useless now. They passed

through the secondary defense line and surprised a sentry who was running with his dog to a guard post. Buey Dan twitched his finger on his AK-47, sending three rounds into the young man's chest. They emerged from his back in a welter of blood and splintered spinal column bones. He was dead before he dropped his rifle and flopped to the ground. The German shepherd emitted a screaming snarl and leaped at Tui, who was closest. His leash was still wound around his dead handler's wrist so that the dog flipped upside down from the momentum of his lunge. Scrambling to his feet, he dug his paws in to lunge again at Tui. He scrabbled from side to side, like a sled dog in harness, towing his master's inert body by its outstretched arm that pointed at the dog with each sideways lunge. Buey Dan gut-shot the crazed animal as he and Tui ran by.

Air policemen in guard posts beside the fuel and ammo dumps triggered their Totem Poles, lighting up their area brighter than the sun at high noon. The brilliant white light from the burning magnesium aerial flares overpowered natural color to illuminate the scene in stark black and white. Sentries fought to hold back their snarling dogs, which had become so frenzied by all the noise and rush of battle that they were foaming at the mouth and crazy to attack. One broke loose to dash out and sink his teeth into the throat of an attacker who had been momentarily blinded by the burning white light. Both dog and VC died along with two other attackers as withering fire from two well-placed M-60 machine guns swept into them, hammering into their bodies long after they fell.

Buey Dan could tell by the sounds of firing and lack of satchel explosions that the attack was being badly blunted. He instinctively measured the distinctly heavier volume of fire of the American M-16 against the sporadic noise of the Soviet AK-47. He had heard only two of the peculiar blatting/ripping sounds of satchel charges going off when he should have heard nine or ten. The helicopter pad holding the Huey gunships of the American Army's 12th Aviation Group should have been hit by now. Instead, Buey Dan heard the sound of their turbine engines starting, which meant the gunships would soon be in the air.

In the confusion he lost Tui, but kept on course toward his target, Bunker 6, known to be a place for pilots to seek shelter. Buey Dan had often tried to convince his superiors it was more important to kill pilots than to destroy airplanes that were so easily replaced. He dodged around an abandoned jeep that was in flames, and slid with oiled precision into a drainage ditch barely fifty yards from Bunker 6.

As Buey Dan cautiously raised himself up and peered over the lip of the ditch, he spotted the outline of a man on top of the bunker, positioned behind a shoulder weapon of some kind. While he watched, another man came out of the bunker and climbed the sand-bags to the top.

"Get your head down, kid," Wolf Lochert growled at Toby Parker as the young lieutenant climbed up next to him.

"How's it going inside?" Wolf asked, his eyes sweeping the area in front of the bunker.

Toby told him about the bandaging of Nancy Lewis, then asked Wolf what he could do to help.

"See that fuzzy line down there in the dark?" the Wolf said, indicating the drainage ditch where Buey Dan lay. "Keep an eye on it. Look sideways. Watch for movement. It's the closest place for logical attack position."

Parker said he would, then almost went straight up in the air when a voice behind them at the base of the bunker spoke.

"Hello up there, Bunker Six. We're two air policemen on bunker defense. Take it easy, we're climbing up."

The two men, both with M-16's, one with a Prick 25, squirmed into position on either side of Wolf and Toby. The leader, a staff sergeant, eyed Wolf and his M-16.

"You know how to use that thing, sir?" he asked, thinking Wolf was a pilot untrained in such low-caliber plebeian things. As he spoke, an overhead flare popped from Spooky, just arrived on station.

The Wolf turned his head toward the staff, who drew back slightly when he saw Wolf's toothy leer and tiger suit.

"Yessir," the staff sergeant stammered, "I guess you do," and turned to face the direction of attack. At that point, he didn't feel like telling the unarmed lieutenant to go below.

The unarmed lieutenant was staring fixedly at an object in the shadows to one side. He thought it had moved. He knew it couldn't be a VC because it was between Bunkers 6 and 7. Maybe, Toby thought to himself, it's merely someone caught out, perhaps even wounded. Then, motivated from somewhere deep, he had a vision of his rushing out to save whoever it was. He rolled past the air policeman to his left, and jumped to the entrance pit of the bunker.

"Must be going inside," the Wolf muttered.

Instead, Toby leapt over the low sandbag retaining wall to make a dash to whoever was down. Just at that time, the downed figure jumped up and ran in a kind of sideways lope toward Toby and the bunker. Toby skidded to a halt.

"Don't shoot," he yelled back to the men on top, "it might be somebody wounded."

His cry held up the three guns that swung to the sudden target long enough for the running figure to get within 10 feet of Toby, close enough for him to recognize the advancing figure.

"Tui," he cried. He took a half step toward her, not really seeing the black pajamas and the khaki straps of the satchel charge. Her right hand was across her body grasping the wooden ball of the detonating lanyard as she had been taught. She had lost her floppy hat. The left side of her thick dark hair was streaming behind her, the other had swung forward to lie under her chin and over her shoulder, framing her expressionless face.

Tui ran toward Toby, faster and faster. Her eyes came alive and truly focused on him for the first time. Her thin mouth started to smile. She released the ball and stretched both arms out to Toby.

"Tow-bee, Tow-bee," she cried, a split second before the three M-16's from atop the bunker opened up and pummeled her frail body backward in a rubber-legged dance until she collapsed in a crumpled mound of black.

Buey Dan saw his chance as all the attention from atop Bunker 6 was focused to the side on Tui. He leapt to his feet and ran to within ten yards of the bunker. Laying down his AK-47, he unslung his satchel charge, pulled the lanyard, and pitched the explosive into the mouth of the bunker. Continuing through in the same pitching motion, he whirled, snatched up his AK-47, and ran back to the ditch. He had gotten close enough to recognize the awful face of the *mui lo* who had killed his son. He felt some satisfaction knowing he would soon see him die in a volcano of flame and concussion.

The three men on the roof, shocked at seeing Tui's shattered body, did not notice the khaki satchel slung through the air behind them. Wolf was the first to recognize the soft thump as it fell inside. He knew with dreadful certainty what it was.

Before he could react, a figure carrying the satchel charge burst from the bunker at a dead run and nearly made it to the ditch before evaporating in a round red explosion that made a three-foot crater oozing yellow smoke.

Overhead, Spooky's miniguns moaned and flicked through the enemy positions.

22

3000023Z DEC 65
FM: 7TH AF HQ MACV TAN SON NHUT AB RVN
TO: RUEDHQA/CSAF
RUHLKM/CINCPACAF
RUWAB/82ND COMBAT SP WING
INFO: RUEDNBA/TAC
BT
S E C R E T   2BV   XXXX
SUBJECT: 7TH AIR FORCE/IGS DISUM

A. (U) TACSITREP
B. (U) OVERVIEW IN TWO PARTS.
    PART I: JOINT-USE USAF-VNAF BASE, BIEN HOA, BINH
    HOA PROVINCE, III CORPS TACTICAL ZONE.
    PART II: 7TH AF COMMAND-WIDE PROSPECTIVE
C. (U) PART I BIEN HOA AB, RVN
D. (U) MAP REFERENCE: SHEETS: XT6361 III/IV
E. (S) GENERAL ENEMY SITUATION:
    1) ENEMY-INITIATED CONTACTS NIL THE PREVIOUS
    WEEK VICINITY BNH. HOWEVER, HEAVY FIGHTING IN
    WAR ZONE C (REF LOC NINH MAP SHEET 6245 II AND
    DISUM 20-01-66) THOUGHT TRIGGERED BY SF MOBILE
    REACTION FORCE PRELUDE TO COORDINATED ATTACKS
    OF COMBINED VC/NVA ON MAJOR US/SVN INSTALLA-
    TIONS. BNH SAPPER PENETRATION THOUGHT DRESS
    REHEARSAL AND PROBE SINCE ENEMY FORCES SUR-
    PRISINGLY INSUFFICIENT AND EASILY REPULSED.
    2) NORMAL ENEMY HARASSMENT AND PROPAGANDA OP-
    ERATIONS SHOW INCREASE IN OUTLYING VILLAGES.

   3) ENEMY UNITS IN 20 KM RADIUS BNH:

UNIT	STRENGTH	DIST/DIR
1ST MF BN	150	8 KM S
2ND MF BN	200	7 KM S
BIEN HOA SAPPER BN	250	7 KM S
SEE 2-224		

F. (S) ENEMY OPERATIONS:

   1) EASTERN PERIMETER BNH AB: AN ESTIMATED ELEMENT BNH SAPPER BN LAUNCHED A COORDINATED ATTACK COMMENCING WITH AN ESTIMATED 25 RNDS OF B-40 RNDS, EST 40 122MM ROCKET RNDS, EST 30 60MM MORTAR RNDS. OUTER PERIMETER PENETRATED. SPECIAL SELF-HELP DEFENSE DEVICES PREVENTED FURTHER PENETRATION.

G: (C) DAMAGE

   1) AIRCRAFT:

USAF F-100S	1 DEST	USAF F-100	2 DAM
USAF A-1	0 DEST	USAF A-1	3 DAM
VNAF A-1	1 DEST	VNAF A-1	1 DAM

B707 ON FIELD OVERNIGHT FOR MAINTENANCE: NO DAM

   2) EQUIPMENT:

   2 JEEP M151 DEST; 1 P/U DAM; 1 CRANE DAM

   3) FACILITIES

   CONTROL TOWER, EM BARRACKS, SQDN OPS SLIGHT DAM

H. (U) CASUALTIES

   1) FRIENDLY:

   THREE (3) OFF WIA; ONE (1) OFF KIA; FOURTEEN (14) EM WIA; TWO (2) CIV WIA

   2) ENEMY:

   TWELVE (12) KIA BODY COUNT; EST TWENTY-FOUR (24) WIA

I. (S) OTHER INTELLIGENCE FACTORS

   1) NEW ENEMY UNIT IDENTIFICATION; THE 9TH ARTILLERY BN REPORTEDLY NOW LOCATED IN DELTA AND CHARLEY REGION. STRENGTH, CAPABILITIES, AND EXACT LOCATION UNK. FURTHER INFO TO FOLLOW FUTURE DISUMS.

   2) FRIENDLY GROUND ACTIVITY

A) MAJOR OF THE CONTACTS WITHIN 20 KMS WERE BY US FORCES WITH SMALL ENEMY UNITS. HOWEVER, ONE ARVN CONTACT WAS REPORTED TO BE WITH ESTIMATED COMPANY SIZE VC UNIT.

B) US FORCES UNCOVERED THREE ENEMY CACHES

YIELDING FOLL ITEMS: FOUR AK-47 RIFLES, TWO 9MM
PISTOLS, FOUR SKS CARBINE, ONE M-79 GRENADE
LAUNCHER, TWO M-16 RIFLES, TWO 81MM MORTAR
CANISTERS, 5000 RNDS AK AMMO, EIGHT HOMEMADE
GRENADES, SEVENTY LBS RICE, TEN LBS SALT, THREE
VC FLAGS.

J. (S) COUNTERINTELLIGENCE:
1) SECURITY: DOCUMENTS CONTINUE TO BE CIRCULATED
   FROM VC/NVA HQ TO FIELD UNITS INDICATING A)
   SECURITY OF VC UNITS ENDANGERED BY CONTINUED
   SEARCH OPERATIONS OF US/RVN FORCES IN III AND IV
   CTZ. THESE DOCS TELL VC/NVA QUOTE: THIS OVERALL
   THREAT TO THE LIBERATION OF SVN MUST BE MET
   WITH RENEWED VIGILANCE. B) A RE-EMPHASIS ON
   THE WATCH SYSTEM WHEREBY ONE SOLDIER WILL
   WATCH AND REPORT THE ACTIVITIES OF ANOTHER. NO
   SOLDIERS WILL LEAVE UNITS IN LESS THAN GROUPS
   OF THREE. ANYONE ATTEMPTING TO DESERT TO CHIEU
   HOI WILL BE SHOT. INCREASE THE AMOUNT OF TIME
   DEVOTED TO POLITICAL INDOCTRINATION ENDQUOTE.
2) ESPIONAGE: POW REPORTS AS WELL AS CAPTURED DOC-
   UMENTS MENTION ESPIONAGE SCHOOL CONDUCTED
   FOR VC AGENTS IN CAMBODIA. THE STUDENTS AT-
   TENDING ARE YOUNG MALE AND FEMALE TEENAGERS
   MOSTLY FROM SAIGON AREA. TRAINING EMPHASIS ON
   MALES HAS BEEN DEMOLITIONS WITH PROJECTED
   ASSIGNMENTS TO SAPPER/SABOTAGE UNITS. FEMALES
   ARE BEING TAUGHT TO DRAW PICTURES OF MILITARY
   INSTALLATIONS AND EQUIPMENT. FEMALE TO BE TAR-
   GETED AGAINST US INSTALLATIONS. ONCE EMPLOYED
   ON US BASE, SHE WILL SELECT TARGETS AND BE PRE-
   PARED TO LEAD SAPPER/SABOTAGE UNITS TO IT.
   REASON GIVEN FOR YOUTHFUL EMPHASIS IS US MIL
   PERSONNEL KNOWN TO BE RELAXED AND FRIENDLY
   WHEN DEALING WITH YOUNG VN GIRLS AND ARE KNOWN
   TO ALLOW THEM SOME FREEDOM OF MOVEMENT.

K. (C) NEW ENEMY TACTICS, WEAPONS, EQUIPMENT:
    ONE VC FEMALE CARRYING SATCHEL CHARGE KIA IN
    BNH ATTACK. IDENTIFIED BY USAF OFF AS UNMAR-
    RIED SAIGONESE INDICATES UNUSUAL VC USE OF
    PERSONNEL POSSIBLY DUE TO LACK OF RECRUITS. NO
    NEW WEAPONS OR EQUIPMENT FOUND.

L. (S) ENEMY CAPABILITIES:

1) THE ENEMY IS CAPABLE OF INCREASING TERRORIST ACTIVITIES, CONDUCTING MULTI-BATTALION SIZE ATTACKS AGAINST BIEN HOA AND LOCAL FWF, AVOIDING CONTACT, INCREASING HARASSMENT OF INSTALLATIONS AND INTERDICTING LOCS, ESTABLISHING SUPPLY POINTS AND BASE CAMPS IN UNPOPULATED AREAS, INCREASING ROCKET AND MORTAR ATTACKS, INCREASING SAPPER/SABOTAGE ACTIVITIES.

M. (S) FRIENDLY FORCES IN 20 KM RADIUS:

1) US: TWO BNS 196TH INF BRIG, THREE BNS 199TH INF BRIG, ELEMENTS 1ST AND 25TH INF DIVS TO INCLUDE TWO AIR CAV BNS, ELEMENTS 173RD AND 82ND AIRBORNE

2) ARVN: FOUR BNS 5TH RANGER GRP, THREE BRIGS MARINES, THREE BRIGS AIRBORNE.

N. (S) CONCLUSION:

BIEN HOA ATTACK THOUGHT TO BE SECOND PHASE OF ATTEMPTED AMBUSH OF 1ST INF DIV ARMORED COLUMN. AMBUSH OF ARMOR THOUGHT TO 1) DETERMINE HOW FAST LEAD ELEMENTS 1ST INF DIV CAN RESPOND AND 2) DRAW DEFENDERS FROM BIEN HOA OPENING HOLE FOR SAPPER/SABOTAGE ATTACK. ENEMY RECCE AND PENETRATION EFFORTS INDICATE INTENT OF A MAJOR ATTACK TOWARD MAIN US/SVN INSTALLATIONS IN NEAR FUTURE. YET POW INTERROGATIONS, RELIABLE AGENTS, AND DOCUMENTS INDICATE ENEMY HAS NOT COMPLETED FORCE POSITIONING OR RECCE FOR SUCH AN ATTACK. ESTIMATE UPCOMING MAJOR GROUND OFFENSIVE WITHIN THE MONTH.

O. (UNC)ADDENDUM CSAF EYES ONLY:

RECOMMENDATION BEING FORWARDED MOST EXPEDITIOUS MEANS FOR MEDAL OF HONOR FOR MAJOR HAROLD L. RAWSON, FV224109, 531ST TFS, BIEN HOA AB, RVN, KIA. SYNOPSIS: ON NIGHT OF 29 JAN 66 AT APPROX 2345L HOURS, MAJOR RAWSON PICKED UP A VC SATCHEL CHARGE THROWN INTO A BUNKER AT BNH CONTAINING EIGHT (8) MIL, FIVE (5) CIVILIAN PERSONNEL AND WITH COMPLETE DISREGARD FOR PERSONAL SAFETY HE EXITED THE BUNKER WITH THE CHARGE AND RAN WITH IT FROM THE AREA UNTIL IT DETONATED.

ENDMESSAGEENDMESSAGE

At first light the day after the attack, three platoons of fresh troops
from the 173rd arrived on the air base. They were under orders to
tour the battle sites (there were three penetration sites), clean up any
pockets of resistance (there were none), and reestablish the integrity
of the inner perimeter defense (it was never lost). Bare-armed, wearing flak jackets and steel pots, they carried their weapons at the ready
as the USAF air policemen and augmentees led them around the
charred and devastated battle sites. The soldiers shook their heads as
the skinny clerk and cook augmentees explained about the Totem
Poles and the ruination caused by the Fire Drums. Lieutenant Colonel Fox Bernard and Master Sergeant Booker Washington Smith
purposely stayed in the background, smirking only slightly as the
soldiers of the 173rd were led to believe the battle had been won
entirely by the augmentees.

Just after 1200 a large contingent of personnel from the 3rd Tactical
Fighter Wing gathered at the main ramp on the flight line to see the
Braniff crew board the Army helicopter set up to take them to Tan
Son Nhut. Sally Churna and Tiffy Berg were working hard to hold
their brave smiles in place through the tears that came afresh every
time another airman or pilot embraced them and said goodbye. Their
arms, and those of the other three girls, were full of small presents
and flowers. Their flight purses were stuffed with bits of paper with
names and telephone numbers so they could fulfill the wishes of the
young men who wanted "just a short call to mom, will you, to tell
her I'm okay." They had no such requests to call wives.

Colonel Friedlander was flying, as were Darlington, and Higgens
the homeless sex maniac, and Freeman. Fairchild was off looking for
Ramrod, who had disappeared during the attack. Toby Parker stood
with Wolf Lochert off to one side. Wolf, facing Parker, was talking.

"Toby," he said, "you got to knock this heavy face stuff off."
He stopped abruptly as he realized he had spoken as if he were giving

a direct order to a recalcitrant private. He resumed in a more fatherly tone. "You volunteered to come over here. You told me that yourself. What did you expect to find? Some Hollywood movie with a happy ending? This is a crappy war. All wars are crappy, but this one is more crappy than most." He couldn't help himself, his voice became harsher. "You're here because you wanted to be. I know what you've seen has been a shock. But you got to learn something, dammit. You got to learn to accept the crap. Put it in a box in a corner and never open it again. Pretty soon, it'll go away." He knew that wasn't true, at least not for himself. He still saw the death throes of every man who had died by his hand.

"Think it out," Lochert resumed in a kind voice. "You can leave it all behind. Your boss is sending you to Phan Rang to the FAC school."

Parker stirred. "I'm not going to be a FAC," he corrected, "just the school executive officer."

"Yeah, but you are getting out of here. New faces, new places. You'll forget all this." Lochert paused. "And her," he added softly, remembering Parker's near catatonic state after seeing Tui so gruesomely killed. Wolf had slapped his face twice to bring him around.

"I suppose you're right, Wolf," Parker said, "about this being a crappy war, anyhow. But who says I have to accept it?"

"I didn't say 'accept' it, I said forget the crap."

"Yeah, sure," Parker said, rubbing the jade earring between left thumb and index finger. "Sure." He looked down at the jade piece for a long moment, then put it into his fatigue blouse pocket. He sighed, and turned to face Lochert. "What about you, Wolf, are you staying on here?"

"No, I'm not," the burly man said. "I'll be at Fifth Special Forces Group in Nha Trang for a few months, then . . ." He didn't continue.

"Then," Parker said.

"Then what?"

"Come on, Wolf. You've been chewing me out for being uncommunicative, and now you won't talk."

"You ever heard of MACSOG?"

"No. What or where is it?"

"Oh, it's down there in Saigon." The Wolf's voice was unnaturally light.

Parker looked at him. "Oh, it's down there in Saigon," he mimicked. "Just what is a MACSOG that has you so evasive?"

"I'm not being evasive. Who says I'm being evasive?" the Wolf boomed, back in form. "MACSOG is actually the Military Assistance Command Vietnam Studies and Observation Group. You leave the V out and call it MACSOG."

Parker lifted an eyebrow. "Studies and observation? You're going to study and observe something?"

"Yeah."

"Like what?" Parker persisted.

"Oh, I don't know. Ethnic indigenous internecine intransigence toward insurgency, maybe." The Wolf's face was as guileless as that of an altar boy serving his first mass. Parker nodded. "Ok, Wolf. No more questions."

Standing next to them just out of earshot was Court Bannister. His flight suit was dark with sweat, and the strain of the mission he had flown was etched on his face. He stood with his foot on the small running board of the jeep, talking to Nancy Lewis seated inside. She wore new USAF fatigue pants and a white blouse. The pants were split up the left leg, allowing room for the bandage on her thigh. A pair of crutches was propped in the back.

"Doctor Russell said I could have the bandage off in about a week. He's so sweet. He gave me a kiss and asked if I'd call his wife and tell her he's alive and well," Nancy said. She looked at Court, "Where are your brother and your wife?" She frowned. "Nuts. I mean where are your half—," she started again, "Where are Shawn and Charmaine?"

"They left for Saigon about an hour ago on the Air Force bus. Colonel Friedlander had it set up for them on this helicopter." He nodded at the Huey slick standing by. "But Shawn said he preferred to bus so he could 'talk to the troops,' as he put it. He was put out. Seems he lost some film rolls and part of his equipment when a rocket or mortar round blew down half the wall of his room in the BOQ."

He and his brother had had a bad scene that morning. Correlli had developed the negatives of the film from Shawn's camera. Though they had to be enhanced in processing, they clearly showed the holed hulls to be M-113's and not buses. Court had presented the pictures to Shawn and said he had done him a favor by getting them developed and he might want to include them with his article. Shawn, knowing this would spike the napalming civilian portion of his article, had been furious and accused Court of being a thief. Court had not told him about Correlli. He felt halfway between sheepish at the method and relieved at the outcome of Correlli's action.

Court took Nancy's right hand in both of his. She was startled, but didn't withdraw. She looked into Court's eyes for a second, then turned away.

"Court, I don't want to get involved. I can't," she said, her voice low and hesitant. I'm lying to him, she thought to herself. I want him so badly. I could love him. I want to love him. Her bottom lip trembled.

"I can't," she repeated, with resignation.

"I know," he said. "I guess I really don't want to get involved, either." He helped her out of the jeep and reluctantly let go of her hand. Damn, he thought, I can't let her go like this.

"Give me your address," he demanded. "I want to write you."

She flashed a half smile. "You sound like a certain lieutenant we know." She fumbled in her purse for her card and scribbled an address on it. "He never wrote, though." She nodded to where Parker stood with Lochert.

"I will," Court said. He took her bag as they started for the helicopter. She used only one crutch. When they passed by Lochert and Parker, Nancy impulsively kissed and hugged them both. She thanked Wolf for his words about Brad. "And you," she said to Parker, "have got to stop frowning." She reached up to smooth his brow and kissed him again on the cheek. "Goodbye, good luck," they said to each other.

The Huey crew chief gave the windup signal with his right forefinger. The turbines started rotating the blades of the slick and its gunship escort. The other girls, with Sally and Tiffy, scrambled on board, the captain, engineer, and first officer right behind. The captain reached back to help Nancy as Court aided her up the step. The hissing whine from the Huey turbine was getting louder. Impulsively, Nancy held back.

"Oh, Court, oh yes, write me," Nancy said and brushed her lips to Court's ear. "I want to get involved," she said. She turned and grasped the outstretched hand of her captain. She settled in and looked out as the helicopter lifted off. She saw Court mouth the words "I do, too" just before the helicopter dipped its nose and sped off with its escorting gunships. The crowd of airmen who had gathered to see them off slowly dispersed.

Parker, Lochert, and Bannister stayed on the line until the whopping sounds from the two helicopters faded and were replaced by the thunder from the afterburners of three F-100's taking off at ten-second intervals. Lochert said he'd drop Bannister off at the squadron and Parker at wing headquarters. They climbed into the black jeep.

"That girl, you know, the one with the green eyes," he said to Bannister.

"You mean Charmaine?"

"Yeah. Someone said you were once married to her. That true?"

"Yes."

"She married now?"

"No, why?"

"No reason. Just wondered," Wolf said, the lie as readable on his face as a telegram. Folded in his blouse pocket was a sheet of commercial black-and-white composite photographs of Charmaine in various poses. On the back were dance and action shots. On the front was a full-face head shot, which Wolf could barely stand to look at. Charmaine's wide-set eyes seemed to peer into his very being, promising unthinkable ecstasies. Across the bottom she had scrawled in green ink the words, "Just for you, Wolf. Just for you."

23

☆

"I appreciate your coming in, gentlemen, and I'll be brief. We have lost over thirty 0-1E airplanes, and twenty-three FAC pilots are dead or missing. The biggest shoot-down rate is in the DMZ, Route Pack One north of the DMZ, and Laos. The war is escalating and we cannot continue to send tiny backyard Cessnas into such places. Although we must stop the men and materiel going down the Ho Chi Minh Trail, we cannot do it with slow FAC's. To improve the survivability rate, the planners have come up with a new method, they call it Commando Sabre. It's a fast FAC concept." The general looked at his two staffers, who were busily taking notes. His face and features were thin. His sparse hair was brown, shot through with streaks of gray. He sat tall and straight behind his desk. He tried not to think of his son.

"I want you to set up and coordinate the support, the airplanes, and the orders. We will start with a planning group in the FAC school at Phan Rang. While they are setting up, I want an experienced F-100 pilot to learn the Trail and the guns so he can report to the group the level of ground fire such a mission would reasonably be expected to receive. He is to go out and deliberately entice the guns to shoot at him. He is to fly every day, day after day, in the same places and in the same way, to see what guns he can bring up once they get used to him."

The two staffers looked at each other. "Sir, isn't all that exposure a little dangerous for just one pilot? Wouldn't you like us to schedule three or four?"

"One is sufficient. I have, in fact, just the man for the job. Once you get the program underway, notify him where and when he is to begin flying. Make a note that I want him to fly up North, over Hanoi. He would need this as a base point of reference for his summation of antiaircraft fire. Here is his name, rank, serial number, and current unit of assignment. Do you have any questions?"

"Yes, sir," the heavier of the two full-colonel staffers said. "Do you have any preferences for the other members of Commando Sabre?"

"No. Choose them as you see fit. If you have no further questions, you are clear to leave."

Outside in the hall, the two colonels looked at the name on the paper. The heavier one shook his head.

"I don't know who this guy Bannister is, but General Austin sure must have it in for him. There's nobody that can survive this one."

> 1530 HOURS LOCAL, 6 SEPTEMBER 1966
> MOBILE CONTROL FOR RUNWAY 27,
> BIEN HOA AIR BASE, REPUBLIC OF VIETNAM
> ☆

The underside of the thick cloud layer was so low, Court felt he could reach up and touch it. It was not a day conducive to safe flying below a thousand feet. A running cloud-pack of lean and gray mongrel scud-dogs sped over the antennas of the control unit, scratching themselves, then blew into ragged oblivion to re-form farther down the runway in furious haste. Court Bannister was in mobile control, a six-by-eight glass-enclosed minicontrol tower mounted on wheels so it could be towed to the side of the approach end of the active runway.

The unit had to be manned by an experienced pilot during all times that F-100's were flying. This was on orders of a TAC regulation that paid off almost daily as the man in mobile control assisted pilots with emergencies by calmly reading instructions from a handbook; or told them to take it around if their landing pattern was too dangerous; or frantically fired a flare and yelled into the radio if someone was on final approach without lowering his landing gear.

In bad weather there wasn't much the man in mobile control could do, as all the landing airplanes made a straight-in approach controlled by ground control approach radar. An airplane would come plunging out of the clouds a half mile away, gear and flaps down, the pilot frantically searching for a glimpse of the runway as he got closer to the ground. Usually his pulse rate was in an indirect ratio to his altitude.

There could be two airplanes, one flying formation on the other. Both flying slow and nose high, with gear and flaps hanging, looking like two bush turkeys flapping and tossing their heads as they skim the jungle forest looking for a safe place to alight.

At the moment, Ramrod 44, First Lieutenant Donny Higgens, was under GCA control as number one to land. He had been on a single-ship Skyspot mission, bombing a target in II Corps. The controller was still smiling over his nonstandard check-in—"Ramrod Four Four QUACK." He was on course and on glide path for Runway 27.

The rain drummed on the roof of the mobile control unit. Court yawned and wiped the moisture from the glass, facing final approach. He had reread the latest letter from Nancy Lewis. Like the other three he had received over the eight months since the Bien Hoa attack, it was cheery and full of humorous anecdotes. Her leg had healed quickly with barely a scar, she said—her only reference to her time with Court—and her trips were long but interesting. Sometimes they carried military dependents in place of G.I.'s. Her letters were sunny and uncomplicated. Not once had she so much as hinted at anything stronger than kind feelings toward a G.I. serving in an overseas warzone. She had reached Court on the phone once from Tan Son Nhut, but had quickly demurred when he said he could come down there to see her.

He thought how quickly the time had passed since he had seen her. Now he had flown over 190 missions and had only three months remaining in his tour. The weeks and months that had passed since the Bien Hoa attack were marked by Court only in terms of missions flown, as his sortie count rose to 50, then 75, then 150. His short-cropped hair had been bleached almost white and he had lost more weight until he leveled off at 165, about 20 pounds underweight.

Each day had gone by in a blur of two and sometimes three missions. He was so much at home in the big fighter that he felt almost naked when he had to climb out. Ground fire had picked up all over South Vietnam, particularly around War Zones C and D. He knew it had gotten rougher up north, as well.

He was startled out of his reverie by the strident shriek of the land line from Bien Hoa tower.

"Mobile," he answered.

"Sir, the plane on final, Ramrod Four Four, said he has an unsafe nose-gear warning light."

Court acknowledged, and switched his radio to GCA frequency and called Ramrod 44.

"Did you 'push to test' the green bulb, Four Four?" he asked.

"Roger, mobile, it checks okay."

"All right, Donny, pull your emergency-gear-lowering lanyard." The T-handle attached to a fifteen-inch cable would be a last-ditch attempt to unlock the door and provide a shot of hydraulic pressure to lower the nose gear. After a pause, Donny Higgens radioed back.

"No luck, mobile. She's still up." When he heard that Court told the tower to scramble the crash crew.

"Fuel state?" Court transmitted. There was a pause.

"Four hundred pounds."

"All right, Donny, bring it on in. No time to go around and play. Don't drop the hook. Don't make an approach-end engagement. Land normally. Hold the nose off as long as you can, then ease it down. Once it touches, pop your drag chute."

If Donny lowered his hook and made an approach-end engagement, the rapid deceleration would slam the nose down, maybe breaking the plane apart right at the cockpit. Easing the nose down on the rollout would minimize damage. There was nothing particularly dangerous about landing an F-100 without the nose gear in place. No panic—a little finesse and an easy touch would do the job. Donny listened to the calm voice of the GCA controller.

"You are on glide slope, you are on glide path," GCA said. "Weather now is 800 overcast, 400 broken, one-mile visibility in moderate rain, wind from 300 degrees at fifteen knots gusting to twenty-five. I understand negative nose gear. Crash crew is notified. Turn right heading 278, maintain rate of descent. You are cleared to land on Runway Two Seven. You need not acknowledge further transmissions." GCA released his microphone key for an instant, in case Court had a transmission, then continued his patter, bringing the plane to the threshold of the runway.

It was a one-shot deal. Donny flew on, nose high, holding 175 knots airspeed and 500 feet per minute rate of descent. He broke out of the cloud layer at 250 feet above the ground.

"Runway in sight," he transmitted, fast but calm, and only slightly high-pitched. He had crabbed his plane five degrees to the right to compensate for the crosswind. Close to the ground he straightened it out and lowered a wing into the wind, so as to not drift off the left side of the runway. It was tricky at nearly 200 miles an hour, as the gusts buffeted and tossed the plane. With the gear and flaps down at the slow landing speed, it was not half as responsive to the control inputs as when flying fast and clean. With everything hanging, it wallowed in exaggerated motions. Immediately after touchdown Donny held the nose off as long as he could, then eased it down and pulled the drag chute handle.

The crash crew and the ambulance roared by mobile control, chasing after the landing F-100. Court could see the plane decelerate rapidly as if jerked back by a string, because the cable attached the drag chute to the airplane at a point just under the rudder. The violent crosswind into the chute pushed it downwind, tugging at the tail of Donny's F-100 and causing the nose to weathervane into the wind. The wheels started hydroplaning on the rain water and the F-100 plunged across the runway and turned upside down in a ditch full of water.

Immediately, the radio became a jumble of frantic voices and commands.

"He's off the runway—"

"There is no fire, repeat, there is no fire—"

"—and under water . . . I can't see . . ."

"He's upside down—"

"—in the ditch."

"All right, knock it off. This is Fire Chief One. Shut up and stay off frequency. Only respond if I ask you something. I am on scene, and I want radio silence." The voice, unmistakably deep-South Negro, was measured and heavy with authority. There was instant silence.

"That's better. Base, you read?"

"Roger, chief."

"Get the crane out here. We got an F-100 upside down. The cockpit is under water. Move."

"Moving, chief."

"Tower, you read?"

"Roger, chief."

"Divert or hold all inbounds till I tell you. Probably 30 minutes before we clear the runway."

"Copy, chief."

In clear violation of the regulations, Court threw down the microphone and ran out of mobile into the soaking rain. He motioned an armorer's truck to pick him up and told the driver to take him to the crash site.

The armorer sped the pickup along the shoulder of the runway, throwing up water like a speedboat. He began to slow as vehicles appeared in the murk. A crumpled fuel tank lay on one side of the runway.

"Over there," Court shouted, pointing to the rain-blurred shape of an F-100 that was upside down in a small lake of pooled rain water. The main landing gear and one underwing fuel tank protruded from the flat slab of wing and bottom fuselage. The rain thrummed on the hulk and splashed the water of the lake so heavily the airplane appeared to be floating. Several firemen, their heavy gear discarded, stood waist- and shoulder-deep in the red-brown water. Their hair was plastered and streaming. They were bent and straining in the cockpit area. Suddenly two figures popped to the surface between them and the fuselage. One was Doc Russell, the other was the fire chief, a small and wiry black man. The two stumbled through the pond to the shore. Doc Russell was coughing and spitting. He had what appeared to be a red grease pencil streak down the left side of his face.

"He's alive," the chief shouted, "where's that crane?"

Court waded out and helped Doc Russell ashore. The mud sucked at his boots. The two stumbled and slipped as they climbed the greasy mud bank. They sat, side by side. Court saw the grease pencil mark was blood flowing from a slash on Doc Russell's left temple.

"He's alive, oh God, he's alive," the Doc said. He pulled out a bandanna and wiped the watery blood from his face and head. "I squatted down there, underwater, in the mud, then wedged my shoulder and arm underneath. The canopy was crushed. When I cocked my arm up inside and felt his helmet, it moved. As I slid my hand up across his face and felt his hands pressed against his mask, he wriggled his fingers. At this point, he's got oxygen so he's still breathing. But I don't know for how long, with the plane busted up like that. The oxygen tank could be ruptured or he could be badly hurt and pass out and drown." The Doc drew a breath, then looked at Court with sudden horror.

"His seat won't go off, will it?" he said, grabbing Court's arm. The vision of the seat exploding Donny Higgens into crushed oblivion fleeted behind Court's eyes.

"No," he said, taking Doctor Russell's hand, "no chance." He didn't want to add that under the twisting movement when the crane lifted the plane, anything could happen.

Two of Doctor Russell's corpsmen, wearing Army rain ponchos and carrying a third, came over. They both helped drape it around their doctor. The taller of the two, a staff sergeant, spoke.

"Come on, Doc, we'll fix you up in the ambulance."

"No, no. I've got to stay here. Just let me get my breath. I'm going back down there." The Doc's body seemed to be vibrating. His chubby Baby Huey face looked strained and ashen.

Court and the two medics looked at each other. Court put his arm around the Doc's shoulders.

"You don't have to. See, the crane is here." He pointed down the runway as the giant yellow crane lumbered into view through the rain like a prehistoric monster. The surging roar of the diesel engine grew louder, overpowering the constant drum of the rain. Court took the Doc's arm to urge him to the ambulance.

"No, no," Doc Russell cried, tearing away, "I've got to be there." He splashed off through the muck toward the inverted airplane. Court jumped in and waded after him. As they arrived at the inverted plane, a man surfaced from near the cockpit area. His fatigues were soaking wet and mud slimy. He was the crew chief for the F-100.

"Oh, help him, help him," he shouted, "he's not moving." He looked about wildly.

"Get him out of here," the wiry fire chief said, motioning one of his men to escort the distraught airman to the shore. "And you, too, sir, we need room," he said to Court. The crane was grumbling into position on the banks. "Doc, you can stay. The pilot might need you."

Court splashed ashore and stood with the two corpsmen. The wing commander's jeep splashed up. Colonel Friedlander, stubby cigar clamped in his mouth, came up next to Court. He returned Court's salute with a wave of his hand. They watched the men detach the sling and wrap the chains from the crane around each main landing gear. The men involved looked grim and determined as they moved with efficient haste. There was no consultation about how to raise the expensive F-100 without doing further damage. They needed to pull the plane up just enough to expose the cockpit and they needed to do it immediately. A nasal roar sounded from the diesel lifting engine. It spouted a plume of black smoke that was torn off and absorbed in the wind and rain. Following hand signals, the operator put a strain on the lines attached to the landing gear. As the forward section of the inverted F-100 emerged, streaming water, the arms of Donny Higgens dangled lifelessly through the shattered canopy.

Doc Russell and two firemen crouched and slid under the battered cockpit. The fireman quickly undid Higgens's helmet and mask, exposing his pale and lifeless face. His lips were blue. The Doc clamped an oxygen breather mask from a fireman's walkaround bottle to his mouth and nose. The two firemen motioned to a third, who waded up with a pair of bolt cutters. He crouched down in an awkward bending position to cut the gas lines in the seat ejection system, so that even if the charge fired the propelling gases would be harmlessly vented. As he withdrew his arms from over his head, he slipped backward in the mud and instinctively threw his arms wide to regain his balance. The heavy head of the bolt cutters slammed into Doc Russell's mouth. Both Court and Jake Friedlander involuntarily groaned as the smack of steel into teeth carried over the sound of the rain. The Doc's knees buckled slightly and he shook his head. He still held the mask to Higgens's face. The offending fireman thrashed up from the water, begging the Doc to forgive him. Nodding his head, the Doc gave him a wink; and bared his teeth in a broken red smile. The apologizing man's face looked aghast at what he had done.

The other two men told Doc they were almost finished unstrapping and cutting Higgens away. He took the mask down and lurched to one side. The fireman cut the last strap holding the unconscious pilot and eased his body down through a slow motion somersault to the waiting arms of the fire chief, who splashed ashore cradling the pilot to his chest. Doc Russell, his mouth dripping red gore, splashed and stumbled alongside, holding the oxygen mask to Higgens's face.

The corpsmen on the shore had a stretcher ready. Court and Friedlander stood aside as the chief laid Higgens down on the canvas. Doc Russell lifted the mask, and the taller corpsman, already kneeling, pinched Higgens's nose shut and started blowing air into his blue-lipped mouth. The Doc squatted back and clamped his fingers on Higgens's wrist to search for a pulse. It was the first chance he'd had to see if the pilot was still alive. He cocked his head, then nodded.

"We got a pulse," he said. Through his crushed lips, it sounded more like "We oughtta ulse."

Court felt like cheering. Friedlander, working his lips, tried to roll his cigar from one side of his mouth to the other. The stogie was a pulpy mass, so he spat it out. The standing corpsman gave the thumbs-up sign to the men at the airplane and the crane, who had been standing frozen and poised at their tasks, waiting to see how the pilot was faring. They broke into wide grins and went back to work.

The corpsman said something about the possibility of brain damage, because no one knew how long the pilot had been without air. Friedlander and Court exchanged glances. After a few minutes, while Doc Russell was probing and examining his body for breaks or other damage, Donny Higgens fluttered open his eyes. They were unfocused and doubtful.

"Sally," he said, "is that you?"

After the ambulance departed with Higgens for the base hospital, Colonel Friedlander gave Court a lift in his jeep to the 531st. They walked in, Court holding the screen door open for the colonel. The pilots, grounded until the heavy rain passed, were grouped around the ops counter, waiting for news of Higgens. The early-morning frags had been canceled one after the other as the rain storms persisted.

"Squadronnn, tench-HUT," someone shouted. The men popped to.

"At ease," Colonel Friedlander said. "Higgens will be all right." He looked around and spotted Demski. "Serge," he said, "let's go someplace where we can talk." He turned to look at Bannister. "You," he said, "stick around." He and Demski walked out of the ops room to Demski's office. The pilots gathered around Court. The PE sergeant handed him a towel. Court told them the story. They howled as he finished with the quote, "Sally, is that you?" Smiggenhiggens, old Duck Call Donny, had done it again.

A moment later, Court and Jack Laird were having a smoke from Laird's fresh pack and a quiet coffee, when Bob Derham said Court was to report to Colonel Friedlander in Demski's office.

"Sit down, Court," Friedlander said to him as he walked in. In this case, Court decided, a salute would be inappropriate. Demski nodded. Friedlander reached for a cigar from his drenched flight suit. The pack was crushed and soggy. Court shook out a cigarette from the pack Laird had given him and offered it to the colonel.

"No, thanks," Friedlander said, "never touch 'em." Demski handed him a cigar from a rectangular pack he kept in his drawer. They were the same brand as those the colonel smoked. All the squadron CO's kept them on hand, knowing Jake Friedlander was impossible to communicate with unless he had a cigar in his mouth. Friedlander lit up with his own Zippo and blew great clouds into the air. Then he took the cigar from his mouth, examined the end, and tapped an ash into the ashtray on Demski's desk. He and Demski stared at Court with fixed interest.

"Who have you pissed off lately?" the colonel asked.

Court's eyebrows shot up. "No one that I know of." He paused. "Well, Major Rawson, I suppose."

"I don't think he is a factor in this. Anybody higher up?"

The only "higher-up" Court knew was his Dad's cousin, Major General Albert Whisenand. He knew of no problems there. He hadn't mentioned this relationship to anyone in the USAF, and saw no reason to start now.

"No, sir," he said.

"Look, Court," Serge Demski said, "we're not trying to be mysterious. It's just that an unusual by-name request came down for some hairy work up North and it has your name on it.'' Demski looked at Friedlander.

"What do you know about Project Commando Sabre?'' Friedlander asked.

"Nothing, sir,'' Court said.

Friedlander continued. "Commando Sabre is the code name for some gun trolling the Pentagon wants done in the high-threat areas of North Vietnam and Laos.''

"Sounds interesting,'' Court said, and grinned.

"Bannister,'' Friedlander said, his cigar leaving contrails as he waved it about, "usually a request comes in to the wing saying, 'Nominate one pilot to perform duties as such and such.' We pick one depending on the qualifications required. You don't have any special qualifications or background for this job, Court, so maybe somebody who doesn't know much about fighter pilots thinks he is setting you up.'' He took a long pull on his cigar. "So, I feel the same way about this request as I did about that PIO guy asking for you to fly your brother. I don't like being told which of my guys is to do what. You don't have to leap at this until I get it checked out.''

For a fleeting second, Court thought about it. Maybe he was being set up, and just maybe a hot-line patch to Whitey in the Pentagon would get him out of it. But that wasn't his way, and Court dismissed the thought before it developed further. He had made his decision to go balls-out a long time before, before he earned his wings, before he even put on a blue suit. He had made that decision when he found himself slipping all too easily into the fatuous life of a rich man's son jetting between Hollywood and the Côte d'Azur. Although he didn't know the name of it at the time, his fighter-pilot mentality had been surfacing even then. That mentality, that attitude, was what pushed him into always trying to go just a bit further than the next guy, and then even a bit further than he thought he was capable of.

"Colonel,'' Court began, "maybe somebody does think he's setting me up. I don't. I'm a fighter pilot, and this sounds like a great job. Let me have it.''

"Thought you'd feel that way.'' Friedlander stood up and smiled. "Serge says he can spare you. Taxi up to wing headquarters and pick up the orders I already had cut on you. You're relieved of duty here to go on temporary duty to Commando Sabre.''

"Yes, *sir,*'' Court said, and saluted.

24

☆

"Whitey, I can't agree with you," the President said. "A total assault on the North like you propose would be rape, not seduction.
I want to seduce those little fellas. You got to understand, bombing
the North is a political tool that I am using to convince old Ho to
quit, and I can't use it up all at once. If I went all out, why, the
Rooskies and the Chinese would be all over us. So I've got to pick
these targets, one by one, in such a way as to show that rascal Ho
we're serious, while making sure you and the other generals don't
get us into the Third World War." The President waved his heavy
glass of Fresca at Whitey Whisenand. "That's why I won't let you
flyboys bomb the smallest crapper up there without checking with
me."

LBJ hadn't been too specific about the job when he asked Whitey
to be a special adviser for air to the National Security Council, nor
had he since clarified his duties, other than to ask his overall assessment of the progress of the Vietnam war. This arrangement of having
another military man in the White House was one more piece of
evidence, so it was said in the Pentagon, that LBJ did not trust
military advice given to him via the Joint Chiefs of Staff.

Today, Whitey was seeing the President about a specific Navy strike
request, not a "total assault," as LBJ had put it.

Both men were standing in front of the fireplace in the Oval Office.

Walt Rostow, who bore the weighty title of Special Assistant to the President for National Security Affairs, sat on the couch facing them. More or less considered a hawk, Rostow was nonetheless known unfavorably in the back rooms of the Pentagon for once having thrown a water pitcher at a colonel with whom he had disagreed. He and Whisenand wore dark suits, white shirts, and the distinctive slanted red and blue stripes of school ties. The President had removed his gray suit coat to reveal his red suspenders. Rostow nursed a lukewarm coffee.

Neither Whitey nor Rostow quite knew what his relationship was to the other, except that Whitey had to accede to Rostow as a member of the Executive Branch. As yet, the assessment Whitey was compiling for the President was just that—for the President. It did not have to be cleared through Rostow or anybody else. With the exception of today's request for an audience, Whitey had been quietly busying himself studying previous reports in his small office in the White House near the Situation Room.

As he researched and jotted down his conclusions, he had realized the mistakes the executive branch and the military had made regarding Vietnam that had contributed to the current morass. Foremost was the lost chance at having an *éminence grise* in the Vietnamese hierarchy, someone such as USAF General Ed Lansdale, who as a colonel had done remarkable things helping Magsaysay against the Communists in the Philippines. He had later been immortalized as Colonel Hillandale in Charley Lederer's book *The Ugly American*.

Had Lansdale been in the palace with Vietnamese President Ngo Dinh Diem before the coup that killed Diem in 1963, scant weeks before Jack Kennedy himself was assassinated, things might have been different. In all likelihood, Lansdale would have prevented the monastic seclusion into which Diem had entered with the eager help of his brother Nhu and his brother's wife, Madame Nhu. Whereas Lansdale had helped Diem secure the presidential election in 1955, by the early sixties he was no longer in favor with the U.S. State Department and could no longer influence Diem. Thus a political handle on South Vietnam was lost by the United States.

Although the U.S. had not engineered the coup that killed Diem, it was perceived to have given tacit approval. What no one in the Kennedy regime at the time had even considered was: Who was going to pull the country together after Diem was ousted? After his death, a series of presidents and prime ministers following on each other in a matter of a few months made the situation worse. Only the seizure of power in 1965 by Vietnamese Air Force General Nguyen Cao Ky had ended the anarchy.

Whitey wrote in his notes that the first mistake was to have no power behind the power. Mistake 2 was to have no strategy. He was appalled. The United States simply had no strategy for the war in Vietnam. There was a vague goal of keeping the Communists out of South Vietnam, but no rational method to reach that goal.

Whitey studied the territorial maps and concluded that Mistake 3 was to believe in the boundaries of Vietnam as shown on the maps. Whereas Ho Chi Minh was using all of the territory in Indochina, including Laos and Cambodia, to fight his war, LBJ and the SecDef only saw the war zone in terms of the territorial boundary line around Vietnam. What little CIA and U.S. Army action LBJ had so far sanctioned in Laos was not even close to cutting the Ho Chi Minh Trail supply route. Further, LBJ was doing nothing about Ho's open use of Cambodian seaports and roads to truck war supplies to South Vietnam.

While reading old memos, Whitey saw that one man in the civilian hierarchy, John McCone, seemed to have realized the problems and had come up with a solution. McCone, Director of Central Intelligence, had told Secretary of State Dean Rusk and Secretary of Defense Robert McNamara that he had grave misgivings about sending American men into ground battle while shackling the use of air power up north. McCone said he thought the Communists were counting on world pressure to stop the limited air strikes that were happening up there. Before that pressure came about, either unshackle the air to go North, or don't commit ground troops in the South.

Whitey took it all in and was drafting a paper that played on one dominant theme: fight the National Liberation Front Viet Cong in South Vietnam, and fight the North Vietnamese Army in North Vietnam.

These assessments, however, were not the reason Major General Albert G. Whisenand had requested an audience with his Commander in Chief. Rather, it was about an urgent message from Task Force 77, the U.S. Navy contingent positioned on Yankee Station in the South China Sea off the coast of North Vietnam. The urgent Ops Immediate message said that 111 surface-to-air missiles had been photographed four hours earlier on rail cars northeast of Hanoi. No guns had come up on the Navy RA-5 Vigilante that took the photos, and the weather was clear and due to remain so for the next six hours. The commander of TF 77 requested permission to strike within the hour. He said his attack aircraft were armed and poised for an instant launch and he needed an immediate answer. He had no way of knowing his request had been lost for twenty-two minutes in the White House pipeline. Whitey had grabbed it. He had sur-

reptitiously made sure that such things were brought to his attention. He was now personally pleading the case to destroy the SAM's.

"Mr. President, I'm not asking for total assault. All I'm asking is
for your immediate permission to destroy 111 SAM missiles where
they sit instead of having to fight them one by one as they are
launched at our aircraft." Whitey stood facing the President. He
held a clipboard with the enacting message for the President's signature.

The President slammed his Fresca glass on the mantel and strode
rapidly to his desk. "Is the 'perfessor' still in the building? Get him
up here," he barked over the intercom. He remained behind his
desk and turned back to Whitey. "Bomb, bomb, bomb, that's all
you generals want to do. You just don't understand."

Whitey walked to stand in front of LBJ's desk when it became
obvious the President was not coming back to the fireplace. Walt
Rostow stood, but didn't take sides, mainly because he had yet to
be asked. The door to the Oval Office opened. The Secretary of
Defense, Robert Strange McNamara, whom LBJ labeled the "perfessor," walked in with short and purposeful steps. His black suit
was a shade darker than the others', his Harvard tie discreet, his
shoes polished to a high gloss. His black hair was combed straight
back. His face was clear and unlined; his eyes bright and hard behind
his glasses. LBJ motioned him over and handed him the Navy request while he continued to talk to Whitey.

"You just don't understand how to send the proper signals, general," the President said. "I'll explain it to you. We won't bomb
the SAM's, which signals the North not to use them. You see? They
know we could hit them today, but we don't. Because we let their
missiles go, they won't shoot them at our boys." He hitched at his
suspenders, then sat in his leather swivel chair behind his desk. "You
tell him, Mac."

The SecDef sat down in the straight black chair to the right of the
President's desk. He looked up from the TWX at Whitey and spoke
in a soft but crisp voice.

"Those surface-to-air missiles, and the others at the sites under
construction, are flashpoints we must avoid. We cannot hit them,
not only for the reason the President told you, but additionally because there are Soviet technicians servicing them. Any surprise attack
might incur Soviet casualties and that would lead to greater Soviet
participation in the war." He cocked his head at Whitey. "You can
understand that, can't you, general?"

Before Whitey could answer, LBJ said, "There you have it. The answer is no, and now you know why." He smiled as he stood and walked around the desk. He took Whitey cordially by the elbow and escorted him to the door. "I knew you'd understand once we explained it to you." Rostow beat them to the door and opened it. LBJ paused and clasped Whitey's hand in a firm shake while holding his elbow. "Anytime," he said, giving Whitey his broad smile and crinkly eyes, "anytime you want something explained about this war, you just come right on in. You hear?" LBJ snapped his fingers in remembrance. "One more thing, general. I want your personal attention in studying a way to reduce our pilot casualties in Vietnam. We must take care of our boys, you know." At these words, Whitey felt himself going purple with rage, but managed through supreme willpower to keep his mouth shut.

That night, to his wife's consternation, Whitey closed himself in the music room and drank two bottles of a robust Burgundy. In the background he played over and over Stanley's "I Am the Very Model of a Modern Major General" from Gilbert and Sullivan's *Pirates of Penzance.*

"We're going to pay for all this," he said to himself for the dozenth time. "Oh God, how we are going to pay."

1230 HOURS LOCAL, 12 SEPTEMBER 1966
HEADQUARTERS, 7TH AIR FORCE,
TAN SON NHUT AIR BASE, REPUBLIC OF VIETNAM
☆

Court walked down the steps from VNAF headquarters, where he had just visited two Vietnamese officers he had known at Squadron Officer's School. Colonel Vo Xuan Lanh and Major Ut, while glad to see him, had talked at length about the way the U.S. was handling the war. They were not pleased. They told him to read everything the author Bernard Fall had written, so as to better understand the Communist methods. As he left they gave him a book written in French by Jean Lartéguy titled *Le Mal jaune,* loosely translated as *The Yellow Sickness.* They explained that the book would give their good friend Court a better understanding of the Vietnamese way and how they interacted with Westerners.

He started to walk the long distance from the VNAF headquarters area to the 7th Air Force headquarters. He had placed Lartéguy's book in the old leather navigator's kit he used as a briefcase. Already in the case were his pay record and his TDY orders assigning him

first to the 366th Tactical Fighter Wing. The 366th flew F-4's from
Da Nang Air Base, located north up the coast from Saigon. At Tan
Son Nhut he was to report to the officer in command of the Bravo
Division in the Directorate of Combat Operations, listed as DOCB
on the 7th Air Force command chart.

He was wearing his one pair of khaki 1505's. The pants were already baggy at the knees, and the center of the shirt was dark with
sweat. Captains don't rate staff cars, and the base bus had just made
its half-hourly run past the VNAF building. After 10 minutes of
breathing dust and having it crust on his uniform, Court gratefully
accepted the offer of a ride to 7th Air Force HQ from two air police
sergeants in their jeep. He shared the back with a bare pole that
could accommodate an M-60 machine gun. The jeep lurched into
the heavy military traffic flow.

They were halfway past the French *cimetière militaire* when the AP
in the right seat nudged his partner.

"Hey, look over there." He pointed toward the rear of the cemetery, where the gravestones ended at a high red brick fence. They
saw furtive movement where there shouldn't have been any, by an
eight-foot mausoleum. The driver spun the wheel and braked on the
shoulder. The two men grabbed their M-16's from corner mounts,
dismouted, and leaped the drainage ditch between the jeep and the
cemetery. They ran to the scene, dodging from tombstone to tombstone as if wary of rifle fire. One ran to two figures struggling on the
ground, while his partner covered him.

Court climbed out, stepped across the ditch, and moved closer.
The tombstones were gray and seemed weathered far beyond the
dates of only fourteen or fifteen years before.

A khaki-clad figure on the ground was moaning and thrashing
away from the AP who was trying to lock his wrists behind him in
handcuffs. A thin, barefoot girl with dirty legs scrambled to her feet
and ran like a jack rabbit, disappearing between the tombstones. She
looked about twelve.

"GAWDDAMM," the soldier on the ground bellowed and
lurched to his feet. He was a big man and his eyes were wild and
unfocused. "GAWDDAMM," he said again, and before anybody
could move he ran head on into the side of the mausoleum and fell
back among the tombstones, unconscious and bleeding.

"Shee-it," the AP who had been trying to handcuff him said. He
got to his feet, pulled out a bandanna and wiped his forehead. Then
he knelt, rolled the man over, and placed the handcuffs on him far
up his forearms, grunting as he squeezed them shut with a loud
clack.

He turned the man face-up and thumbed open an eye. "He'll live, but I don't know what for."

"*Dinky dau* cigarettes?" the covering AP questioned.

"Shee-it, no. This ain't no Mary Jane. This one's on smack. Third one this month," he said. "And that kid probably sold him the stuff, then tried to steal it back when he got stoned." He motioned toward the jeep. "Go call the desk and have 'em get an ambulance over here." He turned to Court.

"Sorry, captain. You still want a lift, we'll get you to Seventh." He wiped the sweat and dirt from his face and wrung out his bandanna. "This stuff is coming into Veetnam fast and cheap and these here Saigon commandos are going nuts over it, I tell you."

Court looked down at the unconscious soldier. His head was cocked at an angle at the base of a dirty tombstone. He wore khakis, dirty and torn now, with only a National Defense ribbon pinned above his shirt pocket. He wore Adjutant General Corps collar brass.

Court looked closer at the tombstone and read the inscription.

Ici repose un pilote de chasse mort pour sa patrie pendant la guerre d'Indochine.

Court presented himself at the DOCB office and was ushered into the august presence of Colonel Donald Dunne, whose office walls held many guns and other war trophies. Behind his desk was a wall map of Indochina. A chromed fake hand grenade housing a cigarette lighter stood on his desk, next to a two-foot carved teak affair on which his name and rank were embossed over a giant pair of carved command pilot wings. The colonel wore immaculate pressed and starched olive-drab USAF fatigues. The eagles on his collar were sewn with white thread and seemed outsized. His name was stitched over his right chest pocket flap, with command pilot wings over his left. The colonel had a high forehead topped by crew-cut black hair interspersed with gray. He appeared fifty or so, Court thought, a little old for a full bull. Court handed him his orders. The colonel glanced at them.

"What do you know about Commando Sabre?" the colonel asked Court.

"Very little, sir," he replied.

"It is not an F-100 refresher or instrument training course, I can tell you," the colonel said with an air of great importance. "That was printed on the orders as a cover." He rose to stand next to the wall map and spread his legs.

"What I am about to tell you is classified secret," he said. "Commando Sabre is a program of out-country sorties to direct and control

TEMPORARY DUTY ORDER-MILITARY

TO: 3rd Cmbt Spt Gp (CAS)	FROM 3rd Tac Ftr Wg (DO)	DATE 6 Sep 66

1. INDIVIDUAL(S) wp on TDY as shown in items 5 through 21.
2. ISSUING OFFICIAL: Lawrence L. Emmett, LtCol, USAF,
                Asst Deputy Commander, Operations
3. SIGNATURE: 4. PHONE: 7108
5. GRADE: Capt   6. NAME: Bannister, Courtland EdM., A03021953
7. ORGANIZATION: 531 Tac Ftr Sq   8. SECURITY CLEAR: TS
9. EFF ON OR ABOUT: 7 Sep 66   10. Approx No. of Days: 30
11. PURPOSE OF TDY
     Commando Sabre F-100 refresher and instrument training.
12. ITINERARY
     FROM: Bien Hoa AB, Vietnam

     TO: Tan Son Nhut AB, Vietnam, 7AF/DOCB
                Da Nang AB, Vietnam, 366TFW/DO
                Tahkli RTAFB, Thailand, 355TFW/DO

     RETURN TO: Bien Hoa AB, Vietnam
     VARIATIONS: Authorized
13. THEATER CLEARANCES: Obtained
14. MODE OF TRANSPORTATION: Military Aircraft
15. AUTHORITY: AFM 35-11
16. SPECIAL ORDER NO: T-768
17. DESIGNATION AND LOCATION OF HEADQUARTERS
     Department of the Air Force
     HQ 3rd Tactical Fighter Wing (PACAF)
     APO San Francisco, 96227
18. EXPENSES CHARGEABLE TO:
     5763400 306-7442 P458 213804 (48.00)
     S599500W OA-T-66-131 (CUSTOMER ID CODE)
19 TDN. For the Commander   20. DISTRIBUTION "D"
21. SIGNATURE ELEMENT OF ORDERS AUTHENTICATING OFFICIAL

                W.R. Montell, 1stLt, USAF
                Chief, Administrative Svc

AF FORM 626
     MAY 63 PREVIOUS EDITIONS WILL BE USED UNTIL STOCK IS EXHAUSTED
                *GPO 1963-690-033.

strike missions against enemy targets of opportunity. Each sortie will be flown in a two-seater jet aircraft with FAC-qualified fighter pilots in both seats. We are considering this program to use jet FAC's because we are losing too many slow FAC's in Laos along the Ho Chi Minh Trail and in the Route Pack One southern portion of North Vietnam. These are high-threat areas for the slow FAC's and they are not surviving. Systemwide, we have had some bad losses. We've got to get some eyeballs up there that are both maneuverable and fast enough to avoid ground fire, yet low enough to see what's happening on the ground.''

The colonel looked at Court with eyes that began to light up as he warmed to the subject. His voice rose and he began to speak faster.

''You see the dichotomy here? We can't have it both ways, so we put two people in a fast airplane. The pilot in back looks around for targets, maybe uses binoculars, while the pilot in front flies. The only two-seat fighters we have are F-105F's and G's, F-4 Phantoms, and F-100F's. The 105F's are allocated to the special Wild Weasel mission, and the Phantoms are all tied up and critical because they have so much electronic gear in back. That leaves the F-100F, which is the airplane we are considering. We have several in-country.''

The colonel had been talking fast, with a strange staccato emphasis on each word that at first seemed out of character. Then Court caught on that the man was acting. He was imitating the mannerisms of actors from various war movies. Right now he seemed to be Gregory Peck in *Twelve O'Clock High*. The colonel took a cigarette from a pack in his desk and lit it with the chromed grenade. He puffed quickly without inhaling.

''You will go first to the F-4 fighter wing at Da Nang for indoctrination, then the F-105 fighter wing at Tahkli. Both are flying over the DMZ, Tally Ho, and other areas on preplanned fragged missions. In those areas there are many enemy targets of opportunity, primarily rolling stock, that need to be sniffed out. The F-4 and F-105 pilots fly in so many different areas, they don't know any one area well enough to find these fleeting targets. The trucks in particular have hidden parks and revetments, according to agent reports. You will go to each wing and fly with them in the mission aircraft to find out how it is up there. You will also brief them on how to use a FAC and how a FAC will use them. You have been flying totally under FAC control, except for Skyspot, for some time now.'' The colonel snubbed out his cigarette and pointed at the upper reaches of the wall map.

"The program hasn't started yet, as we are still gathering information. You are to fly here"—he tapped the map—"in North Vietnam, and here"—he tapped the map again—"in Laos." He faced
Court.

"Your mission," he cracked out each word, "is to get in there to
determine the volume of enemy antiaircraft fire at low altitudes where
the Commando Sabre aircraft will fly. In other words, you are to
troll for guns."

Court almost shook his head at the man. My God, he thought,
now he's acting the part of Clark Gable in *Command Decision*. Colonel Dunne caught something in Court's expression.

"Did I say something funny, captain? For if you think I did, you
are sadly mistaken." Colonel Dunne passed a hand over his crew
cut. "This is no joke, I assure you."

Court stood. He tried to assume a look of earnest concentration
while thinking that the colonel probably even dreamed in clichés.
Colonel Dunne continued.

"You will dispatch nightly summaries to our office, DOCB, with
info copies to the 37th Tactical Fighter Wing at Phu Cat, who has
the action for Commando Sabre."

Court decided he had better take Colonel Donald Dunne seriously. Trolling for guns was not a throwaway line.

"Tomorrow you will proceed by military air to Da Nang, where
you will report to"—Colonel Dunne glanced at a message on his
desk—"Major Ronald E. Bender, the 366th Wing weapons officer.
After sufficient missions to learn your trade as a FAC, you will report
to Major Ted Frederick, the weapons officer of the 355th Tactical
Fighter Wing at Tahkli, Thailand."

Colonel Dunne looked at Court and leered. "The 355th," he said
with relish, "is currently flying F-105's over Hanoi. Our combined
F-4 and F-105 loss rate is wicked, positively wicked. About five planes
a week. Now that's not very funny, is it?"

1645 HOURS LOCAL, 12 SEPTEMBER 1966
MILITARY ASSISTANCE COMMAND STUDIES AND
OBSERVATION GROUP, SAIGON, REPUBLIC OF VIETNAM
☆

Major Wolf Lochert adjusted his beret and stepped out of the low
front end of the pedicab as the long-legged Vietnamese peddler slid
it to a stop, bicycle brakes squealing, ten feet from the Nungs guarding the gate to the unmarked MACSOG complex on rue Pasteur.

Wolf gave him 20 P, reached back for his rucksack and M-16, and shook his head as the man sped off down the sleepy, tree-lined street, his ropy-muscled calves pumping, only too anxious to get away from the fearsome Nungs. Shouldering his weapon and holding his ruck on his back by one strap, Wolf strolled along the cream-colored stucco wall topped by green tiles and coiled concertina wire. He motioned toward the fleeing cyclist.

"The *dan ong* has fear," he said in a Chinese patois to the AK-47-laden Nungs as they opened the big wooden gate for him.

"More of you than us, *thiêu tá,*" one of the guards responded with a toothy smile, scuffling his rubber-tire sandals on the ancient French concrete.

Wolf passed the giant tamarind tree on his right and strode across the compound, digging in the heels of his jungle boots as if passing in review, and entered the two-story building on his left. In the coolness he crossed the linoleum flooring, passed the bar where an enshrined old hat of Maggie's awaited her return, and entered through an unmarked door the office of Lieutenant Colonel Al Charles, a black man taller and wider than Wolf.

"MIGWAD, YOU'RE STILL UGLY," the Wolf boomed as the two men embraced and commenced a ritual that left them wrestling each other to the hardwood floor, smashing a cheap lamp and corner table in the process. Each had grabbed the other's right hand in a deadlock to prevent him from sticking a spit-laden thumb in his ear. Neither could get an advantage.

"Let's break on three," Charles said. Although panting from exertion, his voice was deceptively soft. They were lying flat on the floor, arms entwined as each man's huge hands pinned the other's.

"Nothing doing," the Wolf said. "The last time we did that you broke the truce and stuck your thumb in my ear anyhow." He tried to shift his grip to better advantage. Charles countered by swiftly swinging his body and getting a leg lock on the Wolf. Wolf reacted by suddenly pulling Charles's arm to his mouth and grabbing a chunk of forearm in his teeth and applying pressure just short of breaking the skin.

"All right, all right. On the count of three, and I promise I won't give you an ear job."

"Unh-huh," the Wolf agreed, shifting his body to test Charles's leg lock.

"One," Charles said, tightening his leglock. "Two." The Wolf increased his pressure on the forearm. "Three," Charles said. Nothing happened.

"All right, I give," Charles said and released Wolf. With a howl,

Wolf released his holds on Charles, spit on his thumb and started to grab the colonel's head. He felt his own head grabbed at the same time, and each man suffered simultaneously the indignity of having a soggy thumb stuck in his ear. They stood up, pulses returning to normal, and brushed off.

"Lochert," the colonel said, "I'm so glad you're here, I could puke. Siddown." He kicked the broken table and lamp into a corner and sat at his desk. Wolf pulled up a tattered vinyl-and-chrome recliner and fell into it.

"Charles, I'm so glad to be here, I'd eat it. I had to get out of Nha Trang or I'd blow it up. Fred Ladd is an okay guy, but I can only take so much desk time." He leaned back and studied Al Charles. "I know what the official story is. How about telling me what this is really all about? What the hell is the MACV Studies and Observation Group? Why study and observe the slopes when killing 'em is so easy?"

"Wolf, don't act any more stupid than you were at Bad T, when you decked that burgomeister giving you autobahn information because you thought he called you an *Ausfahrt.*"

The Wolf grinned. "You're just hacked because it screwed up your messing with his daughter. Now tell me about the orders bringing me down here. Not that I mind. I was afraid they were going to leave me at Nha Trang."

"Not a chance. By the way, I read your after-action report last spring about the battle in War Zone C. Sorry to lose Haskell. He was good. Deserved the Medal. Spears came through here. He's lost some upper shoulder motion, but he'll be okay for duty. That Air Force guy Parker did a hell of a job. But, you know, I think there's a lot more activity going to happen."

"Is that why I'm here?" the Wolf asked.

"No. We are getting into some new out-country missions that should appeal to you. Here's how it is." Charles leaned back in his chair, his eyes serious. "MACSOG is a joint service command with the Air Force and Navy. We took over the old CIA mission of supporting the Viets doing sabotage and cross-border ops. Now we do more than support. We've got good assets; Navy SEALs and USAF special ops people with C-123's, C-130's and Green Hornet Hueys. We even have some Chinats flying unmarked C-47 Goons and 123's."

"Yeah, I heard a few things. You the guys that put those rigged mortar rounds in the VC supply system? Don't you do assassination and counterterror?"

"Yeah, but those are just minor ongoing ops. We have five primary missions: cross-border ops into Laos, Cambodia, and North Vietnam; running black-and-gray psy-ops; setting up resistance groups in North Vietnam; planning and conducting POW rescue raids; and setting up a net to grab shot-down aircrew and get them out before they get captured."

"Everything except psy-ops sounds great to me. Where do I fit in?" Wolf asked.

Charles stood up. "In the rescue net for shot-down aircrew. We've got a problem. We've yet to get one pilot back from Southern Laos, the area along the Ho Chi Minh Trail we call Steel Tiger." Charles sat on the edge of his desk facing Wolf.

"Here's the gen, classified of course. Bright Spot is a pilot pickup op we run out of FOB-4 at Da Nang under CCN—Command and Control North. We've tried to infiltrate indidge teams with radios, rations, and medical supplies around the hot spots where the AAA is bad up north, and along the Trail through Steel Tiger in Laos." Charles got off the desk and walked to the far end of the room. He faced Wolf. "But we have never gotten one word back from any of the two teams we've sent into Southern Steel Tiger. Never."

"The answer is simple," the Wolf said, lounging back in the cracked vinyl and crossing his legs. "Send at least two Americans with each team. Or won't the Pentagon let you do that?"

"There's never been a problem with Fort Bragg or the Joint Chiefs at the Pentagon. It was McNamara and Johnson; they wouldn't let American ground troops into southern Laos. Afraid of being accused of invading, I suppose. But that's changed. They just now said we could beef up our efforts to get downed pilots back because we are losing so many."

"Did they specifically agree in writing to us going up there?"

"You just put your thumb in my ear, Wolf." Charles looked rueful. "No, they didn't. They just said to make the maximum possible effort to collect downed aircrew before they got captured and to rescue them if they were."

"And you interpret that as the green light to send some of our guys with the teams, right?" Wolf uncrossed his legs. "Like me, right?"

"Like you, Wolf, like you. Normally, I wouldn't send field-grade—"

"What's that supposed to mean?" Wolf spat out. "That I'm getting too old?" He glared at Charles.

"No, goddammit. Normally a major would be in charge of all the teams, not on one."

The Wolf relaxed. "Okay. I want to pick my own Number 2,"

he said, "an NCO named Menuez. You know him? He's kind of slopy-looking."

"That's not the only reason you want him, I hope."

"No, he's got Hatchet and Spike experience." Wolf was referring to clandestine operations.

"Sure, Wolf, I know him and we'll get him for you. But I reserve the right to supply you a new indidge we think is right for your team. I've got him standing by to meet you. He's older, but knows his way around the boonies and the Commies."

"How's that?"

"He's from Hanoi. Fought against the French as a Viet Minh. Rallied to the South in the early sixties and has been here ever since. Excellent English and French. We ran a full background on him and have run a few local recce ops with him to see his ground savvy. Even Westy thinks he's okay. He thinks like a VC and can smell them, I swear. I went out with him one night and we got three who never should have been there, just outside the Michelin Plantation. You should have seen this guy light up when he greased 'em. He's tough and he loves zapping Commies. There's only one thing," Charles said.

"What's that?" Wolf asked.

"He's pretty intelligent and acts like a general sometimes. He doesn't like to be ordered around. But it's not too bad, he's so smart, he can usually figure out what you want before you do."

"Well, I'm here and ready to go to work. Bring him in and let's get started."

Al Charles picked up the land line and called an office across the compound. Five minutes later, he called, "Entrez," in response to a firm knock on his door. Wearing a sun-bleached tiger suit, a tall Vietnamese man entered and looked squarely at the big black man, Lieutenant Colonel Al Charles, who motioned toward Wolf and said, "This is Major Lochert, the officer I told you about."

The tall Vietnamese looked at Wolf. His face cracked in a half smile as he said, "I am honored to be working with such a famous warrior. I am Buey Dan."

25

☆

Court Bannister sat in the plain plywood-paneled office of Major
Ronald E. Bender, weapons officer for the 366th Tactical Fighter
Wing. They had known each other since pilot training days when
they shared the same T-6 instructor at Columbus, Mississippi. At
the time, Court had been an aviation cadet, and Bender, a Naval
Academy graduate who opted for the Air Force, a second lieutenant.
Later, they had gone through the F-86 fighter program at Nellis
together.

The two men greeted each other with pleasure.

"I've been hearing good things about you," Bender said. "Jack
Laird was through here on his way to R-and-R in Hong Kong and
said you were tearing 'em up down there at Bien Hoa. Called you
Crash Bannister. Said you were one of their top jocks and had the
highest BDA."

"Did you expect anything less?"

"I suppose not, since I wasn't there to show everybody how to
do it." He grinned. "What about this 'Crash' business?"

"Forget it, Bender. I brought in a Hun I should have jettisoned.
Sprinkled it all over the runway. Jack was making a funny."

"Okay, *Crashie*," Bender said with a smirk, then looked serious.
"Jack told me about Rawson. I hear Seventh put him up for the
Medal."

"Maybe so. I haven't heard. I guess by the books he deserves it. But he really was a dork."

"Saved your life, didn't he?"

"That he did. That's an action I'll accept from anybody, even dorks." Court pulled down his left-sleeve zipper and took out his cigarettes and lighter. He offered one to Bender.

"No, thanks," Bender said. He tilted his gray steel chair back against the plywood.

"I've got a bird lined up for us for several missions starting this afternoon," he said. "It just has tanks and a pistol so we can look around some and not be fragged on a target. You must rate, the authorizing TWX came in with a lot of horsepower behind it."

Bender grimaced at the smoke from Court's cigarette. Court stubbed it into the prominently displayed Number 10 can painted fire-engine red.

"Here's the scene," Bender said, standing up in front of several aeronautical charts taped to a wall. He pointed to a dark line dividing North and South Vietnam. "That's the Demilitarized Zone, the DMZ. It was established by the Geneva conference in 1954 as the zone of demarcation between North and South Vietnam when the French pulled out. Most people think it's set at the 17th parallel. The truth is it's actually the Ben Hai River running east and west. U.S. policy forbids ground or artillery attacks into it, so naturally the NVA has moved heavy artillery, rockets, and about four hard-core divisions into the southern half." Ron Bender paused.

"Now," he said, "comes the Pentagon mess. It seems our illustrious Air Force and Navy leaders cannot agree to have all the air strikes in North Vietnam come under a single manager. So they have divided North Vietnam into six different areas called Route Packages, which are split up between the USAF and the Navy." Bender moved his finger along the outline of North Vietnam.

"Pack One starts here at the DMZ and runs north for about 60 miles, then Two, Three, Four, and Five. The Hanoi area is split into Six Alpha, which the USAF is responsible for, and Six Bravo, which the Navy has. The USAF has Packs One and Five, in addition to Six Alpha. The Navy has the rest. Of course, this means there isn't always a combined effort against Uncle Ho. Targets for all North Vietnam except Pack One come from the President to CINCPAC, who assigns them to Seventh Air Force or the Navy's Task Force Seventy-seven on carriers off the coast. Missions in Pack One and Laos can be fragged by Seventh."

"That means without Presidential approval we can't fast-FAC anything other than Pack One and Laos," Court said.

"That's right," Bender agreed. He pointed at the outlines of the heavily traveled supply roads from Hanoi and Haiphong that exited North Vietnam into Laos via the passes at Mu Gia and Ban Karai in Pack One, code-named Tally Ho. "Since we can't hit the rail lines that came south out of China or the seaport at Haiphong or even completely take out the marshaling yards near Hanoi, we have to go after the trucks as they come down these roads in Pack One and through the passes into Laos. The code name for that whole panhandle area of Laos is Steel Tiger. The public doesn't know we are hitting there."

"I had no idea it was this screwed up," Court said.

"Yeah," Bender said. "You Hun drivers down there in the Delta had it easy." He walked toward the door. "Let's go aviate so I can show you some of the big stuff. I filed our call sign as Snoopy."

> 1330 HOURS LOCAL, 13 SEPTEMBER 1966
> F-4 FROM PACK ONE TO MU GIA PASS,
> ROYALTY OF LAOS

☆

They were over the dusty brown roads that headed south along the coast, and then west through the scrub jungle of Pack 1 toward Mu Gia and Ban Karai passes, through the Annamite Mountain chain into Laos. They made several high-speed runs at 3,000 feet, jinking across the roads, drawing heavy fire that widened Court's eyes. From the backseat of the F-4 he was trying to note the position and intensity of the bursts.

"How do you tell the type?" he asked Bender in the front cockpit.

"By the burst color and size. You saw the 23's—they go off never over nine thou with a string of white puffs. The 37's you just saw, they're kind of a reddish-white burst. The 57's are orange in black, and the 100 mils are red in black, you never forget that. And of course a SAM is a big, white, fire-farting telephone pole shot at you. Their warhead is 286 pounds."

"Do you really count the bursts?"

"Naw. You don't have the time or eyeballs to spare. After fifteen or twenty bursts you just sort of estimate by groups of twenty or so."

They plunged down the roads at even lower altitudes to log the ground-fire response. That night it took Court a long time to compose his first TWX to DOCB at Tan Son Nhut. He said in his final paragraph that speed and movement was the key to survival. Dunne's answering TWX let Court know that he wasn't interested in survival methods, just ground-fire rate and accuracy.

The missions over the next few days went by in a blur of sweat and jinking and heavy ground fire. The six-gun 57mm pits directed by radar were the worst, Court and Bender agreed. Each plane they flew had to go into the hangar for battle damage repair. Each crew chief let them know he was mightily pissed that *his* airplane was holed without causing any hurt on the bad guys. Whatever this Snoopy stuff was, they said to each other at the NCO Club, it was sure tearing up airplanes. Court's TWX's became shorter. He listed only position, rate, and accuracy. He did place addendas on his info TWX's to the 37th at Phu Cat, listing the survival methods he and Bender were developing. The 37th Director of Operations phoned in his thanks.

One afternoon, before their final mission, Bender said he was going to show Court exactly what the Russian SA-2 Guideline SAM with a 286-pound warhead was like. Bender explained how the F-4 could protect itself from SAM's by using the radar homing and warning gauges, the RHAW gear, as he called it.

"When you eyeball your first SAM rising," Bender said with a knowing smile, "your sphincter will up and grab your adam's apple."

"Ten o'clock," Court yelled two hours later, his adam's apple suddenly enlarged, "I've got a lock-on at ten o'clock." They were just east of Quang Khe at 35,000 when Court saw the lights on the RHAW dial in the rear cockpit.

"Rodge," said Ron Bender in a far less excited voice, "take a look out the window."

Court looked out and down to where Bender dipped the wing low to the left. He saw a long white smoke trail leading from a cloud of dust on the ground to an orange trail of fire. He could barely make out the shape of the rising missile. His bowels jumped as his buttocks involuntarily clenched.

"The whole trick is seeing 'em," Bender said, "let them get close, then do a flight maneuver they can't follow. Those little stubby wings are just guide vanes. There's not much lift at all."

When the SAM was in position, Bender faked it down, then he pulled hard on his F-4.

"Watch the SAM," Bender grunted through teeth clenched against the brutal load.

"Shit, I lost it. I can't turn my head," Court grunted back, his head almost to his knees, helmet twisted, "You racked it so hard I'm looking into my headset."

Six seconds later, they heard and felt the muffled explosion as the SAM self-destructed when its fusing said it had lost its target.

This time the crew chief was really pissed. His airplane had twelve holes and was starting to leak.

"It's unusual," the intelligence debriefer said, "for that SAM site at Quang Khe to come against just one airplane. You say you made no passes. Were you ever in a position where it looked like you were going to make an ordnance pass?"

"No, not at all," Bender said with some impatience. "Like I told you, it must of been an inadvertent firing or a new guy on a practice shot. You got to realize the gomers make mistakes, too. They're not ten feet tall and their equipment can screw up just like ours."

The Intel officer looked unimpressed. "We have to make just the opposite estimation," he said, "because there is no way we know which SAM site or gun pit is in a training status or has faulty equipment or error-prone gunners."

"Maybe so," Bender said, "but when I run across a bad gunner, one that shoots too early or too late, or has bad aim, I don't kill him. His replacement might be better."

"Major Bender, if you are that discerning when multiple guns come up, you've got to be the coolest man alive."

"Wel-l-l-l . . ."

0915 HOURS LOCAL, 18 SEPTEMBER 1966
F-4 EN ROUTE FROM MU GIA PASS TO DA NANG,
REPUBLIC OF VIETNAM

☆

That morning, after several hairy runs through the passes at Mu Gia and Ban Karai into the Steel Tiger section of Laos, they were checking in with Panama for final radar clearance to Da Nang when a new voice cut in.

"Hey Snoopy, this is Trot One One. You read?"

"Trot One One, got you loud and clear."

"Snoopy, we got a little problem here. You're close to Da Nang. How about a join-up and look us over. I'm on the 352 radial for 40 miles off Channel 77 at flight level 340." The instant Trot One One said he had problems, the air was full of transmissions, some blocking others.

"Trot One One, Panama. Are you declaring an emerg—"

"Trot One One, this is Crown on Guard, are you declaring an emergency?" Crown was the call sign for an orbiting rescue-coordinating aircraft.

"Trot One One, Snoopy, we'll find you. Panama, give Snoopy a vector to Trot One One."

"Trot One One, Crown on Guard. Come up 256.4, repeat, 256.4."

"Negative, partner. Can't switch frequencies. Radio's acting up."

"Snoopy, Panama, Steer 142 for 10 to Trot One One."

"Snoopy copies."

"Let's stroke the burner and catch those guys," Court said on the intercom to Bender.

"Rodge. Just be ready to land from a flameout pattern, we're pretty low on fuel," Bender said as he moved the throttles outboard. "God, the radio goes ape with all these guys trying to help."

When Bender reached 600 knots he came out of burner. He looked at the fuel gauge and did some rapid calculations. "We've only got twelve more minutes and that's only if we stay at altitude until we're right over the field."

"Hey, over there at ten o'clock," Court said. "We've got a smoker." The two pilots saw a lone F-4 trailing a thin wisp of white smoke. Bender manuevered into a position just off its right wing. "I'll fly, you handle the radio," he told Court. The plane, a Marine F-4B with Chu Lai markings, was steadily losing altitude.

"Trot One One, Snoopy here on your right wing."

"Rodge, Snoop. Check me for battle damage, will you, partner?"

Bender slowly slid their F-4 under and around the crippled airplane, then maintained a parallel position off its left wing. Court transmitted.

"Trot, you've got smoke coming out of some holes underneath your forward electronics bay."

"Thanks, partner. I thought it was getting a bit warm in here. Did you know you've got a few holes in your own rudder? They look clean."

"Everything looks okay on the gauges up here," Bender said on the intercom.

"Must have been that zipper at Mu Gia," Court said back to him, then he transmitted to Trot 11. "Okay, thanks."

"Just thought you'd like to know, partner . . . oh shit, our hydraulics are even lower now and we just lost our Tacan. What's the heading and distance to 77?"

Court checked his navigation instrument. "Hold 170 for 30," he said, "you're doing great." Then he saw a trickle of flame from underneath. They were down to 14,000 feet, where the oxygen content was higher, allowing flames to ignite.

"Okay, Trot. You just got some fire now," Court said as Bender slid twenty feet away from the burning airplane.

"Yeah, partner. We might just have to leave . . . oh, oh. Just lost a few more pounds of flight control pressure."

Bender slid another twenty feet off to the side. A burning airplane with control problems can explode or suddenly roll in any direction to collide with whatever is in the way.

"Trot, you got a long trail of fire under there, now. Look, we're over good-guy territory. Best you punch," Court said.

"Crown, Panama. We've got a fix."

"Trot One One, Crown. Are you going to eject?"

"Well, partner, guess we'll have to. I'll have my backseater go out here over land, then I'll get this beast out over the water where it won't hurt anybody when I step out."

Bender and Court followed the burning Marine F-4B as it turned east toward the South China Sea just a few miles away.

"We're down to five minutes, Court," Bender said about their fuel situation.

"We got to stay with these guys," Court said.

"Yeah, I know. You want to bail out in formation with them, too?"

The rear canopy of the Trot 11 aircraft suddenly flew off and the backseater was rocketed out in his ejection seat. Court looked back and saw the figure separate from the seat then jerk upright as the canopy blossomed open.

"Trot One One Bravo's out with a good chute. Trot One One Alpha is still in the bird," Court transmitted, then looked at the front cockpit. It was gushing flame with blowtorch intensity.

"Trot, get out, get out, GET OUT," he yelled over the radio.

"Christ, yes," Bender said. "When that back canopy went, it created a terrible fucking draft." They heard Trot 11's mike button key.

"Can't . . . can't . . ." they heard the pilot's tortured voice, "ahhhhHHHH GOD . . ."

The plane slowly nosed down. Bender and Bannister followed until it impacted in a great spray of water just off the beach north of Da Nang.

"Snoopy, Crown. Did Trot One One Alpha get out?"

"Negative, Crown," Court transmitted, "he went in with his airplane. Give us a snap vector to Da Nang. We're on fumes."

"Steer 185 Snoopy. Can't you cap the backseater?"

Bender broke in. "Shit no, we'd fall on him."

Court twisted in his seat to look back. "There's an A-4 circling the chute," he told Crown.

"Okay guys, go home," Crown said. "One down is enough this afternoon." Then on Guard Channel Crown called: "A-4 circling the chute north of Da Nang, this is Crown on Guard. Come up 256.4 . . ." Bender switched to Da Nang Tower and got permission for a straight-in landing.

During the postflight inspection they found the two holes in the rudder. The crew chief said it didn't look as if anything vital was hit and he'd have it repaired by morning.

Court and Bender debriefed with Intel, then gave them all the Trot 11 information they could. The Intel officer said Trot 11 Bravo had been picked up by a Jolly Green Rescue helicopter. The two pilots went to the wall map and retraced the route they had taken. When Bender was satisfied Court had absorbed and played back all the gun and route information he could absorb, he called it a day. He looked at the clock above the map.

"Damn near seven. Lets fold it. Go write your TWX. I'll meet you at the O-Club at eight." They never spoke of Trot 11 again.

A large sign, supported on three-inch bamboo poles, proclaimed the low wood-and-screen building painted dull green to be the DOOM CLUB, the acronym by which Da Nang Officer's Open Mess was known. A silly journalist had written that the name was the product of the pilot's fatalistic frame of mind, brought about by the rigors of combat.

After that, the F-4 jocks told any newsie dumb enough to listen that the heaviest casualties of the air war were caused by napalming beets and carrots, and cratering bridge approaches.

The B-57 jocks told tall tales of the doom pussy scratching at their canopies at night over the Trail.

The Marine A-4 jocks found sticking their fingers down their throats a more warranted and suitable response.

Inside, Bender's squadron mates waved them over and shoved two Budweisers at them. Bender made the introductions. Everyone wore his green-bag flight suit.

"What brings you to Dang Dang by the Sea?" a tall captain asked.

Court, trying to preserve the security classification of his mission, said it was just for local orientation rides.

"You must be that Commando Sabre guy, the one working on the fast-FAC program," the captain responded.

"The very one," Court said, eyebrows raised. "How did you know?"

"Some Hun jocks from the Thirty-seventh at Phu Cat were in here the other day. They told us about it."

"So much for security," Court said.

"Security, hah," the captain sneered. "No point in classifying anything. The gomers are tapped into all our nets. Those that aren't got their sisters and cousins working here on base." He guzzled down half the beer from his can.

"Heard you're up from Bien Hoa. You know that guy that used to be there named Parker, Pistol Parker?" he asked.

"*Pistol* Parker?" Court said.

"Yeah, he really is, you know. He was in here with some Phan Rang guys, flying around with them in the backseat of an F-model. He's wild. He drinks a lot, throws beer cans around. He even tried to start a fight. That guy's a real pistol."

Later, over dinner in what passed for the dining room, Court brought up Toby Parker.

"Yeah, I heard about him," Bender said. "Killed some FAC, didn't he?"

"No, goddammit, he didn't kill some FAC. He saved a bunch of guys, in fact." Court told Bender about Parker. Bender pursed his lips.

"Well, I wasn't impressed. He was pretty wild here. We all get a bit wild, but with him it was different, somehow." Bender was silent for a moment. "He wasn't having any fun, doing what he was doing, no fun at all."

After they ate, Bender led Court back to the bar for one more beer. It was nearly 10 in the evening and they were both blinking with fatigue. The boisterous bar had calmed down, now that many of the pilots had gone back to their hootches. Those with a three a.m. getup for Pack 6 mission briefs had been the first to go. The rest, scattered in two's and three's at the bar and tables, were exhausted from their day's work. The Tijuana Brass on the Doom Club's sound system tooted to no avail. Court noticed the difference between the Da Nang Club and that of Bien Hoa.

"You know," he said, as they walked back to the hootch in the dark, "I think you guys work harder up here than we do at Bien Hoa."

"Yeah, different airplane, different missions, and we get rocketed, too," Bender responded.

Court didn't mention the mortar attacks on Bien Hoa.

☆

By seven o'clock they were airborne on their last mission, a road
recce south of Mu Gia in Laos. They spotted many fleeting targets
they could have destroyed if they had had strike birds on call. Court
logged where they could easily fly at 1,500 feet and where they had
to fly above 4,500 feet because of ground fire. All told, as they sped
up and down the road system, Court counted over eighty puffs of
flak, mostly the white basketballs of 23mm. They finally pulled up
and headed back to Da Nang.

"It's good for you to get shot at like this," Bender said, over the
intercom.

"Yeah, I know. I have to log all this for the fast-FAC stats."

"I mean in addition to that."

"Oh yeah? Why?"

"Keeps the adrenaline flowing, and that's good for your pecker."

"Whaaat?"

"Adrenaline makes you horny, everybody knows that. Then all that
inflating and deflating of your pecker makes it a more useful tool."

"Bender, you are so full of crap, I don't see how you get airplanes
off the ground."

The club was half full with pilots drifting in for early lunch. Bender
drew two coffees, sat at Court's table, and handed him two TWX's
he had picked up. "I saw part of one. You've got a two-seater Hun
due in."

Court picked it up and read that, indeed, an F-100F was due in
from the 37th at Phu Cat. Tomorrow morning at 0900, as a matter
of fact. In the backseat would be FAC Instructor Jack Barnes from
the 504th FAC School at Phan Rang. He was directed to fly three
missions with Court to give him a preliminary FAC checkout. Under
no circumstances was Captain Bannister authorized to direct strikes.

A second TWX, a nicer one, was from the Director of Operations
at Phu Cat. It said that one each Captain Courtland Edm. Bannister,
AO 3021953, was authorized upon completion of the training missions to return Barnes to Phan Rang, then ferry the F-100F he had
to Clark Air Base in the Philippines for time-required depot maintenance. Once there, he was to wait three days and ferry another
bird back. Court grinned. He recognized the message for what

it was: a sneak R&R at Clark as a reward for his Commando Sabre missions.

Court and Bender met the F-100F the next morning. It came in with another F-model with an empty backseat to take the ferry pilot back to Phan Rang. Jack Barnes was a pleasant young lieutenant who had volunteered for FAC duty after 152 F-100 missions in South Vietnam. He had another 124 missions in the 0-1E as a FAC.

They holed up in a corner in the wing headquarters' main briefing room, where Barnes gave Court the equivalent of two weeks of FAC ground school in two days. On the third and fourth day they flew with the Snoopy call sign in Pack 1 to Mu Gia and on the Trail into Laos, where Court gave Barnes his first look at North Vietnam and Barnes gave Court some FAC techniques. Barnes said there wasn't much he could teach Court on recce flying, just what to look for on the ground like dust, tracks, turned leaves, different camouflage, or suspiciously new trees or bushes that indicated enemy troops, supplies, or trucks. The guns were self-evident.

Then the temporary-duty assignment was completed. Their time was up, the missions were flown, the reports were made, and the F-100F was due at Clark.

Court called down to 7th and pleaded with DOCB for another airplane to replace the one that had run out of time, and to be allowed to start putting in strikes. He said he knew his areas well and where the guns and trucks were. Negative, DOCB told him. Snoopy operations would not commence until such time as the concept was approved by 7th AF, MACV, CINCPAC, and the CSAF. Then, and only then would the full complement of airplanes and men be assembled at one base to perform on a full-time, daily basis. Tentative plans were to run it out of Phu Cat under a Major George Day, using the call sign Misty.

"Okay, okay," Court had said when the major had run down, "just asking."

Court thought for a few minutes about his upcoming trip to Clark Air Base, then spent a half hour getting Lieutenant Toby Parker, executive officer of the 504th Theater Indoctrination School, on the line.

"Hey, Toby, it's Court Bannister. Pack your gear and I'll take you to Clark for a few days."

Parker hesitated, then spoke. "How did you arrange that?" he asked. His voice sounded deep and measured.

Court explained where the F-100F came from and that he had an empty backseat in which Toby could ride. He said Toby would have to get a survival check and a backseat checkout so he'd be cleared per PACAF Regs for flight in a jet fighter.

"I've done all that and even have a current altitude chamber card."

"How come?" Court asked, surprised.

"So I could fly F-100 missions with these guys. I've got five now. The O-1 got a little slow. I also fly some missions with the helicopter people."

Court told him he was impressed and that he'd see him next day. Toby said fine, and that he was sure he could get away.

Court spent the next two hours at the Mars station, trying to get a ham radio hookup to Nancy Lewis in Los Angeles.

"Do you hear me?" he repeated several times after finally getting patched in. The static sounded like bacon frying. They had to say "Over" at the end of each sentence to allow the operators to switch their transmitters off and on.

"Oh, Court, I hear you. Are you all right?"

"Sure. Listen, I'll be in the Philippines at Clark Air Base Wednesday or so for a few days. How's your schedule? Can you be there? Hello? Hello?" The call faded, then just as suddenly came back.

". . . leave tomorrow and I want so desperately to see . . . letters just not . . ." The connection faded. Court handed the microphone back.

"Sorry 'bout that, sir," the Mars operator said. "Sometimes these connections just zero out."

> ### 1915 HOURS LOCAL, 21 SEPTEMBER 1966
> ### SAIGON, REPUBLIC OF VIETNAM
> ☆

The black Mercedes 240D sped down rue Antoine, swerved sharply to miss two female bicyclists in flowing *ao dais,* and crossed an intersection, barely missing two Honda motorbikes and a pedicab. The driver, Bubba Bates, pounded futilely on the horn ring on his steering wheel. The horn, as it had since the day after he bought the car, either made no noise or else gave a feeble and fading beep.

"Goddamn car," Bates said to himself, "paid seven grand green dollars and the frapping horn sounds like a butterfly fart. You can't trust those goddamn East Indians worth spit." He dragged heavily on the soggy cigar in his mouth. It was a Cuban hand-wrapped Corona Especial costing two dollars green. Bubba had two boxes, as a gift of good faith from the East Indian, who had sold him the $4,000

Mercedes 240D for $7,000. He did admit to himself it was a big Texas jump over that little French heap Alpha Airlines gave him to drive. So what if the horn didn't work. Another deal like what was coming up and he could buy three more, all brand-new from the real Mercedes Benz dealer, not that pockmarked Indian dickhead.

Bubba squinted over the cigar smoke as he looked for the unobtrusive gate to Lim's villa. Dissipating black clouds of the late afternoon thundershower intensified gloom on the rue des Trois Fleurs, in the exclusive northeastern section of Saigon. Large villas with tile roofs crouched unseen behind tall barriers of brick and stone topped by broken glass and barbed wire. All the villas were guarded by privately hired armed men whose immunity from military draft was assured by a fee paid to a small man at a large desk in the Ministry of Defense.

Bubba Bates spotted number 13/2 and honked impatiently to be let through the paneled steel gate. The guards peered in the car, and waved him in.

A male servant in slapping sandals led Bubba across marble floors to a small teak-paneled room in the back of the house and bade him wait. Bates noticed they had passed by several larger and nicer rooms. Within moments he heard approaching footsteps. He started to put his mashed cigar in a tall ceramic vase, thought better of it, made a pass at the pocket of his white sport shirt, and put it in the pocket of his black trousers. Two people walked into the room.

"Mr. Bates," Lim said, extending a hand thin and withered. Bates grabbed at it with both paws as if fearful it would fly away. He grinned and pumped. Lim's arm moved in jerks within the wide sleeve of his silk vestment.

"Mr. Lim, a pleasure. A real pleasure to see you again. And you too, general." He extended his hand to the second man, a tall Caucasian.

"God rot it, Bates, don't call me by my rank," the general, a sparse American, said. He wore tan slacks and a short-sleeved white shirt open at the throat. "I told you that. You want this arrangement to continue, you go by the rules. Call me John, that's all you need to know." Bubba Bates lowered his hand when the general made no move to shake it. When the general moved his hand, Bates raised his in expectation, but quickly put it down when the general reached for his rear pocket and pulled out a handkerchief into which he sneezed heavily several times.

"God-rotted allergy," he said. He sniffed, examined the contents, and put the hanky back in his pocket. "I called you here because we are entering a new mode of logistics operation. We wish to increase our out shipments and disperse more quickly what comes in.''

Bates stepped back. ''General, I mean John, I just can't add any more unmarked outbound suitcases, and it's already looking suspicious, the unclaimed inbound bags that pile up in the luggage area. No, sir, I can't—''

''Bates, you'll do as I tell you, because if you don't, Mr. Lim will send some people to have a little chat with you. And I swear to you, they will feed you your balls one by one.'' Mr. Lim nodded, a thin smile moved his lips.

Bates swallowed. ''Sir, I—''

''Shut up. Listen to me. From now on, a courier will accompany the baggage on your planes to and from Bangkok. There will still be unmarked bags both ways, but he will be carrying two more in and out. It is your job, as usual, to see that they bypass inspections.'' The general retrieved his hanky and sneezed again.

Bates nodded his head. Bypassing inspections was the easiest part of the operation. He personally on-loaded the bags with special tags on the ramp at Tan Son Nhut, to be claimed by who knows who at the Bangkok end. He had to personally supervise the off-loading of luggage from the cargo hold of the Alpha Airlines DC-3's and DC-4's to intercept the inbound bags or packages that had distinctive markings. As to what was in the bags, he wasn't sure. He guessed, by the difference in weight, there was money going outbound and maybe jewels and drugs inbound.

Two hundred dollars in green spread around the customs officials and ramp inspectors each week solved any security problems before they occurred. Soon, he knew, the price would go up. His had to, anyway. He was starting to run through his $250 per week too fast. ''Damned woman,'' he thought of Tui, ''if she hadn't run out on me I wouldn't spend so much chasing tail all over Saigon.'' He realized the general was talking.

''The passenger will always be a Caucasian male or female, not necessarily an American, who will ask you if you have any flights after 1500 on Sundays, which you do not. You merely say no, and take the usual precautions. Do you understand?''

Bates nodded, his mind already on Lim, who produced a brown envelope from his robes. He tried not to look.

''Any flights after three on Sundays,'' he said, already mentally counting the 40-percent profit he could make with currency manipulation of the American dollars in the envelope.

''No, god rot it, 1500 military style, 1500.'' He rolled his eyes.

"The first one will be around some time next week. And this is the last time we meet. Things are getting bigger, now. Lim here will be your contact." With a sudden motion, he grabbed Bubba Bates by his shirt front and pulled him close. "Don't ever, repeat, don't you ever contact me for any reason. You got that loud and clear, Bates?"

Bubba nodded. The general spun and walked out. Lim gave Bubba Bates the package and escorted him to the door.

"Mr. Bates, it is always a pleasure to see you. We are very pleased with your work. You will find a little bonus of 50 dollars in the package. You may expect that each week from now on."

Bubba nodded. He could hear the rain beginning in the darkness beyond. Deep in the house he thought he heard a sneeze. He started out.

"Oh yes, one last thing," Mr. Lim said. 'In the future, I will have a courier deliver your weekly package to your apartment. Please, it will be better if you do not come here again."

26

☆

The next morning, Court and Barnes were airborne in the F-100F by 0700. Court leveled at 30,000 feet. The sun was well clear of the horizon formed by the South China Sea. Low scud drew gray dashes along the coastline that lay beneath their left wing. The northeast monsoon season would soon be starting.

"Quite a guy, that Major Bender," Barnes said from the back-seat.

"That he is," Court agreed. They had eaten breakfast with him at five o'clock. He and nine other F-4 crews had a Pack 6 counter coming up. There were no big farewells between Court and Bender, or promises of keeping in touch. Fighter pilots know they will see their friends again, someplace on the circuit. They pick up conversations, sometimes after years of absence, as if interrupted just the day before.

Court wondered if Nancy Lewis would really be at Clark, and what would happen if she was. Their letters had been so insipid. Thirty minutes later he was taxiing in to a revetment at Phan Rang.

After briefing several captains and a major on the virtues and dangers of the new Misty FAC program—"I had no idea there were so many people up there with guns who want a piece of our ass"—Court headed over to the FAC school to see Parker.

Toby Parker smiled, shook hands, and appeared to be pleased to see Court. He was wearing neatly pressed khakis, but Court saw lines on his forehead and bags under his eyes that hadn't been there when he'd departed Bien Hoa seven months before.

"It's all set," Toby said. "The boss gave me the time off. First I've had since I got here."

In the revetment Court had Toby explain everything he knew about the backseat of an F-100F. Court was happily surprised at his depth of knowledge. He knew about as much as any F-100 jock.

Court let Toby take the controls after they leveled at 37,000, heading toward Clark Air Base via Cow Shark Airway to the Lubang intersection, where they would cut northeast for Clark. The total distance was 682 nautical miles.

Toby flew for over an hour without saying a word. At first Court monitored how well he held his heading and altitude. For the first twenty minutes he was ragged. He would porpoise through his assigned altitude by two and three hundred feet and chase his heading up to ten degrees on either side. Then he settled down.

Clark weather reported a cloud layer from 25,000 feet down to 3,000 feet. Court decided to let Toby make the penetration and approach, to see how he hacked instruments, then checked in with Clark Approach Control on 261.4.

"Roger Air Force 723, Clark Approach has you loud and clear. Squawk 45 for positive identification. You are cleared for penetration and low approach at Clark Air Base when you arrive over the high cone. Altimeter 29.96. Air Force 723, when you are inbound from your penetration turn, contact Ground Control Approach on 263.7 for further clearance and landing."

Court read back the instructions, then added that if the weather was clear below 3,000, they'd break it off once they had the field in sight and contact Clark Tower for permission to shoot some landings. Clark Approach rogered the plan.

Toby began his descent, with Court taking him through it. Toby was fairly steady until they entered the cloud layer at 25,000 feet, then he got rough.

"Okay, partner, keep your cross-check going. Don't concentrate on just one instrument. Keep them all in your mind—altitude, heading, airspeed. Watch your rate of descent." In the procedure turn, the bank angle got away from Toby. Court let him go as they tipped from a 30-degree bank to 60 then nearly vertical at 80 degrees before he recovered for him.

"God, Court, I didn't even see it," Toby said. He gave an exaggerated "whew" when they broke out and had the field in sight. Court called the tower for him.

"Clark Tower, Air Force 723, I have the field in sight, canceling IFR. Request landing instructions for one Fox one hundred."

"Air Force 723, Clark. You are cleared on to initial for Runway 24, left-hand pattern. Altimeter 29.96, wind is 210 at six. We have a flight of three on short initial. Report the break."

"Roger, 24, left break, 723."

Court returned to the intercom. "Okay, Toby. Heading 240, altitude 1,500, airspeed 350. That's it. Now we're over the approach end of the runway, give me a nice tight 180-degree turn to the left. Put the boards out. That's it, I'll handle the throttle, gear and flaps for you."

Toby made a credible left break and rolled out on downwind. "Good, hold 230," Court said. "Gear and flaps coming down. Hold the nose up; trim it up. Reduce speed to 190. Start your base turn . . . now. Very nice, bring it around; watch your airspeed; keep it turning; roll out."

"Clark Tower, 723 turning final, gear down, pressure up, touch and go."

"Roger 723, cleared touch and go. No other traffic."

Court helped Toby move the stick and rubber pedals around while they shot two touch-and-go practice landings and one full stop. They taxied in behind a follow-me to the maintenance hangar, then shut down and climbed out. The grinning Toby was dripping wet with perspiration.

"Good God, man," Court said, "you been taking a bath back there?"

"Court, it was great. Geez, *I loved* it. Can I fly on the way back?" In spite of the oxygen mask crinkles on his cheeks, Toby looked ten years younger. He babbled all the way into the hangar, while Court turned the airplane over to the maintenance officer. When the paperwork was finished, they were told the BOQ was full, but the van would run them over to the Skyliner Motel just outside the main gate. Toby kept up his excited chatter all the way to the Skyliner. Court barely listened as he again heard Nancy Lewis's voice on the Mars connection saying she wanted to see him. He felt his breath catch as he wondered if she had gotten her flight.

When the picture of a starving soldier crouched in a cage tried to enter his mind, he quickly tuned in on Toby's chatter.

☆

"What about that second landing? You weren't on the controls that much were you? On the penetration, do you put the boards out before you bring the throttle back or after? How do you know when to engage the nosewheel steering on landing?" Court patiently answered all the questions. Toby wound down as the van stopped at the motel, where they were assigned adjoining rooms. They showered and changed into light slacks and sport shirts. Toby wore a piece of jade set in gold on a thick gold chain around his neck. They walked out to the terrace lounge by the pool and had the waiter bring beer. Toby expertly lit a cigarette but coughed slightly at the first inhale.

Court went over the flight with him. He covered the fundamentals of aerodynamics, engine malfunction procedures, even how to make radio calls. Toby soaked it up and showed by his questions that he had a good understanding. He's really alive again when he talks airplanes, Court mused. He glanced at Toby.

"Tell me something, Tobes. Are you going to accept that pilot training slot or are you going to get out?"

Toby looked up. "Why do you ask?"

"You seem awfully hipped on flying and, face it, you're a natural. Yet you haven't once mentioned going to Randolph or what kind of an airplane you want once you get your wings."

Toby took a long pull at his beer, and stared off at the darkening sky. His face looked thoughtful.

"It's this way," he began. "The folks have expected a little more out of me. They've got a few bucks and they figured I'd have my fun in college and then come into the family real estate business. They sort of own a few things, and hoped I'd do some managing. They were pretty surprised when I went into the Air Force Officer Candidate School." He snorted. "Even more surprised when I graduated. They about washed their hands of me when I volunteered for Vietnam. They actually seemed angry." He shook his head, finished off his beer, and waved at the waiter for more.

"I guess I just wanted to do something on my own for a while before settling down. It's not a bad life back there in Virginia, you know. Fauquier County; horses and Cadillacs, long-haired blondes from Sweet Briar and Hood driving their convertibles around to horse shows. Lunch at the country club. You know what I mean."

Court knew what he meant. He had consciously chucked a relatively comfy life as the great Silk Screen Sam Bannister's son to carve his career out of the Air Force. There were few scions from wealthy families serving as career officers in any military service. The State Department, yes; the military, no.

Court looked more closely at Toby and thought he had never seen him quite so introspective.

"So what are you going to do?"

Toby looked him in the eye with sudden resoluteness. "I'm going to do what Phil Travers wanted me to do. Stay in and fly."

They talked and drank beer until long shadows inched over the terrace and the waiters began to light candles on the tables. Toby fought his way through two more cigarettes.

Court told Toby about the book he was reading, *Le Mal jaune*. "I think Lartéguy has his characters represent parts of the French being, and parts of the Vietnamese. One Frenchman is a tired colonial type, another a young hustler, a third is a liberal. The Vietnamese represent the nationalists, the Communists, and those who align with France. But I can't figure out the Vietnamese girl Kieu, who sometimes wants to be called Claire. Maybe by the time I finish, I'll know what both Lartéguy and my friends Lanh and Ut are driving at. It's in French and I'm pretty rusty." He took a lingering drag on his cigarette. Toby looked bored.

"Do you want to eat here, or over at the O-Club?" he asked. "The motel has a bus that makes the round trip every thirty minutes. I checked."

"Let's go to the club," Court said. "I hear they have great steaks, and I'm ready." They finished their beer and walked through the small lobby to the canvas-covered portico outside the main entrance. Bert, the desk man, assured them the bus would be along any minute. They lit cigarettes while they waited in the dark. The stored heat from the driveway surrounded them like steam from a grate. It was barely eight o'clock. Headlights from a Volkswagen bus lit them up as it swung up the curving drive of the motel and stopped in front of the door. They could see it was packed with civilian aircrew and luggage. They stepped back as the passenger door slid open and found themselves staring at Tiffy Berg. Next to her sat Nancy Lewis.

Thirty minutes later, Court and Toby stood by at the bar at the Skyliner pool waiting for the girls to join them. They had switched to scotch. After the beers, Toby could feel his.

"Hey, Court. That was a great flight today, wasn't it?" He wobbled slightly as he focused his eyes on his watch. "But we've got to eat pretty soon or I'm going to fall over."

"Then don't drink doubles. Shape up. Besides, didn't you see the way Tiffy looked at you? I think she wants your body." Court grinned.

"You and Nancy sure stared at each other for a long time. At first I didn't think you were even going to say hello. You both looked pretty serious." He put his drink down. "So you think Tiffy gave me the old come-on." His face looked rumpled. The whites of his blue eyes were tinged with tiny red veins. He screwed his brow into an exaggerated wrinkle of concentration. "You don't suppose . . . no, no." He shook his head. "No, you don't. And I don't suppose either."

"Toby, old pal, you're not making much sense," Court said. He looked up to the top of the steps. "Here they come," he said. "Here they come, and, God, don't they look great?"

Both girls wore white linen wrap-around miniskirts that smoothed down over their hips and ended well short of their knees. Tiffy wore a blue modified polo pullover that clung tightly to her breasts as if stitched to her brassiere. Her brown hair was short and lustrous. Nancy Lewis wore a blouse of Thai silk that couldn't quite hide the fullness of her breasts. Her hair was brown, now long and combed smoothly over her shoulders. Both had bare legs and high heels.

Court and Toby met the two girls halfway and walked them to a table they had reserved for dinner. It was set with white linen, stemmed wine and water glasses, reasonable china, and shiny stainless-steel flatware. Placed in the center of the table were a large candle, whose flame flickered slightly in the cool breeze, and a curved bowl holding a floating chrysanthemum. The waiter, a slender boyish Filipino, took drink orders and passed the menus. Both girls started to talk, Tiffy Berg first—"I simply couldn't believe my eyes—"

Then Nancy Lewis. "I never thought we'd make it—" They stopped at the same time and laughed. Tiffy turned to Nancy. "Never thought you'd make it? Did you know Court and Toby would be here?" Nancy's smile was her answer, as Court explained the Mars call.

"Nancy," he said, before any further conversation could develop, "I want to know about your leg."

"Like I wrote. I threw the crutch away in a day, and had the stitches out in a week. I was stiff for another week. That's all."

The waiter brought the drinks, wine for the girls, scotch for the men. Without Toby noticing, Court took his double. Everybody ordered lumpia, then Australian beef. Court and the two girls talked about the weather, shopping at Clark, and how nice the Filipinos were. Tiffy said the frug and watusi were still the latest dance rage in the states. Nancy indicated the dance floor, "We'll teach it to you guys tonight," she said, looking from Court to Toby. "Great," Court said. Toby nodded. Nancy looked at him.

"The last time we talked was at the club in Bien Hoa. How have you been, Toby?" she asked.

"Hey, Court," he said, his voice loud, "tell them about that great flight today. Was I great or was I great?"

"You were great, Tobes, just great."

"Toby," Tiffy said, placing her hand on his wrist, "there was a big write-up in the newspapers in the States about how you saved some men and an airplane; about how you won the Air Force Cross, and all. I think that was just marvelous. You must be very proud."

Toby stared at her. "Oh, I'm proud, all right, boy, am I proud. I'm so goddamn proud, you can't believe it." He said the words like bitten-off snarls. Then he worked his face into an exaggerated grin, and tilted his chair back. He waved his glass and started to sing. "Off we go, into the wild blue yonder—"

"All right, Toby, that's enough," Court said.

"—climbing high, into the sun—"

"Parker," Court's voice lashed out like a bull whip, "Knock—it—off."

Toby rocked his chair forward and slammed his glass down. Tiffy put her hand to her throat. Crew members at other tables glanced over.

"Come ON, we're having a party. Right?" He grabbed Tiffy's wrist and looked her in the eye. "A party, got it?"

Court reached over and wrapped his big hand around Toby's wrist. He applied just enough pressure to make Toby let go of Tiffy.

"Bannister, let go or I'll pop you one."

"I'll let go if you behave, otherwise I'm going to dump you in the pool." He tilted Toby Parker's arm in the direction of the pool.

"All right, I get the point. There will be no party. I'll be quiet. Now give me my damn arm back." Court let go.

Toby looked at Tiffy. "You wanna dance?"

"Do you think you can?" Tiffy asked, concern on her face.

"Sure," Toby said. He stood up and squared his shoulders, suddenly looking boyish again. "Just watch me." He held out his hand, and led Tiffy to the dance floor. She looked back at the table and shrugged.

Court and Nancy Lewis watched them take their place among the scattered couples. They danced slow, and close. The orchestra played easy songs for the dinner crowd.

"Oh, Court," Nancy said, "I feel so sorry for Toby. He is so unhappy again. I thought after that talk at Bien Hoa he was coming around. He told me about the girl, Tui, in Saigon, and about Phil Travers. I thought he was getting over it. What happened?"

"Tui was one of the sappers that night you got hit. She got cut in half by M-16's right in front of Toby. She had called out to him. It happened right outside our bunker."

"Oh, no! How terrible. He's so young to be so sad. What can we do for him?"

"Not much. Try to protect him from himself, I suppose, and hope he'll ride it out."

The waiter wheeled up a cart and served four platters of sizzling Australian steaks. Court ordered a bottle of wine.

"Tiffy kind of likes him. Maybe she can help."

"Maybe," Court said. "How about you? Any news about your husband?" As he chose the word, Court realized he didn't want to bring the man to the table by saying his name.

Nancy took a sip of her wine. "Yes, I've had some word." She pressed her lips together for a minute. "Tom Myers wrote me a few months ago. He said he reported Brad's death, based on the evidence given by Wolf Lochert, to the Department of the Army, but they haven't said a word to me yet." She took a deep breath. "Oh, Court, I feel so awful. Part of me wants him alive and part of me wants him declared . . . declared . . ." She shook her head, her eyes full.

Court took her hand. He wanted to cradle her in his arms. He lifted his other hand to her chin, and gently tilted her head up. He wanted her and wanted her bad, but couldn't bring himself into the pursuit mode.

"Maybe Brad is alive," he said, kicking himself for trying to be so righteous but unable to stop. In calling Brad by name and implying he was alive, Court brought the slain soldier to the table and sat him right down between himself and Nancy. She looked away.

"He isn't," she said.

The breeze was warm and scented. The moon hung fat on the horizon. Tiffy and Toby came back to the table holding hands. Toby's face was pleasant and bright.

"I apologize," he said, "for being such a loudmouth." Nancy and Court told him not to worry about it. He looked at them and grinned. It was the Toby Parker of better days. "This is some girl," he said, holding up Tiffy's hand in his own from under the table. "Some girl."

They relished their steaks, and savored the wine, which was kept flowing throughout the meal, and the big chocolate desserts. When they weren't laughing uproariously at funny flying stories, they were enjoying the dance floor. Nancy and Tiffy got the giggles while telling airline stories, and Court went off on some long tale about falling off a horse into a pile of manure when he was a kid.

Later, Toby and Tiffy came back from a dance to announce they were going down to the bar in the basement of the Skyliner; they strolled off, arms around each other.

"Maybe there is a thing going there," Court said.

Nancy nodded and smiled. "Let's you and me dance," she said, looking at Court with half-closed eyes.

They danced apart at first, then closer as the orchestra did a passable job with American prom songs from the forties and fifties. Without speaking, they swayed though a ten-minute medley. The sax player was particularly eloquent.

Nancy snuggled closer. "Hold me," she murmured, laying her head on Court's shoulder. Court, at tent-pole size again, made no move. Nancy tightened and pulled him close. "Court, oh Court, take me home."

"Are you sure?" he asked into her hair.

"Yes. It's all I could think of flying over here."

"But your letters were so noncommittal."

"You never read the ones I tore up."

They took what was left of the wine and went to his room. Inside, he turned the bedside radio, volume low, to some slow music, threw a towel over the lamp, and poured the wine. Before he could pick up the glasses, she slid her arms around him and kissed him. He put his arms around her and was roused beyond measure. They kissed gently at first, feeling each other's lips and faces. Then the kisses became harder, harder and longer; then deep and hard and long, feeling and kneading, pulling and clutching and pressing together until Court lifted her up and onto the bed. He lay on her and began to move his hips, felt her respond under him with undulations and surges of her own. They breathed in gasps and moans, smothered each others' mouths and faces with their lips and tongues, their need for each other blazing and throbbing now.

He started to slide her panties down. She lifted her hips to help and tugged at her skirt. Then she sat up and pulled her blouse over her head, tousling her hair and exposing the brassiere that held breasts far larger and firmer than seemed possible for the blouse to have hidden. She leaned back, arms straight out behind her, hair tumbled over one shoulder, eyes half-closed with want and desire, her moist mouth slightly open. Her nipples were erect and large, her breasts and her belly glowed sun-brown, then white at the triangle of pubic hair glistening blonde and full and moist. Her long legs were knee-bent over the edge of the bed.

Court stood and looked down at her.

"My God, but you are beautiful." His voice was thick and hoarse. He undressed quickly. He felt he had never been this gorged and hard in his life. He went to her, and stood in front of her, bent over and gently eased her down. She breathed more calmly now. He knelt and started to guide himself into her. She gasped, and her legs convulsed together. Court began to pull away.

"No," she said, "stay there, I'll be all right." She put her hands on him to hold him in place. Court touched her. She felt dry and closed.

"Court, it's all right. Please, go ahead."

"No," he said, and pulled away. "It's not all right. I'm not, shall we say, up to it." He stood and quickly turned away from her to grab his pants, but she saw he was more than up to it.

"Oh, Court, you don't have to pretend it's your fault. I'm so sorry. I really wanted to." She sat forward, still naked. She had no pretense at false modesty and made no coquettish grabs for clothes or bedsheet.

With difficulty, Court pulled his pants on over his nakedness.

"Do you want me to—"

"No," he said, interrupting her. "It's okay, really. Don't worry about it. I'll just go in the bathroom and slit my wrists."

"I really wanted to make love, or thought I wanted to. I hope you don't think I . . . am a . . . a girl who teases."

"No, I don't think that. Not at all. I know what the problem is." Court lit a cigarette.

"So do I," she said. "It's too soon. Maybe it will always be too soon." She moved to the side of the bed. "Now that you've got some clothes on, I feel naked." She pulled a sheet around her and leaned back against the headrest.

Court poured them both a glass of wine, then sat in the lounge chair and propped his feet on the bed. He thought he heard Toby enter his room. He studied her profile as they sipped their wine. Mantovani on the radio seemed to soothe her. Court felt disgustedly righteous but terribly frustrated. He took a deep breath.

"I meant what I said. You are beautiful."

"But not sexy."

"Wrong. You are very sexy."

"But not tonight." She took a sip of her wine.

"Wrong again. You are *always* sexy to me, you just don't feel sexy about me."

"Oh, Court, now you're the one who is wrong. I do feel . . . sexy about you. It's just that something locked up at the last minute. I don't know if it was my mind or my body, but all of a sudden something clicked off and I just shut down."

They were silent again as Mantovani played on. Court held up the empty wine bottle. "More? I can get some at the desk."

"No, but I want to ask you something. May I?"

"Sure, go ahead."

"I want to spend the night with you. May I?"

"Sure, go ahead."

"No, I mean in bed with you, with your arms around me."

"Sure, go ahead."

"Dammit," she said, "you're not making things easy for me."

Court looked at her. She looked tired and helpless and hurt. He pulled his feet off the bed and leaned forward.

"I'm sorry," he said. "You're right, I'm being an ass."

She giggled. "Not quite," she said, "not quite."

It began as the first glow of dawn softly restored form and substance to the room. And to their desire. They were slow and gentle with each other. This time it worked. They joined with gentle magic. They spoke each other's names in hushed and reverent tones. And it worked again, the gentle magic. And again.

Later, they fell asleep.

"I feel awful," Toby said the next day. It was nearly noon. Earlier he had bought a bathing suit in the motel shop, and now he and Tiffy had adjoining wooden lounge chairs, the kind with rollers at the big end, in the shade of the palms at the Skyliner pool. Each lay back on a white beach towel, thick and rough with nap. They were glossy with sweat and smelled of coconut oil from Tiffy's suntan lotion. Several empty Bloody Mary glasses were on the low wooden table between them. Toby held another on his chest. He leaned forward and took a swallow.

"It's not your fault," Tiffy said in a soft voice. She leaned over and stroked Toby's hand.

"The hell it's not," he said.

She leaned over him. "Look, you, there's always tonight, you know. This afternoon, for that matter. We'll try again."

"God almighty," he said in a caustic voice, "how many cherries have you copped from twenty-four-year-old male virgins before?"

"Toby Parker, you just stop that kind of talk right now." She took her hand away.

"How many men have you been to bed with before?"

"That's none of your business." She sat back with her arms folded.

"I want to know. Tell me," He propped himself on an elbow to look at her.

"Not very many."

"Come on, how many?"

"What good will it do for you to know?"

"How many? How old were they? Did any of them do what I did?" He tossed down the last swallow of his Bloody Mary and banged the glass down on the table between them.

She turned to him, her eyes soft with compassion. "Oh, Toby, you didn't *do* anything—"

"You got that right," he interrupted. "I didn't *do* anything, did I? You know what it's called?"

"Toby, stop it."

"It's called premature ejaculation. I shot my wad the minute I touched you, before I could even get it in." He shook his head.

"You were," she chose the word carefully, "anxious. I was in a hurry, too. We'll try it again."

"You mean that, don't you?"

"Yes, I do."

"How about right now?" he said, with a smile both apprehensive and eager.

She sat up and looked at him. There were thin beads of sweat on her upper lip. She leaned forward and saw his eyes flick to the cleavage between her breasts. She smiled and her eyes were bright. "Yes," she said, "right now."

Toby had to wrap a towel around his waist to walk from the pool to his room.

Under Tiffy's directions, they took their clothes off quietly and without haste. At first Toby was very hard. "Sit on the bed," she said, "like this." She sat cross-legged with her hands on her knees. Toby sat across from her in the same style. He had started to go soft. He reached out to touch her breasts. She took his hand away.

"Not yet. Let's just look at each other." She held his eyes for a few minutes then looked down at him. He became very soft. His face was flaming.

"You have never been naked around a woman before, have you?" She put a hand on his knee and looked into his face. He produced a crooked grin.

"No," he said, and sighed, "I haven't. I guess you think I'm pretty much of a kid?"

"No, I don't think you're pretty much a kid. Pretty, yes, kid, no. Now just relax, will you? I want you to look at me, and I want to look at you. In a little while, we'll touch each other, slowly and in careful places."

For over an hour Tiffy guided Toby around her body, first directing his eyes, then his fingers. Soon he did the same to her. She paced his sensations with slow advances and planned retreats. She lowered his consuming fervor from a flame to the warm coals of affection; from overexcited craving to steady and controlled ambition to please and be pleased. From instinct imprinted in her body from the time of primordial woman, she knew when it was time. And she was right.

Court helped him on takeoff, then Toby flew the entire route from climb-out to letdown on the return flight to Phan Rang. Except for navigation and airplane performance comments, they spoke little. After three days at the pool and in the rooms of the Skyliner, they felt salty and vaguely uncomfortable in their flight suits. Once settled in, however, both gave little sighs and hums of contentment. The flight was smooth and clear. The engine on the newly overhauled F-100F purred and responded to the slightest touch. Past the coast of Vietnam, Court decided they had the time and the fuel and the weather in the Phan Rang local area to cancel IFR and indulge in some aerobatics. He spent ten minutes indoctrinating Toby in the delights of effortless rolls and loops and wingovers, then talked him to the point of touchdown on Runway 34 at Phan Rang. It was late in the afternoon when they taxied to the revetment.

1700 HOURS LOCAL, 27 SEPTEMBER 1966
PHAN RANG AIR BASE, REPUBLIC OF VIETNAM
☆

Jack Barnes met the airplane, he looked grim.

"Ron Bender and his backseater got shot down south of Hanoi," he said. "It was a big raid, the Da Nang guys were capping Thuds.

Someone heard him say he was hit and would have to get out, but nobody saw his plane or chutes or heard any beepers. I'm sorry. I knew you guys were close."

Court turned aside for a second. He shook his head in an unconscious act those in combat perform in one fashion or another to shake off the emotional burden of the loss of someone close. The job at hand, whether hurling twenty-five tons of steel at the ground as a pilot or creeping vine-snarled through the wet jungle as a soldier, required unencumbered attention, or one would join one's comrade in death or captivity. There would be time later to purge the mind of all but good memories of the fallen friend.

Court joined Toby and Barnes in the jeep. They drove over to the FAC school. "Oh yeah," Barnes said as they walked into his office, "there's a TWX for you." Court lit a Lucky and read it.

It was from DOCB. Court was to report to Major Ted Frederick, weapons officer of the 355th Tactical Fighter Wing located at Tahkli Royal Thai Air Force Base, Thailand, for further observations and experience pertinent to Commando Sabre. The 355th flew the sturdy F-105 fighter on daily raids over North Vietnam. He finished up the paperwork, and met Toby at the club for a fried rice and beer dinner, at which time he told him about going to Tahkli.

"I hear it's pretty rough over there," Toby said.

Court shrugged. "I'm like everybody else," he said, "it won't happen to me." But inside he wasn't at all sure. The next day the T-39 Scatback dropped him off at Tahkli.

> **1630 HOURS LOCAL, 28 SEPTEMBER 1966
> 355TH TACTICAL FIGHTER WING,
> TAHKLI ROYAL THAI AIR FORCE BASE,
> KINGDOM OF THAILAND**

☆

Court had never met Ted Frederick before, but what he had heard about the pilot was legendary. Frederick had gained his reputation as an F-105 fighter weapons school instructor. There were two camps: those who loved him, and those who thought him a flaming asshole who had nothing good to say about practically everything and everybody. Those who loved him thought he had a dry, sardonic wit that went over the heads of his detractors. Nevertheless, the two camps had one thing in common: They agreed he had a rare command of the F-105, and knew the tactics to use it as a weapon better than any other Thud driver in the air since Jim Kasler had got shot down.

"Somebody up there must like him," Court's escort, a former Air Training Command (ATC) instructor pilot, told him at the Tahkli O-Club bar. The escort, a captain, had picked Court up from the T-39 in front of base ops and gotten him a bunk in the squadron hootch. From there they had gone to the 354th squadron, where Court was rigged with the gear necessary to fly in the backseat of an F-105F. The captain told Court that Frederick was on a late-afternoon strike and would meet them at the club following debriefing. "Yep, somebody must like him," he repeated.

"Why do you say that?" Court asked.

"He just came out on the below-the-zone promotion list to lieutenant colonel. That's fast-burner stuff."

"It is," Court agreed. He hadn't decided which camp the captain was in, not that it made much difference. Court glanced around the noisy and crowded bar. A loud hullabaloo at the main entrance caught his attention. A young captain flanked by friends swaggered in and rang a bell hanging over the bar to announce he had just completed his 100th mission over North Vietnam. The pilot was flushed and already a little tight. As was the ritual for such an occasion, his commanders and fellow pilots had met his F-105 when he landed. They had rolled out a red carpet for him to step onto when he climbed down the ladder from his cockpit. Champagne was uncorked; smoke bombs set off; the knight victorious feted. That the enemy was as yet undefeated was unimportant; the victory celebration this day was for surviving 100 missions.

The sun was down by the time Ted Frederick walked into the club, accompanied by two other pilots, all in flight suits. Frederick was easy to spot. He walked in front of the other two as if he were leading a flight into enemy territory. He had thick black hair, still sweat-glued to his skull. His jaw was square and ridged with what could be muscle lines or jowls. His broad shoulders pivoted forward with each step, causing his arms, sharply bent at the elbow, to rock back and forth in front of his waist. His swinging hands curled naturally into partial fists in a way that reminded Court of Jimmy Cagney getting ready to belt someone.

Ted Frederick spotted the captain standing with Court, peeled off with a wave to his wingmen, and came over to them. He stopped a foot away. He was three inches shorter than Court, but broader. His brow jutted out over deep-set black eyes. He didn't wait for introductions.

"So you're the movie actor here to fly around with the big boys, eh," Frederick said in surprisingly rich and mellow tones, considering his accent was pure Maine.

"Wrong, major. I'm a fighter pilot here to learn about Thud operations."

"*Fightah* pilot, you call the Hun a *Fightah?*" Frederick said.

"Well now, just what would you call it, major?" Court could feel his blood pressure rising as his pulse quickened.

"What would I call it? I'll tell you what I would call it." Frederick stood back and rolled his shoulders as if warming up for a boxing match. "I'd call it a shovel-nosed, flat-bellied, corner-slicing, ground-loving hoorah. That's what I'd call it."

Court gave a sharp laugh. "Ground-loving whore, don't you mean?"

"That's what I said. It's a hoorah, a ground-loving hoorah. You making fun of me?" Frederick stepped back and rolled his shoulders again. He looked at Court and squinted.

"Movie fighter pilot, come here, over to the table. You and me, we're gonna arm wrestle for a beer." He looked at Court with a curled lip. "Or don't you want to? Guess you heard I was champ around here."

Court had heard no such thing, but decided what the hell, in for a penny, in for a pound.

"Yeah, champ, I've heard all about you. Let's go."

A sizable crowd gathered around the two as they took their places across from each other.

"No wrapping your legs around the table or holding it with your free hand, you heeyah?" Frederick said as they seated themselves. "And keep your butt on the chair. Once we get our grip, Charley heeyah"—he indicated one of the pilots he had walked in with—"will give the go signal."

He held his right arm and hand up, palm left, and looked from under lowered brows at Court. "You still want in, movie pilot? You can pussy out anytime."

Court felt so ginned up to whip this arrogant Frederick that he was ready to bite through a crowbar. He didn't trust himself to speak. "Go. Let's go," he said through clenched teeth. He put up his arm and slapped his hand over that of Frederick, who looked relaxed and confident.

The pilots, clustered around, drinking from beer mugs and cans, made a lot of catcalls and comments about who could take whom.

When Charley said, "Go," Court channeled all the adrenaline and dislike throughout his body into his arm. He simultaneously squeezed Frederick's hand as hard as he could and put all his arm muscle into meeting Frederick's return force. It was almost no contest. There was some initial resistance, hardly felt, then Court slammed Frederick's hand so hard on the table the stocky pilot tumbled sideways off his chair. He got up immediately.

"Huh, you were lucky. I wasn't ready," he said. He sat down and put his arm up again. Charley gave the "Go" signal and Court put Frederick down quicker than before. Frederick got up fast.

"Again," he said. The same thing happened.

"Again," Frederick said. Court deliberately didn't put in enough pressure to tumble Frederick off his chair. They seesawed a bit, then Court eased Frederick's hand down on his knuckles.

Six more times Frederick demanded a rematch, and six times Court eased his hand to the table. His arm began to quiver and buzz from the strain. He found it harder to keep up the steady pressure than to put out the explosive power that ended a match with Frederick on the floor.

"Again," Frederick said.

"No," Court replied.

"What's the matter? You giving up?" Frederick demanded. His face was white, and his jaw was clenched, whether in pain or determination, Court couldn't tell. He decided it was both.

"No, champ," Court said, "I'm not giving up," and put Frederick down, faster than before.

"Again," Frederick rasped. He was panting heavily, not like a runner, but like a man carrying a heavy load. "Again," he said, and put up his arm.

"Come off it, Ted," some of the crowd members said. Others shook their heads and walked away.

Court suddenly realized this man was going to sit there all night and into the next day or until he dropped dead, calling for another match. He put him down two more times, then didn't bring his arm up at Frederick's challenge.

"That's enough, major," he said. He was panting too, and his arm ached.

"You quit?" Frederick asked, in a voice torn by rasping gasps for breath.

"No, I don't quit. I don't want to do this anymore and you aren't going to win."

"Again," Frederick rasped, "I might get lucky." His lips drew back in a grimace, more of pain than humor, Court thought.

"Once more," he said, "and that's it."

They raised arms, Frederick looking strangely bright, as if in anticipation. Court put him down with a quick, hard rap, and stood up. "That's enough," he said.

"You mean you quit," Frederick said, looking up at him.

Court sat back down, oddly reluctant to talk down to this man who sat, back erect and straight, kneading an arm that Court knew throbbed and ached. His own felt on fire. Court looked him in the eye.

"Major Frederick," he said, "I quit. Let's get that beer. I'll buy."

"HAH!" Frederick boomed, and stood up. "I knew it. You're a quitter. Never could stand a quitter." He started to walk away. His face looked almost peaceful. He hesitated, then turned back to sweep an appraising glance over Court Bannister. "You know, you're pretty big. Bigger and stronger than you look. But I knew I'd get you." He shook his craggy head in disgust. "If there's anything I can't stand, it's a quitter."

Court slowly got to his feet. "How about that beer, major?"

"Don't drink," Frederick said. He fixed Court with squinted eyes that were dark with an inner fury. "You better not either. You got to meet me tomorrow at three o'clock down at Wing for a briefing."

"In the afternoon?" Court asked.

"No, Bannister, in the morning. You're going Downtown with me."

27

☆

The ATC captain led Court to his bunk in a large open bay barracks that had bunks separated by steel double-door lockers. Except for the glow from the shower room, the bay was blacked out. The occupants, company-grade pilots (those not above the rank of captain), were asleep or reading by the dim glow of small bed lamps. When Court put down his B-4 bag and pitched his hat on the bunk, the ATC captain hissed and said never to do that, it was a bad omen. Do it and get shot down, was the superstition, he said, just like the guy who had this bunk two days ago.

"You mean he threw his hat on the bunk and got shot down?" Court whispered.

"I don't know about the hat, but he did get shot down on an Alpha strike." Court knew Alphas were the roughest. Alpha was short for Six Alpha, the USAF half of Route Package 6. Six Alpha included Hanoi and the northwest railroad system, where flak was worse than Regensburg or the Romanian oil fields of World War II. He stared at the freshly made-up bunk, trying not to picture the man who had last slept there. He glanced at the locker. Taped inside the door was a large drawing of a seated nude with 100 numbered squares outlined on her body. The last box, labeled with the number 1, ended at her pubic region. Only forty-two of the boxes were penciled in. The pilot hadn't even been close.

The captain said goodnight and walked quietly away between the rows of darkened lockers and bunks. Court sat on the edge of his bunk and slowly removed his boots. One thumped accidentally on the floor, causing a muffled sleep-soaked voice from the other side of the locker to give a short cry. Court carefully rummaged in his B-4 bag. He set the alarm of a small Swiss travel clock in a leather case he had bought years before in Paris. He took out *Le Mal jaune* and tried to immerse himself in the Frenchman's allegory of the Vietnamese-French relationship. In the quietness, he made page notes and decided the French were driven out because of a lack of unity among the military and the people at home. He couldn't comprehend the story of French civilians spitting on their wounded soldiers when they returned from the Indochina war. He thought Lartéguy must have made that up.

He began to nod. Then just behind his eyes, a man in flight gear, whose face was concealed by shadows, stood silent and unmoving. Court saw in detail his worn G-suit, parachute, flight boots, and survival vest. He tried, but couldn't make out the face. The steady buzz of the air conditioners slid slowly into Court's mind, replacing conscious thought with hypnotic humming until, unaware, he fell into a fitful sleep. The book slipped to the floor.

He awoke with a start when his alarm sounded a discreet bell. His mouth felt like an ashtray and his eyes were grainy and sore. He rooted around in his bag for his shaving kit and a fresh T-shirt. Twenty minutes later he walked into the wing briefing room, blinking in the harsh light. His legs were soaked with dew from the knees down because he had cut across the unmowed athletic field separating Wing from the barracks instead of taking the long way around on the sidewalks. It was two minutes to three.

He found Frederick and sat next to him. The force commander, an older lieutenant colonel with squint lines fanning from his eyes, told the assembled pilots that today's force of sixteen Thuds, four flights of four, was going against the rail yards outside of the Thai Nguyen steel mill. Secondary and tertiary targets were farther south in Pack 1. The Wild Weasel pilots, who flew the two-seater F-105F's loaded with electronic gear controlled by the Bear in the backseat, and exotic weapons to suppress flak and SAM's, looked as unconcerned as subway riders. The renowned Weasels were known for having the biggest balls in the SEA. Few survived 100 missions. Court recognized Westcott and Robinson among several others selected by Colonel Gary Willard to be the first Weasel pilots.

The lieutenant colonel was leading the four-ship Pintail F-105D flight, the other twelve airplanes were in Harpoon, Crab, and Waco flights. His briefing covered the TOT, routes, tanker call signs, off-load fuel, and attack headings, and he gave a rundown on the butterfly, the formation he wanted to use rolling in on the target. Using chalk on the board, he described how the four flights, each flying as a corner in a flat, one-dimensional box pattern 2,000 feet on a side, would split, with two flights rolling in on the rail yards from opposite headings. He stressed detailed memorization of the target area to preclude any confusion on target identification and roll-in points. He answered a few questions about radio frequencies, then returned to his seat in the front row and turned the stage over to the weather briefer, a heavyset master sergeant in fatigues.

Using a pointer on the large four-by-eight pull-out aerial map of Thailand, Laos, and North Vietnam, the sergeant began his litany. "Weather in the refueling area will be broken layers between thirty and thirty-three thousand. Over the fence those layers will stay the same, but you will encounter early-morning buildups imbedded in the scattered to broken cumulus ranging from eight to ten thousand. You will reach the target area just after first light, where your visibility will be five plus miles, opening up to ten as the sun burns off the haze. Winds at release altitude will be from 250 at ten, altimeter 29.66."

Court heard a muttered "Yeah, sure" from several of the pilots. He knew winds over a target area were as predictable as the Army-Navy football score. The altimeter was reasonably valid because actual measurements were sent from a weather recce F-4 and unnamed assets on the ground. The master sergeant concluded his briefing with the weather at the primary recovery base, Tahkli, and the other Thailand alternates of Korat, Udorn, and Ubon. He stepped down.

A dark and vivid major from the intelligence section briefed with quick motions and fast words. From the side opposite the weather maps he pulled out a sliding map board with Communist defenses neatly drawn on an acetate overlay. As he pointed to the locations he listed the amount and types of guns and SAM's along the ingress route, around the target, and covering the egress route. He said today's codename for MiG's was Steakhouse.

Everybody laughed, because when enemy planes were spotted, the cry was "MIGS! MIGS!" Why fool around trying to remember a word to classify an event the enemy already knew about?

He said the base altitude was 13,000 feet. He wrapped up his briefing with a reiteration of the safe bailout areas and the Rules of

Engagement: "Don't fly within thirty miles of the Chinese border, thirty miles of Haiphong Harbor, thirty miles from Hanoi, and of course, you can't hit the MiG bases at Phuc Yen, Gia Lam, Kep or Hoa Loc." He stopped and looked about apologetically. "Lastly, gentlemen, you are forbidden to hit the Thai Nguyen steel mill itself. You may only bomb the rail yard servicing the mill."

"Isn't that the shits," a pilot muttered. "I hope somebody is writing all this down," said a second.

The force commander wrapped up the briefing with a final word. He stood, hands on hips, facing his audience. "This is a JCS target today, gents. Let's take it out, but let's get everyone home. No pressing. No radio chatter, No MiG calls, unless you're positive. Always, I mean always, use call signs." He gave a half salute and said, "Go get 'em."

Frederick turned in his seat to stare at Court.

"Listen, movie pilot," he said, "I didn't ask for you, I don't want you, but I'm stuck with you. Somebody even sent over a two-seater from Itazuki to fly you in, otherwise you'd never get off the ground. We'd never put you in our own two-seaters. They're Weasel birds configured with enough electronic crap for the Bear, the guy in back, to light up Times Square for a year. They go along to take out SAM's. It's damn near a kamikaze mission. Damn few Weasel pilots have made it to a hundred missions yet." He shook his head. "So if the Itazuki bird wasn't here, you wouldn't fly." Without another word, Frederick got up and walked out of the briefing room. The other pilots grouped together to head toward their individual squadron briefing rooms. The darkness concealed the faces of those who were apprehensive.

Court fell in step with Frederick, who continued the conversation as if it had never been interrupted.

"I sniveled us the Number Three slot with Pintail, the force commander's flight, today. We'll get off. You watch, though, some coward will find an excuse not to go. But I'll get you up there. I'll get you up where the big boys fly." He punched the night air with his free hand.

Each flight had a fifth man, a spare, who was briefed with the rest, with an airplane loaded for the strike. The pilot would start the airplane, check in, arm, and taxi to the runway in the event someone had to abort at the last minute. In an extreme case, the man even took off to fly just short of the tankers as an airborne spare.

Frederick and Court joined the members of Pintail flight to listen to the final briefing in the squadron building. When it was over,

Frederick pulled Court aside for an individual brief about what he expected of his backseater. They both carried coffee mugs.

"We may be going on a real double-pump mission; that's when your heart has to double pump to keep up with your adrenaline flow. You'll see a bunch of flak when we roll in. That's normal, so don't pay any attention. Start staring at it and you'll scare yourself to death. Cinch up your seat belts. We might get a few negative g's when I maneuver and certainly a lot of positive g's when I pull off target. A lot of g's." He took a long swallow of coffee, gone cold, and continued.

"If we take a hit, don't arbitrarily punch out. We'll talk it over. The Thud takes a lot of punishment. I'm familiar with this airplane, you're not. I'll tell you when to punch. If we're northeast of the Red River, we've got to either get back west almost to Laos, or east out over the water to be picked up. The rescue helicopters can't make it into the Hanoi area. There's too much flak."

Frederick led Court to the PE room, where they started gathering their gear. He handed Court two baby bottles. "Fill these. Use them on the ground if we punch out. In the airplane, you've got a bottle and a hose to suck on in flight. If the crew chief is a nice guy, he'll have them filled with ice tea or lemonade. Don't let your canopy close on the hose or you'll dry out in an hour."

Court put on his G-suit and survival vest, slipped into his parachute, which, like on the F-100, was not built into the ejection seat. He picked up his helmet bag and his purse, a flat kit made in the parachute shop to hold maps, and followed Frederick out the door. They stood with the other pilots waiting for the van to take them to the flight line. No one spoke. The humid cool air reminded Court of an icehouse. Muted humming from APU's firing up for the KC-135 tankers sounded from down the flight line. They made blowtorch hisses as they spat out compressed air for the tankers to start their engines.

B-66's loaded with electronic warfare equipment had taken off earlier to get set up on station over eastern Laos, where they would help flood enemy radar with false signals to mask the inbound Thuds.

The van drove up to the pilots, the headlights illuminating them like deer in a field as it stopped. Each man automatically squinted and looked away to preserve his night vision. Equipment clanging and thumping as they moved, they climbed in and arranged themselves on the benches along each side.

Court noticed the other pilots didn't have much to say to Frederick. Whether it was from dislike or inarticulateness brought on by being around a living legend, Court couldn't tell. One pilot, Pintail Four, a lieutenant, chattered inanely about the low prices at Jimmie's Jeweler. His voice was thin and edged with nervousness. Court knew it was his eleventh mission, but his first in the Pack 6 area. All new pilots usually flew their first ten missions in the relative safety of Pack 1 before being admitted into the fraternity of the men who flew beyond the Red River into the Hanoi and Haiphong areas. The lieutenant's jumpiness is catching, Court thought, as he caught himself in a jaw-cracking nervous yawn.

The van stopped at each of the four planes to let off the members of Pintail flight. There were no protected revetments at Tahkli. Rows of F-105's lined up like soldiers on flight-line parade. Outside of minor and highly unsuccessful sapper attacks, no Communists rocketed or mortared the Thud bases of Tahkli and Korat.

Court felt mounting apprehension as he followed Frederick to their camouflaged two-seat F-105F. The crew chief, in fatigue pants and T-shirt, took Frederick's helmet up the long ladder to the cockpit. Frederick pulled the rolled-up Form One from behind the ladder, found no previous maintenance write-ups, then began to preflight, using his olive-drab Boy Scout flashlight to illuminate dark crevices of the massive airplane. The 25-ton plane stood so tall they could walk under the wings to shake the fuel tanks and inspect the electronic jamming pods. They looked for hydraulic leaks in the aft section. They crouched under the belly of the giant fighter-bomber to check the fuses on the six 750-pound bombs strapped into their ejection racks.

"See heeyah," Frederick said, holding his flash on the wires that extended from the rack into each bomb's fuse, "this ahming wiyah. I found them using the wrong size. Bombs hung. Fixed naow." They checked the pitot tube, engine inlets, and various other items, until Frederick pronounced the plane safe to fly.

Both men stood still, their attention drawn to the runway where KC-135 tankers, each weighing a quarter of a million pounds, took off one by one, sounding like runaway freight trains as they used every inch of the runway to get airborne. The noise of their shrieking engines seemed to vibrate the very ground. Ninety tons of their weight consisted of fuel for the strike force.

"By God, I couldn't do that," Frederick said. Court nodded, unseen, in the darkness. They turned back to their fighter.

It was a long climb, about ten feet, Court judged, from the flight line to the rear seat of the F-105. He settled down as the crew chief helped him strap in. He put on a sweatband, wondering why Hun jocks hadn't discovered that valuable idea yet, and pulled on his helmet. Frederick made an intercom check, got clearance from his crew chief; then punched the starter button to fire the oversized shotgun cartridge that turned the engine over with a roar, venting acrid smoke into night air. Court looked down into his cockpit and saw the throttle move to idle at 8 percent. The big J75 engine rumbled and whined into life as the gauges moved like tiny semaphores. Court went through the checks Frederick had told him to make. He paid particular attention to the Doppler radar, so vital for navigation in the target area away from fixed Tacan stations.

"Pintail check," the force commander transmitted, calling for check-in. His flight and all the rest answered at machine-gun speed.

"Two."

"Three."

"Four"

"Spare."

"Harpoon."

"Two."

"Three."

"Four."

"Spare."

And so on with Crab and Waco. Twenty airplanes had checked with their leader in under ten seconds. Any pilot who broke the sequence would buy a lot of beer that night.

The twenty airplanes taxied to the arming area one after the other, twenty engines blowing gas that could tumble a man at 100 feet, struts chattering and walking back and forth under twenty-five tons of bombs and fuel and airplane. On reaching the arming area, each plane cocked left forty-five degrees and braked to a stop. They formed a long symmetrical row in the harsh glare of the floods. Court saw the armorers and crew chiefs scurry from airplane to airplane, checking, arming, pulling red streamers, and taking a last look. It was here a lowly two-striper airman could signal a full colonel he was not going on this mission in that airplane.

Two men in khaki 1505's walked together past the airplanes. They waved at each one, made blessing signs with their hands, and gave each a thumbs-up sign. "Chaplains," Frederick said, "Baptist and Roman Catholic. They always come by when they know we're going on double-pumpers. I don't much go for that. Why ask God's help to go kill people?"

"Maybe they're only asking for help to get us back safely," Court said. Frederick blew a puff of air into his mike.

When the checks were completed, the F-105's taxied to the runway, lined up, and took off at eight-second intervals. Court had no forward visibility from the rear cockpit, but he could see the glow of the blue-and-yellow afterburner flames on the grass along the sides of the concrete runway. Their airplane shook and shuddered in the buffeting jet exhausts of the 105's in front of them.

When his turn came, Frederick ran it up, told Court the fluctuating oil pressure was normal for a Thud, and released the brakes. Court saw the throttle move outboard, but there were three seconds of waddling along the runway until the burner lit. When it did, he felt as if they had been rear-ended by a Mack truck. At the same time, Frederick flipped the switch to inject water into the flame tubes, allowing more heat and 1,000 pounds more thrust. At 185 knots on the vertical tape speed indicator, Frederick raised the nose, at 195 they were airborne as the 7,000-foot marker flashed by. In seconds, the water burned out; Frederick had the plane cleaned up, unplugged the burner at 350 knots, and told Court to take control and fly 018 degrees for a rendezvous with the tanker on Green anchor.

Four minutes later they slid into formation with the other Pintail Thuds. Lead kept his navigation lights at "bright-steady" as as they flew in a loose five-man fingertip formation, Pintail Lead being the middle finger.

Twenty-five minutes and 140 miles later, Pintail Lead, Two, and Three, Frederick, had taken 1,000 pounds of fuel each from Green tanker as an initial tap to test their systems. Owing to a foul-up in his fuel system plumbing, Four couldn't receive and was directed to RTB by Pintail Lead. RTB meant Return to Base. He put his lights on "bright flash" and peeled away from the flight to disappear quickly in the night air. They heard him contact radar site Dora, which everyone called Dora Dora, to get a steer for Tahkli. "Good luck, Pintail," he transmitted before he changed his radio channel. His voice sounded relieved, yet disappointed he was not logging another counter after getting all psyched up and coming so far on this one. "Pintail Spare, you are now Pintail Four." "Rodge," the spare transmitted and slid into position.

When it was his turn, Frederick dropped into position under the tanker for his full load of fuel.

"Depressurizing," he told Court over the intercom.

Frederick opened a valve to the outside, equalizing the cockpit pressure from 8,000 feet to 13,000, the refueling altitude. One of the intakes for the air conditioning system was just aft of the receptacle and would suck in the fuel invariably spilled at disengage. When that happened, eyestinging fuel vapor was drawn into the cockpit, so the pilots shut the system down during refueling.

The boomer, lying prone in the aft fuselage under the tail of the giant tanker, looked out at the F-105 flying formation a few feet under and behind the giant tanker. He manipulated the controls that extended the telescopic boom, held it steady as Frederick eased his airplane up to the tip, then moved the control handle that operated vanes on the probe to fly the boom to the port in front of the cockpit. He found it, plugged in and started pumping JP-4 fuel into the tanks of Pintail Three.

Court relinquished the controls to Frederick and felt the plane grow sluggish from the added weight. The pilot had to ease back on the stick, which tilted the airplane to an even higher angle to keep flying as the already heavy F-105 filled up with thousands of pounds of fuel. As he did, he added more power to overcome the increased drag caused by the high angle of attack. The four tanker engines could not propel the converted Boeing 707 through the air at a speed much higher than the stall speed of a fully loaded Thud, resulting in some very delicate flying. Behind Pintail flight were four other tankers refueling their fighters.

After they topped off, Pintail led his force to Channel 97, known as North Station. Passing the North Station, he signaled the sixteen ships to form into the giant box pattern and headed them 045 degrees toward North Vietnam.

The glow to the east grew brighter. Below, karst mountains punctuated the green velvet like torn gray boxes. Their shadows pointed west like jagged sharp spears of black.

0620 HOURS LOCAL, 29 SEPTEMBER 1966
F-105'S EN ROUTE TO THE THAI NGUYEN STEEL MILL,
DEMOCRATIC REPUBLIC OF VIETNAM

☆

"Music on," Pintail Lead said as they approached the border, which they called the fence, between Laos and North Vietnam. All sixteen F-105 pilots flipped the switch that activated electronic countermeasure devices that radiated energy from the pods (the pilots called them "whizzies") that hung from their wings. They spread out in formation to maximize the combined ECM to confuse gun-laying and SAM search radars.

The radiated energy blossomed and bloomed on enemy gun-laying and SAM radar scopes like liquid phosphorus poured down a TV screen. Some of the enemy sites would try to burn through the energy glow by increasing the strength of their own pulses. Others would fire their guns barrage-style into what they judged to be the core of the electronic emanations.

Then they were over North Vietnam. "Green 'em up," Pintail Lead transmitted. Sixteen gloved hands reached to the left side of the instrument panel to flip up the red plastic guard and move the MASTER ARM switch on. Now the pickle button on the control stick was electrically hot to drop the bombs in whatever order the pilot had set on his armament panel: single, pairs, or ripple. The Weasels went on ahead to blast the defenses in the target area. On their way in they called the launch of a SAM heading up to Pintail's place in the sky.

"SAM, one o'clock, Pintail," Lead huffed. "Hold it in, let the pods work." He pushed over slightly to vary the altitude from 15,000 down to 12,000, then back up again in undulations that would never give radar trackers a permanent altitude fix. It wasn't much of a defensive move, but it was better than holding steady at an altitude that maybe a trailing MiG could radio back to the Hanoi Air Defense Sector. "Another one right behind it," Frederick transmitted in a ho-hum manner. Court felt his pulse race as SAM's arced up to them, then seemed to push over. He looked at the airspeed. It registered 540 knots as each pilot had slowly inched his throttle up to stay with the force commander. It was daylight now.

They flew straight into the fierce glow of the morning sun rising from the South China Sea. At eleven o'clock low, Court saw the high narrow hill called Thud Ridge rise up in razorback menace, perfectly oriented northwest and southeast. He saw two more SAM's, shining in the morning sun, rise up like smoking javelins thrown by twin hurlers, then three more. They picked up speed as they aligned themselves into a spread pattern. Pintail Lead steadily arced the flight up a few thousand feet. They were close to the rail yards, and he needed the altitude to perform a successful butterfly attack.

Below, the rail lines shone in the early sun to the left of the formation. The Weasels had dashed about attacking the SAM sites like angry hornets. It was a game of diminishing returns; too many sites, too few Weasels.

Pintail Lead held the flight steady for a few seconds. The giant box he controlled was a half mile on a side. He had positioned his own flight of four in the left front corner. He turned northerly, toward the yard, causing the giant box to rotate on the same flat plane as his wings. He rolled them out. The target was starting to disappear under the nose of his airplane. He put his thumb on the mike button and pressed.

"Ready, r-e-eady, SPLIT," Pintail Lead shouted into his transmitter.

The eastern eight ships broke left as the western eight broke right, splitting the box down the middle, with each half racing away from the other at a separation speed of 1,200 miles per hour. At the sixty-degree point in each section's turn, they reversed, pulled up, and rolled in to the rail yards from 14,000 feet on headings exactly opposite from each other.

Two explosions, so loud and close Court felt the concussion in his stomach, blew his feet up from the rudder pedals. Then flak began to bang and boom around their airplane like popcorn. On each side of them, Court saw the big black-and-brown puffs with fiery red-and-orange centers of the 37's and 57's and 85's as they made multiple layers of steel fragments at staggered altitudes among and below the diving airplanes. Muzzle flashes on the ground made the target area look like New York at night.

"I'm hit. Waco Two is hit," a voice shouted over the radio. Court looked back at seven o'clock to see a 105 going down trailing a long plume of black smoke and bright-red flame.

"Waco, SAM, SAM. SAM at seven o'clock. SAM coming up," someone shrieked. There was a sudden pause on the radio.

"Naw, that's Two going down," Waco Lead said in a laconic voice.

After some initial fast stick pumps and rolls, Frederick held the F-105 steady as Court watched the altimeter tape unwind. To improve his bombing accuracy, Frederick had slowed the big craft to 450 knots. Court knew Frederick had his eyes swiftly cross-checking his gunsight pipper drifting up to the target, his airspeed, and his dive angle, which Court saw was pinned at a perfect sixty degrees.

He had set his command marker at 4,500 feet, the absolute minimum pickle altitude for a Thud in a 60-degree dive over downtown Hanoi. The white altitude tape numbers slid down the dial in a blur. The command marker came and went as the ships on each side released their bombs and pulled sharply up and away from Frederick's airplane to start their hard-jinking climb back up to altitude. As they shot through 4,000 feet, Court began to wonder if Ted Frederick was alive and if he was, did he have in mind a suicide dive right into the heart of the Thai Nguyen rail yards? Then he realized Frederick was humming the same tune and repeating the same word, "Downtown," over and over like a broken record.

At 3,500 feet Court felt the ejector cartridges go off, then almost blacked out as Frederick overstressed Republic's best airplane since the P-47 by pulling 8½ g's to escape Russia's best air defense system outside of the Moscow ring. Then he felt the plane leap as Frederick engaged the afterburner for a few seconds to accelerate his jinking maneuvers back up to altitude. Suddenly the radio came alive with calls.

"Four's hit."

"MiG's! MiG's!"

"Four WHO is hit?"

"Christ, look at them."

"Damn it, where are the MiG's? Who called 'em?" a voice that sounded like Pintail Lead's called out in a testy rasp.

Fighting the g-load and the rapidly rotating cockpit as Frederick jinked left and right, Court looked back over each shoulder for their wingman, Pintail Four. Suddenly, on his left at seven o'clock, he saw an F-105 trailing a long sheet of flame. In the same instant it disappeared in a ball of fire and black smoke, from which the cockpit section somersaulted and small parts arced in all directions, then fell rapidly back. There was no chute.

"I think Pintail Four just blew up back off our left wing," Court told Frederick over the intercom.

"Ay yup, saw it. There's Lead and Two at our two o'clock. And, ahhh, lets see, yup, there's a MiG dropping in on them." Court looked high and to the right to see what looked like a MiG 19 swooping down from a position high behind the lead F-105.

"Pintail Lead," Frederick transmitted, "that was Pintail Four that just blew up. You got a MiG on your ass, and I'm pulling up into him." Frederick's voice sounded almost gleeful, Court thought. He looked more closely at the MiG and the airspace behind it. Higher up was a second MiG in position to shoot at anybody who went after the MiG attacking Pintail Lead. He told this to Frederick on the intercom.

"I don't have him," Frederick said. "You keep your eye on him. I'm going to get this first one. With a violent pull he racked the F-105 into a tight climbing right turn to get a quartering head shot at the attacking MiG. Without forward visibility, Court couldn't see the MiG Frederick was after, although he had a good contact on the other enemy fighter higher in the sky.

Berrrrrump. He heard and felt Frederick fire a burst. Then another. Suddenly, Frederick slammed the plane into a left bank so hard that Court's feet flew off the rudder pedals and his helmet cracked the canopy. Only by snapping his head back and to the right could he keep his eye on the high enemy MiG. Frederick fired again.

"Hah, got him," he hollered into the intercom. Court felt the plane jolt as they flew through the debris of the exploded MiG. "Where's that second one?" Frederick asked,

"He's at four o'clock. He pulled up high, off to one side in a modified chandelle, then rolled on his back. I think he's coming in on us." Court could just barely make out the enemy fighter.

"I don't have him."

"He's rolling in now."

"Damn, I don't have him."

"Gimme the airplane," Court yelled. He had his head bent way back over his right shoulder and didn't dare look in the cockpit, knowing he'd lose the tiny speck. By feel, he reached down and grabbed the stick.

"You got it," Frederick said.

"Gimme a few seconds of burner while I unload," Court demanded. He eased off the heavy G-load on the airplane as Frederick plugged in the afterburner long enough to increase the airspeed another 100 knots. "I still don't have him," he said. Their airspeed climbed to 525 knots.

"I'm going to pull around, and put him at your eleven o'clock position, then you take it." Court knew that when he rolled out with the MiG in front, he would lose sight of him from the rear seat, but by then Frederick should have him pinpointed. Without taking his eyes from the MiG, Court pulled the big fighter almost straight up, quickly using up the speed they had gained from the afterburner. Although he had never flown the Thud, he had the pilot's innate feel for how far to take a plane before it would stall. He didn't have to look at the airspeed indicator to know that in a few seconds that point would be reached.

"How the hell will he be at my eleven if he's on my right side now? Don't you mean one o'clock? And look out you don't stall us." Frederick grunted out against the G-load. Court didn't answer. He'd taken enough crap from one each Major Theodore Frederick. Court eased off the G-load as the F-105 pointed straight up. He held the stick with a delicate grip as he babied it through the nibbles of a stall waiting for the right second to swing it in the direction he wanted. He still had the MiG in sight, but now had the eastern sun at his back so that the MiG pilot, if he were trying to track him, would lose him in the glare.

The MiG pilot held his steady-state bank angle, seemingly waiting for Frederick's airplane to stall and start falling, when he would pounce. He's good, Court thought. I'll bet he's got blond hair and blue eyes and is a lead jock in the Soviet *Frontovaya Aviatsiya.*

Just when it would look to an outsider like the Thud had stalled and was going to spin or slide into oblivion, Court started to pull the nose down to the horizon as if coming through the top side of a loop. As the nose fell to a position just above the horizon, still inverted, he quickly rotated his head from over his right shoulder to look forward and down through the top of the canopy at the MiG. Though still upside down, the maneuver placed him up-sun and in the MiG's six o'clock position.

"What the hell?" Frederick said, hanging from his straps.

"Start pulling the trigger, Frederick, he's all yours," Court cracked out as he ruddered the inverted airplane a few more degrees, nose low and to the right. He lost sight of the MiG as it slid behind the instrument shroud in front of him, but directly at Frederick's eleven o'clock position as seen from their inverted position. If Frederick had to roll out to complete the kill, the MiG would be at his one o'clock position.

"You got the airplane," Court said, light-headed from the negative g's. "He's at your eleven o'clock."

Frederick wiggled the stick slightly to show he had control of the airplane and pressed the trigger on the B-8 stick grip. He placed forty-two rounds from the 20mm M-61 Vulcan gatling gun in the left wing root area of the MiG 19. Still firing, he let the pipper of his gunsight slide back to the center of the fuselage to the engine bay. Sparkling impact points lit the path. The MiG gracefully arced over as a great tongue of flame belched from the tailpipe and then the wing root. Frederick rolled to a wing low position, and quit firing as the left wing of the MiG separated in a blinding flash and the fuselage started violent snap rolls to the left. The side-load G-forces were so heavy the pilot would never be able to grab the handles and eject. He'd have to ride it down the remaining two miles contemplating his Marxist belief in no life after death. Frederick and Court watched for about one second, then Frederick stuck the nose down to gain speed and rolled to a westerly heading.

"See any more?" he asked Court.

"As a matter of fact, I do," Court said, as calm as he could, considering his heart was jack-hammering his chest. He had spotted a MiG very low to the east of Thud Ridge. So low, in fact, it looked about to belly in or land on a grass strip.

"Youuuuu got it," Frederick said. "Let's see what you can do for a second act." As cool as both men were trying to sound to each other, they were both panting and sweating and jerking their heads around constantly to keep track of who was where in the swirling air battle. Since their wingman, Pintail Four, had blown up, they had to keep scanning their six o'clock in addition to all the other sectors of the sky.

Court rolled inverted, pulled the throttle back to 80 percent, and pulled the nose through until he was aiming at the eastern edge of Thud Ridge. Unlike with the second MiG, he had to dive straight at this one to get into position, but to do so would hide the MiG behind the instrument shroud in front of Court. The F-105F simply wasn't made to be piloted in combat from the backseat. He had to turn it back to Frederick.

"You got him?" he asked.

"Yeah, I got him. Gimme the airplane."

"You got it," Court said.

"I got it," Frederick said and wriggled the stick.

Frederick held the dive while rolling left and right in a modified diving jink. As he swung back, Court could get a glimpse of the MiG. It was another MiG 19 and its gear and flaps were down. It was trailing a thin wisp of smoke.

"Heh, heh," Frederick said, "I'm not even going to pull the trigger. He's got a little engine fire and has to land. Watch this."

He lowered the nose even more, pushed the throttle up to 100 percent, and held steady until it seemed they would dive into the ground at the side of the hapless MiG. Then he pulled a 5-G level-off to recover at 200 feet above the ground. The airspeed indicator read 762 knots. They were splitting the air faster than the speed of sound. The supersonic F-105 trailed two conical shock waves, one from the nose and one from the tail. Had there been any windows or crockery under the airplane, which there were not, they would have shattered from the overpressure and vibration caused by the successive shock waves.

The MiG was at 400 feet, nose high at 135 knots, gear and flaps down, trying to land. Frederick flashed under it and started an immediate pull to the right as he headed west to fly up and over Thud Ridge. Both pilots looked back over their right shoulders. The MiG, caught in the two shock waves and the violent vortex of the supersonic Thud, was pitched into a position where its nose pointed straight up, and then it made a partial roll, as if the pilot were trying to recover. Out of control, the plane tumbled and fell and slammed into the ground, where it exploded into a ball of red-and-orange fire and black, greasy smoke.

"We got him," Court yelled. "We got him."

In the midst of his elation, Court's flyer's four-dimensional sense of space and time made him look forward just in time to see Thud Ridge begin to fill the side panel of his windscreen. Without time to blink, or shout a warning, his hand shot to the stick and eased it back a fraction. They were so close the speeding plane clipped the top of a tree when they swept over the Ridge. Frederick didn't say anything as he regained control and started a climb to the west. A moment later he put out a call on the outbound frequency.

"Pintail Three's on the way out. Lead, what's your position?" No answer. "Anybody read Pintail Three?" No answer.

"Probably too low," Court said. Frederick grunted. He held the climb headed west toward Laos and Thailand. He leveled at 32,000 feet and switched to tanker frequency. There were no other airplanes, friendly or enemy, in the sky.

"White, you up?"

"Calling White say your call sign."

"White, Pintail Three. I need gas. Gimme a steer."

"Roger, Pintail Three, hold down for a steer."

Frederick pressed the mike button for five seconds, allowing White tanker's direction-finding equipment to home in on his signal. Court had noticed earlier that the fuel gauge registered lower than their scheduled Bingo, the fuel level at which a pilot had either to head home or go for a tanker.

"Gotcha, Pintail. Steer 232. You copy?"

"Roger, 232."

Thirty minutes later Frederick slid the F-105 under the tail of the White tanker. "Balls," he said over the intercom, the first word he had spoken since they had nailed the three MiG's. Court, who had been damn near biting through his oxygen mask to keep from shouting victory yells, had made up his mind he wasn't going to say one bloody word until he absolutely had to. He had long ago emptied his water bottle of lemonade, but his mouth was so dry from the adrenaline surges that he figured he probably couldn't talk anyhow. He wondered what Frederick had seen about the tanker that had made him say, "Balls."

"White, are you a papa?" Frederick asked.

"Roger that, Pintail. Thought you knew. Our frag order shows

Pintails on Green today, not White. You must be a tad skosh on fuel to come to us.'' White was the closest tanker to Frederick and Court's egress point from North Vietnam. Had they come back directly with Pintail flight as briefed, they would have had enough fuel to go to the scheduled poststrike tanker.

Frederick cleared his throat. As they eased up to the tanker, Court saw there was a long hose with a basket on the end dangling back from under the tail, instead of the boom with the flyable vanes that the boomer would plug into the Thud's receiving bay. To get fuel from the basket meant the receiving airplane had to have a probe, a long metal pole to stick into the basket to make connection with the female receptacle at the center. Once plugged in, fuel would flow back through the pole into the receiver's main fuel tank. The system was called probe-and-drogue. It was the method used by the F-100 and all the Navy and Marine airplanes in the air. Only the USAF had airplanes that needed a flying boom to plug into its innards and transfer fuel. The F-4 was rigged that way as well as the F-105, and all SAC bombers.

The boom method required someone to lie down in the rear end of the tanker facing aft and fly the boom tip into the gizzard of the receiver. There could be only one on a KC-135, or any other tanker. The probe-and-drogue method didn't need a boomer, just a big pod from which to reel out the hose with the basket on the end. A tanker could carry three pods, one under each wing tip in addition to the one under the tail. The call sign of any tank with a basket always had the letter P as in "papa" affixed to it. Many times Court had refueled with two other F-100's at the same time on the same tank. Now here they were, Court thought to himself, too low on gas to go any place while flying next to a truck full of it, but from which they couldn't tap.

Then he felt a hydraulic system activate, followed by a roaring sound to the left side of the front cockpit. It was a probe hydraulically moving out from its stowed position. Court hadn't known the Thud had both systems installed. He wondered briefly why no one referred to it as bisexual. He heard Frederick clear his throat again.

''Ah, Bannister,'' he said in a voice like a rich man required to ask a beggar for a dime to place a phone call, ''you do this probe-and-drogue business all the time in the F-100. Get us a little gas, will you?'' Court leaned his head against the left side of the canopy and saw the probe extended into the breeze. He took the controls. By kicking right rudder he could see the basket. He slid up to it, straightened out at the last minute and stuck the probe into the basket without rippling the hose. He was extremely gratified to hear the boomer, who had nothing else to do except monitor the situation, say, "Nice hookup, Pintail. You're receiving."

"Run that by me again," the wing commander said, "about the one you claim to have spun in." The crowd had gathered in the intelligence room when Ted Frederick and Court Bannister started their debriefing. No one else from Tahkli had gotten any MiG's that day. The wing had, in fact, lost two of their own, Pintail Four and Waco Two, and had had one so badly shot up the pilot barely made it to a safe recovery at Udorn, a base close to Laos. Now a pilot was claiming three MiG's shot down.

MiG shootdowns were a great occasion, since only twenty-two had been shot down so far for a loss of sixteen USAF and Navy aircraft to MiG's. The ratio was not good. In Korea, it had been 12 to 1; twelve MiGs shot down for the loss of each friendly airplane.

Current Pentagon policy makers were beginning to dimly perceive what fighter pilots had been trying to tell them for years: To run an aggressive fighter program that turns out top-level fighter pilots, the air combat maneuvering (ACM) portion must be realistic. To be realistic meant procuring airplanes that looked and flew like MiG's, and accepting the peacetime crashes that invariably are a part of realistic ACM training. So far the USAF had done neither, despite the reports from pilots like Boyd, Suter, and Kirk, top jocks from the fighter school at Nellis Air Force Base by Las Vegas who didn't have enough horsepower to change the system, but who had the skill and guts to push for change.

The U.S. Navy had already received Captain Frank Ault's report detailing the needs and was starting to act on his recommendations for more realistic fighter training at its fighter school at Miramar near San Diego.

Frederick again told of the low-level pass at the landing MiG again. Court corroborated the story.

"Your gun camera film will confirm your first two shootdowns," the wing commander said, "but we need another source to confirm your third. Two crew members from the same plane can only file the claim; to corroborate it, film or an independent party must provide confirmation. As it stands, when your film comes back, Frederick will get credit for one and a half, Bannister for one half." He turned to Court. "You're not doing so bad, considering you are only supposed to be flying with us for flak and SAM experience."

His expression became stern. "But that's it. No more chasing

MiG's.'' He looked at Frederick and shook a finger in his face. ''You are forbidden to fly Bannister anyplace but where the orders call for. He is here to learn our tactics, not chase MiG's, and you damn well will teach them to him, or I'll bust you back to flying Blue Four for the rest of your tour. You understand, Frederick?'' Major Ted Frederick informed his full-colonel wing commander that he understood. He had had his turn as Blue Four, the position flown by brand-new pilots, as a second lieutenant.

It was now eleven in the morning. Court and Frederick had another mission to fly at two o'clock, when they were scheduled in the F-model for one plus thirty over Laos into Steel Tiger. Aerial refueling was not fragged.

''Grab a nap,'' Frederick said. ''Meet me in the squadron at twelve-thirty.'' Court went to his bunk, set his alarm, and, to his fading surprise, fell immediately into a deep sleep.

At two-forty he and Frederick were tearing up the Ho Chi Minh Trail from the pass at Ban Raving to Mu Gia with an intermediate stop at Ban Karai. Except for learning the area, the mission was a complete waste. No trucks were caught out, no guns came up, no supply caches were uncovered. Frederick called the C-130 Hillsboro, airborne command and control center, and got instructions to dump his bombs at coordinates WE 73213976, a suspected truck park just off a spur from Route 12. Frederick flew to the target and dropped his six 750's in three passes of two each into the heavy jungle at the foot of a low hill. Only dust and wood splinters erupted from each explosion. ''Couldn't have been anything there,'' Frederick said. ''Nobody was shooting at us. They were probably sitting back laughing while we waste bombs.''

''Just making splinters for Uncle Ho's toothpick factory,'' Court said. ''We have these monkey-killer missions in the South, too. Since we didn't get any MiG's, maybe we should paint little toothpicks and dead monkeys on our airplanes.''

0715 HOURS LOCAL, 30 SEPTEMBER 1966
F-105F EN ROUTE TO ROUTE PACK 1,
DEMOCRATIC REPUBLIC OF VIETNAM

☆

The next morning Court took off shortly after sun-up in the backseat of the F-model flown by the ATC captain. Frederick had said he should get experience with pilots less experienced than he. They flew to Route Pack 1 and found it clobbered by rain clouds and fog from the deck up to 14,000. On orders from Blue Chip, they contacted Hillsboro, who told them to contact a radar bombing site. They did, and were carefully directed by radar to bomb straight and level through the overcast. An hour later they were on the ground with nothing but a set of coordinates to give the Intel debriefer. There was a message for Court to meet Frederick at the O-Club at 1830.

Before his meeting with Frederick, Court went to the O-Club dining room to sketch out his report. The dining room section, which occupied half of the club, was partially filled with men eating a late lunch, having coffee, writing letters, or simply talking. Many had waved to Court when he walked in. He declined their invitations to sit, stating he had a report to grind out. He drew a mug of coffee from the big urn and chose a table off in the corner.

When it came to being controlled on a strike, Court saw little difference between the capabilities of the single-seat Thud and the two-seater F-4, except for speed and armament. Maybe the back-seater in the F-4 could write down target information faster than the single pilot in the Thud, but that seemed about it. What made the difference were the tactics generated by each F-4 or Thud Wing on the basis of that particular Wing's experience. Since they did not have to follow any overall 7th Air Force procedure on how to fly armed road recce, they developed these tactics using the Wing memory of what worked, as interpreted by commanders and weapon officers. Once in a while, a new commander, anxious to make a name for himself by changing things, would challenge the Wing memory and fly a particular formation or approach altitude that had already proved deadly. He would invariably pay for this conceit by losing men and sometimes himself.

Court also noticed that while individual pilot skills varied directly with total flying time, broken down into time in the airplane and combat time, effectiveness at hitting the target was a direct function of aggressiveness. The aggressive pilot, once he became acclimated to his airplane and the combat scene, always turned in better results that a pilot without that spirit, even if the less spirited one had more time in the airplane. No surprises there, Court thought.

In fact, Court noted, except for the high-threat environment, which quickly revealed lack of aggressiveness in the few pilots who would have been better off pursuing another way of life, the Da Nang and Tahkli scenes were no different than that of his F-100 wing at Bien Hoa.

All things being equal, what would make the difference in killing targets in Tally Ho and Steel Tiger, be they trucks, guns, or supply caches, would be the acquisition phase. The Da Nang and Tahkli pilots, and those from Ubon and Udorn and Korat, as well as Navy pilots flying over the Trail, simply weren't able to spend the amount of time cruising up and down to learn what belonged in the area and what didn't, or what had changed overnight and what hadn't. Court wrote that the fast-FAC program should correct that deficiency.

Near the end of his report, he listed with whom he had flown, when, where, with what ordnance, and the results. Before he wrote his conclusions, he sat back and lit a cigarette. The image of the faceless pilot whose bunk he had taken began superimposing over the picture of Pintail Four exploding. At the same time, he heard the voice of Jack Barnes tell him Ron Bender was missing. Before he was finished with his cigarette, he saw again Paul Austin's F-100 shatter and roll into a fireball. He heard the mortars of the Bien Hoa attack and saw Harold Rawson run out with the satchel charge. Briefly he saw the eleven VC he had napalmed.

The sound and images flicked back and forth, as if from a broken projector. To shake off the memories he got up and walked over for more coffee. He concentrated on the mechanics of opening the spigot and watching the steaming brown liquid splash into his cup.

He tried to analyze his feelings. He didn't feel sad, he noted, but he could feel an anger start to well up and that surprised him. Anger about what? He wished Doc Russell were with him to talk it over. He returned to his table and sipped his coffee. He made a conscious effort to suppress his beginning anger. He succeeded, and finished the report by concluding that the fast-FAC program would prove its worth, and should be implemented as soon as possible. There was no place for his thoughts about bomb shortages, wasted bombs, wasted pilots; or his burgeoning anger. He made one last check for spelling errors, put the report in his case, and went to the bar. It would be typed at Phan Rang.

By 1825 he had already had two beers with the ATC captain and another Thud driver who was celebrating his fiftieth mission by drinking salty dogs. The ATC captain was talking about dip bombers. "They are the ones," he said, "who zip into the target area at 650 knots at 15,000 feet, dip the nose of their aircraft slightly, pickle off all their bombs, and scoot home. The best thing said about their accuracy is that their bombs most likely fall on North Vietnamese territory."

Activity in the club picked up as the pilots from the afternoon strike began to filter in. The weather had been fair in Six Alpha where they had hit a rail junction that, as one pilot put it, probably was repaired by the time they landed. One Thud had been shot down by a SAM east of the Red River. The pilot had ejected safely, had a good chute, and had made contact from the ground over his survival radio. After ten minutes he said the bad guys were coming in on him, and he was going to start shooting. There was one more broken transmission that sounded like he said he had been hit, then silence. Nobody saw any MiG's.

At precisely 1830, Major Ted Frederick walked in and ran the big bell over the bar. "Attention," he said, looking around with a fierce scowl on his face. "Attention in the area. I'm buying, so is Bannister." Court stood up at the mention of his name, wondering what the hell it was all about. Suddenly he knew, when a great smile broke out on Frederick's face. "We have credit for not one, not two, but *three* MiG's. Two for me and one for Bannister." He looked around in triumph. "Autographs will be given," he said.

The bar broke into pandemonium. No Thud driver had ever shot down more than one MiG on one mission. Frederick and Court were besieged by well-wishers who insisted on buying them drinks. Corks popped and champagne squirted through the air as Soupy, the pretty little Thai barmaid, presented flower wreaths to the two pilots. The PIO people wanted Court and Frederick to dress up as if they had just landed and come to the flight line for some photos. Just as Frederick leaned forward to tell the PIO people what he thought of their suggestion, the wing commander made the request an order, to be carried out the next morning. Thud pilots needed all the good publicity they could get, the colonel said.

After a really rotten week flying Downtown, some good news was long overdue. That the pilots were jubilant and genuinely happy over the victories was evident. Yet, down deep, each told himself he should have been the one who got the MiGs. When he could finally pull away, Frederick pried Court loose from a crowd listening to his backseat story, and took him to a corner.

"The Board at Seventh reviewed the film," he said, "which came out confirming the two gun shootdowns. Then, a guy in intelligence, a Colonel Norman, filed a Human Intelligence report about his people intercepting North Vietnamese messages saying a MiG 19 had spun in on final at a dispersal strip next to Thud Ridge after an airplane flew under it in the traffic pattern at the same time we said we did. So that's it. I got the first one, half of the second, and half of the third. You got the two remaining halves and that, movie pilot, totals one each MiG to your credit."

Court looked at Ted Frederick for a long time. "You could have claimed all three. I never even pulled the trigger."

"Yeah, movie pilot, but I never saw the second two. As far as I'm concerned, I'd have credit for only the first one if it weren't for you." Frederick stuck out his hand. "Put 'er there, Bannister. You ain't much good at arm wrestling, but you're not bad in the backseat of a Thud. Of course, I'll never know if you are any good in the front seat." They shook hands and walked back to the bar.

The ATC captain had his guitar out and was singing his own words to the tune of Petula Clark's song "Downtown."

> *"When you get up at two o'clock in the morning*
> *You can bet you'll go—Downtown,*
> *Shaking in your boots, you're sweating heavy all over,*
> *'Cuz you got to go—Downtown.*
> *Smoke a pack of cigarettes before the briefing's over,*
> *Wishing you weren't bombing, wishing you were flying cover,*
> *It's safer that way—the flak is much thicker there—*
> *You know you're biting your nails and you're pulling your hair,*
> *You're going Downtown—but you don't wanna go,*
> *Downtown—that's why you're feeling so low,*
> *Downtown—going to see Uncle Ho,*
> *Downtown, Downtown."*

Part ☆ Three

28

☆

Colonel Donald Dunne was shocked at the sight of the first lieutenant dressed in a flight suit standing on top of a stool in front of the
bar at the Phan Rang Officer's Club. In further wide-eyed horror,
the colonel saw that the lieutenant, to the accompaniment of claps
and whistles from the pilots gathered around, was obviously about
to raise his head into the rapidly revolving ceiling fan directly above
him. His face looked blurry and loose. One of the pilots, with a
Green Hornet patch on the left shoulder of his flight suit, had a
stopwatch.

"Three-and-a-half seconds last time, Parker. Another scotch says
you can't stop it any faster."

Colonel Dunne, up from 7th Air Force for a few days to coordinate DOCB business with the FAC school, believed beyond doubt
that the lieutenant's imminent action was sophomoric at best, and
"conduct unbecoming" at worst.

"You there, lieutenant, stop that."

Toby Parker looked down. "Yes, SIR," he said, saluted smartly,
and stuck his head in the fan. The flat side of the blade smacked the
back of his head and stopped in three revolutions, motor humming.

"Best yet, Parker, two seconds," the pilot with the stopwatch said
in admiration.

Parker lowered his head to allow the fan to resume spinning.
"What else do you want me to stop, colonel?"

Noting Parker's name, Colonel Dunne shook his head in disgust and walked out.

Later, Toby Parker stood at the bar with three Green Hornet helicopter pilots from a USAF special operations squadron. The two lieutenants and a captain had come to Phan Rang to give a classified briefing to selected FAC students in the Theater Indoctrination School about their mission, which was to insert Army Special Forces into areas deep inside enemy territory and, later, extract them. Toby was surprised to hear that the Green Hornets, who flew UH-1F helicopters out of Duc Co, worked in Laos as well as in North and South Vietnam. Their mission was so classified no one outside of those who provided direct support knew about it. Not all the FAC students at the school received their briefing, just those who would have Green Hornet missions in their tactical areas of responsibility.

"Why in hell can't I fly with you guys?" Parker asked for the fourth time. He pushed fresh drinks in front of the pilots.

"Goddammit, Toby, we've told you why not a dozen times," one of the pilots said. "When we go out to insert or extract, every seat is filled, either going or coming. We don't have any space. Besides, we can't take anybody that's not trained for the mission."

"You rotor heads give me a pain," Parker said, with a slack grin. "How in hell can I teach the mission here if I don't fly? I teach 0-1E's; I fly 0-1E's. I teach F-100's; I fly F-100's, or at least in them. So how about a hop with you guys?"

The three pilots looked at each other. They knew about the good work he had done with the III Corps Mike Force. "Tell you what," the captain said, "you make it up to Duc Co sometime and I'll at least get you airborne on a test hop."

"Why don't I just ride back with you guys tomorrow?" Toby pressed.

The captain hesitated for a minute. "Okay," he said, "but no sticking your head in the fan."

2145 HOURS LOCAL, 12 DECEMBER 1966
HAWK INN, SQUADRON HOOTCH, 531ST TFS,
BIEN HOA AIR BASE, REPUBLIC OF VIETNAM
☆

It was black outside, and raining. Cool, wet breezes swept through the hootch. Some of the new Beatle music was being aired over AFVN.

"What's your sortie count now, Court?" Doc Russell asked Court Bannister as they stood up to the plywood bar at the Hawk Inn. The Doc's upper lip was pulled up slightly on the right side because the split he'd received rescuing Higgens had not healed properly. He secretly hoped someone would tell him he looked like Bogart. So far, no one had. He just looked like Baby Huey with a split lip.

"Over 250," Bannister said. He had flown missions in Two, Three, and Four Corps in support of U.S. troops, ARVN troops, and even, although only once, in support of some U.S. Marine ground troops. That mission had been due to an aberrational but last-chance request by a Marine ground Forward Air Guide who later would be severely chewed out by his battalion commander for calling in USAF air support. The Marines were paranoically adamant about using only Marine Corps air support, although they would accept Navy air from time to time.

"How is C Flight doing?" the Doc asked.

"Nothing new," Court said. "We've taken a few hits. Nothing too serious. But everybody is pretty tired. Even Higgens hasn't made many duck calls lately."

Rotation to the land of the Big PX combined with shoot-downs had caused attrition within the 531st. As a result, Court Bannister had become the commander of C Flight, one of the four flights within the squadron. Court had six pilots under his command, including Lieutenants Fairchild, Freeman, and now Higgens. Two FNG lieutenants, Vandenburgh and Howard, rounded out his roster along with a Captain Putney he had made his assistant flight commander and was training as a successor.

"I guess you're pretty short, then," the Doc said.

"Ten days and a wake-up."

"Then off to Edwards for the test pilot school?"

"Yup. I barely avoided a systems command job in L.A."

"Yeah? How come not to a fighter outfit if you didn't make Edwards?"

"Since the Air Force sent me to Arizona State University, they want their pound of flesh from me as an engineer. They think a good engineer is harder to find than a good fighter pilot."

"Are you a good engineer?"

"Hell, Doc, I don't know. Never practiced as one. But I'll find out at Edwards if I've learned anything these last few years. If I don't make it through the school, it's a dead-end job in Systems Command for sure."

☆

One slug from a spray of bullets went through Wolf's right wrist as
he lobbed his last grenade. The Nung next to him fell back dead
with two bullets in his chest. The grenade bounced and exploded
with a muffled roar, the fragments slowing the charge of the four
green-clad NVA soldiers dodging and running through a clearing,
firing steadily toward the fallen tree behind which Wolf and the dead
man lay. Above them, a dead pilot swayed slowly in his harness as
the freshening morning breeze tugged at his parachute. He had died
in the air after his bailout from loss of blood through the flak holes
in his legs.

Wolf's eight-man rescue team had been ambushed ten minutes
earlier as they neared the site of the downed pilot. Now five men
were dead, and only Wolf, Menuez, and one other were alive. They
didn't know it, but only four of the NVA remained effective after
receiving the heavy counterfire the highly disciplined team had put
out at the instant of ambush.

Wolf, splattered by the blood and gore of the dead man lying next
to him, struggled in his own blood to put his last magazine into his
M-16. It slipped out of his hands and fell into the grass. The pain
from his wrist felt like high voltage running up his arm into his brain.
It was increasing. He knew he was going into shock. He summoned
up the strength to shout to his sergeant.

"Menuez, you okay? Where are you?"

The Wolf lay back in the torn brush and tried with his left hand
and teeth to wrap a sweat band around his wound. He could hear a
rustling from the clearing, signaling the NVA were preparing their
final charge. This whole mission was snakebit from the beginning,
he thought to himself, feeling fuzzy and faint. Ten days ago they
had inserted, seemingly undetected, into their zone just west of the
Vietnamese border into Laos. But just as their insertion helicopter
was lifting off, it was hit by a blaze of .51-calibre fire and flopped
down into the trees. Wolf and his team had instantly melted into
the jungle away from the gun and toward the burning helicopter.
They found only blackened pygmies slowly assuming boxing poses
in the red flames. They hurried past. Their job was not to engage, it
was to establish a pilot rescue net.

"Menuez, goddammit, answer me," the Wolf's voice was faint
and absorbed by the brush. The grisly pendulum swayed over his
head.

On the second day their HF radios went out, causing them to miss the scheduled contact times to learn where POW's or newly downed pilots might be hiding. All that remained for communications was an Urk-ten survival radio that Wolf had stuffed into his side pants pocket at the last minute. Then the weather had turned more sour than usual. Days on end of torrential downpours had begun to rot even their canvas Bata boots. Lastly, they heard an air battle high up and saw a stick figure in a parachute plummet into the jungle to the north in an area they had been specifically briefed was free of enemy movement.

"Ahh, Menuez, Menuez, can you hear me?" Wolf was going out and he knew it. The steamy jungle was turning cold and dark. He blinked up at the pilot, dead in his harness. "We tried, son, we tried," the Wolf murmured, his last conscious act.

Menuez, as he lay dying, had heard every one of Wolf's cries. He had tried to shout, to warn Wolf, but the air from his lungs bubbled out soundlessly through his throat, which had been cleanly sliced from ear to ear. His eyes rolled as he made one last feeble attempt to raise his gun and shoot the man next to him. Buey Dan patted Menuez's hand and watched his eyes turn dusty as he died. He smiled as he wiped his blade and tucked it away. He knew he would soon have a stiletto. But he would have to act fast.

"Lizard, Lizard, Lizard," he yelled in Vietnamese. He fired three shots in rapid succession from his rifle, paused, and fired two more. "Lizard, Lizard," he shouted again. The jungle fell silent. The advancing NVA lay still.

"Anh thán lán?" the squad leader called. He had been briefed a month earlier that an encounter such as this might occur in his region. *"Anh thán lán?"* "You, the Lizard?" he repeated, and waited for the proper response from this legendary fighter.

"Yes, I am the Lizard from Hanoi's lake," Buey Dan called back. "It is safe. They are dead. Stand up and show yourselves," he ordered.

Reassured, the squad leader and his remaining men stood. "We must see to our wounded," he said.

"Of course, do so," the Lizard commanded quietly. The NVA soldiers moved to their dead and wounded. The Lizard arose from the brush, stepped over Menuez's body, and walked through the grass, his M-16 hanging under his right arm, to where the lifeless Wolf Lochert lay in a welter of gore. With the muzzle of his gun he turned over the body next to Wolf and noted with satisfaction that the Nung was quite dead.

The Lizard slung his rifle behind his back and knelt to take the stiletto he knew Wolf carried strapped to his leg, even in the jungle. His moment of blood revenge on the *mui lo* had arrived. All that remained was to insert the stiletto that had killed his son into the stomach of the already slain Wolf Lochert. The Lizard wished the stiletto could have been the instrument that caused the actual death of the *mui lo,* but that evidently was not destined. *Ai,* nonetheless he would leave the stiletto in the dead man's stomach.

He was pulling up the bloodstained pant leg, when Wolf Lochert opened his eyes.

0600 HOURS LOCAL, 13 DECEMBER 1966
MAC PASSENGER TERMINAL,
ANDREWS AIR FORCE BASE, MARYLAND
☆

Major General Albert G. "Whitey" Whisenand walked into the VIP lounge at precisely 0600 to be greeted by the MAC lieutenant in charge of the passenger roster for special air missions Flight 782 flying from Andrews Air Force Base, Maryland, to Tan Son Nhut Air Base, Republic of Vietnam. Whitey had decided he needed first-hand information from the troops in the field if he was to be worth anything from 12,000 miles away. He was scheduled out on Flight 782, a VC-135, for a quick trip to Vietnam.

The VC-135, a Boeing 707 modified for the Air Force to carry both cargo and passengers, would be making the flight to Saigon by way of Hickham Air Force Base outside of Honolulu, Guam, and Clark Air Base in the Philippines. The regular round-the-world SAM flight providing U.S. embassy support did not go frequently enough or provide sufficient space for the many official travelers to and from Vietnam.

Congressmen, senators, and investigating committees, in addition to members of the military, had begun to overload the SAM facilities with their relentless and increasing flow of traffic between Washington and Saigon. The civilian members were glad this was happening, because it meant they would get certificates of nonavailability of government transportation. Then they could avail themselves of first-class civilian airline travel, which was far preferable to the so-called VIP flights of the United States Air Force . . . unless of course Air Force One or Two was scheduled. In that case the congressmen would fall all over themselves finding excuses to be on board with the President or cabinet member scheduled to fly to Saigon.

This morning, Whitey was the ranking military officer on board. With him on the passenger manifest were eleven officers, sixteen NCO's, and eight men in civilian dress. The next-highest-ranking officer to Whitey was a brigadier being assigned to MACV. The highest-ranking civilian was a portly congressman from Wisconsin who was on a fact-finding tour to see if the latest request for more troops was justified.

The congressman had allotted three days for his trip: one day to visit four major bases to meet with the troops (his advance message had specifically requested he meet with lads from Wisconsin since he had an election coming up in the fall); one day to tour Saigon and receive a one-hour briefing from General Westmoreland; and one day to rest up, shop, and attend an embassy function in his honor.

The ranking NCO was an army sergeant major who was also on a fact-finding trip. His mission was to check increasingly frequent reports of money scams and black marketeering from the PX's and commissaries that fell under army quartermaster corps jurisdiction. Two of the men in civilian clothing were Criminal Investigation Division agents working with him.

| 0615 HOURS LOCAL, 13 DECEMBER 1966
| STEEL TIGER SECTOR, ROYALTY OF LAOS

☆

A second after he saw Wolf Lochert's eyes flutter open, Buey Dan bent over him and pressed a hand to the American's mouth. "Shh," he said, staring into his face, "don't move." Although Lochert seemed to nod in comprehension, Buey Dan could see he was fading in and out of consciousness, not fully aware of where he was.

He sat back for a minute, his hand still on Lochert's mouth, and thought again of his son's ignominious death under the trees in Saigon. He nodded slowly. He would wait, after all. It was necessary for the revolution. His actions today would prove beyond a doubt his trustworthiness to the American enemy. But someday he would kill Lochert under the same tree where his son had died. And he would do it with the same piece of steel that had pierced his son's heart. Lochert's blood would mingle with that of his son in the same earth. He picked up the stiletto and concealed it in the rotted grass at the base of the fallen tree. Then he slowly and silently rolled away to the end of the log out of sight of Wolf. He stood up, unslung his rifle to rest casually under his right arm, and walked confidently to where the NVA soldiers were bandaging their wounded.

"Does it go well?" he enquired politely.

"Yes, Anh. But you killed six of our men," the squad leader said.

"It was necessary," Buey Dan replied, and offered him a cigarette. "Take it," he said when he saw the squad leader hesitate. "Take it," he motioned back with his rifle. "They're all dead." The squad leader lit up, gratefully. They were never allowed to carry tobacco on patrol.

"Where is your main force unit?" the Lizard asked.

"Twelve or so kilometers north, *anh.*" The squad leader spoke more respectfully. "We were most fortunate to see the air pirate come down."

"Do you have a radio?"

"No, *anh.*"

"When are you to return?"

"In two days, *anh.*"

Buey Dan shot the squad leader through the face, then dropped to one knee and emptied his magazine into the remaining three men kneeling over their comrades. Quickly he strode over and put one slug into the forehead of each of the wounded. "It is necessary for the Liberation," he breathed to himself. He walked back to Lochert and took the Urk-ten survival radio from the American's rucksack and extended the antenna.

"Hillsboro, Hillsboro," he transmitted on Guard channel. "This is Bright Spot Three Alpha, Bright Spot Three Alpha. Do you hear me?" He made three more tries before he got an answer.

"Bright Spot, Hillsboro, go."

"Hillsboro, Bright Spot, Condition Fox, I say again, Condition Fox. One Kilo India, one Whisky India. We need emergency Prairie Fire. Do you understand me?" Buey Dan's voice was strained but crisp. His diction was good, but he knew his oriental accent was obvious.

"Hey, boss," the duty controller on board the airborne command, control, and communication C-130 said to his senior, "we got some gook calling for an emergency extraction."

The senior controller took over. He checked his code book and determined Condition Fox meant mission compromised hence of no further value. Prairie Fire meant emergency extraction ASAP. He knew any Bright Spot was an aircrew rescue team and that Three Alpha would be the call sign of the interpreter.

"Bright Spot Three Alpha, authenticate Oscar November, repeat, authenticate Oscar November."

On the ground Buey Dan hesitated. He had watched Wolf use the code wheel and thought he could do it. He found the code wheel in Wolf's upper pocket and aligned the pointer to the letters O and N. The response arrow pointed to G, then T.

"Golf Tango," he transmitted.

"Roger, Bright Spot, confirmed. Stand by," the controller said and turned to his deputy. "What have we got for Steel Tiger?" he asked.

The deputy had already anticipated the question and gotten a readout from the Air Force command post at Tan Son Nhut called Blue Chip. "We got a Green Hornet airborne on a test hop and two on alert."

"Is the test hop a full-up bird?"

"Yessir."

"Vector it over to Bright Spot, scramble the two birds on alert, and get a couple of Sandy's and gunships for cover."

0645 HOURS LOCAL, 13 DECEMBER 1966
UH-1F HEADED FOR STEEL TIGER, ROYALTY OF LAOS

☆

"Parker, the fit just hit the shan," the Green Hornet pilot said on the intercom. "We just got diverted to an emergency pickup and we've got no time to take you back, so sit down, strap in, and shut up."

Toby had been standing between the pilot and copilot seats during the early-morning test hop. He turned and sat down on the red canvas straps of a pull-down seat nearest the right door. The air was cool and calm, and a light mist was just burning off the jungle canopy below as the sun gained height and strength. It looked, Toby thought, like an early-spring morning in Virginia, when soldier-mist rose from the Rappahannock River. God, Toby Parker said to himself as he thought of the old legend that the mist was made of the souls of dead Civil War soldiers looking for their campgrounds. He shivered. For the first time in Vietnam, he shivered.

Thirty minutes later they were orbiting over triple-canopy jungle.

"Bright Spot, Hornet Two-Two, how copy?"

"Hornet, I hear you, I hear you. Come east 200 meters," Buey Dan transmitted over his-hand held emergency radio. "East 200 meters."

The Hornet pilot slid his helicopter 200 meters east. He noted the Vietnamese accent.

"Bright Spot, put the American on the radio."

"Negative, Green Hornet, one American Kilo India, other American Whisky India. I am only the one to talk."

The Hornet pilot requested and received authentication, then asked, "What's the bad guy situation?"

The pilot missed the irony when Buey Dan answered.

"There is no problem here. I am next to a clearing. I will give you smoke." He pulled the ring on a smoke can and tossed it into the clearing. Yellow smoke billowed up.

"I've got yellow," Green Hornet transmitted. Buey Dan confirmed it was his smoke. Two minutes later the UH-1F rested on its skids in the clearing, rotor downwash flattening the elephant grass into green waves.

Parker jumped out to help the small Vietnamese trying to support a big Caucasian. Both men wore tiger suits. He ran toward them, noticing the Vietnamese bend to pick up what looked like a thin knife from beneath a log and tuck it butt down in his right Bata boot. Parker ran up and grabbed the American's arm and looked into his face.

"Oh my God, Wolf," he yelled above the hissing *whop-whop* of the helicopter. He pulled his arm over Wolf's shoulder and, with help from Buey Dan, got him into the helicopter.

Wolf cocked a dazed eye at his rescuer. He muttered in semiconscious slurred speech, "What you doon, what you doon, flyboy?"

0830 HOURS LOCAL, 15 DECEMBER 1966
FLIGHT LINE, TAN SON NHUT AIR BASE,
REPUBLIC OF VIETNAM
☆

After three stops, SAM 782 landed at Tan Son Nhut 37 hours out of Andrews, at 0830 local. Vietnam was thirteen hours ahead of Washington. The passengers were rumpled and stiff. The chief steward requested they remain in their seats until the VIP's departed. The congressman from Wisconsin stood up and walked with a self-important air to the door and disappeared in a welter of immaculately dressed and pressed civilian and military aides. Whitey, to his surprise, was met by a three-star Army lieutenant general, accompanied by a two-star USAF major general whom Whitey knew to be the Director of Operations (DO) for the 7th Air Force.

What ensued was not pleasant. The Army general, tall and impressive with all the right ribbons and badges, extended General

Westmoreland's compliments and a request—a command, actually—for a working luncheon with him to discuss General Whisenand's trip to Vietnam. He handed a schedule to Whitey, which, he explained, would amply fill his time in Vietnam with briefings and tours to the front lines to see how the real war was being fought.

Without looking at the schedule, Whitey handed it back and spoke very precisely. "General, while I truly appreciate the interest from General Westmoreland, as well as the great personal efforts to which you have gone, I cannot remain here at Tan Son Nhut." Whitey smiled politely, saluted, and waited for the return salute.

The MACV general stood a good three inches over Whitey's five-foot-ten. His sharp blue eyes, topped by bushy dark eyebrows, showed none of the earlier geniality.

"I am sorry to hear that, as I know General Westmoreland will be." His eyes narrowed as he stepped closer and asked the question Whitey had been expecting.

"Exactly why, general," he asked with measured deliberation, "are you here in Vietnam?"

"To reiterate my TWX, of which I'm sure you received a copy," Whitey began patiently, "I want to talk with the Blue Chip people in the Seventh Air Force command post and with the fighter wing commanders about our heavy losses over North Vietnam and Laos."

"I saw that TWX, of course," the Army general said, dismissing it with a wave of his hand, "but I have it from the best sources that you work directly for the President and *he* wants your report on the situation here. Although I can't imagine why"—the general took in both Whitey and the USAF DO with a peevish glance "—the President would send an Air Force major general to check on an Army full general in charge of all operations, air and ground."

Whitey held the general's gaze. "Your sources have misled you, sir. I am not here to check on General Westmoreland. As your source may have told you, I am temporarily assigned to the NSC. It is within my duties to investigate with a view toward improving Air Force activities in this war, particularly the losses. I think you can understand that."

Still dubious, though not anxious to irritate a man working directly for the President, the Army general nodded. "Yes, I suppose I understand." He returned Whitey's salute and spun on his heel toward his staff car.

When he and Whitey were settled in the USAF staff car, the shaken 7th Air Force DO apologized to Whitey for his loss of control of the situation.

"It wasn't your fault," Whitey said. "You couldn't have anticipated their scheme to find out why I was here. What surprises me is the paranoid atmosphere I detected." Whitey turned to look at his fellow officer. "Is it that bad in the Air Force side of the house?"

The DO hesitated. That in itself was an answer for Whitey. "Look," the DO said, "as you know, I've got a four-star blue-suit boss to keep happy. If he's not paranoid, then I'm not paranoid." Whitey nodded his head, as if satisfied with the nonanswer.

Five minutes later the two Air Force generals walked into the briefing room of the USAF command post at Tan Son Nhut Air Base.

0945 HOURS LOCAL, 15 DECEMBER 1966
BLUE CHIP COMMAND POST, TAN SON NHUT AIR BASE,
REPUBLIC OF VIETNAM

☆

"You already know, General Whisenand," the briefing officer, a brigadier general, began, "how the Rolling Thunder Coordinating Committee works in regard to the requests for strikes coming in, and the orders to perform strikes going out.

"The people the committee coordinates with are the Navy—who handle the aircraft from Task Force Seventy-seven; the Strategic Air Command Advance Echelon; and Seventh Air Force, which answers to Commander in Chief, Pacific Air Force, for all of North Vietnam, except Pack One, which is under the control of MACV. Strike orders going out come from the President after being passed down through the Joint Chiefs to PACAF to us."

"I am only too well aware of your command process," Whitey said. Privately, he was appalled at the tortuous path of the command structure. Even though COMUSMACV, an *Army* general, was on the scene, he had CINCPAC, a *Navy* admiral, between him and the Secretary of Defense.

"What you may not be aware of, sir," the briefer continued, "is the fact that we cannot in any way, shape, or form hit where and when we feel it is important and timely to do so. As a result, fleeting targets of opportunity, or even longstanding targets of strategic importance, are not taken out. Steel mills, railheads, power plants, and harbor facilities are allowed to stay in operation.

"SAM sites under construction, MiG bases already in operation, and known gun sites cannot be hit when we think they should be. Those air defense–type targets are off-limits until we get orders to strike the odd steel mill or bridge from time to time. Only then can we go after the MiG bases and SAM sites on flak suppression missions to protect the strike force."

"Gentlemen," Whitey said with genuine compassion in his voice, remembering his pleading with LBJ to allow the Navy to smash the 111 crated SAM's, "I am aware of what you can and cannot hit, as I am also aware that you cannot place priority, or even certainty of strike, on targets you recommend. What I want to know is this: Under the current rules of engagement, are there any improvements in the system, bad as it is, that you think should be made?"

"Yes, sir. Smarter bombs and smarter pilots. Smarter bombs for our air-to-ground missions, and smarter pilots for our air-to-air missions. We need weapons that have built-in guidance systems instead of relying on the eyeballs of a pilot who is being shot at. And we need to release those weapons farther from the target to avoid prolonged exposure for the crew to the flak." He paused to see if Whitey had any questions. He didn't.

"I'm serious, general, when I say we need smarter pilots. For years we have been too concerned with flying-safety records rather than realistic fighter-versus-fighter training. The USAF ratio right now between our fighters and MiGs is only about 1.1 to 1. In Korea, we ran that up to 12 or 13 of theirs for 1 of ours. We're not even close now. We need better ACM training at the fighter school in Vegas."

Whitey reviewed what he knew about ACM. Air Combat Maneuvering was the self-descriptive name for the advanced training a fighter pilot is supposed to receive to learn how best to shoot down enemy fighters. In the preceding years, flying-safety considerations had gradually ruled out realistic training because of crashes, mostly in the early and midfifties, caused by overzealous fighter pilots and their instructors, who really didn't understand the finer points of how to teach young fighter pilots how to be tigers—safe tigers. When the massive and frantic flying-safety program took over, the tiger program became the pussycat program. The net results were few crashes, an excellent flying-safety record (wing commanders with bad records were fired), and unforgivable losses in fighter combat with MiG's in the sky over Hanoi. The Navy wasn't doing any better.

Whitey nodded and kept his mouth shut. He felt like the most contemptible of men. Here he was, building hope in these men by the very fact that he, a two-star general from Washington, was asking such pertinent questions. His presence promised changes that he was not at all sure he could even request, much less deliver.

"Anything else?" he asked.

"Just one thing, general," the DO said, "shut off the command link from the White House to us. We're tired of being fragged by civilians.'' They both laughed bitterly at the appropriateness of the double entendre.

1030 HOURS LOCAL, 16 DECEMBER 1966
366TH TACTICAL FIGHTER WING,
DA NANG AIR BASE, REPUBLIC OF VIETNAM
☆

The next day Whitey landed at Da Nang Air Base in the Scatback T-39 placed at his disposal, for a briefing by the commander of the F-4 wing. The diagnosis was the same as that of the 7th Air Force officers: Rules of Engagement and improper targeting were costing lives, yet neither military nor political goals were being attained. They also pleaded for more weapons.

The wing commander invited Whitey to the Da Nang O-club for a late snack before his hop to Tahkli. En route to the flight line after sandwiches and coffee, the wing commander asked Whitey in a more sarcastic than hopeful tone if there was some secret plan devised way up in the ethereal mists to win this mess. From Whitey's lack of response the wing commander surmised, correctly, that there were no changes contemplated, no changes en route, and there sure as hell was no secret plan.

Later, Whitey rode in the T-39 headed toward the F-105 base at Tahkli in Thailand. He had sent a back-channel message to the new wing commander, Colonel Ralph Morgan, stating he desired no arrival honors and no off-base official functions, such as meeting with the Thai official who owned the place. What he did desire was a closed-door session with Morgan.

Twenty minutes out from Tahkli, Whitey's pilot came back and told him they were picking up an escort. ''Damn,'' Whitey thought to himself, ''I said 'no honors.' '' He looked out to see a camou- flaged F-105 flying close formation on the right wing. On the rudder were the letters RM, showing it to be a Tahkli plane. As it slipped in to fly the left wing, Whitey could see it was a Navy A-4D with the NL identification of an aircraft from the carrier U.S.S. *Coral Sea*. As it slid into place about two feet from the T-39's wing, the pilot tossed off a smart salute at Whitey, who returned it with a big grin. Navy Captain Jim Tunner and USAF Colonel Ralph Morgan, each trying to fly closer formation than the other, were his flying escorts.

They tucked in so close that the airflow from their wings disrupted the air under the T-39, causing the pilot to ask nervously on Guard channel for the two escorts to spread it out a little, please. They flew smoothly for five minutes, then Whitey watched the two planes pull up and roll away and streak for Tahkli so the pilots could be on the ground to meet their former boss when he landed.

It must be grand flying those big fighters, Whitey thought to himself. Remembrance and nostalgia for the sensation of controlling an airplane swept over Whitey with an intensity he thought he had buried years ago. His eyes misted. His right hand formed a fist that beat softly on the arm rest. Ah, God, if I could only fly one of those magnificent beasts in combat again.

2030 HOURS LOCAL, 16 DECEMBER 1966
COMMANDER'S QUARTERS, 355TH TACTICAL FIGHTER WING,
TAHKLI ROYAL THAI AIR FORCE BASE,
KINGDOM OF THAILAND

☆

That night, Major General Whitey Whisenand met with Ralph Morgan and Jim Tunner for barbecued steaks at Morgan's trailer. He brought along a fifth of Johnnie Walker Red. They sat outside in the cooling dark while Morgan prepared the steaks on the flaming grill and Tunner made the drinks. They all wore Bermuda shorts and Hawaiian shirts. Whitey noticed that Morgan was so thin his jowls had all but disappeared. The lines on his face were more pronounced and were etched deeper, like the results of long years of erosion on a steep hill. Jim Tunner was tanned and wind-burned. Whitey thought the crow's feet at the corners of his eyes had become denser since their last meeting in the Pentagon so many months ago.

The scotch bottle was more than half empty by the time the steaks were ready. As they ate, the conversation was jocular and light, consisting mainly of the latest flying stories. Jim Tunner said life as a Commander Air Group was demanding but gratifying, like trying to satisfy four nymphos simultaneously. He said if all went well he would get a deep-draft command, maybe the *Coral Sea* itself, right on schedule. By unspoken agreement, they didn't talk about shootdowns. That would come once they were inside the trailer. They spoke, instead, of victories.

Although Whitey knew of the three-MiG victory by Frederick and Bannister, he was delighted to hear the inside story of how the two pilots had spun in one MiG by buzzing it. They laughed loud, and almost too long, as Morgan told the story. Whitey sensed the two men were suppressing something. Still chuckling, they went inside.

The interior consisted of plastic furniture and linoleum flooring made only slightly more homey by the light woven rugs and two Papasan chairs Morgan had bought in the village. The hum and throb of the air conditioners gently rocked the trailer, as if it were a small boat in light chop.

"You know, or maybe you didn't," Whitey began, "that Court Bannister is my cousin's son. Without making any big thing of it, I'd like to know how he did. I heard he was TDY here for a few missions to research the fast-FAC business. And of course I know about the MiG's. Just between us, how was he?"

"He finished up and left for his F-100 unit at Bien Hoa just as I arrived," Morgan said, "so I really didn't get to know him. As to his abilities, our own home-grown terror, Ted Frederick, thinks Court is second only to himself. That's about the highest accolade you can get in this business."

Whitey nodded, satisfied. He added more ice to his drink. "I hear we need better fighter training," he said to Morgan.

"That we most assuredly do," Ralph Morgan answered. "It's pretty bad when pilots of a single seat nuke bomber, like the F-105 was intended to be, shoot down as many MiG's per encounter as the F-4 jocks who have a backseater to help them out. That's not to say we've got better training. We don't. It just means at this particular time we have more experienced jocks in 105's than in F-4's. Certainly the same as the Thud wing over at Korat. The whole situation could change in a month or two, as old heads rotate in and out of Vietnam for both airplanes. But that's not answering your question. Overall, yes, we all need more realistic air-to-air training back in the States."

Jim Tunner agreed, poured fresh drinks, then asked, "How is your new job coming along, boss?"

"About the same way the war is coming along," Whitey replied.

"What does that mean?" Morgan asked.

"I haven't been given a clear-cut mission, I don't really know what the President expects of me, but I could be relieved of my position in a heartbeat for violating rules that aren't even thought up yet." Whitey surprised himself. He didn't mean to go off like that. That damn scotch, he thought. "Enough of that. I'm here to listen to you guys."

Tunner and Morgan exchanged glances. "You first," Tunner said.

Taking a hefty belt of scotch, the USAF colonel, the commander of the 5,000-man F-105 fighter wing, stood up and started pacing the confines of the trailer like a restless tiger in a small cage. His expression was agitated.

"It's like this," he started in a low voice that got louder, "I'm sending all these men out there to die and I don't know what the hell for." He smacked a fist into a palm. "Every day I sweat blood and watch those guys take those big, bomb-loaded beasts snorting and bucking into the air for North Vietnam. Day after day they do it. And you know our losses are terrible. Every week we go against North Vietnam, we, the Air Force and the Navy, lose half a dozen airplanes and nearly as many pilots. Yet our guys keep going back as ordered. Now I know how the Aussies felt at Gallipoli. Let me tell you, boss, our guys are just magnificent." He stopped and glared out the window over the door. "I don't know how they do it. I don't know how they do it," he repeated in a louder voice, smacking his fist repeatedly into his palm.

"Where do we get such magnificent guys and . . . why are we killing them?" He spun around to face Whitey. His eyes were blazing. "I ask you, goddammit, *Why are we killing them? Who is the miserable son of a bitch in Washington that's responsible for this mess?*" He turned to the wall and slammed his fist into the paneling so hard it cracked through to the insulation. He pulled back and absently rubbed his knuckles, while making a visible effort to regain his composure.

"You know it's not you I'm talking about in Washington, general," he said quietly.

"Yes, I know," Whitey said. "I also know you don't just *watch* your men flying those missions. You are out there flying just as much as they are. You're not supposed to, you know. You're supposed to spend more time running this wing. I know," he said holding up his hand before Morgan could speak, "you're going to tell me you can't run a wing from behind a desk."

"That's exactly right, General Whisenand. I've got a great big staff and an exec and a vice-commander to handle the paperwork. I'm here to *command* these pilots; and to me, that means I'm out front leading. Now if the United States Air Force thinks that's the wrong way to go about it, then I'm in the wrong service."

"Ralph," Whitey said, "you know that I agree with your philosophy. You also know with that kind of an attitude, you probably won't ever be on the promotion list to general."

Colonel Ralph Morgan looked at Major General Whisenand.

"Whitey," he said with a twisted smile on his face, "you think I give more than one-third of a fifth of a fuck about a down-line brigadier general list? It's the here and now, with these men, that I'm living. Besides," he broke into a big grin and waved his scotch, "who says I'm going to be alive when the list comes out, anyway?"

Whitey dutifully laughed and looked fondly at Ralph Morgan. You could, he thought, divide the motivations of a combat wing commander into thirds; accomplish their mission, protect their pilots, make ace. The exceptional ones wanted all three. (For non–fighter wing commanders, making general would suffice in lieu of ace. But no fighter pilot would ever trade being an ace for the stars of a general officer.) The truly exceptional ones wanted to do all three in reverse order. Normally, however, accomplishing the mission would be the prime motivator. Yet, as the commanders soon realized, there was no clear-cut mission other than what was teletyped in on the daily frag order. There was no grand scheme or victory plan.

Whitey accepted another drink from Jim Tunner. "Are you gentlemen trying to get me intoxicated?" Both Morgan and Tunner looked at Whitey in mock "Who, me?" horror. "Because if you are, don't try it. I'd put both of you away." All three laughed, Tunner and Morgan shaking their heads.

Jim Tunner leaned back in a Papasan chair. Whitey looked at him.

"It's the same with you Navy guys, isn't it Jim? The problems, I mean."

"Yes, sir, it is. The Navy is having the same trouble. When I got the back-channel from Ralph saying you were coming in, I decided to come here to talk about it with you. I'm not trying to bypass Navy channels, it's just that you are the only person I know who is intimately involved with the highest authority." Jim Tunner pushed himself out of the deep chair and began unconsciously pacing the small confines as Morgan had. "Do the President and the SecDef *know* the Navy has lost over 100 planes in North and South Vietnam these last two years, yet supplies and troops are still going into South Vietnam? Do they *know* the Air Force has lost 280 planes in the same time, yet enemy attacks are increasing in the South? Do they *know* we, the Navy and the Air Force, have nearly 300 pilots as POW's in a captivity more brutal than the Japanese used in World War Two? And do they *know* that in spite of our efforts and all those losses, we see the defenses increasing in North Vietnam? And what about the dead pilots of those 1,000 or so Army helicopters shot down in South Vietnam? Do the President and the SecDef know any of this? And if they do, does it *mean* anything to them?"

☆

After another session at the Tahkli Thud wing, Whitey climbed on board the T-39 bound for Tan Son Nhut. He nursed a light hangover and a heavy sorrow. The rage of the men he had talked with, under the fighter pilot's can-do facade, was unlike anything he had ever experienced. In World War Two, the combatants, while suffering various degrees of fatalism and enthusiasm, nonetheless had believed in the cause they were fighting for, and in the overall decisions of their leaders.

In Vietnam, he was seeing a series of local, wing-level commanders trying to fight the portion of the war they had been allotted without a sense of unity in some overall grand plan. And, at that, the portion of the war they had been allotted was mostly controlled tactically and strategically by unknown persons of dubious ability situated over the horizon in lofty offices more attuned to political than military realities.

At higher command levels found at MACV, Whitey had the distinct impression that harassment and fear were stalking the corridors. It would at least be understandable, if not countenanced, were it harassment by sporadic enemy fire or fear of combat; but it was worse than that. The harassment came from long hours trying to make sense of, and respond to, conflicting and unprofessional orders from Washington; the fear came from knowing the results were not right and never would be, and the consequences to both conscience and career were not pleasant to contemplate.

He was dozing when the T-39 made its steep descent into Tan Son Nhut. He awoke with a start at the roaring sound made by speed brakes, as the pilot extended them to slow the airplane to traffic-pattern speed. As arranged with the DO, he was met without ceremony and taken to his previous VIP trailer. The interior decor was Howard Johnson Spanish, and cool. Whitey pulled the blackout shades, showered, and lay on the bed.

He missed his wife Sal's soothing presence and her way of gently making him come to the point when he would explain his perceptions of events to her. He wanted to discuss with her what course he could take that would help the United States resolve this dilemma. In her practical manner, she would say, "You don't mean the United States, you mean the United States government, don't you." "Yes," Whitey would say. "Because," she would continue, "the United States are the people; the government is the leadership. You want to help our leaders to find a way out of this mess, don't you?" "Yes," Whitey would respond. "Well, it's simple then," Sal would say, "there is only one leader who really controls the prosecution of the war, and that's the President, so it's him you must assist, isn't it?"

Yes, it was the President he must get to, Whitey knew. That would be like getting to a mammoth frozen in tons of ice and asking it to meow like a cat.

The irony of it was that Whitey had both the mandate and the instrument to get to the President. The Man himself had asked for Whitey's assessment of the Vietnam war, and that was that. Yet the past actions of the Commander in Chief of the American Armed Forces seemed to indicate he wasn't about to act on any input from the military, be it Whitey or the Joint Chiefs of Staff.

He remembered a few days earlier when he had been summoned to the Oval Office. Told to enter, he had walked in to hear LBJ, who never looked up, in the middle of a monologue to one of his aides.

". . . and the generals. Oh, they'd love the war, too. It's hard to be a military hero without a war. Heroes need battles and bombs and bullets in order to be heroic. That's why I'm so suspicious of the military. They're always so narrow in their appraisal of everything. They see everything in military terms." The President had then dismissed the aide, greeted Whitey with great charm, and had gone on about his business at his desk, leaving Whitey to withdraw on his own with the idea that LBJ had wanted him to hear his thoughts about generals.

In view of that, was it possible that the President's request for Whitey's input was just a sop to appease the military and to protect himself from criticism, if it came to that? Whitey sat straight up in the realization that maybe he was being had. His brain began to whirl with sudden alarming thoughts.

Maybe he was being used as a cover against possible fallout from political repercussions when it came time to answer some hard questions as the President prepared to run for a second term. Maybe he was being used as a shield against current unrest from the Joint Chiefs of Staff so the President could point to the assessments and say, "Look, I am getting your military views from General Whisenand here." Maybe he was being used as a patsy to help the President play off one of his internal political factions against the other for some obscure purpose. Maybe . . . maybe his position on the National Security Council was a sham to make the President look as if he had balanced input from the civilian and military members of his staff.

Maybe he had no business being there at all.

29

☆

The mission was nearly over, yet it hadn't quite registered with Captain Courtland Esclaremond de Montségur Bannister that he was about to land from his 254th and last combat mission of his tour in Vietnam. Only when he was leading his flight three miles directly above Bien Hoa Air Base down to the traffic pattern did the stark realization strike him that he would never again fly combat in Vietnam.

In an eerie combination of inside-outside, he saw himself both performing actions in the cockpit while also viewing them from the outside of the plane five minutes in the future. He was going through the motions of landing his airplane on the runway below. He clearly saw his hand tug the drag-chute handle, and from the outside he saw the chute deploy and decelerate the sleek fighter. As the scene of déjà vu played out, he was washed by an unexpected sadness, as if he were about to lose something of immense value.

Unbidden, a memory surfaced of that teenage summer when he had had a brief affair with a girl in France. She had been all Wellesley with dark plaid skirt and knee-highs and flowing black hair curling in wings around her wide brown eyes. Within two days of their meeting at his father's villa at Cap Ferrat they were in steamy, sensual love. Laughter, secrets exchanged, red wine, sleek bodies swimming in the moonlight, candles, chest-aching love, moist skin joining on the warm beach. She had been a houseguest along with her aunt. Then she was gone; a Hutton-DuPont, her future was as preordained as that of a Mayan high priestess. For weeks after he had been empty and sullen. Now he had a presage of the same feeling of loss, a presage of sadness at never again doing a thing that had—the realization startled him—become the most important thing in his life.

These thoughts and emotions swept Court in an instant, leaving him with the realization of how much he loved and needed his airplane and the altitude and the sky and his wingmen and the pure sense of flight, and of how exhilarated he felt while flying a combat mission, and of the joy he felt upon his triumphal returns to base. He would have laughed and blushed if pressed to put these feelings into words.

He shook his head and looked up through his visor. The day had at once taken on a new meaning. The colors and the sounds in the cockpit intensified. The white of the clouds became whiter in contrast to a sky that became a deeper and darker blue. The outlines of the two planes in echelon off his right wing became more distinct. The details of the runways and taxiways of the air base below became vivid and sharp as he had never seen them before. The sound of his engine and the wind rushing over his canopy were as much a part of him as his own heartbeat. He and his big ugly-beautiful fighter were one.

This airplane, this *particular* airplane, knew who he was. They could not separate. This could not be the last time he soared far above the clouds in this fine craft that he loved so. And it loved him. He knew it. It recognized him and sent smooth signals of responsiveness to his slightest whims.

A moment before, he had been fully occupied in leading his flight of three F-100's back from attacking a target in the Mekong Delta. Then, with that terrible wrench, awareness had struck him that he would never do any of this again. It simply could not be. There had to be more.

Neither of the other two pilots had called Bingo, so he knew they had a few minutes' extra fuel. For a moment anyhow, he could prolong his last combat mission. He gently porpoised his plane as a signal for his two wingmen to slip back into the trail position. No words were necessary. He eased the throttle forward a few percent of rpms, knowing they would follow as soon as they detected his plane creeping away. They would fly such a tight formation their feet would vibrate on the rudder pedals as their planes were buffeted by the exhaust from the tailpipe of the plane in front.

When they were tucked in, he gently pulled his plane up and, lowering the right wing, rolled easily about the horizon and let the nose fall through, until they were inverted over the earth with the sun shining on the flat underside of their planes like a spotlight on ballet dancers. Then, still lazily rolling, they were pointed straight down with speed building up to 1,000 feet per second. For a few heartbeats, he watched the mottled green earth grow larger in detail, then pulled up with increasing force until they were headed straight up the side of a newly birthed cumulus too painfully white to look at. Under his guidance, they rolled together and soared effortlessly over the top, to hang motionless in the sky for long seconds like seagulls painted on a canvas. Then, carefully, he rolled them level and gradually vanquished gravity by pushing the nose down until they were loose in their straps, and their pencils floated up from their sleeve pockets. They flew behind him as tight as links in a chain. When they were a few degrees below the horizon, he eased in back stick, then pulled them up crisply and rolled them twice to the left.

Then it was over. "Bingo minus two," Ramrod Number Three transmitted in a voice quiet and apologetic. He had just told Court Bannister he was 200 pounds under what he should have to return to base from a 100-mile distance.

Court had one last trick to squeeze every sensation out of this day. He told them to switch to tower frequency.

"Bien Hoa Tower, Ramrod Two One approaching initial with three. Call the command post and ask them to clear us for a flyby then a tactical pitch-up for landing."

"Ramrod Two One, you're cleared," the voice of Frank Darlington, the new commander of the 3rd Tactical Fighter Wing, shot back. As he did with all pilots on their last mission, he was in his command jeep in preparation to meet Bannister in the revetment, where fellow pilots would pop champagne and douse the man who had just flown his last combat mission and was going home.

Bannister gratefully acknowledged. He put his flight into a V formation and led them, engines screaming above the wind, down Runway 27 at 200 feet indicating 530 knots. At the end of the runway he pulled them up into a tight left-climbing turn and gave the wing dip to signal the left wing man to slide over to echelon right. They zoomed up to 3,000 feet, stayed within the boundary of the air base, then dove down in a left turn to roll out once again onto the initial approach for Runway 27. He throttled back to indicate 450 knots. He revolved his gloved forefinger alongside his head, then held up two fingers in the signal to his wingmen to pitch up after him in two-second intervals. Two repeated the signal to Three to maintain perfect radio discipline.

They streaked up initial at 200 feet. As they flashed over the beginning edge of the runway, Court racked his F-100 up left in a tight five-g climbing turn, and at the same time blew his speed boards out into the wind. The sudden deceleration threw him into his harness as he pulled the fighter farther up and around to level off at 1,500 feet on the downwind leg of the landing pattern. When he had slowed to 230 knots, he threw the gear handle down, followed by the flap handle, and started a left turn onto the base leg. Behind him, in precise two-second intervals, Two and Three had zoomed left and up into the same pattern. The engine scream and the wind roar and the boom of the speed boards as the planes, one after the other, flashed low over the field to climb to pattern altitude let everybody know this by God was a fighter base and three pilots had just returned from combat.

The wingtips of each plane trailed gossamer threads of white from the vortices created by the wracking turns in the humid air. The vortices faded quickly, to be replaced by white puffs of smoke when rubber met runway, as each pilot set his plane down on the same place as the man landing in front of him. Each man pulled his handle at the same spot, deploying his drag chute to billow and spin white behind him as he rolled down the runway, decelerating rapidly. After turn-off they aligned perfectly with each other in the de-arming area. Upon unspoken agreement, Two and Three opened their canopies at the exact moment their leader opened his. The de-arming crew looked at each other; this was one sharp flight.

After de-arm, Court Bannister taxied with his hands and forearms resting on the rails beneath the open canopy. He had loosened his mask so that it hung to one side of his helmet. The melancholy strains of "Yesterday" came over his earphones from the AFVN station he had tuned in on his ADF. He waved to the company of troops from the 173rd, their faces so young, who sat on the brown sunburned grass bordering the taxiway to await airlift to a remote jungle battle zone. They waved back and stared at the jeep trailing smoke leading Court to his parking place.

This can't be it. This can't be the end, he thought as he taxied behind the jeep. There has to be more. They can't expect a man to live 365 intense days, flying combat with some of the best men ever made, then expect him suddenly to pack up and go home. It's all over for you, many thanks, see you next time. No, that couldn't be the way it was supposed to be. There has to be a period of . . . of transition, or change, or something. Christ, he wasn't ready for decent society. Just look, everything was yellowed about him. His fingers were stained yellow from his Luckies. He had no clothes that weren't yellow and worn from too many pounding coldwater naphtha-soap washings. Even his skin was tight and yellowish. Hell, he bet his teeth were yellow, too.

Maybe something was wrong with him, he thought. He'd seen all the others, they had seemed happy enough to be going home. So why wasn't he? Now that he thought about it, he did recollect seeing a certain something, was it mist or nostalgia, in the eyes of those who had flown their last mission. Was that what he was feeling? Whimpering nostalgia?

Nuts, he hadn't even left yet, so how could that be it? Was that how he looked now to an outsider? Did he have that odd look in his eyes, too? Just what *did* he look like, he wondered. For months he hadn't looked in a mirror except to shave. Had someone told him, he would know his eyes were now cold and hard. But no one told him because they all looked that way, the combat fliers, and no one could see anything different about themselves. Nor did they know they were more cold and hard inside than when they had arrived young and eager a year earlier. The faint image of the eleven VC he had napalmed appeared for an instant, then faded.

He came out of his reverie when he became aware the jeep had led him to the revetment. He saw the group of squadron pilots he didn't really know waiting for him. All his buddies had either gone home, or were dead. Jack Laird, Joe Howard, Fairchild, Freeman, had gone home. Phil Travers was dead. Ron Bender was missing in action. Bob Derham was in Command and Staff, Colonel Jake Friedlander, whose name had just come out on the new BG list, was at TAC headquarters. Baby Huey was back at Brooks for some refresher training. Even Ramrod the snake was long missing. He didn't even know the wing men he had just flown with, except that they were two fine pilots. The only person he really knew in the squadron now was Bob Putney, his replacement, and Colonel Frank Darlington, who had replaced Jake Friedlander as wing commander.

He pulled up and tapped the toe brakes lightly to bob the scoop-shovel nose of his fighter as a salute to those waiting. The crew chief positioned the ladder and ran up to help Court unstrap and climb out.

Corks popped and champagne spewed. The pilots applauded and cheered and rubbed it in his hair, then gave him the bottle to drink. Court was pleased at the reception by these new guys. How times had changed from that day one year ago when he had first walked as a new guy, stiff and aloof, into the 531st.

Court Bannister didn't realize it, but he had become a well-known and respected fighter pilot. His exploits in F-100's and F-105's and F-4's to help set up the fast-FAC program were considered top staff work done under formidable conditions. His MiG encounters with Frederick were legendary. Now it was only incidental that he was the son of a famous movie actor.

Colonel Frank Darlington got out of his jeep and walked up to the crowd of pilots, who made way for him as he went straight to Bannister. He had a stern look on his face and some official-looking papers in his hand. Court looked at him, surprised he wasn't smiling.

"Bannister," Darlington snapped, "do you know the minimum altitude for a flyby?"

Court furiously searched his memory. It occurred to him he hadn't the faintest idea if there even was a regulation or Standard Operating Procedure on the subject. The other pilots stood still, looking at one another. It was plain they didn't know either.

"No, sir, I don't know," he replied.

"What was your altitude and airspeed on your first pass?" Darlington asked, as stern as before.

"Two hundred feet and 530 knots, sir," Court answered.

"Gentlemen," the Colonel said, turning to the crowd, "you all heard that." His face broke into a broad grin. "From now on, no one will perform a flyby at less than 200 feet or more than 530 knots. As of now, that is the newest; and, I might add, *only*, SOP on the subject of flybys."

It took a second for the news to dawn on Court and the crowd that he wasn't really on the carpet. Another bottle of champagne magically appeared. The colonel was given the first drink. He took a swig and handled the bottle to Court. Flashbulbs went off when he tilted the bottle up, while many pilots took pictures of the man with whom, they knew instinctively, they someday would want to say they had flown with.

The colonel assumed an expression more stern than before. He peered at the sewn black stripes denoting captain on each of Bannister's shoulders. He shook his head in mock sorrow. The crowd grew silent again. Now what?

"It is my sad duty to inform you that you are out of uniform, *Major* Bannister."

30

☆

Shawn Bannister sat at a wrought-iron table on the covered terrace of the Continental Palace Hotel overlooking the traffic bustling back and forth across Freedom Square and around the fountain. A haze of exhaust smoke reached almost to the level of the heavy concrete railing surrounding the terrace. Shawn, wearing aviator's sunglasses, was dressed in his trademark khaki safari suit with wide cargo pockets. His shirt lay open to the navel, exposing the many gold chains he wore around his neck. One of the chains supported a little gold alligator. He had sent an identical one to his father. He hummed happily to himself as he reflected on his life in the Vietnam combat zone. To help him reflect, he smoked a joint of Thai Buddha weed—killer stuff, he thought. He finished the joint using his roach clip—the gold alligator.

He recounted his assets. He had several girls—Oriental and Caucasian, American and foreign—on the string for romp and randy at just about any time of the day he cared to indulge. He had an unlimited supply of dope from his good friend Bubba Bates. (For an airline employee, Bates seemed to have an excess of money that he spent on lavish parties.) He had journalist cronies who doted on his every word.

Best of all, his article "Pandemonium Prevents Rescue" had been picked up by the wire services and trumpeted in the liberal journals and magazines. In it, he recounted his experience with a maniac USAF fighter pilot—his own brother, no less—who, in concert with a madman armor officer, conspired to blow away civilian buses and their passengers one fine day along Route 13. The *California Sun* touted the story as the real truth about murderous American interference in Vietnam's civil war. Despite being shown photos to the contrary by Court, Shawn had long ago decided to write the article as a "composition" of what probably happened every day throughout Vietnam.

Shawn Bannister was now a *correspondent célèbre* from Berkeley to Paris—he was also selling photographs with limited text to *Paris Match,* a French magazine that wasn't about to let up on the upstarts who thought they could accomplish in Indochina what *la belle France* could not. Not that he needed the money. The hundreds of thousands settled in trusts and municipals provided by his parents yielded a tidy monthly income.

With one exception, war photographer Shawn Bannister wasn't bothered by the fact that all the pictures he took in Saigon were of drunken G.I.'s and whorish bar girls. The exception was the one he had taken of a suspected VC hanging by his ankles while the ugliest cook of the Mike Force Nungs waved a knife under his nose. The suspect had been found with three cartridges in his pocket near a civilian hospital that had just come under sniper fire. The Nungs, under command of an American, were doing their best to scare the truth out of the upside-down man when Shawn asked if he could take a picture of the scene . . . for his private collection, he had promised. Well, hell, the sergeant thought, Sam Bannister is an okay stud, so his son must be too. Sure, go ahead.

As soon as the picture was processed, Shawn had sold it to a wire service, from which it had been picked up in all its glossy eight-by-ten glory by most major newspapers in the U.S. for their front pages. That ensured that the American, Sergeant First Class Johnson, would never make it to master sergeant; in fact, he narrowly escaped a court-martial over the affair.

That Shawn was even on the one-hour operation was because the trusting Special Forces Sergeant Johnson had met the famous actor's son in the Butterfly Bar on Tu Do a few nights before and had actually agreed to take him out on a close-in patrol. After that incident, Shawn had decided that it would be in his best interests to avoid the Butterfly for a while.

Shawn looked out over the street and saw a staff car he figured was carrying his godfather. He quickly licked his fingers and killed the roach, then pocketed it and stood up and waved a casual hello to his godfather, Albert Whisenand. Whitey wore a short-sleeved white shirt, dark slacks, and a broad grin as he walked up and shook hands.

"Shawn, it's good to see you." He stepped back to look at his godson. "You look tanned and healthy. Tell me, are you eating well? You don't forget to take your malaria pills, do you? What about your shots, are they up to date?"

"Whoa, Uncle Albert. I'm fine. Really I am." They sat across from each other, careful to position themselves to see the street.

"Your dad would be very angry if I didn't ask those questions," Whitey said with a smile. He leaned forward as the smell of burning rope assailed his nostrils. He raised his eyebrows at Shawn, who raised his own eyebrows at Whitey.

"Dad knows," he said, "so no lectures. Okay?"

"No, no lectures." Whitey sighed. "Actually, I'm pleased you look so good. You must be doing something right." He regarded Shawn's perfect teeth, firm jaw, and bold eyes. My God, he said to himself, this was Sam twenty-five years ago in all his swashbuckling glory.

They passed a few minutes catching up and talking about how Sam was doing in Las Vegas. Whitey said he'd seen him in Washington shortly before he left for Vietnam.

"Shawn, your father asked me specifically to ask you about your plans. How long will you remain in Vietnam? If you leave, where will you go? Back to France?"

Shawn leaned back and made a snorting sound. "I'm never going to leave here. I, ah, have a lot going besides the magazine. I'm not about to peel out." He looked at his watch.

"Listen, Uncle Albert, it's nearly time for the Five O'Clock Follies at JUSPAO. You know, that's the Joint U.S. Public Affairs Office, where the embassy and the military gives us journalists daily briefings on how they want us to think the war is going. I usually go to it. Mostly they're howlers. It's just up Le Loi, about a five-minute walk from here."

Whitey told the airman driver to have a couple of Cokes on him over at the PX snack bar and to pick him up at JUSPAO in an hour. The driver smiled, and politely refused Whitey's offer of a script dollar. Once the general was out of sight, he planned on a beer or two at Mimi's Bar on Nguyen Hue just down from JUSPAO.

Shawn and Whitey walked up Le Loi, threading their way around the black-market goods spread out nearly to the gutter, on sidewalks that had been tiled in the best French fashion but were now chipped and stained. The vendors, mainly women dressed in thin black trousers and white blouses, squatted on mats next to their wares, patiently waiting for the sales they knew would come.

Twice the two Americans were approached by little boys who asked them if they wanted to make boom-boom with their virgin sisters for 200 P. From the street came smoozy castor oil exhaust fumes and raucous taxi and cyclo horns, sad adjuncts to a city that once was rightly called the Pearl of the Orient. Saigon had become the classic example of abandoned courtesan reduced to abuse in the hands of the lower caste.

Suddenly, in front of them, a black Mercedes 240D came screeching around the corner. Behind it were two Army sedans that quickly bracketed the Mercedes and forced it to a halt by driving into each side of the front fenders. The Mercedes driver tried to wiggle out the window of the jammed driver's door but was caught by three beefy Caucasians in civilian dress who jumped from the sedans. Whitey recognized them as having been on the plane from Andrews. One had been in the uniform of an Army sergeant major.

Hey, I know that guy, Shawn thought, looking at the struggling man from the Mercedes. It's Bubba Bates. He fingered the roach in his pocket. Damn, he thought to himself, there goes my supplier.

A jeep with MP markings pulled up behind the three cars. From the back stepped a tall, sparse Army brigadier general.

I know him too, Shawn thought. He's the provost marshall for MACV.

The general walked up to the men holding Bates.

"Good job, men," he said. "We've finally caught this God-rotted smuggler. Take him to the Long Binh stockade."

The excitement over, Whitey and Shawn walked on, Whitey lost in his reflections about the underlying problems in the war zone; Shawn wondering where his next civilized connection would come from. He disliked buying his stuff from street urchins. It was of terrible quality.

An hour later their driver met them at the door of the JUSPAO building and drove them to the Caravelle Hotel. He exuded just the faintest odor of beer. Whitey told him he had an hour to get a Coke before they had to leave for Tan Son Nhut. Then he took his godson to a place he hadn't seen in years, the Champs-Élysées Restaurant on the Caravelle's rooftop terrace on the ninth floor. From up there they had a panoramic view of Saigon and the environs.

"Uncle Albert, do you mind if I light up?" Shawn said, after they seated themselves. Shawn took a joint from his pouch.

Whitey eyed his godchild. "If you mean marijuana, yes, I do. Very much."

"Well, you've just ordered a scotch, so what's the diff?"

"It's illegal. That's the difference." He ordered Shawn a beer.

From their table at the edge of the terrace, they watched the war outside the city. Streams of slowly rising and falling green and red tracers duelling each other gracefully arced to and from ground positions. The approaching night softened the sharp outlines of the city beneath them, so that Whitey felt as if they were on a tall ship watching a naval battle on a far wave. Soon, Spooky arrived to lick the earth with its fiery tongue, and the green tracers stopped. Behind them, from the dance floor on the terrace, there was shrill gaiety and shrieks of laughter. A Filipino band wailed about the "Gleen, Gleen Glass of Home."

Whitey thought about the scene earlier that day at the embassy. He had paid a visit to the ambassador, who had pointedly questioned him about what proposals he was going to make to the President.

Whitey had told him they were classified, then held up his hand in response to the reddening of the ambassador's face. "In truth, sir, I have a jumble of ideas that are not fully thought out, much less in a presentable form. What I can say is this: Our Air Force and Navy air crew members are going up against air defenses in many areas worse than anything mounted in World War Two. In spite of heavy losses, they go out day after day in a display of courage and professionalism seldom equaled, never bettered."

While the ambassador nodded in agreement with Whitey's dramatic observations, his eyes appeared puzzled, as if he were wondering just what the Air Force general's point was. He didn't wonder long.

"What I haven't deciphered yet, Mr. Ambassador," Whitey said quietly, "is to what purpose these men are being sent into that inferno."

Whitey wondered the same thing again now as he watched the evening fall and listened to the revelry from the rooftop.

"It's not the same, Shawn," Whitey said.

"What isn't?"

"The war. I was in London in the early forties when the blitz was on. You could watch ack-ack and tracers, and searchlights, and the high flames of fires started somewhere in the city. It was not a graceful thing to see. But the people were; they were graceful. Here"— Whitey stared out over the rail, his voice thick—"here, God help us, it's just the opposite."

Shawn had no comment. Whitey fell silent. He wondered if the ambassador would cable his remark back to State and, if so, if State would pass it on to the President. He surprised himself by realizing he didn't care. He shifted in his chair on the balcony.

By the end of the hour, the two men, godfather and godson, were lost in their own thoughts. Shawn had tossed off several beers. He wanted to get away and light up, but was afraid of what Uncle Albert would tell his father if he forced a departure. Whitey stared morosely over the rail at the night battles while he sipped the worst scotch he had ever tasted. Finally, they took the elevator to the lobby.

The buck sergeant met them and ushered the general to the car. Shawn, suddenly feeling his beer and his independence, stopped his godfather at the car by grabbing his arm.

"Uncle Albert," he said, "tell me, when are all you military bastards going to get the hell out of Vietnam and leave it in peace?"

Whitey narrowed his eyes. He disengaged his arm. "Goodnight, Shawn, and goodbye," he said in a voice like a file on steel. He climbed into the car without shaking hands. The sergeant closed the door for him. As the sergeant backed away, he spun around and grabbed Shawn by his lapels.

"Listen, you little weasel, you'd better stay the hell out of my sight, because the next time I see you I'm going to beat the living crud out of you. You're the one who better get the hell out of Vietnam and leave us in peace." The buck sergeant got into the car and started the engine. He smelled as much of beer as Shawn did.

"Sorry, general," he said. "Guess I pure got carried away. That wasn't anybody important, was it?"

Whitey still didn't have an answer to that question when the driver dropped him off at his trailer.

Washington was cold and rainy when the SAM flight brought Whitey home. He stared down through the dark mist at the red and white bands of taillights and headlights as the evening traffic streamed along the Washington, D.C., Beltway. He knew he would have to have a long talk with Sal about retiring from the Air Force.

31

☆

Wolf Lochert sat with Al Charles in the MACSOG lounge, drinking Bamuiba.

"No, Al, regardless of what you say, I blew it. I don't know why, but I blew it." The Wolf's body looked ravished and twenty pounds lighter. His right wrist was tightly bandaged and in a sling. His tan was long faded and his skin was pallid and wrinkled. His eyes flicked at the slightest sound and his mouth twitched.

Al Charles looked at him with great compassion in his black eyes. "Ah, Wolf, take it easy. You said yourself that pilot was already dead. Menuez and the others could have been greased anyplace. You got back alive."

"Hah," Wolf barked. "Not without Buey Dan. He saved my life. I passed out, he broke the ambush and called the Hornets in to get us extracted. I owe him a lot. Lost my lucky knife, though."

"Wolf," Al Charles said, his mahogany face crinkled in thought, "you have any, ah, misgivings about that guy?"

"Misgivings? What do you mean?"

"Well, I mean, do you completely trust him? He used to be Viet Minh at one time, you know."

"Yeah, I know that. He converted a long time ago. He's Catholic, you know. We're going to Christmas Mass together next Sunday at the cathedral on JFK Square. Says he wants to show me something."

"Wolf, I'm afraid you won't make that mass."

"No? How's that?"

Charles dug into a folder at the side of his chair. "I got a TWX message from the Department of the Army. You're to report to some general in the Pentagon. It's maybe kind of a highly classified rescue-planning group. According to this, they want a first-hand account of your story. I've got you a seat on a MAC flight to L.A. You leave Friday morning, the twenty-third." He stood up. "Oh yeah, one more thing." He flipped to Wolf a small piece of blue cardboard with two silver oak leaves pinned to it.

"Merry Christmas, colonel."

0745 HOURS LOCAL, 23 DECEMBER 1966
CAMP ALPHA PROCESSING CENTER,
TAN SON NHUT AIR BASE, REPUBLIC OF VIETNAM

☆

Camp Alpha more resembled a dusty Texas feedlot than a processing center for G.I.'s bound for the U.S. Hundreds of homebound soldiers, carefully separated from those just coming into Vietnam, milled around the fenced enclosure—as if anybody would want to escape. A drooping green Christmas garland with splotchy needles hung over the Camp Alpha sign like a tired fat snake with hives. Scratchy Christmas music from a far-off transistor clashed with the heat and dust.

Most of the men, about 80 percent, were dressed in clean, well-tailored and beautifully fitting uniforms, with all their brass and stripes and Vietnam war campaign ribbons carefully fastened exactly in place. Their faces and boots were clean and shiny, their suntans dark and even, and their haircuts a beautiful sight to behold. Their eyes were relaxed and happy.

In wretched contrast were the remaining men. They wore ill-fitting uniforms that were too large—because the wearer had sweated off so many pounds in the jungle—and creased, from resting a year at the bottom of a duffel bag. Some khakis were stained with mold. Most of the men's suntans were abominable. Their foreheads were a sickly white, and their skin looked soggy and ragged, as if they had recently suffered severe cases of rash and pustules. Somehow, these men looked older than the others, whom they regarded with wary and slitted eyes.

There were a few officers with this ragged bunch. One of them, a fierce-looking lieutenant colonel, scowled at a broad-shouldered, stocky master sergeant whose face resembled a map of Ireland after somebody had wiped his cleated logger's boots on it. They both squatted, Vietnamese peasant–style, with their backs against a wall.

The lieutenant colonel, in fact, was not scowling at the master sergeant. Wolf Lochert's wan face was actually framed in a smile, his first in weeks. Jim Mahoney was relating his tale of how he and a few of his green beanie buddies had cleaned out a whole bar full of REMFs the night before. Both men knew that REMFs were worse than Saigon Commandos, who were mostly postal and admin clerks. A REMF was a rear-echelon motherfucker who fiddled with war plans but never visited the battlefield. A REMF could be officer or enlisted, civilian or military.

The REMF contingent Mahoney and crew had cleaned up on were civilians hanging out at Mimi's Bar on Nguyen Hue. Mahoney said he thought the civilians were some State Department guys. At any rate, they had been put out when Mahoney shot their toilet to ceramic bits. Mahoney had tried to explain to them he needed a bullet hole in his trousers and thought this was a quiet way to do it. He certainly didn't want to hose off a round outside. Besides, he thought the water would just, um, *cushion* the bullet. He needed the bullet hole in his trousers to match a hole in his leg that he got when— "I'll tell you the rest on the airplane, Wolf." He pointed toward the door. "Look who just walked in."

Court Bannister spotted the two Special Forces officers lounging against the wall. He was appalled at how thin they looked when they stood up to greet him.

"Hey, Captain Bannister," Mahoney said in his usual breezy voice, "who'd you swipe those major's leaves from?"

"The same guy you swiped that extra stripe from, Master Sergeant Mahoney." He shook hands with him and turned to Wolf. "Congratulations, Lieutenant Colonel Lochert, you look great under those things."

"Yah," the Wolf growled, "you don't look so bad yourself, major. Kind of thin, though." He examined the gold leaves on Court's collar and felt the material of his uniform with two fingers. "Fancy stuff," he said.

Only mildly embarrassed that his tailored 1505's were of a finely woven silver-tone material, Court said, "You bet it's fancy. Our hootch maid had a cousin whose uncle made them for us. Cost twenty bucks."

"What plane you on, major?" Mahoney asked. Court noted the sergeant called Wolf by his first name, but still referred to him by his rank. They examined each other's papers. They were all on the same American Airlines flight due to take off in thirty minutes. Before Court could ask Mahoney what had happened to his face, a commotion by the door attracted their attention.

"Lieutenant," a harried-looking MAC sergeant was saying to an Air Force officer in a rumpled uniform who stood feet apart and swaying, "if you don't throw that bottle away, I'm not going to let you get on the airplane. If you give me a hard time about it, I'll get the Military Police over here."

"At ease, sergeant," the lieutenant said, "it's a flask, not a bottle. Here, have a drink." He held out a small, silver hip flask to the sergeant, who waved it away. With a look of disgust plainly visible on his face, the sergeant started toward the pair of military policemen standing by the processing counter.

"Well," Wolf Lochert said as they observed the scene, "I guess we'd better go straighten up one each Toby Parker before he really steps in it. Mahoney, stop that sergeant before he gets the MP's. Tell him we'll take care of this."

Court and the Wolf eased up on either side of Toby Parker and took his elbows. Court took his flask.

"Hey," Parker yelped. He swung his head back and forth. His eyes were bloodshot and his fingernails were dirty and ragged. He didn't wear a nametag or any of the decorations Court knew he had earned. A piece of jade hung from a chain around his neck. He recognized Court and Wolf and smiled at them with breath evidencing a week's debauchery in Saigon. "Well doggone, if it isn't old home week. . . ." He stopped and looked suddenly vague. His eyes started to roll up. "Grab him," Wolf said as Parker's knees began to buckle. They put their arms around his waist and, without letting him sag and draw attention, supported him into the latrine. Court glanced at Wolf. His expression was as tender as a father's with a baby. Mahoney had maneuvered the MAC sergeant around so he didn't see the sodden man being dragged away.

When it came time to get on the airliner, they had straightened Parker up enough so he was able to hand over his boarding pass without incident. They pushed him all the way to the rear and settled him in a corner seat next to the window before covering him with a blanket. Wolf sat next to him, and Court and Mahoney took the two seats in front and buckled in. Parker fell asleep. When the big jet broke ground, the G.I.'s cheered and stomped their feet. A few extra quiet ones only stared at the ground they were leaving behind.

Court thought about Nancy Lewis and how disappointed they

were that he wasn't scheduled back to the States on a Braniff flight. They had written each other a few times since Clark, but the words hadn't been right.

He lit a Lucky, put his head back against the seat rest, and watched the stewardesses pass out frozen washcloths to the grateful G.I.'s. One of the girls got on the PA, wished them the merriest of Christmases, and welcomed them on behalf of American Airlines MAC Contract Flight A6T7 to the first leg of their flight to Los Angeles, California.

"We have a surprise for you," she said. The men looked up in anticipation. "Here it is, direct from the Unites States. Ta da . . . fresh milk." Two other girls brought out the ice chests filled with milk cartons they had carefully lugged around and kept cool for the five days since they had left the States.

It wasn't airline milk. The girls themselves had bought both the milk and the ice chests after a few trips during which they'd heard that the thing most sought after once the returning G.I.'s were on the plane was not an alcoholic drink, which was illegal on board anyhow, but fresh whole milk. The Braniff girls had started the custom. As they spoke of the G.I.s' love of milk, the custom spread throughout the MAC contract system.

The men—boys, really—went wild at the prospect of downing a tall, cool glass of fresh milk made in the U.S.A. Some actually had tears in their eyes as they had their first taste of real American milk in over a year. Oh, the memories it brought flooding back to them: Mom, home, fresh-mown grass. Every stewardess, even though she said she was used to it and swore it wouldn't happen again, felt hot tears spring to her eyes as she saw the incredible joy such a simple American product brought to these young warriors.

Wolf took two. Jim Mahoney was asleep. Court gave his to a G.I. across the aisle and wished he had a beer. He stubbed out his cigarette and fell asleep. One of the girls tucked a blanket around him. She stood looking at him for a long minute.

By Guam, Parker was sober and coherent. Wolf had insisted he drink the two milks and a lot of coffee heavy with sugar. At Hickham in the latrine at the MAC terminal, Parker stripped off his shirt and took a French bath in the basin. Next to him, in a row, were Lochert, Bannister, and Mahoney, with their shirts around their waists, shaving. Mahoney was explaining the cuts and bruises on his face.

"—so when they realized I had just shot the only real American toilet south of the embassy, that's when it all started. Imagine, those REMF's don't like those French bombsight johns."

"Yeah, but I don't understand why you had to put a bullet hole in your pants," Court said.

"Simple. It had to match the one in my leg. You see, when I got shot, I had on civvies."

"What in hell does *that* explain?" the Wolf grumbled.

"I thought you knew. If you're gonna be WIA, you got to be in uniform. Those were my tiger suit fatigues I shot up. When the holes matched, I went to the Third Field Hospital on Tan Son Nhut and got patched up. See." He dropped his trousers and showed them a bandage with dried blood taped to his thigh. "Only a flesh wound," Mahoney said, "but you're not authorized even a flesh wound on Tu Do, especially when you kill somebody."

"Kill somebody? Mahoney," Wolf rumbled at him, "if you don't explain what in hell you're talking about, I'm going to rip your damn leg OFF and beat you over the head with it."

"I'm trying to explain. Some Saigon cowboy groped me and I backhanded him silly. A few minutes later he came roaring by on a Honda and took a shot at me. This was on that side street behind the Sporting Bar. He hit me in the leg, so I plugged him. You know how bad the paperwork would be on that. So I had to rig something before showing up at the hospital to get it patched. I told 'em I took a sniper round along the Bien Hoa–Saigon Highway and fell down and scratched my face." Mahoney laughed. "Oh yeah, let me show you something." He dug into his pocket and pulled out a Purple Heart medal. "I was laying in the ward with the rest of the guys about to be med-evaced, just resting up from my hangover, when some general comes through and pins these to our pillows. 'God bless you, son,' he said to everybody."

1330 HOURS LOCAL, 23 DECEMBER 1966
AMERICAN AIRLINES 707 EN ROUTE TO
LOS ANGELES INTERNATIONAL AIRPORT, CALIFORNIA

☆

They slept most of the way on the final leg. Court had tried to finish *Le Mal jaune* but couldn't concentrate. He had figured out the French had offered Vietnam concubinage instead of marriage, and that hypocrisy was rampant in metropolitan France. He still didn't see how it tied to the United States' position of offering Vietnam freedom from Communism.

Toby and Wolf talked about the Green Hornet helicopter extraction from Laos.

"I'm telling you, Parker," the Wolf said, "you got to stop this finding-me-in-the-jungle routine. You're spoiling my reputation. It's undignified."

"Yeah, right," Parker said. "Say, Wolf, that Viet you were with . . . the one you said saved your life in the ambush."

"Yeah, what about him?"

"He picked up a knife or something just before we got you on the helicopter."

Wolf Lochert looked at Toby with narrowed eyes. "Hah," he barked, and turned to look out the window.

"Gentlemen," a stewardess said over the PA as they flew over the California coastline, "let me welcome you back to the good old U.S.A." Her voice was husky and warm as the sun. She was a tall, leggy girl with that special look of confidence worn only by the ones who live on the beach.

The men cheered and looked out at the incredible expanse of sprawling Los Angeles, slightly fuzzed by smog, that was their first sight of the U.S. in a year.

The beach girl came back to talk to Court.

"Hi, I'm Susan Boyle. I know who you are." She held out her hand for Court to shake, and sat on his seat's armrest. Court felt the warmth of her on his face. "I wondered what happened to you. I saw those beach movies, and the Westerns, and the one where you were a Winsockie cadet. They were a lot of fun to watch."

"They were a lot of fun to make," he said. He liked her directness. She wore her long sun-bleached hair in the regulation bun. He could imagine how it would look flowing down her tanned, sleek back as she lay in the sun on the beach. She had warm brown eyes that crinkled and promised fun when she smiled, which was often. She had taut impressive breasts, and as she sat close, he smelled her musky-sweaty scent, and became instantly and wildly aroused. He was glad there was a blanket on his lap. She eyed his wings and ribbons, and the new major's leaves on his collars.

"You married?" she asked.

"Not any more," he replied.

"I like your eyes. Sort of a strange marble-y blue, aren't they?" Susan Boyle looked directly and boldly into his eyes. "I would like to eat hamburgers, and drink beer with you at Donkins some day," she said, naming a popular Marina del Rey bar and restaurant.

"I'd like that," he said.

She handed him a folded piece of paper. "Please call me."

"I will. I'd like to drink beer with you at Donkins."

"And eat hamburgers."

"Yes, and eat hamburgers."

"One thing," she said, "I remember your face and marvelous body very well from the movies, but for the life of me"—she threw her head back and gave a throaty laugh—"I can't remember your name."

All the passengers were wide-eyed and ready when the airliner was on final for Runway 25 left at Los Angeles International. The approach had been long and curved as the airliner descended east and then turned back over the city, coming in over Downey and Watts. The soldiers could see the Forum and Hollywood Park off the right wing. The plane settled lower and lower as the pilot worked the controls. Soon they could see the automobile traffic clearly as their flight path paralleled Century Boulevard. The plane continued down until they could see the license plates on the cars flowing north and south on the San Diego Freeway, and then they were on the ground. They all cheered, many through tears. They had survived, and they had come home.

Getting their luggage was such a fouled-up mess that the four men decided to hit the bar on the top floor overlooking the airport and retrieve their bags later. The bar was festooned with tinsel and shining silver stars.

What the hell, they decided. This was a celebration, so they ordered champagne cocktails all around. So what if it was only ten in the morning? This was an occasion. The bartender served them with practiced skill, and they touched their wide glasses together and laughed and drank.

The Wolf made a face. "This is awful," he rumbled, "tastes like angel piss." He turned to the bartender. "Gimme a double JD, straight. NOW." The bartender jumped to obey.

Court and Mahoney switched to beer. Toby Parker decided to try California white wine. He expertly lit a cigarette and inhaled deeply.

Their laughter and banter died away as each became lost in his own thoughts about where they had been and what they were coming back to. It wasn't as if they were expecting a band or anything like that, but a small welcoming committee of one or two would have been nice.

"So it's off to test pilot school for you, Bannister, and pilot training for you, Parker," Wolf Lochert said, finally breaking the silence. Court nodded, relieved to stop the onset of what seemed to be not exactly a bad mood, such as anger might cause, but rather a feeling of dejection caused by lonesomeness, disappointment or . . . he didn't know what.

They talked about the two schools. Court's test pilot school was at Edwards Air Force Base, beyond the mountains north of Los Angeles. Toby was to report in for pilot training at Randolph Air Force Base outside San Antonio. Both men had three weeks' leave before they had to report for duty. Lochert had a few days for Christmas, then had to report to Washington for the rescue planning conference. Mahoney had a flight connection from L.A. to Florida to spend Christmas with his brother.

They were in the middle of their third round when the Wolf slapped Bannister on the back. "Listen," he said, cocking his head. They all listened.

". . . pick up the white courtesy phone. Will Mr. Courtland Bannister please pick up the white courtesy phone. You have a message."

Court found the nearest phone. "Hello," he said, wondering what it was all about.

"Hi, Mr. Bannister?" said a light and vaguely familiar male voice.

"Yes, this is Major Bannister."

"My God, a major yet. Congratulations. This is Terry Holt." Terry Holt was an actor from his dad's old days who never could act, but had become Sam Bannister's shrewd and valued business manager. He was bouncy and never seemed to age.

"Terry Holt," Court said. "What a coincidence. What are you doing here?"

"It's no coincidence, Major Bannister. Mr. Bannister sent me over with the Lear to pick you up. We had to hold over San Bernardino, otherwise I'd have met your plane. I've got the studio limo at the American arrival door. Tell me where you are, and I'll come get you. Your Dad has a big welcome-home and Christmas bash planned for you in Vegas; girls, orchestras, the works."

Court explained he was about to get his luggage, and would meet him at the limo.

As Court walked back to the bar he looked at his three companions. The grinning and irrepressible Jim Mahoney was obviously telling another of his wild war stories, which were invariably humorous and gory at the same time. Grizzled Wolf Lochert listened, with wary eyes searching incessantly for ambushing Viet Cong. Toby Parker, looking young and sleepy now, struggled to follow Mahoney's meandering tale.

On Court's urging, Toby had pulled shiny new ribbons from his kit and put them on in the latrine at Hickham. The Air Force Cross, next to the Purple Heart, was authoritative and new. Court felt a wave of affection for these men. If only Jack Laird and Doc Russell were here, along with Ron Bender and even Ted Frederick. God, they'd have a good time. It would go on forever, he'd see to that. He stood still for another minute, then made up his mind.

"Come on guys, you're coming to Las Vegas with me. My Dad's got a plane waiting, and a big blowout ready when we get there, so let's get a move on."

The three men sat in surprised silence at such an expansive offer, until they suddenly remembered that their pal was the son of a rich and famous man; a man who could send out a private jet to bring his warrior son to a party. Somehow, it was hard to reconcile that a combat veteran actually came from a famous family. "Silk Screen Sam, the ladies' man. If he can't get in, no one can." Court saw all of this in their eyes, and he waited.

Wolf Lochert broke the silence. "Let's hump," he said, with a smile and a nod. "Sounds great," said Parker. Mahoney reluctantly said he had to see his brother and might come out later. But the tension had been broken, as each man reminded himself that this wasn't Sam Bannister's son, this was Major Court Bannister, shit-hot fighter pilot and Vietnam veteran. They splashed down their drinks with noisy vows of eternal friendship and split for the baggage room. The bartender shook his head as he mopped up after them.

The four thin and hardened combat veterans, hats and berets cocked proudly, strode line abreast down the wide hall to the baggage carousels. They made an impressive sight in their khakis, resplendent with badges and ribbons, trousers bloused on the Special Forces men. The civilians in the terminal smiled as they passed, and thought how handsome they looked.

Nobody saw the girls in granny dresses and beads or the long-haired boys in sandals and torn pants along the wall where the passageway opened to the luggage concourse. They wore MERRY HASHMESS headbands. One of the boys had an American flag sewn to the seat of his pants.

They watched and waited, and suddenly dashed forward and splashed a red liquid at the four men, screaming all the while, "PIGS! PIGS! BABY KILLERS! MURDERERS!" One girl, with limp yellow flowers in her hair and dirty bare feet, dashed up to Lieutenant Colonel Wolf Lochert.

"Murderer," she screeched, and spat in his face.

Instantly there was a tableau. Nobody moved. The girl saw a flicker in the Wolf's eyes that chilled her almost beyond reason. Her companions poised themselves to flee. Both Mahoney and Bannister moved to restrain Wolf from doing what they knew he was about to do. Still the Wolf stood there without moving; a glaring man with spittle running down his cheek. A jaw muscle jerked. Then with articulate dignity, he thundered, "I AM NOT A *MURDERER,* YOUNG LADY, I AM A *KILLER.* THERE *IS* A DIFFERENCE."

1545 HOURS LOCAL, 23 DECEMBER 1966
LEAR JET EN ROUTE FROM LOS ANGELES
TO LAS VEGAS, NEVADA

☆

Mahoney had separated from the three and caught his flight to Florida. Later, in the Lear Jet over the desert, Terry Holt was still badly shaken by what he had witnessed earlier at the airport. The scene with the hippies had been bad enough at the time it was happening, but this delayed reaction he was feeling now was worse, much worse. He was so insulated in Las Vegas; everybody was. They didn't hear about protesters, or much about the war, for that matter. And that gruff Colonel Lochert; Terry Holt stared at him with fascination. In Las Vegas he had seen his share of hard men who had earned their bones, but none of them had piercing, blazing eyes like this colonel. They looked as if they could burn through a wall at fifty feet.

After takeoff, the men had removed their uniforms stained with red dye and changed into what they could find in their luggage. Parker and Bannister had on T-shirts and Bermudas. Lochert picked out the cleanest fatigues he could find.

Terry had fixed them tall glasses, dark with scotch. In an effort to be of service he had handed them the first stateside newspapers they had seen in a year. Now, selected portions of the paper were spread over the floor of the plush jet as the three men studied them from their chairs.

Page one of the *Los Angeles Times* had a full shot of a bent-over man identified by the Democratic Republic of Vietnam as Air Force Major Ronald Bender. His flight suit was torn to his waist; his head, wrapped in drooping bandages, hung so low his chin touched his chest. His arms were twisted behind him in such a manner they had to be bound together past his elbows. A tiny girl wearing a pith helmet pointed an SKS rifle with bayonet at the barefoot pilot. She held it so awkwardly, with both hands palms down on the barrel and stock, it was obvious she had never seen one before.

The accompanying story quoted Hanoi's *Nhan Dan* newspaper as saying that Major Bender was now a criminal being held in Hanoi. If he confessed his crimes against humanity, he would receive the lenient treatment given by Ho Chi Minh to all who confessed and were truly repentant of their sins.

Other stories glared out from the papers.

SIX PLANES LOST IN HANOI-HAIPHONG RAID

Saigon—One of the heaviest attacks of the war against the Thai Nguyen steel mill complex cost the U.S. at least six warplanes, military headquarters announced Tuesday.

AIR FORCE PILOT STRAFES SOVIET TRAWLER
ONE KILLED; SOVIETS PROTEST

Moscow—The Soviet Union has alleged that an American F-105 strafed and badly damaged the cargo ship *Turkestan* in the North Vietnamese port of Cam Hoa, 50 miles north of Haiphong. Two crew members were badly wounded, one was killed in the unprovoked attack.

OFFICIAL RELEASES NAME OF PILOT WHO
KILLED RUSSIAN SAILOR

Washington—A congressional source who prefers to remain anonymous today released the name of Major Ted Frederick as the pilot said to be responsible for the strafing of the cargo ship *Turkestan* in a North Vietnamese harbor. The source reported the major will undoubtedly face a court-martial for his flagrant violation of the Rules of Engagement and unprovoked attack against a peaceful ship.

COLLEGE STUDENTS PROTEST VIETNAM WAR

Washington—Last weekend more than 15,000 college students carrying signs, guitars, and paper peace doves paraded in Washington to protest this nation's involvement in the war in Vietnam. They carried "I will Not Fight in Vietnam" signs, and threw eggs at policemen.

They stared out the windows in silence. Below, the green San Bernardino mountains that for an instant reminded them of Vietnam disappeared under the wings as the Lear flew over the sand and desert that led to Las Vegas.

"We land in ten minutes, gentlemen," the pilot announced over the intercom.

The Wolf held his splattered blouse in his hands. He was slowly unpinning the badges and stained ribbons. He glanced up and saw Menuez and Krocek and other dead comrades watching him. He looked into each one's face and shook his head. "This is no place to be," he told them.

In his hand Court held a small newspaper article the other men hadn't noticed.

FIRST STEP TO MOON

> Houston—The Apollo 7 flight crew are ready to launch in the first manned test of the spacecraft that will carry three astronauts to the moon and return them to Earth.

The accompanying photograph showed a photo, superimposed over the surface of the moon, of an earlier spacecraft lifting off. Court stared at it, his mind starting to range.

Faintly at first, then louder, he started hearing radio transmissions of men's voices that were strained and hard at work: "Two's in . . . take it more to the east . . . MiG's, MiG's . . . Okay Four, Break NOW . . . We got him, we got him . . . I'm hit . . . MAYDAY, MAYDAY. That's not a SAM, that's Two. Hillsboro we got one down at Mu Gia. . . ." He saw Paul Austin's fireball and Pintail Four blowing up over Hanoi. Then, stumbling forward through the swirling mist, he saw Ron Bender, humiliated and hurt. His teeth clenched involuntarily as he suddenly remembered Larteguy's Lieutenant Kervallé, who roamed the streets in a drunken haze looking for his parachute battalion comrades lost at Dien Bien Phu.

"I don't think I'll be happy here," Court Bannister said. The pictures of the humiliated Ron Bender and the smiling Apollo crew alternated in his mind's eye. "Maybe . . . maybe I'll meet you back there." With machine-gun rapidity, he absently flicked the lid of his Zippo with the rubber band around it.

Parker swung around to look at the two of them. "I'll be there," he said quietly, thinking of Phil Travers, "just as soon as I graduate."

The Lear flew on over the brown desert toward Las Vegas, engines purring steadily, away from the green hell of Vietnam.

If we kept on flying, Court thought, we would circle the globe and wind up right back at Bien Hoa.